Richard Marman

McAlister
the
PeaceMaker

MCALISTER THE PEACEMAKER

Published in Australia
by
KEYPRESS CONNECTIONS
PALMWOODS QUEENSLAND

Website
www.richardmarman.com
www.richardmarman.net

ISBN 13: 978-0-6450920-9-7

First Edition, 2021

<u>Glossary</u>

Aircraft Fitter	Aviation engine mechanic
Aircraft Rigger	Aviation airframe mechanic
Ala Littoria	Italy's state run civil airline formed in 1934
Alex	Alexandria, British Egyptian headquarters during WWII
Ack-Ack	Anti aircraft fire
AOC	Air Officer Commanding — a RAF officer ranking Air Commodore or above commanding an area of operations
ASDIC	Anti-Submarine Detection System (similar to US SONAR) what the 'IC' actually stands for is unclear
ASI	Airspeed indicator
ATS	Auxiliary Territorial Service — Women's military support services during WWII
AWOL	Absent without leave
BEF	British Expeditionary Force (British and Empire troops in France 1939-40)
BPBC	British Power Boat Company
Brass Up	Shoot up or strafe a target
Broad Pennant	Admiral or commodore's banner flown from a fleet's flagship
Caique	Mediterranean fishing boat or utility vessel
CPO	Chief petty officer, a naval non-commissioned rank approximately equivalent to an army staff sergeant.
Crate	Slang for aircraft used by pilots of the time
Dog Boats	RN patrol-boats built by the Fairmile Marine Company

EPR	*EjércitoPopular Republicano* — Spanish People's Republican Army
FAA	Fleet Air Arm — Royal Navy aircraft units
Falange	A faction of the Spanish Nationalists often used when referring all Nationalists
FANY	First Aid Nursing Yeomanry formed during WWI
Flank Speed	A water vessel's maximum speed
G-Force	Increased gravity force when a plane manoeuvres aggressively
Hauptmann	German army officer equivalent to captain
Kepi	Military cap worn by a number of services including the French and Italians
Kriegsmarine	*Nazi* WWII Navy literally 'War Navy'
LSO	Landing Signals Officer — trained to guide pilots on approach and landing onto aircraft carriers
Mae West	Life jacket named after busty screen siren Mae West because of the bulky chest-high inflatable float chambers
MPH	Statute miles per hour opposed to knots (nautical miles per hour)
MTB, MGB	Royal Navy Motor Torpedo or Gun Boat
MVSM	Voluntary Militia of National Security (Black-Shirts)
NCO	Non-commissioned officer — lance-corporal, corporal, sergeant and warrant officer
NDB	Non-directional beacon — a radio homing device for aircraft
'O's	Officers' mess or sleeping quarters

Point	Naval jargon 11.25° 1/32 of a compass-rose
RAF	Royal Air Force
RCAF	Royal Canadian Air Force
Regia Aeronautica	Royal Italian Air Force
Regia Marina	Royal Italian Navy
RN	Royal Navy
RPT	Regular Public Transport — referring to airlines
Runway Threshold	Either the take-off or landing end of a runway
Schell-boot	German 'Fast-Boat' similar to British MTB known by the Allies as E-Boats (Enemy-Boats)
Schleswig Holstein	North German province
Stick	Group of paratroopers in one drop
Sudetenland	Eastern Czechoslovakia
Tube	London Underground Railway Network
Under Cart	Aircraft landing gear system
WREN	Member of the Women's Royal Navy

<u>RAF and Commonwealth Air Forces' Unit Formations</u>

Flight	A small number of aircraft flying together led by a flight-lieutenant
Squadron	A number of flights totalling about 12-24 aircraft commanded by a squadron-leader
Wing	A number of squadrons commanded by a wing-commander
Group	A number of wings commanded by a group-captain or air-commodore

Editor's Note

Ten years ago Zach McAlister asked me to compile his notes covering his Grandpa Danny's memoirs into a series of books we called *The McAlister Line*. This stand-alone story results from material discovered a few years later. It records Zach's Great Uncle Callan and Great Aunt Ivy's adventures during the Spanish Civil War and WWII.

Much of the information was gathered from military unit histories, personal diaries and some rare interviews by those who survived that terrible conflict, most of whom have now passed on.

As with his previous investigations, Zach includes a brief prologue.

Zach is still exploring his family history and hopefully he'll discover more hidden anecdotes filled with action and adventure.

I am indebted to my wife Judy for her continual support in bringing *The McAlister Line* adventures to you and Judy Bandidt for beta and proof reading as well as PC guidance.

Richard Marman

2021

McAlister the Peacemaker

Prologue — Merimbula NSW

Hello there, Zach is back. Angela and I have dug up some more interesting factoids regarding Danny's great-uncle Callan McAlister and Ivy Brown. Being based on more recent events, this narrative was easier to research. We were also able to contact Gene McAlister's kinfolk who still run a cattle ranch in New Mexico. Danny actually drove past the place on a road trip with Mad Monty back in the fifties. He recalled the name, but didn't make the family connection.

So let's see how the story unfolds...

<u>Part 1 — Mediterranean</u>

Part 2 — Sea and Air War

Part 3 — Peacemaker

Chapter 1 — Spain

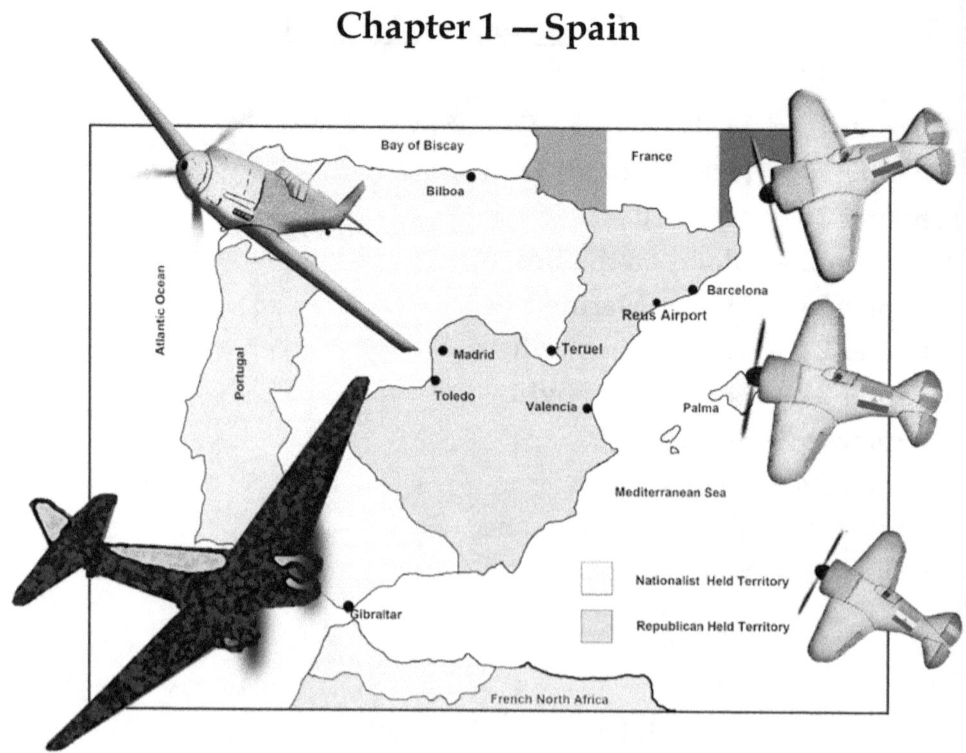

McAlister Field New Mexico, 1937

'We've got a job,' Gene McAlister declared, waving a telegram in Callan's face.

Callan sat at the desk of the *MacAir* admin office reading a pulp dime novel from the pile in the company filing cabinet. He'd pretty well got through the entire collection, because nothing much was happening in Arizona's charter aviation business.

McAlister Field lay on the edge of the vast McAlister beef property started by Gene's parents, Sam and Pepita. His three sisters and their families now ran the property. Despite the Great Depression, the ranch was still making do. Whatever else, folk had to eat.

Although Callan and Gene were distant relations, they'd grown up in different continents. Gene was born in New Mexico and now in his sixties. He still headed *McAlister Aviation* or *MacAir* as it was known, although he left most of the aerial work to his younger Australian cousin-a-few-times-removed.

Both men had flown in combat during in the Great War after which Callan joined Gene during the golden barn-storming era of the Roaring Twenties. But the Depression had taken its toll, leaving only a skeleton company touting for any business it could find. Only a Federal mail franchise kept the planes flying and the bills paid, although not always on time.

Talking of which, right about then a high-wing Ford Trimotor bumped onto the unsealed landing strip and taxied to the hangar. Moments after the engines clattered to a stop a slim woman dressed in leather jacket and riding breeches stepped from the plane cabin. She swept off her helmet and goggles, shook her hair loose and strode into the office.

Ivy McAlister was a stunning thirty-nine-year-old woman and noted pioneer aviatrix. She held several American speed and distance records. The only thing she loved more than flying was her husband Callan. Despite vigorous attempts, the couple remained childless, which gave them more opportunities to pursue their careers.

'You made great time from Austin,' Callan said after she'd kissed him.

'The westerlies dropped to nothing so no headwind for a change.'

'You're just in time to hear Gene tell us about our new contract,' Callan said.

Ivy arched her eyebrows suspiciously. She had a second sense when it came to knowing if Gene was up to something.

'Well, it's not so much *our* contract as *yours*.'

'Oh yes..?'

'It's kinda overseas.'

'OK,' Callan said, 'that's not so bad.'

'Where overseas?' Ivy demanded.

'Marseilles, France.'

'Heck, that's just dandy as you Yanks say. French wines and food, what do you think of that, love?'

'So I'm included?' Ivy said.

'Sure,' Gene said with relief. 'It'll take at least two pilots to keep the roster going.'

'What about you, Gene?' Ivy said.

'I'm too old for that sort of thing.'

'What sort of thing?'

'Just ferrying equipment and personnel...'

'Ferrying them where?'

Gene hesitated.

'Well?'

Ivy folded here arm, which was always the prelude to a challenge.

'Just across the Pyrenees carrying stuff for the Republican Government...'

'Would that be the *Spanish Republican* Government, Gene..?'

Gene nodded.

'Bloody hell, mate, you know Spain's in the middle of a civil war, don't you?'

Another nod.

'I don't go to war anymore, Gene. I came out of the last one as damaged goods. If it hadn't been for Ivy I reckon I'd be a gonna by now.'

Ivy squeezed his hand and kissed him again.

'It was my pleasure to repair you,' she smiled.

'You ain't one of them sissy conscientious objectors, are you?' Gene said.

'Damn right, I am. Even with a loyal wife like Henrietta, my brother Robert couldn't cope after four years in the trenches and tossed himself in front of a freight train. '

'I know and I'm real sorry about that, but you won't be fighting, just hauling freight and mail like we do all the time.'

'It's still a military contract.'

'I prefer to call it humanitarian,' Gene grasped at a straw, 'what with refugees, casualty evacuations and such. Ivy's nursing background will fit to a tee.'

'It's a long time since my FANY days, Gene. I'm a flyer now,' Ivy reminded him.

'And I sorta promised...' Gene said lamely. 'There's a penalty clause in the contract if we don't deliver, so we're kinda committed.'

'Is that a royal "we", Gene?'

'Look it's only for six months and think of the Mediterranean sunshine.'

'There's plenty of sunshine in New Mexico,' Callan replied.

The long and short of it was they agreed to go in light of the fact *MacAir* would fold if they didn't accept the contract Gene had already signed. Callan and Ivy might well have sacrificed the company they worked so hard to keep had they studied the Spanish struggle more closely. The McAlister ranch had subsidised

Gene's aviation enterprise on several occasions, but there was little cash to spare until the cattle business returned to the halcyon pre-depression days.

But Spain was a long way off, especially as The United States, Great Britain and its dominions including Australia were staying strictly neutral. So no one State-Side was taking a great deal of notice. Callan and Ivy held a number of passports and travel documents between them. Due to Gene's sponsorship, they'd been granted Alien Registration Receipt Cards endorsed 'Perm Res', along with their British and recently issued British Commonwealth of Australian series 'A' passports, so their international bases were pretty well covered.

'You can use whatever nationality suits best at the time,' Gene offered helpfully.

So they sailed to Marseilles rather than Barcelona or Valencia to avoid being seen as directly assisting Spain. They weren't fooling anyone, but diplomatic protocol was observed pandering to international preciousness. It was unlikely anyone cared anyway as multi-national forces had fought on both sides since the war broke out.

The previous summer a group of conservative military heavyweights led by arch reactionary and all around tough guy, General Francisco Franco, staged a military coup to oust the socialist Republican government. Franco's faction called themselves Nationalists although they were leaning towards fascism while many Republicans were latent or active communists. That put them squarely at odds with the Catholic Church hierarchy. Spain had never quite shaken off the Inquisition and Cardinals were still a force to be reckoned with.

The coup didn't work out too badly for Franco and by the end of 1936 the Nationalists controlled most of North-Western Spain while government forces dominated the south and east. Both sides got some high-priced outside help. Germany and Italy sent troops and arms to the Nationalists including the fledgling Condor Squadron of aviators and planes. Portugal even chipped in for the Nationals while not surprisingly Russia supported the Republicans with advisors, munitions and aircraft.

Meanwhile a bunch of idealistic Europeans and Americans decided to join the fray against Franco's fascists, forming International Brigades with more enthusiasm than training. Callan thought they were mad, but then remembered how avidly he'd marched to war back in 1914.

By the time Callan and Ivy caught an Atlantic steamer to Europe the war had turned into a nasty affair indeed. Whereas the idea of tens of thousands of people trying to kill one other can only be described as barbaric, the Spaniards took it to new levels of horror. Massacres, rape and torture were more than collateral damage, rather the result of old scores to settle and ancient feuds.

Callan and Ivy were blithely unaware of the Iberian butchery as they sailed eastwards like honeymooners. They danced, dined, romanced and generally played tourists. As they passed through the Pillars of Hercules Ivy's camera shutter worked overtime capturing images of the North African coast and Rock of Gibraltar.

It was hard to imagine the carnage ashore when they sailed north-eastwards along the *Costa-del-Sol* in perfect weather. Occasionally when land smudged the horizon Callan sometimes spotted smoke, but that could have simply been wildfires.

Señor Juan Pablo Vargas was the Republican government factor who met Callan and Ivy when they disembarked at

Marseilles. He was a portly, jovial black-moustached fellow who greeted them like saviours. Perhaps not all pilots were so eager to fly over a war zone, so anyone was welcome and Vargas was keen for his new aviators to start right away.

Ivy and Callan travelled light and their luggage easily fitted into the boot of Vargas' prestigious Citroën *Traction Avant*. They headed for *Marseilles-Marignane Airport* some miles out of town.

'So what's the job?' Callan asked as Vargas drove.

'You will be given instructions when you reach Barcelona.'

'Barcelona? I understood we were to operate from Marseilles.'

'Do not worry, Señor McAlister you will come to Marseilles regularly. The French Government is sympathetic, but must be seen to be neutral in this conflict. You shall be based at Barcelona. It is a beautiful, magnificent city.'

'Flying what to where?'

'Anything and anywhere that is required, Señor.'

'But the entire country is a war-zone,' Ivy said. 'We are contracted for civil operations, not combat.'

'Señor, I am certain you will be perfectly safe, protected by our excellent Republican military.'

Somehow Callan and Ivy weren't over confident about Vargas' assurances.

They had every reason not to be, because the late autumn of 1937 was a bad time to be joining the Spanish Republican forces. However things started out looking promising. They took off in a comfortable DC-2, one of the latest and technically advanced passenger planes flying. The pilot was a cheerful Canadian called Johnny Witherspoon who invited Callan and Ivy to the cockpit for the flight to Reus Airstrip about five miles outside a port town called Tarragona not far from Barcelona.

The plane usually included a co-pilot, but the Spanish Republic was short of pilots. So while Vargas made himself comfortable in the spacious cabin, Witherspoon was more than happy to have two qualified pilots along to lend a hand. Official endorsements weren't always necessary when times were tight.

Ivy bagged the co-pilot seat while Callan occupied the fold out jump-seat.

'She'll go a thousand miles at one-fifty miles an hour,' Witherspoon bragged.

'We've seen some around the States, but never been in one,' Callan admitted.

'*Linear Aéreas Postales Espaolas* runs five of them, although the Glorious One poaches our planes all the time for military work.'

'Glorious One..?' Ivy said.

'*La Glorious* as the Republican Air Force calls itself.'

'From your tone, I gather it's not your assessment,' Ivy said.

'Nope! I'm afraid I joined the wrong side all full of grit and good intentions. The Republic isn't really a government, but a bunch of factions tearing away at each other. Meanwhile Generalissimo Franco bumped off all his opposition and rules like Nero.'

'That isn't necessarily a good thing for him,' Callan observed. 'Look what happened to Rome when Nero ran the show.'

'True, but the Nationalists have some powerful help from the Krauts and Dagoes while the Republic has the International Brigades, Russian backing and some help from Greece who just want to piss off the Italians.'

'I've heard of the Condor Legion,' Ivy said. 'Some say Hitler sent them to Spain to practise for another European war.'

Callan shuddered at the thought. Having fought the Great War continuously in the Sinai, Gallipoli, Dublin Rebellion, and the Western Front, he'd no desire to get caught up in another bloodbath.

'They're better trained and equipped than us. They also out-gun the Republican Army,' Witherspoon explained.

By then they'd reached their nine thousand feet cruising altitude. The aircraft wasn't fitted with an auto-pilot. They were around at the time, but not universally in service, so Witherspoon gave Ivy a course to steer and let her take control.

'You know when I first got here a year ago the *EPR* didn't even have the right ammo for their rifles. Things ain't much better now. They're in hock up to their eyebrows to the Russians for guns, tanks and planes.'

'You don't sound confident about the outcome.'

'You're dead right there, ma'am. When the *Falange* staged their coup they held a bit of Northern Spain. This year they control half the country and then some. The *EPA* ain't doing real well.'

'If you're so unsure, why stay?'

'Money.'

'Yeah, the pay is good...'

'Just make sure you're paid into an overseas bank account and you've got an exit plan,' Witherspoon advised. 'The Spaniards on either side ain't exactly keen on taking prisoners, so you don't want to be on the losing team when this shindig goes pear-shaped.'

The plane cruised on. Ivy thought it a delight to control. After an hour she swapped places with Callan, so he could have a go. It was a fine day with the turquoise Mediterranean below and the Spanish coast clearly visible through the windscreen.

They crossed the coast northeast of Barcelona. Witherspoon pointed out salient landmarks as the city sprawled below. *La Glorious* used Reus field and even managed to erect a locating beacon. Witherspoon tuned the beacon frequency and a pointer flickered ahead on a gauge beside the main instrument panel.

'Cool, eh?' he declared. 'Makes navigation a breeze. Just fly towards the needle and when it swings around you're over the top.'

Ivy and Callan were impressed, not only were they flying a modern plane, but the Spanish ground aids weren't as primitive as they'd been led to believe. Witherspoon did mention the Republican forces still controlled the east coast and Madrid slap bang in the centre of Spain. The capital was under continual siege from Nationalists, but still held out.

'What's all that smoke ahead?' Ivy asked.

'Bugger, so much for intelligence reports,' Witherspoon replied. 'Condor Legion bombing raid.'

To prove his point, Witherspoon pointed across the sky to a smudge of black dots above the western horizon.

'Heinkels and *Stukas*, which means...'

And the DC-2 shuddered as machinegun shells raked the fuselage. Callan grappled with the controls to remain upright until Witherspoon took over. A shadow flashed over the cockpit when a fighter plane swooped by.

'Messerschmitt 109 escort!' Witherspoon declared.

'There'll be more then,' Callan said.

It turned out he was wrong. Three stubby Russian built Republican Air Force Polikarpov 1-16 interceptors shot past giving chase with guns blazing. The Messerschmitt soared aloft with unbelievable power before dwindling to a speck on the horizon.

Apparently the Me-109 was a lone wolf who couldn't resist a soft target. The rest of the escort squadron remained in formation to guard the bombers as they were supposed to.

'The Ruskies won't catch him. The Kraut has twenty or thirty mph on their crates.'

Sure enough the *La Glorious* fighters peeled off, turning back to fly formation on the DC-2's wingtip.

'Our personal escort,' Witherspoon said.

Chapter 2 — Back to War

Reus Airstrip was busy when Witherspoon landed the DC-2. Russian and Spanish pilots were also retuning in their 1-16 interceptors, which looked almost comical compared to the sleek Messerschmitt lines. The planes had scrambled to shoo off the Condor Legion's bombers, but they'd lost two 1-16s in dog-fights with 109s.

Witherspoon tut-tutted as he inspected the bullet holes in his precious aircraft. A 13-mm machinegun shell had pierced the fuselage just inches from Señor Vargas, who although unharmed, was no longer his cheerful, garrulous self.

'The boys'll fix it,' Witherspoon opined, 'but it'll take a few days. 'I guess I'm back to flying the trucks.'

By trucks he meant the assortment of flying machines at *La Glorious'* disposal.

'You know some of our crates are single units — just one of a kind. Can you image the hassles getting spare parts? The 1-16s are the best we've got and the government has hocked itself to the eyeballs to pay the Russians for them.'

'Jesus, Gene's gonna have some explaining to do,' Callan said. 'This place is a basket case. We're out of here on the first plane to France.'

'Good plan,' Witherspoon agreed. 'I'll head back to my island when my contract's up next spring.'

'Island?' Ivy said.

'Sure. I'm holed up at a spec in the Adriatic called Mirios off the Albanian Coast.'

'What was wrong with Canada?'

'Holy crap, have you been there in winter?'

'No but we've been to Montana.'

'Which is mild by comparison — the defence rests. Mostly though the depression hit aviation real hard in Canada,' Witherspoon explained. 'I heard Italy had gone crazy for planes and I heard right. Air races, new designs, air routes and best of all sea-planes.'

Witherspoon had started his career on float-planes because one thing Canada had aplenty was water. So when he heard an Englishman ran a sea-plane service from Mirios to Dalmatia, Greece and Italy, Witherspoon jumped at the chance. He was doing pretty well too until the promise of big bucks lured him to Spain.

Ivy and Callan were given no more time to reflect. They were put to work straight away. A rather curt pair of air force officers appeared and started ordering everyone about. One was Spanish and the other Russian and neither spoke more than a few words of English. As Witherspoon translated, it became clear Ivy and Callan would deal through the Canadian. Their status was still uncertain, but the line between civilian contractor and International Brigade was blurred to the point of disappearing.

As partners Callan and Ivy shared a room at the end of a long barracks hut. It afforded some privacy and opened onto a veranda. After a meal and a good night's sleep Callan calmed down. In fact things worked quite well when they were assigned the daily mail run to Toulouse, which seemed in line with their contracts.

'What are we going to fly?' Ivy asked warily.

She was normally enthusiastic about anything new.

'Well we have a bit of a treat for you both,' Witherspoon grinned. 'You have a unique bird each.'

Their planes were parked close together beside a hangar, control hut, operations centre and air-raid shelter. Both aircraft were modern twin-engine machines, although with a certain down-at-the-heel appearance. One looked like a smaller version of the DC-2 while the other was smaller again, but quite sleek in its way.

'That's the Breguet four-seventy Fulgar,' Witherspoon said. 'The Frenchies only built one and it wound up here. The small crate is an Airspeed AS-eight Viceroy. Some English dude had it purpose-built for air races, but it didn't do so well and was mothballed. Then the Frogs bought it and sold it on to the Republic. It flies pretty well too, but once again only one was ever built. She's a dedicated freighter now — no seats or fuselage windows.'

Each plane came with a pamphlet-size flight manual which only took minutes to read.

So against their better judgement Ivy and Callan started flying the mail run between Barcelona and Toulouse. After a week the post included a letter addressed to Mr and Mrs C McAlister bearing the logo of Gladstone and Trump who managed *MacAir's* legal affairs.

Thinking the letter to be the usual dry official mumbo-jumbo, Callan only got around to reading it after returning to Reus Airfield...

Gladstone & Trump
Attorneys at Law Albuquerque, NMS

Dear Mr & Mrs McAlister,

I trust this correspondence finds you in good health.

Unfortunately the same cannot be said for Major Gene McAlister who suffered a minor stroke just after your departure. I am pleased to report he has recovered well and regained all physical and mental faculties.

However, following his doctor's advice, Major McAlister has decided to retire and take things easy. To this end he has sold the MacAir business which our firm is now in the process of liquidating. As employees, we regret your services are no longer required now the company is being wound up.

The Macalister family are the only shareholders, but wish you to be considered as partners and have made provision for you to receive one sixth of the sell-off proceeds to be held in our trust account awaiting your instructions. The account currently realises interest at 3% p.a.

I understand you are presently engaged in a contract with the Spanish Republican Government. As the company is no longer trading, we must deem that agreement void, freeing you from any further obligation.

The McAlister family has asked me to convey their profound apologies for any inconvenience and wish you well in the future. In recompense they are prepared to offer you a part share in the McAlister Cattle Ranch as silent partners if you so desire.

Please do not hesitate to contact this office should you have any further inquiries.

I remain yours respectfully

Joshua Trump

'Stone the flaming crows! Read this, Ivy,' Callan said, handing the letter to her.

'At least it seems we're off the hook if we want to blow town,' she commented dryly.

'Maybe, but it hasn't been that bad and they're paying big bucks.'

'We can always negotiate our own agreement. It's not like they want us to go.'

As it turned out that was exactly what Señor Vargas had in mind. He accompanied Callan on his next flight to Toulouse and Ivy rode along as co-pilot. They opened a *Credit Suisse* account through a local banking agency into which their monthly salaries were to be paid. Juan promised to provide a transfer statement for every payment.

And that would have been that, but things changed by year's end.

Ivy and Callan were finishing breakfast waiting for the daily postal truck from Barcelona carrying the usual mail sacks.

'Finish your coffee,' Witherspoon said, entering the mess hall. 'Change of plan for you two this morning.'

'Oh?' Callan said suspiciously.

'Sure thing, buddy, you're going to ferry some VIPs up to Teruel.'

Ivy and Callan were pretty well acquainted with the political and military situation by then. Teruel was a Nationalist held hilltop stronghold two hundred miles to the west. The town wasn't particularly important strategically, but it was a salient protruding into Republican territory.

'In case you haven't noticed the *Falange* control Teruel,' Ivy reminded Witherspoon. 'We just fly the mail, remember?'

'That can wait and you're not actually going to land at Teruel, just take a look-see.'

'We don't do military stuff,' Callan insisted.

'This ain't military, it's just a VIP flight and a bunch of hangers-on.'

'How many hangers-on?'

'Can't be more than a dozen — the Fulgar has only got that much room. We'll use the Viceroy to carry their baggage.'

Republican Prime Minister Juan Negrin along with his military heavy-weights decided they'd like to attack the South Aragon town of Teruel. They had their reasons. Teruel was considered a soft target which stood between eastern Spain and besieged Madrid. By taking Teruel, the Republican forces would have a clear run to reinforce the capital. It would also be good PR which the Republicans badly needed to boost their army's flagging moral. General Hernández Saravia headed the push with his Army of the Levant leading and the Army of the East in support.

'The PM wants you to take a couple of his guys along with some foreign news-hounds for an aerial recon,' Witherspoon said.

'Like I said, we don't do military stuff,' Callan insisted.

'It's not like you'll be carrying generals or anything. They've all headed to the battle-front by railroad. So it's really a civilian op, wouldn't you say? And you don't really have much choice.'

'How come?'

'It's best to go with the flow in Spain these days. People who upset the powers-that-be tend to get shot.'

'They wouldn't dare..?' Ivy said.

'Wanna bet? A couple of guys from an International Brigade's French battalion faced a firing squad last month just for complaining about their equipment and rations. Anyway with all those foreign correspondents aboard, you're sure to get a fighter escort.'

As it turned out Prime Minister Juan Negrin's representatives included Señor Juan Pablo Vargas to guide the journalists around. They were accompanied by a mean-looking pistol-packing army officer who was introduced as Lieutenant Garrido. While stashing their gear in the Viceroy, the journalists eyed Ivy with lecherous intent. One of the newsmen was especially interested. He was about her age and quite dashing, sporting a pencil-thin moustache and slick manner.

'Howdy, ma'am,' he drawled, extending his hand. 'You're a right handsome young filly if you don't mind me saying. My name is Hemingway, Ernest Hemingway and I'm mighty pleased to make your acquaintance.'

'Indeed, Mister Hemingway,' Ivy replied coolly although she accepted his outstretched hand. 'I do believe I have heard of you from Toronto or some such place a while ago. However I do not appreciate being compared to livestock. Now if you'll excuse me I will check my plane is loaded correctly.'

'Your plane..? Surely you ain't our pilot?'

'One of them. My *husband* standing over there is the other.'

'Shame, but it still doesn't mean we can't be sociable.'

'I believe not. I understand you may be an able writer, but whatever your opinion, you have yet to prove yourself a ladies' man.'

Ivy elected to fly the Viceroy and avoid Ernest Hemingway. The two planes lumbered airborne and headed west for one of the airstrips in Republican hands close to Teruel. Lieutenant Garrido insisted on occupying the co-pilot seat instructing Vargas to sit in the fold-down jump seat between the pilots. Vargas was nominally in charge, yet it seemed to Callan Garrido called the shots. The lieutenant spoke no English, so it was up to Vargas to interpret.

'Lieutenant Garrido wants you to overfly Teruel so he can check out enemy positions,' Vargas explained.

'Oh, great,' Callan retorted. 'He does know that ground troops have guns and we don't have anything to shoot back with.'

'They won't expect us,' Vargas replied rather too glibly in Callan's opinion. 'We will be gone before they notice.'

The Breguet 470 windscreen wasn't the best for visibility, but Garrido was ready with a camera nonetheless. Meanwhile Vargas instructed the journalists to be ready to snap shots from the cabin windows.

Despite Callan's concerns and Witherspoon's assurances, which he had no way of fulfilling, the fighter escort didn't eventuate. But Condor Legion Messerschmitt 109s were the least of their worries...

North-Eastern Spain was about to suffer its most severe winter in twenty-five years. The coastal plain was spared the worst, but Teruel was perched three thousand feet above sea level where the temperatures were not only colder, but the wind reached gale force with chill factors over minus twenty degrees.

Callan saw the storm clouds ahead some fifty miles short of their destination airstrip and he didn't like the look of it one bit.

'There's crap weather ahead, Ivy,' Callan called over the radio.

'I see it,' she replied through the crackling static of Callan's earphones.

'It's a huge weather system,' Callan said. 'We'll never get around it. Let's head back home.'

'Roger that,' Ivy replied. 'See you back at the ranch.'

She'd flown the Viceroy loosely on Callan's port wing-tip. He glanced through the cockpit side window to see her plane bank sharply left as she set a course for Reus.

'Sorry, lads,' Callan said. 'We'll not be flying to Teruel today. That's a wall of meteorological hate ahead.'

Wisps of cloud began to flash by accompanied by niggling turbulence. Callan concentrated on his instruments and banked his plane. Then he felt cold steel pressing against his temple. Lieutenant Garrido glared down the barrel of his pistol.

'What the blazes..?' Callan said. 'Put that damn gun away, Lieutenant. What's his problem, Vargas?'

'He wants you to fly on to Teruel, Señor,' Vargas explained. 'He is very insistent. He wishes to do his duty... he also fears if we return with no photographs he will be in big trouble.'

'Tell him we can't see anything in this cloud. His camera is useless.'

By now the plane was rocking violently. Callan operated the de-icers to shed build-ups on the leading edge of the wings. He knew the system was mediocre and soon ice would stick to the underwing increasing the plane's weight and reducing manoeuvrability.

'What the devil's going on?' Hemingway yelled from the cabin, but Callan ignored him.

'Tell this idiot I'll stay at six thousand feet. I know that's well above any terrain around here. But when we get to Teruel by dead-reckoning, I'm turning back if we can't see anything.'

Garrido lowered his pistol after Vargas explained Callan's intentions, but the officer didn't holster the weapon. In any event they hadn't far to go and as luck would have it, the cloud broke up as they neared their destination. The weather was still treacherous for flying amongst hills, but Callan glimpsed patches of ground as they sped past.

Garrido waved his pistol around shouting orders to Vargas.

'He wants you to descend.'

'Tell him he's an idiot,' Callan spat back. 'These clouds are full of rocks.'

Vargas stared at him.

'Hills, mountains we can't see.'

'He says you are a coward,' Vargas announced after he and Garrido had exchanged words.

'Maybe, but I'm not a fool.'

More words...

'The Lieutenant says the republic shoots cowards.'

'Yeah, well that's smart. Who does he think will fly the plane then?'

Garrido didn't seem to consider that and aimed his gun at Callan again.

'Tell him I'll go down to four thousand feet and not an inch lower. That will give us clearance above the town, but I dunno about the surrounding terrain.'

'I'm sorry, Señor,' Vargas said with a shrug. 'The lieutenant is a communist first and Republican second. I fear communist zealots trying to make names for themselves don't think like rational men.'

'He'd probably shoot you if he understood what you'd just said,' Callan replied.

Fortunately Callan's navigation was spot on. He ducked and weaved his plane around clouds and emerged into clear air below the base. Teruel was visible, but Callan had to bank sharply to stay away from snow falls scattering the sky

Visibility was so poor it was impossible to assess the Nationalist positions or strength. Teruel was an old walled town clinging to a hill with a church spire at its peak. The buildings were clustered together in a maze of terra-cotta roof-tiles and narrow streets. Nevertheless Lieutenant Garrido kept his camera busy.

'Looks like a fairytale castle to me,' Callan muttered, remembering the bloody hand-to-hand combat through the South

Dublin Union and Four Courts tenements during the rebellion in nineteen- sixteen. 'It'll be a flaming nightmare...'

The control column bucked in Callan's hands as ack-ack shell exploded only yards from the cockpit. Well, you can't go buzzing a Nationalist stronghold in a plane with Republican markings and expect to get away with it. The Nationalists opened up with a 75-mm anti-aircraft gun.

'I don't care what Garrido thinks — we're out of here!' Callan declared, blanking the plane and gunning the throttles prop and mixture levers to full power to gain altitude.

This time there was no argument from the lieutenant although Callan judged he'd made a vindictive enemy. Callan knew his attitude had embarrassed Garrido in front of Vargas, who he considered an underling. It appeared rabid communists were as paranoid about losing face as Southeast Asians.

Chapter 3 — Teruel Under Siege

'What kept you so long? I was worried sick,' Ivy asked at the end of the field telephone line. 'I thought you were flying right behind me.'

'That lunatic Garrido insisted we press on to Teruel just so he could take some photos. As if the weather and terrain weren't bad enough, the *Falange* decided to take pot-shots at us. The Breguet's peppered with shrapnel holes,' Callan replied.

'You let that trumped up peasant bully you?'

'Not him — his hand-gun.'

'Where are you now?'

'I put down at a Republican military field clear of the worst weather. There's a ruddy great army build-up here. Thousands of troops and a bunch of generals just arrived by train.'

'When will you get back to Reus?'

'Dunno. We have to patch up the crate. Can you get Johnny Witherspoon to send our technicians over here?'

Callan had found the strip by chance as he flew back to Reus. The Breguet was flying erratically and Callan suspected some of the control surfaces were damaged. With the huge Republican presence he felt safe enough to land, knowing the strip was one of a number established around Teruel. The Republican Army was building up several corps to prise the Nationals from the town's hilltops.

'You gotta spot to bed down?' Hemingway asked as he approached from the officer tent-line.

'Sleep in the plane, I guess.'

'You'll freeze in an hour. C'mon, we've found some digs with a kerosene heater. It's amazing what a few well placed Yankee bucks and a promised mention in the international press will do.'

Hemingway was right. The reporters had ingratiated themselves into the officers' accommodation in double quick-time. Callan looked around and feared the common soldiers fared far worse with no heating other than wood they could scrounge and barely enough tents for half the men. After a meal of soup and bread, there was nothing left to do but huddle around the heater in a six-man tent.

Callan took his prize harmonica from his top pocket. He carried it everywhere and was pretty good and could bend the notes like a Mississippi Delta blues player.

'Why is the weather during a war always so bloody awful?' Hemingway said. 'Same as the last blast.'

Callan stopped playing

'You fought in Great War?' Callan asked.

'Gung-ho teenage ambulance driver— got wounded in Italy in eighteen and shipped back stateside via Paris after the show was over.'

'Ivy did the same on the western front. She was awarded the *Croix de Guerre* for bravery and dedication to duty.'

Callan was justifiably proud of Ivy's war record even though he was a highly decorated hero as well.

'So we have much in common,' Hemingway grinned.

'I'm sure you do,' Callan said in a tone suggesting it was OK just as long as they didn't have *too* much in common.

The heater was pitifully inadequate and the night bitterly cold as snow storms swept in from the north east. There was a brief break in the weather the next morning during which Ivy and Johnny Witherspoon flew in from Reus. They carried a mechanic and tool-kit along with the journalists' baggage which included Hemingway's whiskey supply.

Ivy had barely landed when the weather closed in and the Viceroy was grounded beside the Breguet Fulgar. Republican troops, tanks and artillery arrived constantly. The build-up continued until mid-December when a youthful imposing fellow turned up. He looked barely thirty, but dressed in a leather battle jacket and hawklike stare marked him as a warrior. A bunch of officers made a great fuss over him.

'Who's that rather dishy chap?' Ivy asked.

'That is General Enriqué Lister,' Hemingway announced.

Hemingway had been hanging around Ivy despite her indifference.

Of course she'd heard of Lister who was the army's rising star and along with General Vincente Rojo, many thought the Republic's best hope.

*

Teruel — Dawn 15 December 1937

'Are you coming?' Hemingway said, peeking through Callan and Ivy's tent flap.

'Where?' Callan grunted. 'It's foul outside.'

He was right. The temperature was way below zero with snow falling heavily.

'Savaria's sending Lister's division to surround Teruel.'

'They're gonna have trouble gouging the *Falange* out of there. When's the push on?'

'Now.'

'Why don't I hear artillery?' Callan asked as the whole military nightmare came flooding back.

Hemingway shrugged.

'Dunno. I just go where the news is and report what I see.'

General Savaria's plan was to send a brigade around the left flank, while the rest of Lister's division would hit the centre and right with tank support hoping to totally surround the town wall. Conditions were appalling with temperatures of fifteen below and a wind chill-factor of goodness-knew-what.

Hemingway had befriended an ambulance medic who drove them to the first city wall where infantry were already deploying through Teruel's narrow streets. It was arduous work with visibility reduced to yards in blinding snow. The first casualties were not from hostile fire, but frost-bite so severe some men were unable to shoot their weapons.

'Many of these guys slept in the open last night with no gloves or adequate clothing,' Hemingway said. 'They'll lose a lot of fingers or worse.'

About then the leading units literally bumped into Teruel's Nationalist defenders and the fight was on. While Hemingway marched on to witness the Republican glory, Ivy and Callan made themselves useful helping casualties, whose numbers grew rapidly.

Teruel houses were jammed together in typical medieval style and there was no way of telling which buildings were occupied by Nationalists, so everyone had to be investigated. Sometimes it was obvious as rifle-fire blasted into the Republicans when they passed at close range. Then it was a matter of kicking in doors and tackling the enemy with bayonets and bare hands.

Republicans and Nationalists slugged it out all day in that bloody house-to-house melee. The ambulance was filled within minutes of the first shot. The Republican medic was one of the first casualties when a bullet took him right between the eyes, so Ivy took over as driver while Callan joined the stretcher-bearers. He salvaged a pistol and ammunition pouch from a fallen officer and took down several Nationalists when they charged the ambulance. Apparently bayoneting wounded was a legitimate Spanish warfare tactic — a wounded enemy might recover and come back to fight another day, whereas a dead man wouldn't.

Bloody hell, just like I figured. It's the Dublin Four Courts all over again only with a flaming snow storm thrown in for good measure. I promised myself I'd never harm another human being...so much for promises...

Ivy never got above second gear manoeuvring the ambulance in Teruel's tight backstreets and it was only the extreme cold that prevented the radiator boiling. Once the truck was full it took fifteen minutes to turn around. Advancing Republican troops from the rear were the main hindrance.

Eventually Ivy drove back to the airfield where several surgical marquees stood. The conditions inside were already overcrowded with hundreds of wounded men lying on frozen ground. Their body heat improved the inside temperature, but turned the floor to a quagmire when the mud thawed. Many others waited outside because there was no room under cover.

Ivy and Callan took over the ambulance by default, but no one objected especially after they refuelled and headed back to Teruel. By then the Nationalists were well aware they were under attack. Sporadic mortar and light artillery shells exploded into the advancing army, but the gunners' vision was blinded by snow and any hits were purely random.

Back in town the fight developed into an amorphous flood of bloodshed. Although the left flank's primary role was to by-pass the town centre and take high ground to the west, including *La Muela de Teruel* — Teruel's Tooth overlooking the central defences. It was an excellent vantage point to co-ordinate artillery into town if of course the snowstorm lifted and they could see anything to shoot at.

Republican spies suggested there were ten thousand people within Teruel's walls. However half were likely to be civilians, while the Nationalist commander, Colonel Domingo Rey d'Harcourt had a relatively small force at his disposal. This became tragically evident when Ivy and Callan returned to the front line — such as it was.

Republican infantry pressed themselves against buildings or scrambled over stone walls into back yards. Then they blazed away indiscriminately and asked questions afterwards. When some soldiers beside the ambulance sensed a movement through the French window of a second story balcony, two events occurred simultaneous:

- A woman holding a baby appeared on the balcony
- A soldier lobbed a grenade through the French window

She screamed a split second before the bomb exploded, blasting the woman and infant over the balustrade. They splattered onto the cobblestones. If the grenade hadn't killed them, they died instantly on impact. The street turned into bedlam when the soldiers realised what they'd done. They may have been ruthless with the enemy, but so far no one had intended to kill innocent townsfolk.

The tragedy was due to the fact that much of the fighting had moved hundreds of yards forward, but pockets of stubborn resistance needled away from individual buildings. Everyone was jittery and trigger-happy. Ivy and Callan could move the ambulance no further past debris and scattered corpses anyway. A burly infantryman crashed through the front door below the balcony with his bayonet-bristling comrades closely behind.

Ivy and Callan entered seconds later to find the soldiers had baled up about twenty emaciated, trembling children. While his men looked on, their sergeant turned shaking his head, signalling them to follow and rejoin the fight.

'*No hay nada que pueda hacer, señora...*' he muttered as he passed Ivy — 'there is nothing I can do...'

Once the soldiers left Ivy tried to reassure the shivering children they were safe, but they didn't understand her.

'Dunno about safe, Ivy?' Callan said 'They're exhausted, freezing, starving and many look sick. See if you can get 'em into the ambulance while I check to see there's no one left behind.'

Pistol at the ready, Callan climbed the stairs, but the grenade had done its work and only shattered corpses lay there. When he returned to the ambulance, Ivy had loaded the children aboard and wrapped the smallest in what blankets she had. Callan sensed the rattle of gunfire and occasional thump of mortal shells seemed no further away, indicating the soldiers were having a tough time advancing.

'You drive,' Ivy said, 'I'll try to help in the back.'

So they inched back to the main Republican headquarters. Even as they reached the rear positions, wounded men still lay exhausted or staggered towards where they hoped to find a medic.

'We don't even have room to pick any of these poor blokes up,' Callan called back to Ivy. 'I hope they make it until we can come back for some of them.'

More advancing troops continued to block the way frustrating Callan's progress. He sounded the horn, but no one took any notice.

Why did they build such narrow streets? I mean even in the Middle Ages knights on horses would have had a hard time getting up here.

And then there was a break in the human traffic, but the way was barred by a group of officious looking soldiers headed by none other than Lieutenant Garrido. Along with their armed unit, the officers were accompanied by two men wearing grey trench coats with armbands depicting a red hammer-and-sickle. Señor Vargas was also present rugged up in a fur-lined overcoat, but still looking miserable.

Garrido stood in the ambulance path with his hand raised. Callan had no choice but to stop the vehicle. Two soldiers broke ranks and doubled to the truck's rear door. They opened up and yelled something to Garrido. Callan could understand no other word other than *niños,* which he knew meant children. Leaving the motor idling, Callan dropped from the cabin as Garrido approached.

'Ruddy hell, Vargas, what's this bugger playing at now?' Callan demanded. 'We have to get these kids warm and cared for pronto.'

Garrido barked at Vargas.

'Lieutenant Garrido says you are under arrest for stealing property of the republic.'

'Stealing..? He's barmy. We've been evacuating *your* wounded from *your* battle after *your* driver was shot.'

'He says there are no Republican casualties aboard now. Just *Falange* brats,' Vargas replied after some translation. 'The lieutenant says you should have handed the ambulance over when you reached headquarters the first time. He says this is not satisfactory.'

'Tough-titty, Señor! What's he gonna do about it and who're these jokers with farm tools on their arms?'

'They are Russian political observers,' Vargas replied sadly.

'Here to see there's no commie back-sliding, I guess.'

Vargas shrugged.

More jabbering from Garrido.

'Alas, the *señora* and you are still under arrest. You must hand over that vehicle and accompany us to headquarters.'

'What about the children?' Ivy demanded.

'He says that is no longer your concern,' Vargas continued apologetically. 'Lieutenant Garrido claims you are capitalist spies who have deserted the International Brigades.'

'That's crazy,' Callan protested. 'Tell him Vargas, we've never been part of any International Brigade.'

Vargas shrugged again as Callan and Ivy were led away. Lieutenant Garrido headed the group with far too smug an expression in Callan's opinion. They were bundled into an open topped truck and endured the bitterly cold journey back to the airfield where General Lister had established his HQ. The only comfort was while the two Russians sat snugly in the heated cabin, Garrido, the military escort and Vargas suffered alongside their prisoners.

Chapter 4 — Interrogation

Garrido looked much happier once they were under canvas in his provost hut. A wood stove stood in the tent centre glowing invitingly. Garrido sat at a single desk while the Russians stood impassively behind him. One of Garrido's minions placed a pair of canvas chairs in front of the desk.

'Please sit,' Vargas said.

Garrido snarled at Vargas. Callan didn't understand, but figured the gist of it was we don't use 'please' and' thank you' when addressing traitors. As far as anyone recalls the interview went something like this:

'We will break you in no time, so you might as well confess,' Garrido began through Vargas.

'Confess to what?' Callan asked — also through Vargas.'

'You are a capitalist spy. I'd recognise your type anywhere. You spread filth and propaganda among our ranks hoping to weaken the will of our glorious comrades-in-arms.'

'I thought propaganda was your department.'

'We know all about you. You are an English Army officer who spied against the Irish.'

This was a bit harsh, because at that stage Great Britain was at least supporting the Republic in principle.

'Blimey, that was over twenty years ago and I was an Australian soldier, not an English one.'

'Ha! Austria allied to fascist *Nazi* Germany. You are condemned by your own words.'

'Au-stra-lia, not Austria, you goose. You know down-under, kangaroos, boomerangs and such like. And I'm blowed where you dug up my military record, but that's ancient history.'

Garrido ignored the insult — or maybe Vargas wisely edited the translation — he indicated the Russian.

'These men have dossiers on all the International Brigades,' Garrido continued. 'Do you not think we know what goes on in Berlin, London and Paris?'

Garrido may have been stretching it a bit, but both Russians, who apparently understood Spanish, glared at him for his indiscretion. Callan and Ivy were unaware at the time that the Communist Party had infiltrated a bunch of impressionable Cambridge under-graduates, many of whom joined the British civil service and supplied the Russians with all sorts of useful information.

One of the most notorious was Kim Philby who posed as a journalist for General Franco, but was in fact a communist agent who would continue undetected for nearly twenty years.

Perhaps getting Imperial war records was easier than anyone imagined.

'What exactly is it you think we've done?' Ivy asked quite reasonably in Callan's opinion.

'Spying of course!' Garrido snapped although Vargas interpreted in a more even tone.

'We were hired to fly the mail between Reus and Marseilles. Nothing more.'

'Yet here you are in a military camp.'

'That was your idea, not ours. We have no desire to be any part of your war.'

In the end it was futile. Garrido kept ranting about treason against the great socialist republic while the Russians nodded with stone-faced severity. After an hour's grilling Garrido closed the interrogation.

'What now?' Callan asked Vargas.

'You will go to Barcelona to face a military tribunal.'

'Come on, Señor. This is nonsense and you know it. What's Garrido's real angle?'

'You defied him for which he will not forgive. He is a proud man.'

'Holy flaming smoke, is that all. This isn't pride, it's bloody arrogance! Surely those Russian stooges won't go along with it.'

'I believe they just like seeing people tried and punished. Russia is a brutal land populated by brutal people who have been through brutal times. There is no pity in them.'

Callan and Ivy were held under guard awaiting transfer to Barcelona by train, leaving Witherspoon to fly the repaired Fulgar back to Reus when the weather improved. The fact that Garrido was plainly unstable and pressed the charges out of personal dislike was obvious, but no one questioned him. Nobody dared question him, which was odd for a lowly junior officer.

'For heaven's sake, Señor Vargas,' Callan pleaded. 'Sort this mess out. You're a government official after all.'

'Lieutenant Garrido has connections in the high places,' Vargas suggested apologetically, 'but I will do what I can.'

Although Witherspoon and his mechanic had patched up Callan's plane, the weather was still so foul aviation was out of the question. Callan and Ivy were confined to their tent. Armed guards attended them continually, although they assigned a butch female to accompany Ivy whenever she visited the ablution pits.

Meanwhile the butchery in Teruel continued. Hemingway returned with horror stories of untold savagery and thousands of casualties. By Christmas the Republicans surrounded the town forcing Colonel Rey d'Harcourt to withdraw his remaining four thousand men into a redoubt surrounding a few government buildings.

Republican propaganda proclaimed Teruel had fallen, but the Nationalists bitterly fought on. Hemingway only stopped long enough to file his report and gather more film for his camera before racing back to glory at the battle front.

Vargas showed up shortly after Hemingway's visit with good and bad news. Garrido had agreed to drop charges against Ivy who he considered a silly woman who'd been subverted by her vile and morally corrupt husband.

'Now we know it's personal, don't we?' Callan said.

Vargas nodded sadly. By then he was sad all the time.

'I convinced him we need *Señora* McAlister to fly the mail. And that is only the truth. Pilot losses are crippling so now every Spanish and Russian aviator flies for *La Glorious.*'

'When are they taking Callan to Barcelona?' Ivy asked.

'Maybe soon, maybe later,' Vargas shrugged. 'The battle is General Lister's top priority and he has given no orders yet. Even Garrido must do as he is bid by high command.'

'What about the Russians? They seem like a law unto themselves.'

Vargas just continued looking miserable.

So Callan languished under guard until General Franco did something unexpected. Until then the smart money was on a Nationalist push into Guadalajara and finally take Madrid, but Franco was determined no Nationalist stronghold would fall to the Republicans, so he sent help.

Nationalist divisions surged eastwards to Teruel with Condor Legion air support. On New Year's Day 1938 the Republicans were in the parlous position of surrounding d'Harcourt's bastion, but under attack on their eastern positions. Then a blizzard set in grounding the Condor Legion, but hand-to-hand fighting continued in the city centre where d'Harcourt's perimeter dwindled inch by blood-drenched inch.

Due to inactivity, keeping warm was Callan's biggest worry even with Ivy to cuddle. There was also little to do between Garrido's grilling sessions, which normally merely entailed the lieutenant ranting and making threats. As the weather still grounded her plane, Ivy was present on many occasions leaving Callan uneasy when Garrido eyed her licentiously.

The slimy bastard doesn't even try to hide his lust. He's positively slobbering at the chops.

Hemingway visited once saying the front was a shambles with thousands dead and the survivors tearing one another apart with bayonets and daggers after their ammunition ran out.

The weather broke a few days into the New Year allowing the Condor Legion to unleash its Heinkels, *Stukas* and Messerschmitts to pound Republican positions surrounding Teruel Citadel where d'Harcourt's men fought on.

8 January 1938

'What's the commotion?' Callan asked as Ivy entered their tent.

There was enormous excitement throughout the HQ base. Troops cheered and fired shots into the air, wasting precious ammunition in Callan's opinion.

'The Teruel garrison has surrendered,' Ivy replied. 'They're bringing POWs in now, including Colonel d'Harcourt.'

Despite his prisoner status no one stopped Callan leaving his tent to join the crowd of support troops and reserves to see the Nationalists marched into camp. A group of a few hundred emaciated, freezing men shuffled between two ranks of Republican escorts who were in little better shape. The victors didn't look elated. They were hollow-eyed, unshaven and exhausted. Many on both sides had limbs bandaged against frost bite, but in many cases it was too late — numerous amputations were to follow.

Two men led the POWs. Perhaps because both wore wire-framed spectacles, neither was particularly warrior-like, but they marched forward with dignity, pride and determination.

'That's Colonel d'Harcourt,' Witherspoon explained.

'Who's the joker with him?' Callan asked.

'Anselmo Polanco, Teruel's bishop. Doesn't look much of a firebrand, does he? But he's been one of the main driving forces among the *Falange* in Teruel.'

'They're in big trouble now,' Ivy observed.

'I know it's unusual for this war, but maybe not. The word is out the military admires d'Harcourt's tenacity and dedication to duty. Y'know, soldier-to-soldier.'

'It will not be up to the generals,' Señor Vargas said, pushing through the crowd to join them.

'These men will be taken to POW camps around Barcelona and may not be treated well. Rations are in short supply and there is little to go round.'

'It can't be worse than Teruel. Most of these guys would have starved to death if the enemy didn't get 'em,' Callan observed.

'Quite so, but I fear the colonel and bishop will be incarcerated within *La Modelo's* walls.'

La Modelo was built at the beginning of the century with the best of intentions as a model modern penal facility emphasising reform rather than punishment. Now it was overcrowded with political prisoners and POWs.

'I fear Lieutenant Garrido desires the same for you, Señor McAlister,' Vargas added in his now permanent apologetic tone.

'Bloody hell,' Witherspoon whispered between clenched teeth. 'There'll be no rescuing from there.'

'Rescue...?'

But Callan had no time to pursue the matter because Garrido turned up in a foul mood. He cuffed the sentry who'd allowed Callan to walk about freely, ordering Callan back to his tent.

The Republican camp celebrated that night. They may have been short of food, but there was no shortage of wine to go around on that particular occasion. The prisoners were herded into holding pens until the morning when General Lister hoped he'd be able to use the railway to get them to Barcelona where they'd no longer be his concern.

Night fell early during those mid-winter days. Not long after nightfall Ivy, Callan and Witherspoon were hunched over mugs of steaming coffee after their evening meal of bread, cheese and rice. After supper Ivy took the dishes to the canteen marquee to wash them.

She was intercepted by Señor Vargas accompanied by a squad of sentries.

'Lieutenant Garrido wishes to speak with you,' Vargas said.

'What about?' Ivy asked with suspicion.

'He has not confided in me, but I understand it concerns your husband's future.'

'Shouldn't we get Callan then?'

'The lieutenant indicated he only wanted to see you. He was — insistent.'

Ivy was left with little choice. She was in no position to take on a bunch of armed men.

When they entered Garrido's tent he stood beside his director's chair in front of a kerosene heater. A folding table, small filing cabinet and camp stretcher were the only other furniture. Despite the cold Garrido stood without his jacket and had unshouldered his braces. An empty wine bottle lay on the canvas floor while another was half full on the table. Two glass beakers stood beside the bottle. Garrido's service pistol lay in its holster on top of the cabinet

Garrido appeared well into his cups and was obviously unsteady on his feet.

To Ivy's surprise, he dismissed Vargas along with the guards.

'You sit,' Garrido ordered in heavily accented English, indicating the chair.

Ivy hesitated, eying him doubtfully, but then obeyed, placing the plates on the table. Garrido smiled slyly. By complying she allowed him to assume he was in control, which was no more than the truth at that point.

'Señor McAlister goes with POWs tomorrow,' Garrido said.

For a man who knew no English two weeks ago, he'd picked up the language remarkably well. Perhaps he'd rehearsed what he had to say and didn't expect any discussion. In any event Ivy's horrified expression pleased him.

'*La Modelo*,' he added.

And then he got down to business.

'I stop that if you good *señora*.'

'What do you mean?'

'You good *señora*. Garrido maybe release McAlister. You drink wine now.'

As he poured the wine, Ivy was in no doubt what being a 'good *señora*' entailed and she was having none of it.

'I will not tolerate this. I shall have Señor Vargas report your unseemly behaviour to General Lister.'

About then negotiations broke down irrecoverably, but Garrido wasn't unduly distressed. Maybe he enjoyed knocking women around, because it looked like that was how it would end up.

'I'll scream!' Ivy warned.

'No one come. Guards are gone. I give them you anyway — *manana*.'

Garrido wasted no more time. He grabbed Ivy, slapping her viciously across her cheek when she resisted. He hit her again when she continued to struggle. She spun around with the force of the blow. Garrido saw his chance to push her to the floor. Obviously the camp bed was inadequate for rough-and-tumble rape.

The table and dishes went flying as Ivy slammed into the filing cabinet and instinct took over. She grabbed for Garrido's revolver and heaved it from the holster. But she lost her balance and crashed to the floor with Garrido writhing on top of her. Ivy was fit and fought like the devil, but Garrido was at least ten years younger and strong for a small man.

He realised Ivy had his gun and instantly clamped his hand around her wrist. His face was inches from hers, reeking of sweat, wine and lust. The pistol was a small calibre double-action Spanish made Smith and Wesson clone.

Ivy had just been slugged twice. Her cheeks stung abominably and her body was bruised in several places. She was no shrinking violet and mad as hell. Garrido seriously under-estimated a woman who'd endured four bloody years during the Great War and was no stranger to violence and death. But his lust took control. As clawed at Ivy's clothing, she jammed the gun-barrel into his belly and pulled the trigger.

Whether she'd intended to merely cock the weapon and warn Garrido off remained unclear, but it was too late. The bullet tore through his belly, lodging in his gut. Garrido stared at Ivy in disbelief as he let her go and grasped his stomach. Blood welled up through his undershirt and fingers.

The shot was remarkably quiet, just a pop smothered by both Ivy and Garrido's close-pressed bodies. The lieutenant tried to speak, but blood gurgled through his teeth as he gasped for air. During her time with FANY, Ivy had seen scores of wounded men and knew when there was no hope. Garrido was bleeding to death internally.

He was on his knees, shaking uncontrollably as shock set in. He slumped across his cot and Ivy managed to lift his feet onto the bed. She felt for a pulse, but by then he was dead. She was unsure of her emotions, but remorse wasn't one of them.

Serves you right, you filthy pig. Nobody interferes with Ivy Brown without her permission.

Which was all well and good, but now what..?

Chapter 5 — Fight or Flight

Ivy wasn't the sort of woman to dither, but she had no idea what to do about Garrido's corpse. The first thing was to tell Callan, although how he could help while under guard was anyone's guess. However when she returned to the tent the guards were some distance away warming themselves by a 44 gallon drum of burning trash.

Callan and Johnny Witherspoon were playing cards seemingly unconcerned about what tomorrow might bring. She rushed to Callan and flung her arms around him.

'Well that's nice...' he began.

'We're in big trouble,' she said, sounding calmer than she felt.

'Yes, I know. I think they're shipping me to *La Modelo* with d'Harcourt's crew. Vargas is trying to pull some strings, but with no luck so far.'

'I shot Lieutenant Garrido. He tried to rape me.'

'The dirty bastard! Are you OK?'

'Not really, but we have to get out of camp. I sort of killed him and someone will discover the body tomorrow morning.'

'Sort of killed him..?'

'Well, killed him a lot.'

'Oh, he's dead then,' Witherspoon said. 'We don't have to get out of camp — we have to get out of the bloody country!'

'That's impossible.'

'Maybe — maybe not,' Callan said after a pause.

'How're the planes?' Callan asked Witherspoon.

'The Fulgur is just about ready and the Viceroy was fine when we flew in. What do you reckon, Ivy?'

As the designated pilot, Ivy was responsible for the plane while away from home base.

'It's serviceable. I ran the engines and swept snow off the wings every day.'

'Fuel?

'Enough to get to Reus — easily.'

'No further?'

'I had to keep the weight down or I'd never get the crate off this strip.'

'What's your plan?' Witherspoon asked.

Callan told him.

'Look Johnny, you don't have to be part of this. We could end up dead for all I know.'

'Count me in,' Witherspoon replied. 'The republic is falling apart. The *Falange* are counter-attacking already. There's no way the commies will hold Teruel. It's the thin end of the wedge and they're shafted. I reckon it's high time to skip town.'

'You might want this,' Ivy said, holding out Garrido's revolver.

'You keep it. I have one of my own.'

'I'm sure that little pop-gun will come in handy against the whole Republican army,' Callan said.

Ivy glared at him, but pocketed the pistol anyway.

They gathered what they could, especially blankets. The Viceroy's fuselage would be like a freezer. Witherspoon peered outside. A few soldiers were about, but they were huddled around a brazier, including the two assigned as Callan's guards. What did they care and where would anyone go on a freezing night anyway? As they left the tent the first person they bumped into was Señor Vargas.

'Bloody hell, where did you pop up from?' Witherspoon declared. 'I just checked the coast was clear.'

'What is going on..?' he demanded.

'Sorry,' Ivy said, sticking Garrido's revolver under Vargas' nose. 'We don't want trouble or to hurt you, but we have to leave town.'

'I understand Señor McAlister's predicament,' Vargas said reasonably enough.

'It's a little more complicated than that,' Callan said.

They quickly explained Garrido was dead and a military court was unlikely to be sympathetic.

'I don't suppose we can ask you to keep this under wraps until we're out of here?' Callan said.

Vargas' reaction was surprising.

'It will be best if you take me with you,' he said.

'Why?' Callan was astonished.

'I shall be implicated.'

'But you haven't done anything,' Ivy said.

'By association, *Señora*,' Vargas shrugged. 'It was I who arranged your employment. I will be held accountable.'

'Maybe that's not a bad idea,' Witherspoon said. 'My Spanish is just adequate and we might need a little authority when we get to Reus.'

As it turned out Vargas thought much the same as Witherspoon. The Spaniard was disillusioned by the way the Republic had simply become a communist dictatorship, little better than Franco's Nationalists. Vargas agreed he could be useful, because foreigners would have difficulty dealing with local authorities. The communist government saw the International Brigades as necessary evils. General Lister hadn't even deployed them against Teruel, hoping for an all-Spanish victory.

On Vargas' suggestion they waited six nerve-wracking hours until pre-dawn when most of the camp was asleep, although the battle raged relentlessly. Gunfire and explosions still rattled from Teruel. If they went straight to the plane and hid inside, not only would it be hideously cold, but they'd be missed if any guards felt inclined to check Callan's tent.

Freeing Callan was ludicrously easy. Vargas simply told the guards Callan was required at Lister's HQ. Witherspoon masqueraded as an armed escort and the bored soldiers merely shrugged and let them walk away. No one questioned the early hour or the knapsack stuffed with blankets Callan carried.

'Now it all depends on the weather,' Ivy said.

'It doesn't look too bad,' Witherspoon observed.

Dawn cracked along the eastern horizon and the cloud base had indeed lifted to a few hundred feet which was good enough to take off. What the weather was like at Reus was anyone's guess, but in this case the old pilot adage: *take-off is optional — landing is mandatory* didn't apply. Right then take-off was mandatory.

They reached the Viceroy easily enough. As the plane had no fuselage windows, it made a good hiding place. With only two transport planes on the flight-line, no sentries patrolled the area. There was no point to delay further, so Ivy went straight to the pilot's station.

Ever mindful of the need for reliable engine starts, Ivy had removed the aircraft batteries from their normal compartment and rewired them inside the fuselage. In this way she could disconnect them when not in use to prevent charge leakage. She also insulated the batteries against the severe cold with several layers of sacking.

'Park brake on, chocks away,' Ivy said softly.

Callan quickly reconnected the battery terminals and took the co-pilot seat. Meanwhile Witherspoon dislodged the wheel chocks. It took several desperate kicks as the plane had rolled slightly, wedging the rear chocks. Finally Witherspoon just removed the front chocks as the plane would taxi forward anyway. He tossed them through the cabin door and clambered aboard just as the starboard engine spluttered into life.

She didn't waste any time. Witherspoon had barely slammed the fuselage door when the Viceroy rolled forward.

'Contact,' Ivy said and there was no need to be quiet this time.

Callan flicked on the magneto switches while Ivy adjusted the throttles, mixture and prop control levers.

The port engines backfired twice and finally settled at idling RPM.

Daylight began streaming across the Republican camp and it was clear the weather had improved, which was good, but also posed a problem.

Soldiers were waking by then and crawled from their tents and dugouts, eyeing the plane curiously.

'Do you think they'll try to stop us?' Ivy asked.

'Why should they? We could be on a legitimate mission for all they know,' Callan replied. 'Now if only these flaming cylinder-head and oil temperatures would rise...'

He tapped the gauge glass while the needles stubbornly hovered below the green-band. It was vital the engine warmed up before Ivy applied full power to allow the lubrication oil to become less viscous and flow where it was needed. Otherwise they ran the risk of the motors seizing or shattering due to thermal shock.

'They'll be alright when I reach the runway threshold,' Ivy said, although Callan wasn't so sure.

'The run-up check will lift the temperatures,' she reassured him..

'Here's hoping, but if one of the engines isn't up to scratch, there's nothing much we can do about it. We certainly can't turn back.'

As they turned onto the runway the oil-temperature gauges had crept into the cautionary amber-band, but still below the green-arc which indicated a takeoff could be safely undertaken. No amount of tapping would budge the needle to move beyond its ponderous inclination.

While Callan and Ivy concentrated on the engine instruments, Witherspoon kept his eyes on events outside the plane.

'Bugger,' he hissed, standing between the pilot seats. 'Looks like we've got a farewell committee.'

Sure enough about two thirds along the strip, which was not much more than a cleared paddock, a troop of republican infantry strolled idly towards them in most unmilitary fashion.

'You reckon they're going to try to stop us?' Callan thought aloud.

'They don't look particularly angry,' Witherspoon observed. 'Maybe they just happen to be passing.'

'Well, I'm not giving them the benefit of the doubt,' Ivy said, pushing the throttles, mixture and prop-control levers forwards. 'Those temperatures are close enough.'

The engines coughed, but responded and the plane lurched forward.

As the Viceroy gathered speed, the oncoming soldiers seemed unaware that they were in its path.

'They must be half asleep,' Ivy yelled. 'Get out of the way, you idiots.'

Of course no one heard her above the roaring engines, but that did get the soldiers' attention. At first they simply stopped and stood still. It seemed like eternity before they realised the danger. When they did, the troops panicked. They ran helter-skelter, crashing into one another and knocking several to the ground.

Men dived aside as the Viceroy sped past. Ivy pulled on the control-column, hoping there was enough lift under the wings to get airborne. The plane hopped over most of the prone men, but one fellow lifted his head and the thump was felt throughout the fuselage. The plane dropped to earth again, bounced and rumbled on.

The bounce knocked the momentum from the plane causing the airspeed indicator to drop by fifteen knots. Ivy was rapidly running out of takeoff distance and trees loomed at the strip end.

'Oh shit...' three voices groaned in unison.

There was nothing for it, but Ivy kept cool. Reefing the plane into the air would have definitely stalled the wings ending in disaster.

Instead she eased the control-column back, finessing the elevators so the aircraft slowly lifted skywards while still allowing the airspeed to increase. As foliage filled the windscreen Ivy eased the plane upwards just enough to crest the treetops. Branches brushed the under fuselage and a few leaves were sprayed to confetti by the props, but the plane was clear.

Ivy flew just above the canopy allowing the plane to accelerate to a safe climbing airspeed.

'Thank heaven the birds have all flown south for winter,' Callan muttered. 'All we need now is a bird-strike.'

Ivy adjusted the engine controls for the climb. She banked the plane to the northeast. Reus next stop.

'Bloody hell that was close,' Witherspoon sighed. 'Excellent work, Ivy.'

'We're not out of the woods yet. What's the plan after Reus?'

'Toulouse seems sensible to me,' Callan said. 'At least we know the way.'

Two hours later in rapidly improving weather they touched down at Reus. In true Spanish fashion the base was in no particular hurry getting started. The tower was still unmanned and no one other than a couple of sentries hung around the flight line. Most of the Russian fighter planes were still parked in revetments and it appeared no missions were planned for that day. Perhaps the squadron commanders thought weather conditions over Teruel were still unsuitable.

'Good,' Witherspoon said. 'The last thing we want is some smart-arse poking around asking questions.'

Without delay, Ivy parked the Viceroy alongside the nearest fuelling truck. Callan cranked the diesel pump, earthed the plane and began filling the tanks. Meanwhile Witherspoon and Vargas scouted around to find something to eat.

'Don't wander too far,' Callan warned, 'we're taking off as soon as the crate's fuelled.'

For a large military unit, Reus was eerily quiet...but not for long.

The Viceroy tanks were full. Temperature affected fuel loads in a curious way. In cold weather you actually got more bang for your buck. Petrol density increased with dropping temperature, making it burn more efficiently and increasing the aircraft range.

Good, we're gonna need to get as far away as possible, Callan thought, *now where the bloody hell are Johnny and...*

A shot echoed between the tower building and one of the arsenal storage huts followed by a ragged salvo. Seconds later Witherspoon and Vargas raced from cover followed by an excited section of armed men. One soldier levelled his rifle, but his sergeant stopped him.

Callan didn't understand what the NCO said, but, *we'll take 'em alive,* was a pretty good guess.

'Crank her up, Ivy,' Callan yelled. 'Looks like word about Garrido is out...'

He turned and, too his dismay saw disaster.

What the...

He spun around again. Ivy hadn't moved.

Bloody hell...

They now faced another squad of infantrymen with their rifles aimed towards him. A cacophony of animated chatter followed, with the sergeant yelling orders and Vargas protesting at the top of his voice. But the soldiers were having none of it and marched the quartet towards the control tower where a very smug looking captain stood slapping his thigh with a swagger-stick.

'Oh bugger,' Callan hissed. 'They know, don't they?'

'Si, Señor,' Vargas replied with a forlorn sigh. 'Word from Teruel came in just as we passed the radio-station.'

'It took 'em about a second to put two-and-two together,' Witherspoon added.

'We have orders to shoot you on sight,' the captain said in heavily accented English. 'Come, we will go to the airstrip. We don't want stray bullets damaging our precious planes, buildings or going through the tents. Someone might be inside.'

He grinned as if he'd cracked a fine joke, but it looked like stray bullets wouldn't be a problem. About a hundred ground and aircrew now gathered around. The shots had roused even the latest sleepers and what better way to start the day than an execution.

'It is a pity about the *señora*,' the captain said with a shrug, 'but we have orders to be prompt. I understand General Lister is very angry...*si*, very angry indeed.'

So Ivy, Callan, Johnny Witherspoon and Señor Vargas were marched to the centre of the airfield as the cloud cleared revealing the first blue sky for over a month.

Chapter 6 — Condor Legion

'I'm so sorry, boys,' Ivy said forlornly. 'I've really got us into a pickle this time.'

'I dunno, we've been in tougher spots,' Callan said, placing his arm around her shoulder.

'In case you haven't noticed, buddy,' Witherspoon said, 'we're surrounded by half a battalion of trigger-happy guys.'

'So what's the plan?'

'Plan? There isn't any plan!'

'Bugger. I was really hoping for a plan.'

'Halt!' the captain barked, bringing his men to a sharp boot-crunching stop although the four condemned shuffled a bit, which was understandable.

They were man-handled into a rough line while the soldiers lined up a few yards away. The troops were armed with an assortment of weapons, many being single-shot breech-loaders, but what did it matter? They couldn't miss at that range. The soldiers were so confident they hadn't even searched their captives. Witherspoon had been disarmed, but Ivy still had Garrido's pistol tucked under her jacket, although there was no hope of drawing the weapon for a shoot-out. One hand-gun against a rifle company wasn't an option.

'So this is how it all ends, darling,' Ivy sighed as she clung to Callan. 'By golly if I could lay my hands on Gene, I'd wring his bloody neck...'

Callan held her tightly while Johnny Witherspoon and Señor Vargas put on brave faces. Whatever else they were going down as men.

'*Escuadrón de ejecución atención!*' the officer bellowed, quite unnecessarily in Ivy's opinion. It wasn't like he was far away.

I suppose things like that make you irritable when you're facing death...

'*Rifles actuales — apunta...*'

Callan and Ivy knew enough Spanish to understand the orders — Execution squad attention — present arms — take aim...

Blam! Blam! Blam!

The ground shook with such force the soldiers staggered to stay upright. Callan, Ivy, Witherspoon and Vargas crumpled to the ground as the earth continued to tremble.

The entire airfield erupted in explosions, spraying debris and shrapnel in all directions. Metal fragments whizzed past slicing into some of the firing squad, ripping them to shreds. The condemned four were spared when the hail of death flashed just inches above their heads.

Men scattered as the explosions kept coming. The noise was deafening and the shock-waves battered anyone in their path.

'Bloody hell, it's an air raid,' Witherspoon yelled. 'Bravo the *Condor Legion!'*

'They're trying to kill us too, you goose,' Callan replied, grabbing Ivy's hand. 'And if they don't, the bloody Republicans will have another go. Come on!'

Witherspoon hauled Vargas to his feet and stumble-ran down the airstrip. He cursed losing his pistol. A few shots might have kept the soldiers' heads down, but it was hardly worth worrying about. The Condor legion was doing the job for him.

Bombs crumped all around. Sometimes the shockwaves buffeted them to the ground, but the four fugitives quickly resumed their frantic dash. Several members of the firing-squad made it to the protection of sand-bag revetments. They fired a few wild and random shots from shelter. Bullets zinged past Callan's ear, but he just kept going ensuring he clung to Ivy's hand.

A bomb smashed into the closest revetment blasting everyone within to scarlet mush and bone shards. A skull rolled past Vargas who, considering he wasn't a warrior, coped commendably. At least the rifle fire ceased from that particular source. The Republican fighter planes were the main target and half a dozen were blasted into obliteration within seconds.

The Viceroy swayed dangerously with every shock-wave. A bomb-blast slammed Ivy against the fuselage, winding her. Callan grabbed her arm and heaved her through the side door. Witherspoon hauled Vargas aboard and slammed the door. He scrambled into the co-pilot seat as Callan booted the engines to life.

Meanwhile the Condor Legion continued its relentless bombardment.

'God knows what state the strip's in,' Callan said, 'but there was no time for speculation.

He opened the throttles and the plane didn't budge.

'We forgot the flaming chocks,' Witherspoon cried.

'No time to fret, I'll roll over them!'

Fortunately the grass at Reus wasn't frozen solid like that on higher terrain near Teruel. At full power the Viceroy main-wheels forced the chocks into the sod. With a thump, the tyres broke free and the plane surged forward.

Once again there was no time for pre-flight checks, it was simply full speed ahead and hope for the best. Callan turned the plane straight onto the runway which was now seriously pot-holed. Ivy was flung across the fuselage as Callan kicked the rudders pedals to avoid a bomb crater. He managed to dodge two more, but then ahead bombs had destroyed the entire runway. A ragged-edged trench lay before them!

'Bugger!'

Callan pulled the control column backwards. The plane had not achieved flying speed, but under-wing air pressure had built up sufficiently to reduce the load on the wheels. The plane glided over the pits before bouncing back to earth. A little energy was lost, but the Viceroy quickly accelerated. Approaching dangerously close to the strip end, Callan eased the controls back once more. The plane rose agonisingly slowly, but brushed over the low vegetation beyond the airfield boundary.

The Viceroy hugged the tree-line as Callan turned eastwards towards the coast. Callan dared not climb because the Viceroy was no match for Messerschmitt 109 interceptors. That tactic proved successful and none of the Condor fighters bothered to take up the chase.

After half an hour, Callan judged it safe to climb to five thousand feet. Witherspoon and Vargas helped Ivy to sit against the fuselage. Other than a bump on her temple and a screaming headache, she was OK. She drank some water and felt better.

'And that is why the *Falange* will win,' Vargas announced. 'Their bombers were ready to strike at the first chance, while our *La Glorious* sit on their hands waiting for nice weather. No planes will be able to leave Reus until they've repaired the strip and that'll take days or weeks.'

'That's if there are any crates left in one piece,' Witherspoon added. 'Lucky we don't want to go back because I reckon there'll be no strip to land on.'

Callan had been steering the Viceroy eastwards, but now it was time for more precise navigation.

'We can't head for France,' he conceded. 'I expect we're wanted by the Republican government and France is sympathetic and likely to extradite us.'

'I know where I'm heading,' Witherspoon announced. 'Mirios!'

'Your island..?" Ivy said.

'Sure, why not. You'll love it there and we can sort out our cash-flow matters after we arrive. I've got a swag stashed away with *Credit Suisse*, and I reckon you'd have a few bucks too.'

'What about you, Señor Vargas?' Ivy asked.

'Spain is over for me,' Vargas replied looking even more doleful than ever.

'What about your family?'

'They are gone, *Señora*. Killed when *Falange* planes bombed Madrid. I was just a simple school master. I was not political, but the Republic summoned me into service because I spoke several languages.'

Ivy embraced him because he simply looked so sad.

'Stick with us, Señor,' Witherspoon said cheerfully. 'You'll love Mirios.'

'I have no money.'

'You won't need any. You're a school teacher you said, we've got plenty of kids. You'll have no trouble earning your keep.'

The idea must have appealed to Vargas, because he actually smiled.

'In that case, it would please me if you called me Juan as I hope we are to be friends.'

So it was first names all round from then.

'There *is* one thing we have to consider though...' Witherspoon began.

'And what might that be?' Callan said, eying the Canadian suspiciously.

'Mirios doesn't have a landing strip.'

'What about your plane?'

'It's a float-plane remember, I moor it in the harbour.'

'So what do we do?'

'Don't sweat it,' Witherspoon said, wrestling with an aviation chart until he'd folded it his satisfaction. He prodded north-western Sicily with his finger.

'How about we head for Catania in Sicily? I know there's an airstrip there. The Ities should be OK. They're in thick with the *Falange.*'

'It's a long way from Mirios,' Callan observed.

'We'll go by sea.'

'What about this plane?'

'We'll sell it of course,' Witherspoon beamed as if it would be the easiest thing in the world. 'Steer ten degrees to starboard and we'll pick up a fix crossing Sardinia.'

The plan went quite well except everyone was hungry. Ivy had nothing more than a bag of barley-sugar sweets to share and the trouble with a long flight is you don't have much else to think about except your stomach. Rotating flying and navigation duties helped pass the time.

They confirmed their position over Sardinia, adjusted their course and crossed the Sicilian coast at Trapani. However they didn't know the *Regia Aeronautica* had recently established a military base at Trapani-Milo. And that would have been OK as they overflew the airfield at eight thousand feet and no one would probably have noticed.

But they reckoned without *Maggiore* Bartolo Grasso.

Judging by his military record, Grasso was something of an ace. He'd been credited with five enemy kills during WWI and won numerous air races in the 1920s and 30s before shipping out to Eritrea in 1936. He downed several Ethiopian mercenary planes before transferring to Spain with similar success. Grasso has been recalled and was preparing a squadron of Fiat C.R. 32 fighters for operational service in Albania.

Il Duce Benito Mussolini had his eyes firmly set on annexing Albania thus controlling the east and western Adriatic shores. Italy's aviation zenith peaked in the 30s, but had declined since then. The C.R. 32 was Italy's front-line fighter, but as a fixed-wheel bi-plane it was already outdated. Although it was a tough and manoeuvrable aircraft it was no match for the emerging military mono-planes. Nevertheless as Albania had nothing to oppose an air attack, the C.R. 32 was up for the job. An upgraded model C.R. 42 was in development, but not yet operational.

Just as the Viceroy cruised over Trapani, *Maggiore* Grasso happened to be air-testing one of his machines. He spotted the unidentified aircraft and swept in for a closer look. Although Grasso was no stranger to air-racing, the Viceroy was a one-off, which he didn't recognise. What he did recognise however were the Spanish Republican markings on the fuselage which intrigued him. The aircraft was a long way from home.

Grasso banked his plane steeply and flew within inches of the Viceroy's port wing-tip. Ivy, who was occupying the pilot's seat at the time, was the first to notice the fighter beside them.

'We've got company,' she announced. 'I think the pilot is trying to tell us something.'

The C.R. 32 was radio equipped and tuned to Trapani Tower's frequency, but the Viceroy maintained radio silence. Callan and his companions had no idea what the tower frequency was and no intention of finding out.

Grasso gestured for the Viceroy to descend and land at Trapani field, but no one thought that was a good idea. So Grasso flew ahead, rocking his plane's wings which was an international military signal for 'follow me'.

'It looks like an air force base down there,' Callan observed from the co-pilot seat. 'I can see lines of fighters along the strip.'

'Probably best to press onto Catania,' Witherspoon said. 'When I was there it was just a small strip. We really don't want to get mixed up with any more military types, do we?'

The C.R. 32 peeled away in a steep dive towards Trapani field.

'What do we do?' Ivy asked.

'Ignore the bugger,' Callan said. 'We press on to Catani.'

'We'll never out-run him.'

'We'll see.'

Callan pushed the throttle forwards, adjusting the mixture and prop-speed levers for maximum speed.

'Fuel consumption will be rubbish, but we still have ample reserves for Catani.'

It turned out to be a good call. Grasso's plane was low on fuel and he'd expended the plane's machinegun magazines during test firing. He was left with no option but to land. He didn't waste time refuelling and rearming his plane or organising a flight to give chase. He simply checked with his ground crew and dashed for the nearest plane with full petrol tanks and ammunition magazines.

Grasso was airborne in less than ten minutes, but the Viceroy was already over thirty miles away. He had to be quick because the C.R. 32 was limited to a range of just under five hundred miles at best cruise speed and petrol-air mixture setting. But even at top speed it meant he could make it to Sicily's east coast and back.

He caught up as the Viceroy approached Mt Etna.

The plane ahead appeared as a speck against the backdrop of the eleven-thousand foot smouldering landmark. This time Grasso had no intention of letting the Republican — ergo communist — interloper escape, even if it meant shooting it down.

Sulphurous vapour oozed from fissures along the mountain peak extending down the slope in places. That was nothing new, Mount Etna was indeed one of the most active volcanoes worldwide, but generally its eruptions were simply moody and only occasionally life-threatening. That was not to say it should be taken lightly.

Grasso considered the Viceroy an enemy plane. He'd learnt it was better to shoot first when in doubt. He'd given them one chance back over Trapani, so they only had themselves to blame, didn't they? He wasn't worried about an international incident.

Benito Mussolini had made it clear Republican Spain was no friend of Italy.

Once the Viceroy was squarely in his gun-sights he squeezed the trigger and four machineguns blazed across the sky. Grasso watched the tracer-bullets streak towards his prey. He wasn't an ace for nothing and could hardly miss at such close range with no other enemy aircraft to worry about.

He saw with satisfaction the port motor burst into flames with debris spewing from the shattered engine cowling.

'Bloody hell,' Callan hissed between clenched teeth. 'We're under attack!'

The Viceroy banked sharply and Callan heaved the control-column to compensate, but the plane refused to respond. The wings lost lift and the Viceroy started to spiral earthwards.

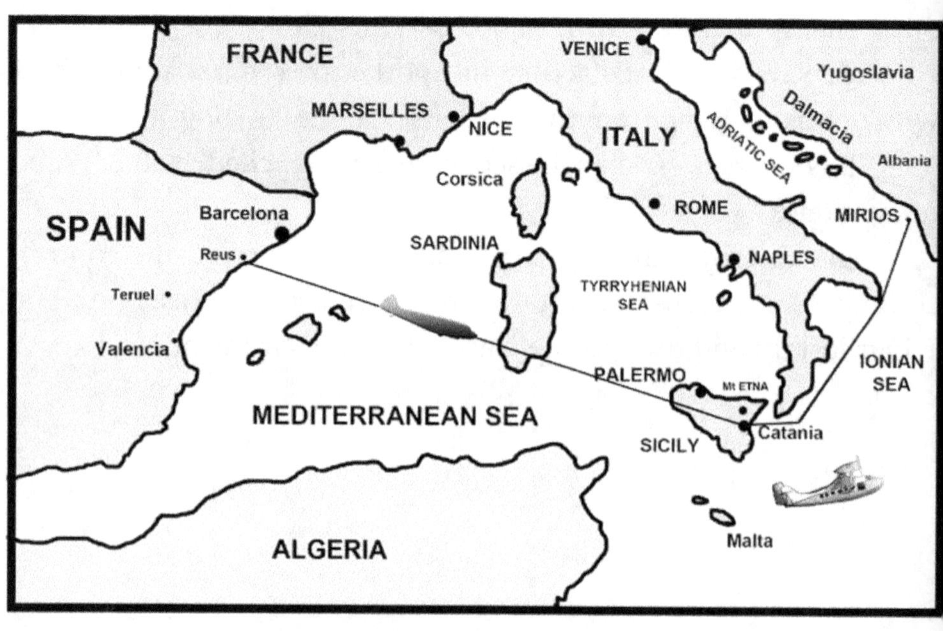
FRANCE
VENICE
Yugoslavia
MARSEILLES
NICE
ITALY
Dalmacia
ADRIATIC SEA
Albania
Corsica
SPAIN
Barcelona
ROME
MIRIOS
Reus
SARDINIA
NAPLES
Teruel
TYRRYHENIAN
SEA
Valencia
IONIAN
SEA
PALERMO
Mt ETNA
MEDITERRANEAN SEA
SICILY
Catania
ALGERIA
Malta

Chapter 7 — Goodbye Viceroy

'I can't hold the wretched thing! The rudder's hard over and she's still turning,' Callan declared. 'Give us a hand on the yoke, Ivy.'

Ivy grabbed the controls from her co-pilot station. She and Callan overcame the wind force of the ailerons and the bank decreased slightly, but the plane kept turning.

'Kill the good engine, Callan,' Witherspoon said with commendable calmness considering the imminent crash. 'The prop force is too great. It's pushing us over. Full rudder-pedal can't stop it.'

Callan pulled the throttles to idle and the Viceroy responded immediately. With no asymmetric power, the plane wings levelled, but of course there was no power left to stay airborne so Callan trimmed the plane for best glide-range speed.

'OK, look for a landing area,' Callan said, 'and we might even get out of this alive.'

As he spoke they all saw the C.R. 32 flash past the window, climbing steeply before turning sharply and come in for another strafing run.

'Cocky bastard,' Witherspoon snarled. 'Brave as hell against an unarmed transport plane.'

Grasso eyed the stricken Viceroy with cool satisfaction. At first it looked like there was no recovery, but remarkably the pilot regained control and steadied the plane into a gentle descent. Aware that if the Republican plane landed safely and the occupants escaped, it was possible he'd never discover their identity. Why not shoot them down and send troops to investigate whenever they could locate the wreck.

Grasso dived his plane past the Viceroy, banked steeply to attack head-on. His target was a sitting duck. The Viceroy and its crew were doomed...

Right about then Mount Etna erupted.

It was neither the largest nor most threatening of Etna's flatulent outbursts, but the two planes were close to the exploding fissure. Lava gouts belched from the crater accompanied by a cloud of sulphurous smoke that drifted south-eastwards with the prevailing wind.

A burst of ash-filled smoke swept over the Viceroy immediately clogging the engine and rendering it useless. There was no motor-splutter or coughing, the engine just seized. The prop shuddered to a stop, but now acted like a brake. There was no way of feathering it and the plane banked alarmingly in the other direction. An acrid stench filled the fuselage, but the ash mostly remained outside.

'Shit,' Callan cursed under his breath. 'Some days you should stay in bed.'

'Not this morning,' Ivy reminded him. 'Look we're dropping below the dust-cloud.'

'I can't see a ruddy thing,' Callan replied. 'The windscreen is coated with ash.'

'I can see a little.'

'OK, take the controls — handing over.'

Ivy was appalled at how badly the Viceroy handled with the prop continually dragging the plane to the right. There was no way of clearing the windscreen wipers as the ash had dried into a solid crust, but a little forward visibility was better than none.

'At least that bloody Itie has buggered off,' Witherspoon observed scanning the sky through both cockpit side windows which were still clear.

Johnny Witherspoon was correct. Grasso radioed his Trapani base, reporting he'd dodged the ash-cloud and left Mount Etna as fast as his plane could fly. He'd lost sight of the Viceroy anyway and who's to say a small eruption wouldn't turn into a massive one. The duty officer immediately telephoned the Eastern *Carabineri* Divisional HQ, advising them to investigate a mysterious aircraft with Spanish Republican livery flying around their area.

As Grasso headed west, Ivy held the Viceroy on its easterly course towards lower terrain. And at that moment the remaining propeller hub sheered, snapping the blades into two lethal missiles, which immediately flashed from sight. The plane bucked, but Ivy was able to gain control and flying was much easier even though the Viceroy had become a glider.

'I never thought I'd say I'd be glad to lose a prop, but that's a relief,' Ivy said. 'Hang on everyone, I see a field ahead. It's not much, but it's all we've got. I'll go for it.'

'It'll be a belly landing,' Callan advised. 'Hydraulics are shot and there's no time to hand-crank the wheels down.'

'Hang on back there, Juan,' Witherspoon yelled. 'We're in for a bumpy landing.'

Ivy focused her attention entirely on the tiny clear patch of windscreen. She saw grass ahead, but was aware that carob and olive trees were common and could be close by, but there were no other choices, so she put the idea of crashing into trees out of her mind. In any event there was no time to worry, the ground rushed up to meet them.

Ivy reduced the plane's descent rate in the nick of time. Even so the impact jarred the fuselage alarmingly accompanied by scraping metal on the rocky surface. They missed the scattered trees but the plane bashed into rocks as it slithered to a halt. A boulder lay to the side, ripping the right wing from the fuselage. The plane spun on its axis, throwing Witherspoon and Vargas across the cabin.

Aviation gasoline spewed from the severed wing tank, exploding into flames. Luckily the rest of the wreck slid far enough ahead to avoid the inferno. The fuel tanks were by no means full but the flames flared and spread to the surrounding dry grass and thorn bushes.

Callan and Ivy were protected by their seat-belts, but both Johnny Witherspoon and Juan lay still behind them. No one moved at first, stunned by the crash, but Callan sprang out of his seat when smoke filled the cockpit.

'Abandon ship!' Callan yelled.

Ivy tried to get up but couldn't move.

'Undo your seat-belt, Ivy,' Callan said.

She fumbled with the buckle and followed Callan to the rear door. Witherspoon staggered to his feet and helped Callan drag Vargas aft.

'Go ahead and open the door, Ivy,' Callan said.

She grabbed the latch, but the door failed to move. Callan and Witherspoon put their shoulders into the job, but with no success.

'The fuselage is buckled, we'll never budge it!' Callan said.

Jonny Witherspoon was in no mood to be roasted then or at any time, but the increasing smoke and petrol fumes clogged their nostrils and it was only a matter of seconds before they'd suffocate or perish in the spreading fire.

'C'mon, let's go forward,' he said.

The Viceroy windscreen was in two panels with a central reinforcing bar. The panes were large enough for a person to scramble through, but although cracked in places, had not shattered. The thing about aircraft windshields is they're built to withstand huge wind-blasts, bird strikes and hail stones, so they're tough. Callan clambered into the co-pilot seat and tried to boot the panel free, but it was almost impossible to find enough purchase for a decent kick in the confined cockpit.

By then everyone was coughing and smoke stung their eyes. Visibility was almost zero, causing confusion and disorientation.

'I've got this,' Witherspoon yelled. 'Gimme your gun, Ivy!'

She handed Garrido's pistol to Witherspoon who fired point-blank into the windshield. The pane shattered which should have been an escape route, but black smoke shot through the gap into the cockpit.

'Hold your breath!' Callan spluttered. 'Go through...and...don't stop...until...you're...clear...'

Ivy went first — it seemed chivalry was alive and well. As the plane lay on its belly, it was only a short drop to the ground, but grass smouldered all around and Ivy singed her hands. Callan landed beside her, turned to help Juan, whose most nimble days were behind him. Mind you, a smoke-filled aircraft moves a man to alacrity. They had hardly scrambled to their feet when Johnny Witherspoon landed beside them.

They rushed through the smoke and flames which mercifully hadn't spread too far. All four flopped to the ground once clear of the blaze. Apart from coughing, nausea, cuts, abrasions and minor burns, they escaped otherwise unscathed.

And then the remaining fuel tank exploded.

The blast wasn't so loud. It was more like a whoosh and rush of hot air. Once the initial burst sucked any nearby oxygen, the fire imploded before settling to a steady, crackling blaze.

'Bugger, there goes our ticket to Mirios,' Callan sighed. 'We can't sell an ash- pile.'

'We're marooned,' Ivy observed forlornly. 'And it won't be long before the authorities start looking for us after that fighter pilot gets back to base.'

'Let's get into town and see what's what,' Witherspoon suggested. 'And talking about ash, that wretched volcano has fizzled out. Talk about being in the wrong place at the wrong time.'

'It's not so bad,' Callan said. 'At least we have our passports. We always carry them in our jacket pockets.'

'And I have identity papers,' Juan added. 'But I don't how well we'll be received.'

'We'll just have to keep our heads down...' Witherspoon began, but halted when he saw a group of people hurrying up the slope towards them.

'So much for anonymity,' Ivy sighed.

Normally those living at the foot of Mount Etna would make themselves scarce or at least seek shelter from the ash shower, but the good folk of Eastern Sicily seemed to have gauged the eruption's power and deemed it safe to venture outside. In this case some members of a small farming community saw the plane crash and being charitable folk, rushed to help — or in the case of a few baser souls, to see what might be salvageable.

It was quickly apparent that only a little scrap metal would be left after the flames died, so everyone turned their attention to the survivors. Amid a cacophony of excited chatter, which Ivy and Callan couldn't understand, Juan explained what had occurred in a mixture of about four Romance languages and multiple gestures.

Ivy thought the Spaniard and Sicilians were pretty good when it came to gestures, because they appeared to be communicating.

'We have to go quickly,' Juan explained. 'These people say the nearest *Carabineri* post is close by and they are sure it won't be long before soldiers or police turn up.'

'Not law-abiding folk then?' Witherspoon observed.

'Not so much,' Juan replied with a shrug.

That was true enough. *Carabineri* policy required its posts be manned by men from distant provinces — the more distant the better — to avoid any felonious collusion with hometown friends and family. Maybe that was good in some respects, but it didn't really foster local empathy.

'Where are we?' Ivy asked.

'San Giovanni,' Juan replied after some discussion with the townsfolk and farmers.

Ivy shrugged. It wasn't overly helpful because hundreds of locations around Italy and Sicily bore that name, which roughly translated to St John in many incarnations.

This particular San Giovanni lay only a couple of miles away and they soon arrived at the town piazza, and centre of social activity — the church. The town itself was unremarkable although moderately prosperous by Mediterranean standards. Narrow cobbled streets weaved through a maze of closely packed stone buildings with terracotta roof-tiles and geranium-adorned window-boxes.

A rather agitated priest met them at the church door and was soon joined by a portly fellow in a crumpled three-piece suit. A heated discussion ensued and soon everyone was yelling at once.

'What's going on?' Ivy asked.

'As far as I can make out, it seems we have a mixed reception,' Juan replied. 'The fellow in the suit is the mayor. He and the priest think we're communists and aren't too happy about it.'

'What about the townspeople?'

'I get the impression they're more or less evenly divided.'

That was pretty much the way of things since Benito Mussolini had proclaimed himself *Il Duce.* Most people were expected to be either rabid fascists or communists when most folk didn't actually want to be either, but that's the nature of political ideology for you.

In the end it didn't matter. *Maggiore* Grasso's message had already reached the local *Carabineri* post. San Giovanni was a small place and word travelled fast. It's not every day a plane crashes nearby and a bunch of foreigners come to town. The soldiers didn't have to look hard. Their barracks were next to the piazza and the uproar was a giveaway something was up there.

A squad of rifle-toting *Carabineri* stalwarts stomped into the square, pushed through the crowd and surrounded the four crash survivors. Their intention was unmistakeable, so Callan raised his hands, followed by his companions.

In a moment, amid jeers and cheers depending on the onlooker's point-of-view, Ivy, Callan, Juan and Johnny Witherspoon were marched away to gaol at gunpoint.

'Is it just me, or is this sort of thing becoming a habit?' Callan sighed.

Chapter 8 — Men of Honour

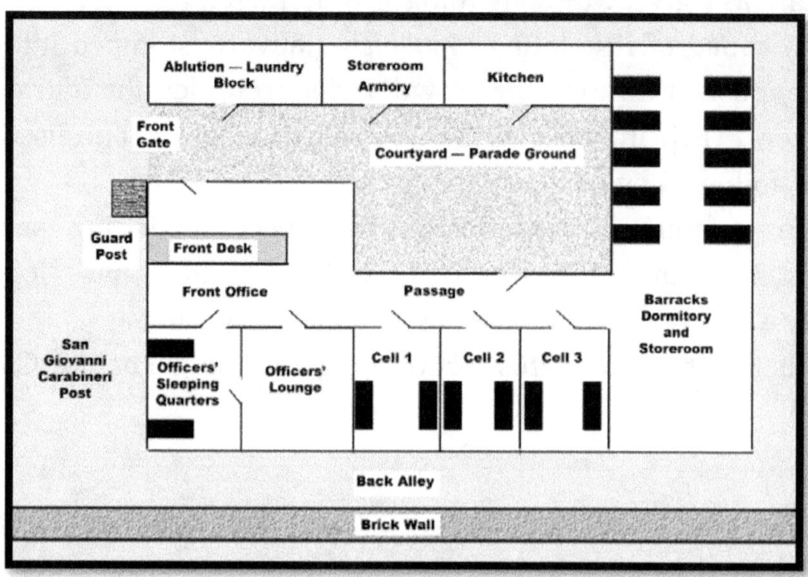

San Giovanni gaol was damp, cold and inadequately furnished. The four fugitives were escorted to a cell with two double bunks with dubious bedding and sanitation. A small, barred window was so high they could hardly see the narrow street beyond.

A bucket in the corner served for ablutions which was OK for the boys, except Johnny Witherspoon who said he couldn't pee with anyone watching. So they dutifully turned and faced the wall until the sound of tinkling stopped. Ivy was having none of it and kicked up a stink until she was escorted to an equally less than sanitary hole in the ground and told she'd either make do or embarrass herself. Lunch was a large bowl of pasta and tomato sauce, which was fine although they had to share a fork.

They appeared to be in one of a row of cells, separated by brick walls so it was impossible to tell whether other inmates were incarcerated.

In time a *Carabineri* officer showed up accompanied by a guard and a rather sleazy young man to act as interpreter. The officer was in his forties with a jaded careworn appearance. His severe look made it abundantly clear he wasn't happy about a crashed Spanish Republican plane in his backyard.

'Howdy,' the young man said with an accent somewhere between Rome and New York. 'My name is Tacitus Sorrentino and may I introduce *Primo Capitano* Abiati.'

Abiati spoke in Italian, indicating he was not prepared to interview prisoners in their gaol squalor so everyone moved into a front office. They sat around a table large enough to accommodate them all while Abiati busied himself by shuffling papers and fiddling with his fountain pen.

He examined what identity papers they had. Callan and Ivy ensured they only showed him their US Residency Cards, distancing themselves from any European ill-feeling. Once satisfied he returned their documents and started a barrage of questions at a speed Sorrentino had difficulty keeping up with.

In the end Abiati did little more than establish everyone's identity. He appeared perplexed as to how a Canadian, two Americans and a Spaniard had turned up in Sicily.

'We have not committed any crimes in your country,' Ivy said. 'I demand our immediate release.'

'*Capitano* Abiati doesn't like demands so much either,' Sorrentino replied. 'He reckons you're trouble and he wants you outa the way. He wants to ship you to Palermo and maybe the mainland. He says for you to keep your identity documents to show to immigration authorities later on.'

'Blimey, that could take months to sort out,' Callan said.

Sorrentino shrugged and said Republican Spain was no friend to Fascist Italy. They could all wind up doing gaol time for no more than being associated with communism. Abiati soon grew bored with the interview and left for lunch, leaving the guard to oversee the prisoners. Sorrentino wasn't in any particular hurry to go, seemingly more interested in the strangers than the authorities.

'We're sure in a pickle,' Ivy sighed. 'It's so unfair. We haven't done anything bad in Sicily.'

'Maybe they will let you go,' Sorrentino offered.

'You think?' Callan replied.

'Not so much. There are formalities, processes. The *Carabineri* likes processes.'

'The *Capitano* didn't seem that interested. He let us hang onto our identity papers.'

'Right now he has a bigger fish to fry in the next cell, which gives me an idea. Maybe I can make you an offer.'

'Offer?' Everybody said at once.

Sorrentino eyed the gaol door, but the guards had returned to the front office for coffee. They couldn't understand the conversation anyway.

'*Si*, I am a *Man of Honour*.'

'I'm sure you are,' Ivy said uncertainly.

'I am from the last of the big Sicilian families. Mussolini's Black-Shirts and *Carabineri* have shut down our business in the west of the island. My family moved to Chicago.'

'Why are you back here then?' Ivy asked.

'Don Rocco.'

They stared at him blankly.

'He is the big fish in the next cell. *Capitano* Abiati will transfer him to Palermo tomorrow — the same as you. Don Rocco will be a big feather in the *Capitano's* hat.'

'What's he done?'

'He too is a *Man of Honour*. He will be the last of our family to be shipped to the mainland and probably a long gaol sentence...maybe he'll face a firing squad.'

'You still haven't told us what has he done?'

'It is enough to be suspected of being a family member. We are discreet, you understand. We keep our business to ourselves.'

'Not essentially within the law..?' Callan suggested.

Sorrentino shrugged, glancing nervously at the guard who was unlikely to understand English, but you never knew.

'*Si* — perhaps. I can say no more,' Sorrentino whispered. 'I must go.'

'What about your deal?'

But Sorrentino was already through the cell door leaving the guard to lock up. So the afternoon dragged on. Abiati returned and spent some time with Don Rocco although no one could understand their muffled conversation. The *Capitano* barely glanced through the inspection plate before returning to the front office.

And that was about that. Only occasional trips to the ablution block under guard relieved the boredom. They all felt better after a cold shower, but a change of underwear would have been nice. Juan tried explaining to one of the guards, but got nowhere.

'At least *we* don't smell anymore,' Ivy declared with some satisfaction.

'I wonder what Senore Sorrentino meant by being a man of honour,'Ivy wondered.

'The Sicilian Mafia, I suspect,' Juan replied glumly.

'You mean the Mob?'

'I believe it to be so.'

'Oh dear, whatever have we gotten ourselves into now?'

But no one had an answer.

Their evening meal was fish and rice, with the ubiquitous tomato sauce, but it was OK. They'd certainly tasted worse. Even though they'd been idle most of the day, they were exhausted by nightfall. A plane crash can do that to you.

'I'm turning in,' Callan said.

He kissed Ivy and clambered onto the top bunk, took his harmonica from his top pocket and blew a few tunes before nodding off. The others weren't far behind him.

*

San Giovanni lockup around midnight.

Boom!

It wasn't so much the noise that deafened everyone, but the shock wave that blasted through the cell block. Callan and Johnny were pitched to the floor as the bunks collapsed, crumpling onto Ivy and Juan below. Masonry tumbled randomly as smoke filled the entire building choking the four cellmates and covering them with cement dust.

No one cried out. They were too stunned to say anything. The cell-block was uncannily silent except the clunk of bricks, wood and iron falling onto the rubble strewn floor. The lights had been blown to pieces, but enough moonlight flooded through the shattered gaol window to illuminate the shambles in the cell. A series of further explosions popped somewhere close by.

Ivy was the first to recover enough to call for help. The bunk had pinned her down and despite her struggling, she was unable to break clear. Juan was in a similar plight, but he remained too dazed to move.

'Callan!' Ivy cried, bringing him to his senses.

He stumbled around, pulling debris from Ivy until she scrambled into his arms.

'What the bloody hell..?' she stammered.

Meanwhile Juan came to and started yelling in panic. Johnny and Callan quickly lifted the bunk frame off him. No one was badly hurt, just shaken and bruised.

And then Tacitus Sorrentino appeared at the cell door. It had been blown from its hinges and hung askew.

'Quickly, before the *Carabineri* recover,' Sorrentino said. 'Come with me.'

No one questioned him. A break-out was on and the four aviators were part of it. But, where to go? They simply followed Sorrentino into the next cell and through a gaping hole into the back-street behind the gaol. It didn't take a genius to work out a bomb had been planted by the adjacent cell window and blown away enough brickwork for their escape.

An open truck was parked where the back-alley joined the main road to the piazza. Don Rocco already sat beside the driver in the cabin. The motor was idling. Two other men armed with Tommy guns stood in the tray.

'Quickly, get into the truck,' Sorrentino urged before he clambered in beside Don Rocco.

Nobody needed any further encouragement, because about then the *Carabineri* piled through the wrecked wall with guns blazing. The two men in the truck opened up, spraying the wall and forcing the guards back inside. Pausing for a moment, one of the gunmen grinned and handed Johnny Witherspoon the pistol from his belt.

Amid the rattle of gunfire the truck sped off as everyone clung onto the sides, although Ivy and Juan still landed on their backsides, luckily with nothing more serious than wounded dignity.

Considering its nefarious moonlit operations and likelihood of a police chase, the getaway truck was indifferently maintained. Mediterranean folk could be infuriatingly casual at times. Ivy, Callan and Johnny Witherspoon were all able mechanics and understood what torture the engine and associated hardware were suffering.

Indeed the chase was on. Police vehicles roared into action, racing after the escapees. The *Carabineri* headlights grew closer after each bend in the road.

'We'll never outrun them in this jalopy,' Ivy cried.

'Too right, and who knows what reception committee will be waiting in town,' Callan said. 'All *Capitano* Abiati has to do is telephone ahead. The place'll be swarming with cops.'

But Sorrentino and his gang had thought of that and blown several telephone phone poles to splinters. Callan had noticed a two-way radio in the police HQ which may well have survived the explosion, but right then no one knew how good communications were between San Giovanni and Catania...or how many *Carabineri* could be mustered in an emergency.

The pursuing vehicles steadily gained, but didn't draw too close as sporadic machinegun bursts blazed from the escaping truck. A sack lay open in the truck bed exposing an assortment of firearms and ammunition including several bolt action hunting rifles fitted with telescopic sights. Callan chose a rifle and managed to stuff his pockets full of bullets. He slid a round into the breech, but the truck rocked so badly he had no chance for an accurate shot, so he bided his time, saving his ammo.

Before long they hurtled through Catania's narrow streets, crashing into urban bric-a-brac standing in the way. They stuck to the main thoroughfares, because back alleys were simply too narrow for the truck and had a habit of ending in high walled courtyards with no escape route.

Callan leaned forward to the driver's cabin.

'Where are we going?' he yelled to Sorrentino over the roaring engine and gunfire. 'How do we escape? If you're thinking of a boat there's no chance. It'll be too slow.'

'No boat, but we go to the sea.'

'But that's where the boats *are*.'

That particular point didn't seem to bother Sorrentino as they sped from the labyrinth of cobbled streets to the water front. Mediterranean lateen-rigged fishing caiques and passenger ferries were moored against the quay while ocean freighters lay anchored off-shore. As Callan feared it would simply take too long to board any of the vessels and even if they did the *Carabineri* must have a speed-boat to give chase.

The truck lurched to a stop and everyone piled out where a jetty stretched into the harbour. As the fugitives hustled along the pier, the driver moved his truck to block the entrance. He jumped from the cab with an oily rag in his hand. Striking a match he lit the rag and stuffed it into the petrol cap just as the *Carabineri* barrelled onto the quayside.

The driver dashed after his comrades. Seconds later the trucks whooshed into flames.

'So much for the getaway vehicle,' Witherspoon lamented.

'Oh no,' Sorrentino said with a grin, pointing to the end of the jetty. 'You play your part now.'

And there it was — under a spotlight an *Ala Littoria* Macchi MC-94 floatplane bobbed on the tide rippling through the harbour.

'It was refuelled last night ready for the first flight this morning,' Sorrentino beamed. 'The crew are staying at a hotel in town. We planned to kidnap them, but then you showed up. Lot less trouble. You have a vested interest.'

Callan rolled his eyes.

'We've never flown this plane before,' Ivy protested.

'Planes are all the same to me,' Don Rocco muttered.

'You speak English..?' Ivy said.

'A little.'

Rocco shrugged.

'Well, all planes *aren't* the same,' Ivy insisted.

'How hard can it be?'

About then the *Carabineri* had organised into a firing line and opened up from the dock. The truck still raged and blocked the jetty entrance. Everyone dived for cover behind crates, oil drums and assorted maritime tackle as lead slammed into the wooden planks spitting lethal splinters everywhere.

'You're the float-plane guy, Johnnie,' Callan said. 'You and Ivy get the crate started while we make things hot for the cops.'

Ivy found a torch and the flight manual.

'Everything's written in Italian,' she declared from the fuselage door.

'I go,' Sorrentino said.

Callan stared at him blankly.

'I translate.'

There were about a dozen *Carabineri* on the quayside, but no doubt reinforcements were on the way. So far Callan and his companions hadn't fired a shot. Each Carcano bolt-action short rifle had a six-round magazine. There were two spare rifles left in the sack. Juan took one while Don Rocco checked the other, snapping back the bolt-action to load a slug into the breech. He looked like he could handle a gun.

Juan looked ready for business and for an office administrator also seemed comfortable handling a rifle. Don Rocco's three gangsters quickly assembled a barricade and started some pretty accurate shooting that sent the *Carabineri* diving for cover.

The burning truck illuminated the docks making for easy targets. Two men fell, but managed to stagger behind some cargo pallets. Don Rocco joined the shoot-out, blasting the spotlight to glass-mist and darkening the jetty.

After that things settled into a desultory stalemate.

'They'll try to surround us with boats when they find them,' Callan surmised.

'Plenty boats,' Don Rocco grunted.

'Not enough people to man them.'

'Yet.'

Indeed the ensuing police report indicated *Capitano* Abiati was in no particular hurry. He had the fugitives bottled up on the pier and the situation contained. Two of his men were slightly wounded and he didn't want more unnecessary casualties. He'd contacted Catania HG to rouse every *Carabineer* in the city and get them to the harbour with as much hardware as they could carry.

During the next half-hour policemen drifted in from side streets where Abiati deployed them along the entire dock. Then a truck rumbled in to view towing a 65 mm mountain artillery piece hitched to the tailgate.

'Ivy, we need to be elsewhere,' Callan called.

More bullets zinged past.

'We've gotta stop them pointing that cannon at us,' Sorrentino observed. 'They won't miss at this range. What we need is something to keep their heads down?'

'Maybe I can help,' Callan replied levelling the hunting rifle, steadying the barrel on the crate shielding him. 'I used to be pretty good at shooting Turks in the Gallipoli trenches.'

Memories of over four years service during the Great War flooded back as if it was yesterday. Nightmares had recurred over the years, but with Ivy's help he'd learnt to deal with them.

'The sight's primitive,' Callan observed, 'but I've used worse. I hope there's enough light on the quay.'

Sorrentino and the others eyed him doubtfully.

Callan aimed and squeezed the trigger...

Chapter 9 — Plan B

Capitano Abiati chivvied the gunnery sergeant to get a move on. It seemed to take ages to assemble the howitzer and it wasn't even very big by artillery standards. Eventually they prepared the weapon and were about to load the shell when a bullet ricocheted off the gun's front plate. The shot did no damage, but the artillerymen ducked instinctively and weren't inclined to raise their heads.

The steel protection shield was barely chest high and of no use to a standing gunner. While shells could be loaded into the breech from a crouching position, one careless move would leave you at risk. Another shot smacked into the steel plate before zinging into oblivion. Two more shots followed discouraging the gun-crew even further.

'Some crack-shot, you haven't hit a thing,' Sorrentino muttered.

'I'm not aiming to hit anyone, you goose,' Callan hissed. 'Do you think I want those blokes' blood on my hands?'

'They're trying to blow us up!'

'Maybe, but they're just following orders. I don't have a grudge against them.'

'You'll change your mind when the first shell comes our way.'

'Hopefully I can keep their heads down...'

An aero-engine spluttered into life behind them.

'Cast off! All aboard!' Ivy called from the co-pilot window.

No one needed telling twice. While Callan fired a last parting shot, the Sicilians untied the mooring ropes and clambered through the entry hatch. As the sea-plane drifted away from the pier, Callan jumped, missed his footing, but Sorrentino grabbed him and dragged him inside.

Capitano Abiati was livid, yelling obscenities to his gunners who now feared him more than incoming bullets.

They slammed a shell into the breech.

'Fire!' Abiati raged.

'Fire now.'

Blam! The muzzle roared, the gun jumped backwards with the recoil as a shot screamed into the night. If the Macchi had still been moored, they'd have been dead to rights, but the shell screeched past the plane's tail-fin. The foot pedals shuddered under Witherspoon's feet as the shell's slipstream buffeted the rudder. He was having enough trouble steering with one engine as it was.

Ivy cranked the second engine over.

'Hooray! Now we're in business,' she cried. 'Give her all she's got, Johnny.'

Another shell splashed into the sea beside the starboard wing, exploding on impact. Water sprayed across the windshield, temporarily blocking forward visibility.

Witherspoon set the mixture and prop levers then gunned the throttles. As they gathered speed, water streamed from the windshield which soon cleared. With moonshine behind the plane, Witherspoon could make out a horizon, but ran the risk of smashing into any boats in his path.

Another shell exploded just astern.

The plane bucked across the swell, which was fortunately less than a foot high.

'A bit of swell is fine,' Witherspoon assured everyone. 'It helps break the water surface tension to get some air under the hull and floats.'

Around fifty kilometres an hour they all felt the plane lift as air pressure built up under the wings.

'We're over the hump,' Witherspoon explained. 'We're planing.'

'That's a good thing for a plane,' Ivy giggled.

'Oh, please.'

Witherspoon rolled his eyes.

The airspeed indicator increased rapidly after that. Witherspoon eased the control column backwards.

'You've gotta be gentle,' he said, 'or the floats and hull will dig back under the surface and cause greater drag.'

Lift off...Blam!

The plane rocked as an exploding shell sent shrapnel streaking through the pilot's side cockpit window. A metal fragment flashed inches in front of Ivy's face and clattered somewhere beside her. Witherspoon grunted and slumped over the controls. The plane pitched forward.

Ivy gripped the control column and hauled back with all her strength. But Witherspoon's dead-weight was too great. The plane dived towards the sea.

'Pull Johnny back!' Ivy screamed.

Callan hadn't had a chance to take a seat in the cabin and was standing between the two pilot seats for takeoff. He grabbed Witherspoon's collar and dragged him from the controls. Ivy pulled the control column into her chest.

Nothing happened.

The plane's inertia kept it hurtling to the surface. The nose rotated minutely upwards just as they hit the water with a spleen-jarring crack. The Macchi bounced, and became airborne once more. Ivy then shoved the stick forwards to keep enough airspeed to stay in the air.

Skimming inches above the waves, Ivy slowly regained control and eased the plane into the sky. Two more shells whistled past, but the inexperienced gun-crew missed. In fairness a moving target is pretty damn hard to hit with a clumsy mountain cannon.

Witherspoon's head flopped back as Callan held him as upright as possible. His face was awash with blood from a six-inch slash across his forehead.

'Is he dead?' Ivy wailed.

'Dunno, but I'm going to have to drag him out of the seat. '

And that posed a serious problem. There was only room for one person in the space between the pilot stations, which was pretty tight. Johnny Witherspoon wasn't a huge fellow, but once he became dead-weight, it was going to take a lot of strength to budge him. Callan leant forward and unbuckled the pilot's seatbelt.

Callan struggled for a while, but achieved little other than bumping Ivy so hard she nearly lost control of the plane. After a few minutes, Callan felt a tap on his shoulder. The Mafia truck driver gestured for him to return to the cabin, before leaning into the cabin and — seemingly with little effort — pulled Witherspoon free and dragged him aft in a trail of blood.

Being an RPT aircraft, the Macchi was equipped with a first-aid kit. Juan unpacked antiseptic and bandages.

'You go fly the plane with Ivy,' he said to Callan. 'I'll do what I can for Johnny.'

'Well, that's a bummer, Muscles,' Ivy said with a dry smile. 'Johnny was the only one who knew where we were going — how is he?'

'Dunno. Juan's taking care of him. There's loads of blood. The floor's all sticky.'

'Sorrentino must have some sort of a plan.'

Callan twisted in his seat and waved to Sorrentino, who was in an animated conversation with Don Rocco. Whether that was a heated discussion or just Mediterranean flair was uncertain. Sorrentino came forward anyway. By this time the plane's rate of climb had dropped off to virtually nothing, so Ivy levelled out at five thousand feet and reduced the throttles, pitch and mixture controls to what she considered acceptable cruise settings.

'Ok,' Callan addressed Sorrentino. 'I presume you had something in mind after Catania?'

'We go to America,' Sorrentino beamed.

'How?'

Sorrentino looked around the plane.

'You're kidding, right?'

'We have a plane, we fly.'

'I don't know how far you think this plane will fly, but it won't get to the States on one tank of petrol. It'll probably take ten tanks of petrol — maybe more. Where will we find somewhere to refuel — and someone prepared to fill up the plane?'

Sorrentino shrugged with an infuriating Latin laissez-faire attitude.

'You haven't forgotten we stole this plane, have you?'

'And, what about Johnny Witherspoon? He needs hospital attention,' Ivy added.

About then Juan squeezed beside Sorrentino.

'How's Johnny?' Ivy asked.

'He lives. I have stopped the bleeding with bandages. He has a nasty cut across his brow. It should be stitched, but he is breathing strongly and I do not think he has lost too much blood. He is semi-conscious and seems to be resting peacefully. He is lying on some cushions in the aisle and we have covered him with blankets.'

'OK, Ivy. Keep flying north-east. Where are the charts and manuals?

'Storage bin behind my seat.'

'I'll need your help, Mr Sorrentino and Don Rocco as well.'

Callan knew exactly what he was looking for. As an RPT aircraft, Italian aviation regulators insisted the plane was well stocked with charts for the area including the Adriatic, Ionian, Tyrrhenian and Mediterranean Seas. They also showed radio beacons and frequencies. Callan scanned the flight manuals. Although they were printed in Italian, he had a pretty good idea where to look.

He flipped through the pages until he found the heading *Prestazione* followed by columns of figures which looked familiar.

'That says "Performance", doesn't it?'

Rocco and Sorrentino nodded.

'Great, now just confirm I've got the cruise, speed, altitude and power settings correct for best range.'

After examining the charts and checking the plane's fuel gauges, Callan explained what he planned. No one objected.

'Do you reckon Johnny will last a few hours in the air, Juan?' Callan asked.

'As I said, I have staunched the wound, but he will need a doctor to stitch it up.'

'OK let's hope there's someone available.

Callan explained his plan to Ivy.

'So it's back to Plan B,' she replied, 'which is really Plan A if you think about it. Mirios here we come.'

*

So as dawn broke, they flew on to Johnny Witherspoon's adopted Mediterranean home. It wasn't too hard to navigate their way. Ivy simply flew keeping the Italian landmass on her port wingtip. Once she cleared the boot heel Callan gave her a course to fly directly across the Southern Adriatic Sea to the Yugoslavia-Albanian coastline.

As far as Callan could ascertain from the chart, Mirios was strictly speaking part of Albania, but the territorial situation along the Adriatic seaboard from Dalmatia right down to Greece was unstable. Mussolini was pushing feelers east trying to scrounge some extra dominions. Italian forces had bombed and occupied

Corfu fifteen years earlier much to the League of Nation's dismay. Its delegates postulated, but weren't prepared to send an allied military force to chuck the Italians out.

Mussolini came out of it pretty well, with boosted national prestige and a huge pay-cheque from Greece to keep the peace. Now with recent *Nazi* and Fascist sabre-rattling, who knew how things would wind up?

But Ivy and Callan had other problems.

Finding Mirios in fine weather was no trouble. Map reading close to the coast proved easy enough and Callan quickly located a landing zone. The island was hilly with a main town serving as a small fishing, freighter and ferry port. The landscape was by no means barren. Ivy identified olive groves, vineyards, cereal patches, citrus orchards and vegetable gardens and meadows where goats grazed.

And then came the part which had concentrated Callan's and Ivy's attention for most of the flight.

'What do you reckon?' Callan asked.

'Do you want to take over?'

'Hell no, you've flown so far and at least you've a feel for the crate.'

'As Don Rocco would say — how hard can it be?'

'It's just another plane, I suppose.'

There was little wind judging by chimney smoke, so Ivy could choose her landing direction. Also there was barely a ripple on the surface, which they both agreed was a good thing, right?

Ivy manoeuvred the Macchi to approach across the harbour and touch-down facing seawards so she had no distance worries. The flight from Sicily had given Callan and Ivy time to study the flap settings and landing speed, so they both felt reasonably confident, right?

However they failed to factor in peripheral vision. Landing at an airstrip provides visual cues from trees, buildings, vehicles and anything around which help the pilot to judge that last few feet of descent. Over water, especially if the surface is calm, those cues are missing and most pilots initially feel they're lower than they actually are.

And that's precisely what Ivy did. She was at least fifteen feet above the water when she cut the power and flared the Macchi.

Nothing happened except the airspeed washed away until the plane stalled and dropped to the surface. The hull slammed down with a spine-jarring wallop...and bounced.

Ivy slammed the throttles forward and the props roared into over-speed. The Macchi hung just inches above the surface as the engines clawed back flying speed. The plane staggered back into the sky.

'That was interesting,' Callan said, turning to check everyone in the cabin was OK. Juan gave him a nervous thumbs-up.

'Bloody hell, Callan. I made a right hash of that,' Ivy said between gritted teeth. 'I can't land this stupid plane. You'll have to do it.'

Ivy looked pretty sheepish because she normally had no trouble landing aircraft. Callan smiled and blew her a kiss.

'Don't sweat it, love. I'm sure you'll get the hang of it. What makes you think I'd make a better job of it?''

Ivy nervously manoeuvred the sea-plane for a second approach...

Chapter 10 — Mirios

'There, I told so,' Callan laughed.

The second landing worked a treat. Initially Callan was worried Ivy would wait too long to flare and arrest the plane's descent, but its hull glided smoothly onto the surface and pulled up remarkable quickly.

'Let's go and see if the natives are friendly, which will make a nice change,' Ivy said.

'You betcha, if one more person points a gun at me I swear I'll grab it and shove it where it fits best.'

'Be nice, Callan dear. This is Johnny's home so I'm sure they'll be delightful.'

'Yeah, we'd better get cracking. I hope he's going to be OK.'

Ivy guided the plane close to the quayside where another sea-plane was moored. Callan assumed it was the aircraft Witherspoon flew when he wasn't away fighting for lost causes. Within minutes a small group of locals gathered. Callan opened the forward cabin door and tossed a mooring line ashore. Someone took the rope and secured it to a bollard. When Ivy cut the engines, Callan hauled the plane towards the seawall.

Sorrentino and Don Rocco's men carried Witherspoon ashore where he was placed in a donkey cart and hurried away, presumably to a doctor. Judging by the concerned looks on the townsfolk faces, Witherspoon was well known and well liked on Mirios. A bevy of young women looked especially distressed as they followed the cart.

'He's quite the favourite, isn't?' A voice spoke urbanely beside Callan and Ivy who, in all the excitement, hadn't noticed anyone approach.

His accent was refined and, oh, so English. He was about fifty, sporting a clipped Van Dyke beard with an ornamental pipe clamped between his teeth.

'Those girls seem very upset,' Ivy ventured.

'Indeed, I believe they have all set their sights on young Witherspoon, but he has managed to evade capture so far. Please allow me to introduce myself. I am Dennis Mortimer, Johnny's partner and dear friend.'

'I hope he's OK,' Ivy said doubtfully.

'He's a tough nut. I'm sure he'll pull through.'

Ivy, Juan and Callan introduced themselves while Don Rocco and his men-of-honour vanished to organise their future as yet undefined business.

'You're a long way from home,' Mortimer observed.

'We might say the same for you,' Ivy replied blandly. 'Are you on vacation?'

She'd picked up a number of American expressions over the years.

'In a way, my dear,' Mortimer shrugged. 'Nothing much left for a baronet's youngest scion. Nothing much left for a baronet's eldest either when I come to think about it.'

'A peer no less,' Ivy said.

'Not quite, dear lady. We slink around with knights and dames just below those exalted dukes, viscounts, earls, and barons. But that is of no matter. The days of noble houses are surely numbered. The war, general strikes, crippling taxation and the depression saw to that. Most estates are so burdened with debt lords are selling slices of their manors just to make ends meet.'

'So you came here for a cheaper life?'

'Precisely, not to mention the weather is so much more agreeable.'

'Much as I enjoy standing chatting,' Callan ventured, 'but, what do we do now? I'm sure *Ala Littoria* wants its plane back and I don't think we can keep our arrival secret.'

'I'll have a word with the local clergy,' Mortimer said. 'They're mostly Catholic and Orthodox around here so the priests are still pretty influential.'

'Yeah that's fine, but the authorities have probably started looking already and we can't risk them turning up here sooner or later.'

'Perhaps we can help one another....'

All heads turned to face Don Rocco and Sorrentino who'd returned from wherever they'd been.

'I have discussed our options with my associates,' Don Rocco continued, 'and certain arrangements may be acceptable. We simply return the plane and disappear.'

'What do you mean, put it back where we found it?' Ivy said.

'Precisely,' Don Rocco replied. 'Right now if I were searching, I'd draw a circle on a map based on the plane's range from Catania and send word to every *Carabineri* station, army post, naval ship and airfield within that area and start tightening the net.'

They sat at a quayside cafe where Mortimer ordered breakfast and coffee.

'That's a lot of territory,' Callan ventured. 'It'll take 'em ages.'

'They might get lucky,' Sorrentino said. 'Even if they don't it's only a matter of time.'

'We could always sink it,' Callan added, but everyone frowned and shook their heads. The idea of wilfully destroying a beautiful flying machine was against all they believed.

Also Don Rocco wasn't keen and they were under no illusions who called the shots. He may have been a man of dubious moral calibre, but needless waste wasn't his style. Even when it came to disposing of troublesome rivals, Rocco did so sparingly. Generally there were less severe methods of discouraging troublemakers.

'In any event,' Don Rocco said,' I have business on the mainland and I need a lift back there. Had we not left Catania in such haste, we may have done thing differently. So this is what I have in mind...'

*

The plan was to land right at sunrise. It was risky, but there were no landing lights, so a night approach onto water was impossibly dangerous. They refuelled the *Macchi* and Witherspoon's sea-plane which turned out to be a single-engine Fairchild-82 Witherspoon had shipped from Canada when he teamed up with Mortimer. Other than a broken side window the Macchi looked OK, especially when Mortimer organised a clean-up team to wash away Johnny's bloodstains.

Witherspoon was in good hands and looked like making a speedy recovery. The doctor had extracted several shrapnel fragments from various parts of his body. He'd lost some blood and suffered mildly from shock, but with tender loving care, his prognosis looked good. And there was no shortage of dedicated and adoring nurses volunteering to help.

They loaded the Fairchild with *Wehrmacht-Einheitskanisters* which were brilliant new 20 litre fuel containers. They'd only been developed for a few years and were reserved for the German military. The Spanish Nationalists were supplied by Germany, so they were well stocked, but the Communists could only use the ones they captured, and they weren't doing a lot of capturing lately. Dennis Mortimer didn't mention where he'd procured his stock.

'Jerry Cans, eh?' Callan said with a grin.

Ivy stared at him blankly.

'Why not, I heard some Tommies refer to the Hun as Jerries at the end of the war. They're a German invention — ergo: "Jerry Can"! It sounds kinda neat, don't you reckon?'

Jerry had not been widely used until late in the war and Ivy was unaware of the term. Her father had made sure she was sent home once he discovered Lady Dorothie Fielding had posted Ivy to the front as a FANY nurse and ambulance driver.

There was only a single telephone connection from Mirios to an exchange on the Albanian mainland, so Don Rocco was on the line all day. By the time he finally slammed the speaker and earpiece down, he'd threatened to kill a number of people on the other end of the line.

But he was satisfied his plan was set in motion.

Callan, Ivy and Juan had no difficulty finding somewhere to stay. Although there was no hotel on Mirios, householders were more than happy to welcome them, especially as they'd brought their darling aviator home safely. So they filled in the day exploring around town, napping and eating extremely well. They turned in early until Mortimer woke them just after midnight. Their hosts were also awake and brewing coffee.

Mortimer ran a professional outfit and held a useful library of aviation material in his office. Among the publications were charts for determining first light for different latitudes and longitudes. After a quick study and estimation of flight time, Callan calculated a take-off time based on the slower Fairchild speed.

Ivy piloted the Macchi with Don Rocco and his gang as passengers, while Callan accompanied Mortimer in the Fairchild loaded with full Jerry Cans. Juan offered to go with them, but wasn't particularly disappointed when Ivy suggested he stay behind to save weight aboard.

After lift-off they navigated in moonlit formation to an inlet north of Catania where Don Rocco had arranged a motor boat to meet them.

After landing Ivy moored the Macchi while Rocco's henchmen made short work of refuelling the plane. Once the tanks were full, Ivy wasted no time boarding the Fairchild while Don

Rocco and company bid everyone farewell and took off in the motorboat.

Before leaving he handed Ivy an envelope.

'Inside are Sicilian and mainland telephone numbers and addresses,' Don Rocco explained. 'You have done me a great service. Men-of-Honour do not forget. If you ever need a favour the people you contact will know where to find me.'

'You're just an old softie,' she said as she embraced him.

'Don't tell anyone,' he grinned.

'Or what?' Ivy challenged.

'Oh, I'll have to kill you. I have a reputation to uphold, you know.'

Ivy laughed as she waved goodbye, but thought it best to take Don Rocco at his word anyway.

By the time Mortimer eased the Fairchild skywards Don Rocco's motorboat had cruised around the bay's northern point and disappeared. Just in case anyone was paying attention, Mortimer flew north for a while then turned right on course for Mirios.

*

Meanwhile *Capitano* Abiati was not a happy man and unhappiness put him in a foul mood. The previous morning had revealed Catania dockside was a mess of wreckage and spent machinegun cartridges. The phones rang all day with *Ala Littoria* managers demanding to know where their plane was, while his superiors wanted to know what he was doing about it.

Doing about it? Well, searching would be a good start, but where? The plane headed into darkness and could have gone in any direction. Damn them all, why can't they stop calling and let me think!

Now over twenty-four hours had passed since the waterfront fight, and if anyone knew where the fugitive aircraft was, they weren't telling. Abiati had dragged in the usual suspects when it came to underworld skulduggery. His men roughed up those miscreants during questioning without success, so they were either genuine tough-guys or genuinely ignorant — Abiati was pretty certain it was the latter.

Abiati had slept little during the previous night. It was now a couple of hours after sunrise and he felt like hell. He was a fastidious man and knew when he needed a bath, shave and fresh clothes. He was about to rectify all of the above shortcomings when the phone rang.

'*Capitano*, you might want to come and see this...' one of his patrolmen said.

Half an hour later Abiati drove to a cove several kilometres north of central Catania. No one lived there as the approaches to the shingle beach were precipitous. Sometimes fishermen sheltered their caiques in the cove and right now there were two dinghies drawn up on shore.

'Local fishermen rowed in after dawn to chase herring, sir,' the patrolman said. 'That's what they found.'

The *Ala Littoria* Macchi bobbed at anchor in shallow water.

Abiati was certainly surprised, but showed no emotion. Police officers were expected to be stoic fellows.

'Did they see the plane arrive?'

'No, *Capitano*. The fishermen arrived about an hour after first light and the plane was just there. They saw no one and it wasn't here yesterday because my section patrolled this coastline.'

'Well, it didn't fly *itself* here, did it? Get every available man and all our transport — trucks, automobiles, motorcycles — and we'll comb every inch of the area. They must have landed after sunrise. They can't have gone far.'

'Yes sir, but it's puzzling, isn't it.'

'What is?'

'Why did they come back so close to Catania? I mean if they'd had engine trouble, or the plane was damaged they'd want to put it down as soon as possible, but as I said it wasn't here yesterday. They've returned almost to the scene of the crime.'

'It is a mystery indeed,' Abiati sighed. 'But we'll catch them and beat the truth out of them. I do not like being made a fool of.'

'No sir.'

'Contact all units to rendezvous here and tell them to be quick about it.'

So the search for the mystery aircrew began.

During the day an *Ala Littoria* maintenance team arrived with two pilots to reclaim their plane.

'They didn't go far,' the aircraft captain observed. 'The petrol tanks are completely full and other than the broken side window, the plane is fine.'

'I wonder how they hid the plane for a day with half of Catania looking for it,' the co-pilot said.

'Beats me, but our engineers are satisfied it's in perfect working order, so let's get the window replaced and have this aircraft back in service.'

A week later the *Carabineri* had still found no clues to investigate — nothing. The mystery crew had disappeared into thin air. The official search was abandoned as police units were called to other duties. Abiati however wasn't going to let the matter rest. The case-file remained open in his eyes and it wouldn't be closed until he'd solved the mystery.

Chapter 11 — Lull Before the Storm

Mirios 1938-1939

Johnny Witherspoon recovered quickly and asked Callan and Ivy to join his company as pilots and mechanics. It was a time when pilots working for small operators serviced their own machines or the job wouldn't be done at all.

There was no reason to return to America. *McAlister Aviation* had been liquidated, so Callan and Ivy were reasonably cashed up. When they felt the dust had settled regarding their Sicilian adventure, they organised their finances through Swiss bankers and brokers. Mirios was a happy place with fair weather and people of pleasant dispositions.

With four pilots the Fairchild was fully utilised, carrying passengers, livestock and freight throughout the Adriatic coast. Juan proved his worth as an agent and factor securing contracts in Yugoslavia, Greece, Italy and especially the Albania cities of Durrës and Vlore. There was no indication the Italians were still interested in Callan and Ivy's flight from Spain, while the Spanish Republicans were in dire straits. Setback followed setback and by mid 1938 it looked like the Republic's days were numbered.

To give them their due, in July the Republicans tried one last serious push across the Ebro River in the country's north. They stuck it out for a few months, but by the end of November the offensive ran out of steam and collapsed. About half way through the campaign Republican moral was shattered when British Prime Minister Neville Chamberlain signed the Munich agreement with Adolph Hitler allowing the *Reich* to swallow the Sudetenland. Granted, much of Sudetenland's population spoke German and thought of themselves as Germans. But it was the thin end of the wedge as Czechoslovakia was to discover in March 1939.

For some inexplicable reason Chamberlain believed Hitler when he said he was an all-around good guy who didn't mean any harm. Apparently no one had anything to fear from the Third *Reich*.

The Spanish Republicans had hoped for Britain's continuing support, but saw the pact as abandonment. Now Callan and Ivy had little reason to worry about Spain and so began their halcyon days, for some months anyway.

Mortimer owned a large villa on a hill overlooking the main town and harbour. He called it *Bella Vista* which may not have been very imaginative, but described the beautiful view over cypress trees, terracotta roof-tops, across the bay and out to sea.

The property had numerous bedrooms and large grounds staffed by a cook, house-keeper and gardener. Mortimer apologised for his small household, but times weren't as prosperous as they had been. However he invited Ivy, Callan and Juan to be his house-guests while they worked for his business.

'We wouldn't wish to impose,' Ivy said.

Callan rolled his eyes. Of course they wanted to impose. Who wouldn't jump at the chance to live in a handsome villa with a good cook and maid to make the beds?

Luckily Mortimer insisted.

'The staff go home to their families at night,' Mortimer explained, 'so I'd be delighted to have company after dinner.'

Nevertheless, Mortimer was an enlightened and decent boss when it came to staff-relations and asked Fausto the gardener, Adela the maid and most importantly Carmela the cook, if they had any objections. They were a cheerful trio and saw no hardship.

'We can help out,' Ivy suggested.

But that was unnecessary. It was a matter of professional ethics, Mortimer explained. Fausto, Adela and Carmela took great pride in their work especially as they were employed by a generous and easy-going boss.

Witherspoon's lodging arrangements remained mysteriously variable.

Life was carefree and spiritually fruitful, although not particularly profitable.

The Adriatic Sea supplied all the fish the islanders needed, while goats and chickens provided protein galore. In fact so many goats grazed on Mirios, they'd become a nuisance and could easily wreck crop fields, especially those who'd gone feral and roamed everywhere.

'Juan and I think we have an untapped resource,' Mortimer declared one lunch time as he helped himself to more goat stew. 'We've been talking to a chap who supplies restaurants and markets on the mainline.'

'And..?' Ivy eyed him suspiciously.

'Lot's of folk think Italy's doing fine.'

'The trains and buses run on time since Mussolini got things organised.'

'Yes, my dear,' Mortimer said, 'but there is a cost. *Il Duce* wants to build an empire, but there's not much left to colonise. Britain, France, Germany and the Dutch had pretty well grabbed everywhere by the turn of the century, and Italy didn't really pick up anything useful after the Great War.'

'They got Abyssinia in '35,' Callan said.

'Yes and what's there? Minerals, but no one knows in what quantity or how to mine them. The rest is desert and it's costing a fortune to keep troops there. Italy is up to its eyeballs in debt.'

'All I know is every time we fly to the mainland there are Black-Shirts everywhere,' Ivy said.

'Yes, and they've taken over everything worthwhile. The economy is a shambles and common people are having a hard time of it.'

'So what's your idea, Dennis?' Callan asked.

'What have we got in excess, dear boy?'

Callan stared at him.

'Goat meat! In fact they're a pest.'

'Your point is..?'

'Cull 'em and fly 'em to the mainland by the plane-load.'

'You've got to catch them first,' Ivy said.

'That's where your beloved comes in. I believe you were quite the marksman during the 14-18 conflict...'

'You want me to shoot goats?'

Mortimer nodded.

Callan had no qualms about hunting. Food was food after all, and there was a need, not to mention a lira or two.

'Won't the Black-Shirts be guarding the airstrips and confiscate our cargo?' Ivy asked.

'That is where Don Rocco's people come in,' Juan said. 'I've been on the phone over the past few days and it seems we can come to an arrangement.'

So ex-sniper Callan McAlister became a goat hunter.

And the plan worked pretty well. Callan was able to bag goats by the cart-load to be quickly flown across the Adriatic. That could have been a problem because Mussolini's Fascists patrolled the ports and airstrips, but a phone call to Don Rocco's men-of-honour seemed to clear the way. The fascist inspectors found it convenient to take their lunch breaks when the Fairchild flew in.

So let the good times roll...

*

Mid-Afternoon Durrës, Albania 6 April 1939 — Maundy Thursday

'Time to shove off if we want to get home before dark, my darling,' Ivy announced as Callan practised his Italian on a major who commanded a number of mixed Albanian units including an infantry company and local *Gendarmerie*. Although Albania had its own national language, Italian was widely spoken.

Despite the fact Mirios was officially Albanian at the time, most folk had strong Italian family ties and favoured that language.

The Fairchild was moored at the main wharf loaded with miscellaneous cargo ordered by Mirios citizens. Unlike the Italians, Albanian authorities had no objection to free trade. The major was also interested in any news from Italy which had been sabre-rattling for months, making Albanians decidedly nervous.

The officer shook Callan's hand, saluted before returning to his troops.

'Major Kupi was pretty chatty today,' Ivy observed.

'Sure is. He's got a feeling the Italians want to take over Albania. They haven't been living happily together recently. Apparently Mussolini is spitting chips because King Zog keeps giving him the royal finger. Kupi's in change of defending Durrës and he doesn't have much to work with. He also reckons there are way too many Italian officers in the Albanian armed forces for his liking.'

'The enemy within, eh? Mind you it looks to me like there are plenty of Albanian soldiers and sailors around town right now,' Ivy observed.

'Our good major reckons he's got about five hundred men, a couple of mountain artillery pieces and four patrol-boats with a single machinegun between them. They won't be much use against warships, planes, tanks and a ruddy army.'

'Do you think the Italians are planning an invasion?'

'Could be. After the *Reich* took over Czechoslovakia, Mussolini is hankering to do a bit of empire building of his own. Albania is close and pretty rich in resources, which would be handy for *Il Duce's* prestige.'

'It's barely twenty years since the war and all Europe is at one another's throats,' Ivy sighed. 'It feels like 1914 all over again.'

'Hitler and Mussolini are certainly up to no good, and from what I read the Japs are being thoroughly unpleasant in China. They may not want to stop there either. These things have a habit of escalating. It looks like getting American residency was a good idea. That should keep us right out of it.'

'I'm with you. We don't have an argument with anyone.'

They boarded their plane with Ivy in the pilot seat while Callan checked the load was tied down securely.

'Fire her up, sweetheart,' he called once he was satisfied and clambered into the co-pilot seat.

They were airborne in moments. Ivy turned the plane west for the journey back to Mirios, but they didn't get more than ten miles before Callan spotted something on the horizon.

'Now what do you suppose that is?' he wondered. 'Turn right fifteen degrees, Ivy. Let's take a look.'

At first Ivy couldn't make out anything, but after the plane flew several miles, it became all too obvious they were approaching a fleet of not only warships, but transport vessels as well.

'Blow me down, it's a bloody armada,' Callan said. 'Take her down and we'll check this out.'

'Are you sure that's a good idea?'

'Why not?'

'It looks to me like they're Italian ships and they're heading for the Albanian Coast. We're steering clear of trouble remember.'

'We'll just take a teeny-weeny peek.'

Ivy pushed the control column forward and dived to five hundred feet. They were skimming above the fleet in just minutes and saw Italian colours flapped from every sternpost.

'Crikey, there are a dozen warships down there. Cruisers, destroyers and those smaller vessels are torpedo-boats if I don't miss my guess.'

'What about the transports,' Ivy added, 'the decks are crowded with what look like troops to me.'

'It's the invasion Major Kupi was worried about. Do you think we should go back and tell him?'

'We're not getting involved — *remember!* He'll find out soon enough anyway.'

'Yeah, but every minute will be precious for him to prepare his defence.'

'What defence?' Ivy banked the Fairchild for another pass over the fleet. 'You told me Major Kupi only has five hundred men. There are more than that on just one of those transport ships and I count ten of them.'

'All the more important to warn him. If I was him I'd skedaddle and take the fight into the mountains.'

'So much for remaining neutral. You can't help yourself can you, Sir Galahad?'

'Your call, you're driving.'

'You're impossible,' she sighed.

Suddenly the choice was made for them. A massive cloud of smoke erupted from one of the destroyers. The Fairchild bucked as a shell exploded way too close for comfort. Next tracer bullets streaked from machineguns mounted on the torpedo-boat decks.

'Time to go!' Ivy announced.

And they nearly cleared the danger zone, but a last burst smashed metal fragments through the Fairchild fuselage.

'Bloody hell, give her all she's got, Ivy.'

Ivy didn't need telling, she slammed the throttle to full power, diving just above the waves, willing the plane to fly out of range. As it turned out the Italian gunners must have thought it too difficult to hit the fleeing plane and stopped firing.

Major Kupi met them as Ivy drifted the plane close enough to the quayside so Callan could leap ashore and tie the mooring hawser to a convenient bollard.

'Is something wrong?' Kupi asked.

'For you I think something is very wrong,' Callan said. 'It looks like the whole flaming Italian navy is just over the horizon. I reckon your invasion is on its way, Major.'

Kupi took the news rather too calmly in Callan's opinion, but Albania was going to need cool customers very shortly. Kupi questioned Callan and Ivy about the fleet size and enemy strength. He listened without interrupting then thanked them both, saluted and strode back to his men, issuing orders as he went.

Within minutes men and women were constructing barricades along the waterfront, using anything available — cargo, vehicles, packing cases even straw bales wherever they came from.

'We'd better get going,' Callan said to Ivy. 'We can still make Mirios easily before last light.'

'I dunno, sweetheart,' she replied. 'You'd better come and check the fuselage. There are a few bullet holes and I think one of the elevator cables is damaged.'

Sure enough Callan inspected the cables that ran along the fuselage to the tail controls surfaces. The rudder cables looked OK, but the elevator conduits were frayed and ready to snap apart.

'Yeah, we're going to have to fix those cables before we take off. If they let go before we reach home, there'll be no altitude control other than throttle power which will make it damned difficult to maintain altitude let alone climb and descend. I don't fancy ditching in the Adriatic either.'

'I don't think we carry spare cable on board,' Ivy said.

'You're right, we'll have to ask around and see what we can scrounge.'

Finding suitable wire wasn't as easy as Callan thought. The tumult caused by Major Kupi's men preparing the town defences made progress difficult. There always seemed to be someone in the way wherever Callan wanted to go. Fence wire was pretty readily available, but unsuitable for aircraft control cables which need to be flexible.

Callan eventually settled for a brake cable and several jubilee clips from a car repair shop. It took a couple of hours to splice the cables together and secure the clamps. Callan and Ivy were ambivalent about the jury-rig repair, but remained sanguine as there was no alternative.

'It's too late to fly home now,' Ivy sighed.

'If we sleep on board we can get away at first light.'

'What about the Italians.'

'I don't think they'll try anything tonight.'

Indeed the Italian ships were now moored a mile or so off-shore and seemed content to stay there for a while.

So Ivy and Callan ate supper in a dockside cafe before turning in. Callan slept remarkably well and before he knew it, Ivy shook him awake.

'It's dawn,' she announced.

'Time to hustle then.'

'We have a problem, come and look.'

They stepped onto the dock which was shrouded in thick fog.

'Bloody hell, we can't take off in this soup. Goodness knows what we might run into.'

Chapter 12 — Invasion

Durrës Waterfront 5:00 am 7 April 1939 — Good Friday

As Ivy and Callan tried to peer through the fog they noticed a shadowy form emerging only a few yards from the jetty. Soon they made out a steam pinnace crowded with about twenty Italian soldiers.

Major Kupi saw it too and led an infantry squad to the pier end where the boat was now being moored and several officers disembarked. Kupi drew his service pistol and immediately fired a shot into the air which stopped the Italians in their tracks. A heated and animated discussion followed, but the outcome was the officers reboarded their pinnace and steamed back into the fog.

'I wonder what that was all about.' Ivy said.

'I think the good major just told the Ities where they can shove their invasion,' Callan replied.

'I don't think that'll deter them.'

'Too right, they'll be landing as soon as this fog clears when they can see what they're doing.'

Major Kupi had other problems.

'They demanded we surrender,' he hissed as he walked past Ivy and Callan. 'To make things worse my Italian officers have all disappeared overnight.'

'Maybe they don't want to kill fellow Italians,' Ivy ventured.

'More likely they don't want to be killed by fellow Italians,' Callan said. 'Maybe you should take to the hills and choose your battle grounds.'

'I'll be damned if I let those bastards land unopposed. We'll fight here, Senore,' Kupi snapped. 'I suggest you make yourselves scarce as soon as possible.'

'That's our plan...' Callan began, but Kupi was already half-way to his barricades.

The fog was lifting and Callan and Ivy were appalled at what they saw. The large warships lay pretty much where they'd first anchored, but the freighters now edged towards the quay escorted by half-a-dozen torpedo-boats. No one could stop the merchant ships drawing alongside the quay. As soon as the first ship docked, its crewmen lowered stairways and gang planks. Immediately troops disembarked and formed into companies on the wharf.

But Kupi and his men weren't waiting to be overrun. They opened up with machineguns and rifle fire, killing a number of Italians and sending the others scurrying for cover, although there wasn't a lot around so many troops simply dropped onto their bellies and soon traded shots with the Albanians.

The Italian position was tenuous and officers ordered their men back aboard the freighter. But it wasn't long before they reformed and were joined by other rifle units from the next ship to arrive. The Italians held tight formation and began to advance.

Bullets were zinging everywhere from both sides.

'Bloody hell! Ivy, we can't stand around here,' Callan yelled above the din of explosions and rat-tat-tat of machineguns.

'We can't take off. The whole wretched Italian Navy is in the way.'

'Take cover,' Kupi yelled from behind a barricade before waving for more men to move from the rear to man the forward positions close to the pier.

Troops raced from nearby buildings to bolster the defenders' numbers and fire-power. The plan worked. At close range the Albanian riflemen were carving the Italians to pieces. Sergeant Mujo Ulqinaka commanded the only Royal Albania Navy patrol-boat armed with a machinegun considered it ineffective. So he transferred the gun to the central town defences. He fired with deadly accuracy, giving Ivy and Callan a brief respite to dash for cover.

They dived over Major Kupi's barricade followed by a trail of ricocheting bullets.

'Blow me down,' Callan said in English because he couldn't think of an Italian equivalent. 'Those jokers mean business, but you've got them pinned down on the wharf, major.'

'We have only so much ammunition, Senore.'

Nevertheless the Albanians were giving a good account of themselves. The Italians were reluctant to advance along the narrow jetty without a chance of out-flanking their enemy.

Reluctant or not the Italians did advance, albeit slowly. As more soldiers disembarked, the increased firing rate kept Albanian heads down, reducing their opportunities.

Major Kupi turned to Callan and Ivy.

'Senore, Senora, you must not be here,' he said. 'It is not safe.'

'Looks like you need all the help you can get,' Callan replied.

'It is not your war!'

Ivy urgently tugged Callan's arm.

'Come on,' she cried. 'Remember Teruel...and Ireland. Let's help with what we know.'

She was of course referring to the Dublin uprising during Easter 1916, where wounded were thick on the ground and someone had to care for them. So far the Albanians were lucky and their casualties low, but there were still wounded men to be helped to the rear for treatment.

An army surgeon, nurses from the hospital and a couple of local doctors tended wounded men a safe distance from the firing-line. So while Ivy went back into FANY mode assisting the doctors, Callan returned to the front to help anyone too badly wounded to continue fighting. Even though casualties weren't numerous, the Italians had only just started.

Some of the invaders closed on the barricades, but Kupi's men drove them off with furious rifle fire and Sergeant Ulqinaka's deadly machinegun bursts. After the Italian second wave was beaten back to their ships, there was a lull in the exchange, but not for long.

While the initial units regrouped a runner reported more Italians were approaching in shore-craft via a beach on the Albanian right flank.

'Get over to the artillery battery and tell Major Jorgo to concentrate on those landing craft,' Kupi ordered the soldier who raced away.

The Albanian defenders had just four Skoda howitzers which although no match for a naval bombardment, could trouble the landing. The Italians seemed to anticipate Kupi and right then warships fired their opening salvo.

Grump! Grump! Grump!

Three explosions blasted the houses just behind the Albanian position. The shock waves rattled the defenders.

Major Kupi knew he couldn't hold the Italian advance much longer. He reloaded the magazine of his Ruby pistol before slamming it into the butt— nine rounds and two spare clips in his pocket.

'Fix bayonets!' he yelled.

And then the Durrës waterfront dissolved into bedlam. Callan hardly knew what was going on around him as more shells exploded way too close for comfort. Shrapnel, debris, masonry and occasional body parts erupted as deadly missiles. Callan felt dizzy and disorientated by a blast close by. Nevertheless he kept searching for wounded men.

Despite Major Jorgo's artillery efforts, the Italians landed in strength all along the beach. In a co-ordinated effort, the men from the first two waves gathered heart and once again advanced towards the Albanian barricade. This time the fire was diverted to the right flank and the frontal attack was less hazardous. Worse still a shell blasted Sergeant Ulqinaka's position to splinters and mush, killing him instantly and permanently silencing the central machinegun.

Heartened by the reduced gunfire, the Italians rushed forward and quickly assaulted the Albanians on two sides, forcing their way through the barricade. It was small arms fire and hand-to-hand combat from then on. There was no holding the flood of

Italian troops. Kupi saw his position was hopeless especially when the Italians began rolling out small tanks from ship holds and lighters coming ashore on the beach. The tanks were not heavily armed, but they couldn't be stopped by small arms fire and their guns caused havoc among the defenders.

'Pull back!' Kupi yelled.

Callan withdrew with the Albanians, carrying a wounded man on his back. He reached the aid-station where Ivy helped him make the casualties as comfortable as possible. The doctors, nurses and wounded were oblivious to the battle around them. It didn't last long in any event.

The Albanian position was desperate and they quickly withdrew beyond the town, retreating to the surrounding foot-hills and mountains beyond. The Italians made no effort to pursue them. Their orders were to take Durrës, and they'd done precisely that. Nor were they particularly interested in wounded Albanians and simply passed by the aid-station.

It was all over. By nine o'clock Italian infantry marched through town to secure a perimeter. Shortly afterwards tanks rumbled past also heading eastwards. Great excitement ensued when a group of officers strode by while men snapped to attention and made it their business to get out of the way. As they reached the aid-station, the central figure waved the riding crop he carried and his party jerked to a halt.

There was some chatter among the group, but the senior officer ordered quiet and strode inside.

'You men fought bravely,' he announced to the wounded, who probably weren't that interested anyway, but the speaker wasn't just anybody.

'I am *Generalissimo* Afredo Guzzoni,' he said. 'I command the Italian Expeditionary Force.'

Callan noticed he didn't say 'invasion force'.

'Your valour is noted and praiseworthy,' the general continued. 'You will be treated with honour. We have not come to conquer...'

Bloody liar, Callan thought.

'...but to unite Albania and Italy to our mutual benefit.'

Guzzoni eyes flashed past Callan to Ivy. He pondered for a few seconds before addressing Callan.

'You don't look like an Albanian to me,' he said.

'I don't know how you can tell, General. I'm so covered in dust and grime I could be anyone.'

'Now your accent betrays you, so can you explain why you are fighting against Italy?'

'I'm not fighting against Italy or anyone, nor is my wife over there,' Callan said. 'We're just helping these wounded men like any decent person would. We're American residents caught in the wrong place at the wrong time.'

Callan was going to mention the Fairchild now moored alongside the Italian ships, but thought better of it.

Don't give 'em any information unless you have to.

'You have papers?'

Callan handed the US permanent resident card he always carried to the general who barely glanced at it before returning the document.

'You still haven't told me why you are here.'

'Tourists,' Ivy said quickly realising the Italian authorities mightn't appreciate their nefarious trading operations. 'Your ships' guns damaged our plane. We had to make an emergency landing here.'

'Ah yes, I saw your plane spying on our fleet yesterday.'

'No one was spying, general,' Ivy said. 'We were just curious. I mean a large fleet isn't something you see every day, so we took a look. Sightseeing is part of being on vacation after all.'

'You know I could have you shot as spies, don't you?'

'Shooting two innocent American holiday-makers would no doubt cause an international incident your government may prefer to avoid, general.'

Guzzoni considered that while his aides nodded sagely.

'Perhaps so,' he said, 'I have more important things to do as it is. You are free to continue your...holiday.'

'Can we ask you to make sure your gunners don't fire at our plane again, please,' Ivy said.

The general smiled.

'*Si, senora,* I will tell my men not to shoot your plane.'

To Callan's relief one of Guzzoni's aides tactfully reminded him they were due to press onto Tirana twenty miles inland and speed was the essence. Guzzoni nodded, raising his whip in a salute.

'I shall send some of my medical team to assist when they have treated our own wounded. *Buon giorno,*' he said to the doctors and was gone.

'Blow me down, Ivy,' Callan sighed with relief, 'that was too close for comfort. Let's make tracks for home.'

'I'm with you, sweetheart. I've done all I can to make these poor fellows comfortable and General Guzzoni has promised help.'

'If he meant it.'

'The general struck me as a man of his word.'

Which was indeed so. On their way back to the Fairchild, Callan and Ivy passed three nurses and a military surgeon heading for the Albanian aid-station.

*

Squeezing the Fairchild through the jumble of Italian shipping was tricky, but Ivy got it done with Callan hanging out of the cargo door yelling instructions to ensure the wing-tips didn't collide with any military hardware.

Once they were airborne, Ivy and Callan saw the full extent of the Italian task-force. Ships were moored off-shore for miles along the coast. It turned out about 20,000 men were involved in the initial invasion, but it looked like there was plenty of support. Additionally bomber formations now flew overhead and Albania had no fighters to intercept them.

'Poor Albania doesn't stand a chance,' Ivy Lamented. 'It's such a lovely place and the people are sweet.'

'The Ities mightn't have it all their own way once they get into the mountains,' Callan said. 'It'll be a different story against guerrillas, because somehow I think there are enough blokes like Major Kupi who'll put up a fight.'

When they touched down and taxied into Mirios harbour the invasion was already old news. Dennis Mortimer had already heard it all on the long range low-frequency wireless transceiver he used for communicating with fellow expatriates worldwide. He powered the set by an ingenious foot-pedalled generator which operated in much the same way as a sewing machine treadle.

'What do you make of it, Dennis?' Callan asked. 'It's more than sabre-rattling, isn't it?'

'I believe so, dear boy, I think Mussolini is trying to show the *Nazis* he is just as big a cheese as Hitler in the Pact of Steel.'

'Are they going to try to conquer all Europe?' Ivy wondered.

'It looks like a good start.'

'Surely the French and British will stop them dead in their tracks.'

Mortimer shrugged.

'I wouldn't be too sure about that if I was you, my dear. Winston Churchill has been urging Britain to re-arm to a war footing for years, but no one seems to be listening. He's furious with Chamberlain's appeasement policy towards the *Nazis*. He reckons we're not nearly ready for war and I'm inclined to agree with him.'

'Yes, and don't forget the last big show started in the Balkans,' Callan said.

'And guess where we are...' Ivy added.

Chapter 13 — Phoney War

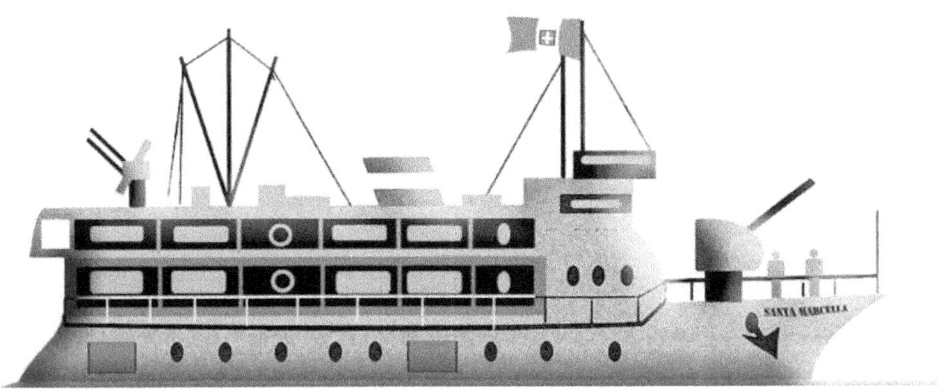

Naples Waterfront — September 1939

'Now you look after the old crate,' Johnny Witherspoon admonished, shaking Callan's hand vigorously. 'Are you sure you don't want to come with me?'

'No thanks, Johnny, I'm too old for that sort of caper. Like I said I don't fight wars anymore.'

'Although they have a way of chasing us around,' Ivy reminded him.

She embraced Witherspoon, squeezing the breath from his lungs.

'Take care and write,' she said.

'Absolutely, but it'll all be over by Christmas. I'll be right back to life as usual before you even know it.'

'That's what they said back in '14,' Callan said grimly. 'But, you'd better get on board. The ship won't wait — not even for potential fighter aces.'

'I can't wait to strap on a Hurricane or maybe a Spit. There are more coming off the production lines every day.'

Johnny Witherspoon's enthusiasm didn't infect Callan. His brushes with the Spanish and Albanian conflicts hadn't altered his opinion of warfare. The lure of flying a high performance Hawker Hurricane or even better a Supermarine Spitfire may tempt young Witherspoon, but Callan was more circumspect.

Witherspoon joined the eclectic crowd shuffling up the gangway. Despite the Pact of Steel signed by Mussolini and Hitler, Italy had not yet declared war and seemed to be fence-sitting for the time being. Nevertheless prudent British expatriates were making themselves scarce to avoid internment.

There were also large numbers of Jewish refugees who'd heard about the German concentration camps which had been in operation for six years. Mussolini made no secret of the fact he felt empathy towards the *Nazis* when it came to Jews. So many wisely decided to leave town before the inevitable round-ups should Italy enter the war as part of the Axis alliance.

The freighter Witherspoon sailed on was part of a flotilla heading for Malta where it'd pick up a frigate and corvette escort to cross the Western Mediterranean, past Gibraltar, through the Pillars of Hercules to the Atlantic en route to Plymouth. Although something of a vacuum occurred after the *Nazi Blitzkrieg* into Poland, no one was taking any chances when U-boats could be lurking with an eye for the main chance.

It was also no secret the *Reich* had commissioned a fleet of heavy cruisers known as pocket-battleships. *Admiral Graf Spee, Admiral Hipper, the Blücher, Scharnhorst* and *Gneisenau* all prowled around the world's oceans looking for an opportunity to blast unprotected merchantmen to the bottom of the sea.

'Aren't you a wee bit jealous of Johnny?' Ivy asked from the co-pilot seat.

Callan stared at her blankly.

'I mean flying those beautiful new fighter planes.'

'You're kidding me, right? Dog fights are just plain scary and I never want to get into another, especially as those Hurricanes and Spitfires probably go four times faster than a Sopwith Camel. I'd never keep up. At my age I'd be dead on the first day.'

'You're not that decrepit. In fact you're in pretty good shape for an old guy.'

'Less of the old guy or I'll put you across my knee and paddle your bottom.'

'You never know, I might enjoy that.'

'I think I'll just concentrate of flying now...Anyway I think it's swell we're under the American umbrella. I reckon the US will stay neutral for this one and I'm content to sit it out too.'

Back on Mirios life returned to normal after the eligible girls finished lamenting Johnny Witherspoon's departure. The Italian army held the Albania border against the Greeks, but nothing much happened. No one was interested in Mirios, which was now part of Italy by conquest, although no one had actually conquered it. Mirios simply went about its daily business with quiet discretion.

Callan did notice Dennis Mortimer had moved his radio to the attic and had become secretive when he used it.

Life was still sweet on Mirios so Callan and Ivy stopped paying attention. The islanders came to rely on their aviation service in many ways, especially for mail and medical supplies. The fact that many of the island's trading activities were facilitated by Don Rocco and his men-of-honour didn't bother anyone. A bottle of cognac at a discount price was more than enough to make Mirios citizens look the other way. It had started in such a small way that Ivy and Callan hardly noticed until the demand for contraband became almost as great as legitimate trade.

'You know we're smugglers, don't you?' Ivy admonished as they flew home one evening after a particularly lucrative day's business.

'You're such an honest soul,' Callan replied, 'but it's all Mussolini's fault for being such a pain in the arse.'

'And those beastly Black-Shirts just love pushing honest folk around. I don't feel badly about pulling the wool over their eyes.'

'Especially as we provide a service for those honest folk.'

'It's our civic duty.'

She giggled.

'Don Rocco has totally corrupted us.'

'Justifiably so.'

There was a moment's interest when Mortimer reported the German pocket-battleship *Graf Spee* had been sunk somewhere in South America called the River Plate. Then in the spring of 1940 everything changed. The Germans decided to explode everywhere at once.

'Blow me down,' Mortimer declared, 'Jerry has decided to invade the world. They've smashed into France and bottled our boys with the Frogs at Dunkirk and sorted out Denmark and Norway in short order. I guess the *Nazis* think they need to protect their north border.'

'At least they're not heading this way,' Ivy said.

Maybe not the *Nazis*, but actually the Italians were...although it took them over a year.

Benito Mussolini had been spoiling for war ever since the Germans marched into Poland to kick the whole thing off. Unlike Hitler, Mussolini didn't call the shots when it came to the military. King Victor Emanuel III was still commander-in-chief of the Royal Italian Armed Forces. His majesty was concerned Italy wasn't prepared to take on a long-lasting conflict. It was a judgement that was to prove fundamentally correct.

But after the German *Blitzkrieg* sliced into France like a knife through very warm butter, Victor Emanuel saw the chance of occupying southwest France, which he'd coveted for ages. So Italy charged in boots and all even though it still wasn't ready for a protracted struggle.

Meanwhile the British and French managed to evacuate over three hundred and thirty thousand men from Dunkirk and stem the Luftwaffe over Britain's skies. British cities, especially London endured the *blitz* started by an off-course German bomber, but setting off a chain reaction. Churchill gave Air Marshall Arthur 'Bomber' Harris *carte-blanche* to unleash his Vickers Wellington, Short Stirling and Handley-Page Halifax bombers on residential as well as industrial targets. Harris was only too happy to oblige.

Johnny Witherspoon made a name for himself as a Hurricane ace and now commanded a fighter flight.

1940 dragged on into what had become a spiteful stalemate. By autumn rumours began to surface that the Axis powers might set their sights on the Balkans, North Africa, Greece for fuel and food. Maybe Russia was even a possibility, but no one believed Hitler would be silly enough to take on the Communist Bear.

'It makes you wonder where the hell do they find the men and equipment,' Mortimer remarked.

The Italians were committed to North Africa and Greece, but weren't doing very well. They met stubborn resistance at the Greek border and by December British Commonwealth forces put the Italian 19th Army out of business in Africa, capturing 130,000 prisoners who were shipped to POW camps in South Africa and Australia. So now Italy needed all the military manpower it could muster.

*

San Giovanni Police Barracks — December 1940

*C*apitano Abiati considered himself a policeman and not a soldier even though *Carabineri* were technically military police who'd seen active service. Abiati fought in the Great War and didn't care much for the experience. Now a second war had erupted he was happy to do what he knew best, which was keeping the peace. Unfortunately those in high places had other ideas. Once Italy had officially joined the Axis powers in war, Mussolini's Black-Shirts started rounding up Jews in earnest just to prove how helpful they could be.

Abiati didn't have anything against Jews. In fact he couldn't recall meeting any, although the strictly orthodox men looked out of place in their black clothes and distinctive haircuts. But they were by and large law-abiding and certainly far less trouble than communists or the criminal families who were still up to mischief and damned illusive because no one dared to testify against them.

So he was pretty miffed when an arrogant black-shirted individual stomped into his San Giovanni police station. The

MVSM officer who looked about nineteen snapped a *Nazi* salute, which irritated Abiati who thought it pretentious.

'Lieutenant Enzo Viola with orders from the Albania Division HQ,' the officer announced, far too loudly in Abiati's opinion.

'I really don't have time for this, lieutenant,' Abiati sighed wearily. 'And if you haven't noticed we're in Sicily not Albania.'

'You would defy *Il Duce's* orders?' the lieutenant replied in disbelief. 'You are to accompany me to Catania Wharf. We shall round up the Jewish scum from the islands. There is no escape for them.'

The police chief read the orders, which didn't totally agree with Viola's interpretation. They were signed by a colonel Abiati had never heard of on behalf of the Albania Division top brass. The papers also included authority to commandeer whatever he needed and government vouchers to pay for it. There were many other documents, including radio frequencies and a code-book. In fact all he needed to administrate an independent command.

'It says here I'm to command a seaborne detachment and patrol the eastern Adriatic and Ionian Seas,' Abiati said. 'Don't we have sailors enough?'

'Enough to man our assigned patrol-boat maybe, *Capitano*, but not for shore operations. The *Regia Marina* needs every man for the Mediterranean fleet.'

Abiati's orders were irregular, but he figured irregularities were something he'd have to get used to in wartime. God knows, there were enough of them in the last war. Lieutenant Viola was nothing more than a courier after all, even if he was a trumped-up pompous Black-Shirt bastard. Apparently Abiati's detachment awaited him at the docks.

Abiati packed a duffle bag. It didn't take long to gather his meagre possessions. There was no family to farewell. He'd been married long ago, but his flighty wife quickly grew bored of provincial life and left for cosmopolitan Verona. Abiati's sometime mistress probably wouldn't notice he was gone for a month or two.

Viola rode a Moto Guzzi 250cc motorcycle. Abiati clambered into the side car with his duffle squeezed between his chest and knees. It was a short, but uncomfortable ride and Viola rode like a maniac, so Abiati was in a foul mood when he arrived at the dock. And he didn't cheer up at what he saw.

Abiati had visited the waterfront frequently since Ivy and Callan's escape and always wondered what had become of the Americans who'd been missing for nearly three years now. At first he was vehement, but with limited resources he'd prioritised. Matters only grew worse when the Army, Navy and Air Force systematically poached his youngest, fittest and most able men as Italy prepared for war.

A converted tourist cruiser was moored among fishing caiques, freighters and military patrol-boats. *Santa Marcella* had been stencilled on her bow and the only signs she was a warship were an anti-aircraft gun mounted on the forward deck and twin machineguns astern.

About thirty men lounged around the port-side cafes, smoking and drinking either coffee or wine. They were a mixed bag, some being barely more than children while others were reaching retirement and beyond. To their credit they were reasonably turned out, although some uniforms were ill-fitting, but they'd done their best.

'Who are these men?' Abiati demanded. 'They don't look like regular servicemen to me.'

'Neither are they, *Capitano*,' Viola replied. 'Some are reservists while others have been conscripted.'

'How did such an obviously ambitious young fellow like you get assigned this detail? Surely there are more glamorous battles for you to fight.'

'Indeed, but I'm not at liberty to discuss matters with you,' Viola replied smugly.

Abiati felt like smacking him in the mouth, but was saved when two trucks rolled to a stop a few metres away. The drivers explained they contained weapons ammunition and rations for his platoon. Next, an impossibly young naval ensign snapped to attention in front of him.

'*Guardia marina* Angelo Russo, *Capitano*. I command the *Santa Marcello* and await your instructions.'

Abiati smartly returned the salute.

'First we'd better get the men out of the bars and start loading this gear aboard. Then we'll sort out quarters aboard before we organise a work schedule, guard rosters, catering provisions.'

Russo and Viola stared blankly as Abiati rolled off a dozen tasks required to get the men ready as an operational unit. Viola was young, arrogant, spoilt and used to others doing the heavy-lifting. Russo was just green and barely out of training. Well, all he and his ten-man crew had to do was drive the boat where Abiati told him while Viola had better get used to becoming an officer and not just a strutting peacock.

Meanwhile the troops had seen the officers arrive and formed themselves into two ranks beside the trucks. They tried their best, but didn't look particularly warlike, but neither did Abiati although he'd seen his share of action both on the battle front and as a policeman. He may not be fond of bloodshed, but he'd do his duty.

Santa Marcella was large enough to accommodate everyone. The two upper decks consisted of five large cabins each which slept three men comfortably. The naval men shared the below main-deck cabins and Abiati, Viola and Russo had a cabin each.

Abiati appointed the eight most likely men to act as NCOs — two sergeants as platoon leaders and six corporals to command the three ten-man squads in each platoon. After a few days of onboard drill, the men were ready to sail. Russo's crew were assigned the task of provisioning the ship because they knew what to do as the cook and his assistant were sailors. Abiati was amazed how much they took aboard.

He assembled the men on deck before they sailed.

'Men, our task is to patrol the Eastern Adriatic. We're to keep an eye on these waters while the rest of the fleet fights the British on the high seas. Our boys are also advancing to Greece and we must protect their rear echelon against partisans. We shall be patrolling ashore as well from this vessel, so you will remain alert and your weapons must be kept in inspection order at all times...'

'And the Jews...' Viola blurted.

'Lieutenant, you will remain silent while I address the men,' Abiati said without raising his voice.

The following dawn *Santa Marcello* cast off and sailed to war.

Chapter 14 — Dennis Mortimer's Secret

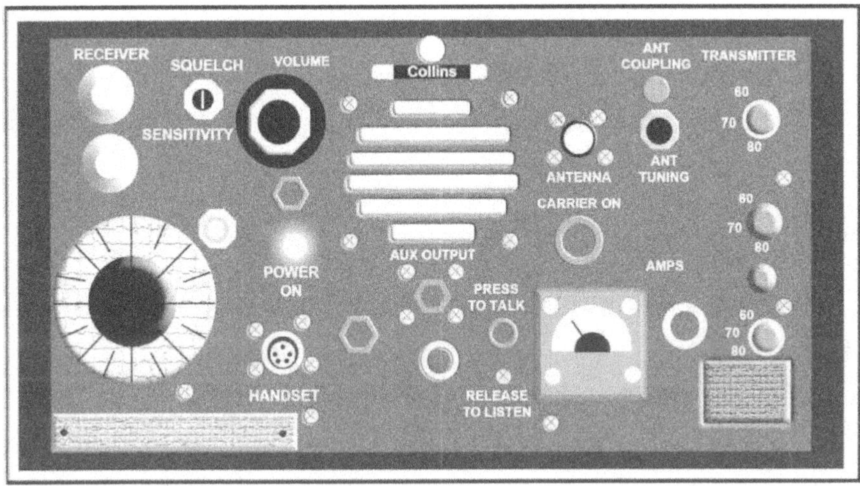

Santa Marcello wasn't the only vessel patrolling the East Adriatic. There were a number of other ships in a loosely co-ordinated flotilla. Some were converted pleasure craft, caiques or freighters, while others were purpose-built torpedo and patrol-boats. Their task was both marine and shore based.

With the Italian Army now poised on the Grecian border, Albanian partisans had taken the opportunity to step up their operations. Sabotage, mines, booby traps and hit-and-run ambushes were all on the increase. Abiati often took his men ashore to sniff out trouble. But word soon got out and the miscreants were pretty cagey and hard to find. Viola was still eager to round up Jews, but Abiati discouraged him, saying they didn't have time to continually ferry prisoners back to Italy.

Although Abiati was unaware he even existed, one unlikely trouble-maker was Dennis Mortimer. He'd disappear to the attic and operate his radio for hours.

'What's Dennis up to?' Ivy wondered as she and Callan strolled back to the villa after supper in town.

'None of our business,' Callan replied, rather too self-righteously in Ivy's opinion.

'We live under the same roof.'

'As guests.'

'We make enough money for the business to earn our food and board.'

Matters came to a head the following day when *Santa Marcello* drew alongside the Mirios sea-wall and troops disembarked. Juan was stitching up a deal in one of the waterfront offices. He excused himself and walked straight into *Capitano* Abiati as he left the building.

Juan muttered a quick apology and rushed off, before Abiati had time to connect him with the San Giovanni gaol-break. But three years had passed, surely not. Abiati stared after Juan for a second, frowned, shook his head and turned to his men.

There was no reported rebel activity on Mirios, but Abiati decided to march the men inland to keep them fit and explore the terrain. He planned to return to the ship before dark as the idea of bivouacking under the starts held no appeal at that time of year.

Meanwhile Juan hot-footed his way to *Bella Vista*. If Abiati didn't remember him, the same couldn't be said for Ivy and Callan. So he was in a right old flap when he reached the villa.

'Italian soldiers!' he managed to blurt out after gulping two glasses of lemonade.

'What do they want?' Ivy asked, realising what a silly question it was as soon as she'd spoken. Of course Juan didn't ask them.

But why hadn't he? It would have been a reasonable question.

'It doesn't matter,' Callan said. 'We hold US permanent residency cards, but Dennis had better make himself scarce.'

'Yes, I don't fancy an internment camp,' Mortimer said.

'I think we may all be in trouble. That police captain in Sicily...what's his name...is in charge as far as I can see.'

'Abiati..?'

'*Si*, I don't think he recognised me, but he might when he thinks about it.'

'We'd better *all* make ourselves scarce...'

Ivy's voice trailed off as she spied Abiati's column marching out of town. They'd have to come right past the villa to the road inland.

'Quick! Into the house,' Mortimer said. 'There's no time to head for the hills.'

They hurried inside. Mortimer called for Adela, Fausto and Carmela. Anxiety showed on their faces when they assembled in the entrance hall.

'There's an Italian patrol heading this way,' Mortimer explained. 'They can't find us or I'll be interned and our guests apparently have...history...with their leader.'

'Go up into the attic,' Fausto said. 'We'll keep them occupied.'

'Or maybe they'll pass us by,' Adela said hopefully.

'You might get into trouble,' Ivy reminded them.

'No time to worry now,' Fausto said. 'We'll be fine.'

'Fascists don't frighten us,' Carmela added, although Adela didn't look so sure.

Access to the attic was via an extending staircase that folded into a trapdoor in the top-storey ceiling. Fausto lowered the step-ladder with a boathook. Mortimer led the way and the others clambered up after him.

'Keep the pole up there, Senore,' Fausto said. 'If they can't see a way up, they might not bother.'

Ivy and Callan expected to see the attic cluttered with the usual bric-a-brac people have no use for, but can't bring themselves to toss out. That wasn't the case at all. Mortimer's attic looked like a military command centre. Maps covered much of the wall-space while book-cases lined any clear spots. A large table strewn with papers and manuals stood in the centre of the room. A desk was pushed against a wall bearing Mortimer's Collins radio transceiver, high-powered binoculars, an expensive 35mm SLR camera and several detachable telephoto lenses.

'Blow me down, Dennis,' Callan declared, 'you've got some pricey kit here for bird-watching.'

'I'll explain later, dear boy,' Mortimer said peeking through the garret gable window. 'If I get the chance, those bloody Dagoes are coming onto the grounds.'

*

The attic trapdoor hadn't even closed before Fausto headed for the gate where Abiati and his men stomped to a halt just as he arrived.

'What is this place?' Abiati demanded.

'Why, it is a house, *Senore Capitano*,'

'I can see that.'

Abiati refrained from adding 'you idiot' because he'd asked the question and received an answer.

'I mean who lives here?'

'Just two housekeepers and me,' Fausto replied.

Abiati looked Fausto over, taking note of his well-worn shirt, corduroy pants tied below the knees with bowyangs and his dusty boots.

'I see. You seem well accommodated for a man dressed like a peasant.'

'You would not tend your garden in opera clothes, would you, *Senore*?'

'You don't employ a gardener, then?'

Now Fausto had to start thinking on the fly.

'Oh no, *Senore Capitano*, I am just a retired veteran,' Fausto was looking for some military empathy there. 'Fourth *Alpini* Regiment. I was wounded at Monte Vodice. Look.'

Before Abiati could stop him, Fausto untied his left bowyang, rolled up his trouser-leg to expose a scar where a decent chunk of his calf had been shot away.

'So you got a job here after the war?' Abiati asked.

'*Si, Senore.*' Fausto beamed.

'Then who owns this villa?'

Fausto was wise enough to know when lying, it's best to stay as close to the truth as possible.

'Rich Englishman. He comes here for holidays, but now he is away. We don't know when he'll be back.'

'I don't expect he'll come back at all now we are at war, do you?' Abiati said. 'But I think we'll take a look around anyway. Lieutenant Viola, take a squad and check out the grounds. Sergeant

Vanni, bring six men and follow me. Everyone else stay on guard here and keep your eyes open...Open the gates, *Senore.*'

The gate wasn't locked and before Fausto could think of any further delaying tactics, Viola snapped opened the latch and pushed past him. His squad fanned out and picked their way through the gardens. The soldiers didn't expect to find anti-Fascist partisans lurking in Fausto's neat flowerbeds and produce-laden vegetable patch. So their search didn't go beyond pilfering a few ripe tomatoes until Viola ordered them to stop.

'We are not common looters,' he snapped. 'Save your energy for partisans...and Jews.'

The sheds and garage of course revealed nothing.

Abiati marched through the front portal. Fausto noticed Carmela and Adela were nowhere to be seen, which was a relief because there was no way the soldiers could avoid finding signs of habitation if they searched the bedrooms. He also remembered the table had been set for four people. The latter he could explain away, but not the former.

Abiati dispatched men upstairs. They returned shortly reporting all was clear. Fausto heaved a sigh of relief when he saw the dining table was completely bare. Abiati seemed satisfied and ordered his men outside.

'*Grazie, Senore,*' Abiati said touching his cap-peak before he led his men away.

Fausto rushed back inside. There was still no evidence of either Carmela or Adela, so he assumed they'd escaped through the small back gate and made their way through the trees to town. But that wasn't the case...

When Fausto went to meet Abiati, Carmela cleared the dining settings and stashed everything in the nearest kitchen cabinet, while Adela rushed upstairs. The beds were already made and she prided herself in their neatness, so they didn't look as if they'd ever been slept in. She pulled one of the pillow cases free and stuffed everything lying on the dressers into it.

She had to be quick because she had three bedrooms to clear as well as the bathrooms. She emptied the vanity drawers of razors, toothbrushes, combs, ladies toiletry and any other evidence which all went into the pillow case. She had no time to empty the bedroom drawers when she heard Abiati's men clump up the staircase. She scrambled under Ivy and Callan's double bed and held her breath.

The door eased open and Adela saw a pair of boots move across the room. The soldier stepped to the window and peered through before casting his eyes around. Nothing looked out of place and after a cursory scan he was satisfied and left. Maybe if Viola had been leading the indoor search, Adela might well have been discovered, but the soldiers barely glanced in each bedroom.

'No one here,' one soldier called.

'Same here,' came one reply after another.

Fausto was unaware of that when he took a broom from the closet, climbed the stairs and thumped on the attic trap door, which opened immediately. Ivy led the others down.

'Blimey, that was close,' Callan said. 'What were those jokers after, Fausto?'

The gardener looked puzzled as *Jokers* didn't really translate well in Callan's intended context.

'Soldiers, Fausto. The soldiers. Why are they here?'

'The *Capitano* he did not say. He didn't seem too clear himself.'

'Let's hope he doesn't decide to come back,' Ivy said, turning to Mortimer. 'And Dennis, what exactly was all that stuff in the attic?'

'Well, I suppose I'll have to come clean sooner or later, my dear...'

'And..?'

'I'm afraid I might be a wee bit of a spy...'

Mortimer looked decidedly sheepish about it.

'It sort of came with the territory when I decided to live here,' he added. 'I served with a Navy chap called Jimmie Matthews during the last show, you see. He introduced me to his boss the late Sir Mansfield Smith-Cummings who was head of the British cloak-and-dagger department.'

'I met Lieutenant-Commander Matthews briefly in Ireland in '16,' Callan said.

'Yep, same fellow. Anyway Cummings, who started calling himself "C" for "Chief" or "Controller" or some such or maybe it was just his surname initial. Anyway he recruited agents worldwide and I was one of them. When I shifted here he asked me to keep an eye out and report any fishy business by the wireless set upstairs. I've been able to provide a few tit-bits, especially when flying around, but it's mostly small fry and I hope it stays that way.'

'*Capitano* Abiati might be about to change all that,' Ivy said.

'Then we'd better take steps to make sure he doesn't. Now where the blue blazes are those two girls?'

After clearing the kitchen table, Carmela had indeed raced through the back gate and hidden in the cypress grove beyond. Once she saw the soldiers march off, she returned. Everyone was much relieved when she came through the door, looking a little nervous.

'It's alright, Carmela,' Mortimer said. 'The soldiers have gone, but where's Adela?

Carmela stared blankly.

Ivy went up the stairs to search and found Adela who was still under her bed and too scared to move. With a little coaxing Adela crawled out and told Ivy what happened. Ivy, who was a pretty huggy person anyway, embraced the maid.

'Well done, you brave girl,' she gushed. 'Jolly quick thinking.'

'Oh. *Senora* Ivy, I was so frightened.'

'Trust me, Adela, you weren't the only one.'

'So it looks like my staff earned their wages today,' Mortimer said when all the stories were told. Fausto hinted at a rise. Mortimer told him not to push it, but brought out a few bottles of his favourite vintage.

'Work's over for today,' he declared. 'Let's celebrate. Don't worry, Carmela, we'll all lend a hand to prepare lunch.'

Celebrations aside, the entire household stayed alert for any returning soldiers, who took an alternative route back to town. Abiati's men spent the evening at the cafes wining and dining in true Italian fashion. Much to Lieutenant Viola's disgust, this meant they made a late start the following day. Finally the *Santa Marcello* cast off and steamed into the Adriatic, leaving Mirios residents with some serious concerns.

The Island was very much a multi-cultural community. The population of only a few thousand was made up of Italians, Greeks, Albanians, Montenegrins, Yugoslavians, Cypriots and North Africans, all of whom had found a haven during the Adriatic's turbulent history.

About half the population lived in town, while the rest owned farms and market gardens throughout the island. They acknowledged a selection of religious beliefs: Catholic, Orthodox Christians, even a few Protestants, Moslems, Atheists and Jews.

No one on the island seemed to care and everybody got along fine when centuries ago Islamic worshippers agreed not to wake everyone with a call to prayer and just turned up at their modest mosque when they felt the need. Most islanders relied on one another and traded nearly every day at the quayside market where vigorous haggling was the most friction found on Mirios.

But Mortimer soon heard from townsfolk they'd been quizzed by the black-shirted officer who was interested to locate any Jews on the island. Luckily it had been the Sabbath. With their synagogue devotions over, the Jews had all gone home. But if the black-shirted officer returned and started looking in earnest, the Jews would soon be discovered. Everyone now had a pretty good idea what happened to dissidents, including Jews even though they weren't particularly dissident.

Mirios' citizens didn't want their Jews deported to goodness knew where, because they included the doctor, pharmacist, and baker along with quite a number of other useful and respected people.

It was time for a town meeting, which showed how seriously the townsfolk took the military's appearance. No one could remember when the last town meeting had been called, but now there was a lot to talk about.

Meanwhile *Capitano* Abiati didn't forget *Bella Vista* villa with its stunning views, tranquil grounds stocked with produce often in short supply on Sicily and mainland Italy.

Chapter 15 — Fascists' Return

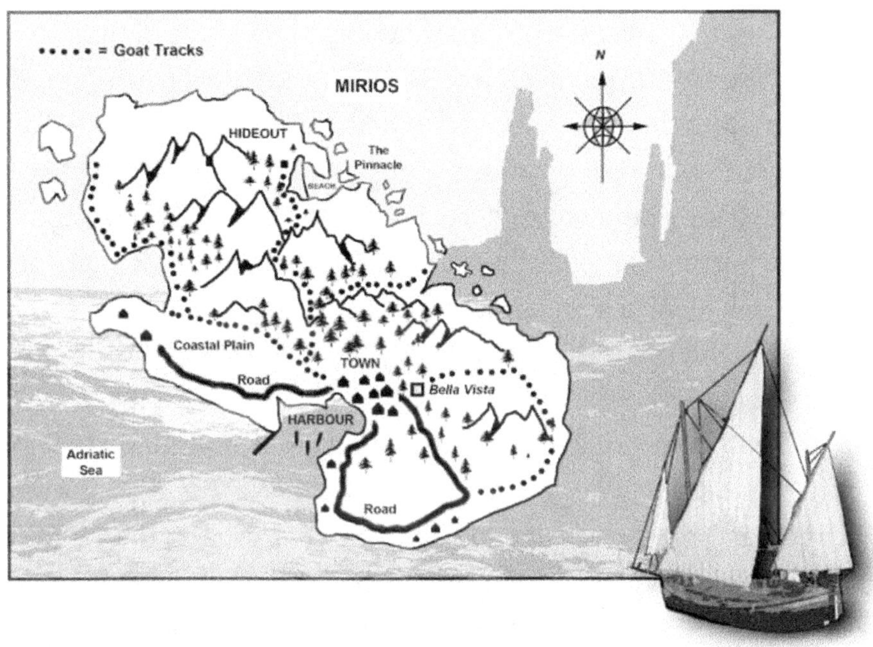

The town meeting lasted all day, but it took time to iron out contingencies and there was a lot of wine involved. Every solution usually posed more possible threats, so little was actually achieved although they did agree ethnic minorities might be in danger, but what to do about it? They were on an island and from what they heard about the mainland, things wouldn't be any better for Jews who the Axis had taken a particular disliking to.

Someone pointed out Italians hadn't been too bothered about Jews or anyone else until the Axis was formed, so maybe things wouldn't be as bad as they were in Germany...or Poland...or Czechoslovakia...and pretty much everywhere else under *Nazi* domination. But no one was in any doubt about who pulled the strings when it came to Axis control. Ivy, Callan, Juan and Dennis Mortimer left the meeting before anything was resolved. Everyone else drifted away shortly afterwards to consider their options Mirios style — over a meal, more wine and a good night's sleep.

'The first thing we have to do is move my stuff somewhere remote,' Mortimer announced when they returned to *Bella Vista*. 'Not just the communications equipment, but anything that might give the Ities a clue we're here. Intelligence reports have confirmed several patrol-boats are operating in the area, and if that lot don't come back, chances are another boat-load will.'

'What about the plane?' Ivy asked. 'They didn't take any notice of it before they left.'

That may not have been as odd as it sounded. Italy was a power-house of aviation after the Great War. It had hosted four Schneider Trophy events and won three. Perhaps the heyday was waning, but five years earlier a Macchi M.C. 72 float-plane had broken the 700 km/hr barrier, utilising counter-rotating propellers. This was over a 100 km/hr more than the Supermarine aircraft that won the last Schneider Trophy in 1931.

So planes were common enough, but they were a resource the military might want to exploit.

'Maybe we should take it as far from the town as possible,' Fausto suggested. 'I might know a place on the far side of Mirios.'

After Mortimer unfolded a map of Mirios Island, Fausto pointed out a sandy cove protected by a pinnacle and rocky shoals.

'It would take over a day to trek there overland. The terrain is too rough. A small boat and the float-plane should be able to squeeze in on the high tide. A Navy ship will go aground if it tries to enter the cove.'

'Looks like I'm moving house,' Mortimer sighed. 'I'll miss your company.'

'We may be joining you,' Ivy reminded him.

It took over a week to sail all the kit Mortimer needed to survive. The cove turned out to be a pleasant enough spot. Fausto skilfully navigated his caique past the pinnacle and rocky outcrops that flanked the bay inlet. He explained the swell and wind direction controlled whether anyone could enter the bay or not. An ancient ruin stood on a headland overlooking the beach. It may have been a temple or gathering point, but no one knew for sure. Only the pillars remained intact, but Mortimer decided it was a good spot to camp.

Callan flew the Fairchild loaded with Jerry cans across Mirios, touching down just beyond the bay and cautiously taxied the plane through the entrance.

'There, that wasn't so hard,' he said smugly.

'It doesn't take much to make the passage impossible,' Fausto reminded him. 'Also you'll run aground at anything much below high tide, so it's a pretty good spot to take shelter.'

They erected a couple of tents within the temple ruin which had been encroached upon by a cypress grove. The temple had originally been built to overlook the sea, but trees now veiled the view so the camp was hidden from any passing seafarers. The trees also made excellent masts for the radio aerial. At first they thought fresh water would be critical, but a creek rippled down from the central high country into the bay. Firewood was no problem and it was unlikely smoke would be considered remarkable or even noticed through the trees.

Fausto said he'd return in a week while Ivy and Callan remained to help Mortimer set up camp.

They hadn't moved any time too soon. When he returned Fausto informed them *Capitano* Abiati had already returned with the intention of making *Bella Vista* his headquarters. Patrol-boat life bored him to distraction, so he decided he'd become a land-based commander and leave the dreary routine to Viola and Russo.

He felt no guilt about making himself comfortable. His orders were vague at best and after weeks of patrolling, they'd turned up very little that posed a threat to Italy. Viola was a total pain complaining continually about being wasted and why wasn't he fighting with the Germans who knew what warfare was all about. Abiati saw himself as a policeman, dammit, and all he was doing here was disturbing people who hadn't committed a crime between the lot of them.

They hadn't even found any wretched Jews, who'd either been swept up by other patrols or were very good at staying hidden. Mind you Viola was the only person complaining about that. Well, he'd finish going on wild-goose chases until someone came and told him otherwise. Now it was time to inspect *Bella Vista's* wine cellar.

'It looks like you'll be living off the land for a bit,' Fausto told Mortimer, 'so I've brought you something to help.'

He unpacked several cartridge boxes for Callan's rifle and an assortment of vegetable seeds and cuttings.

'The soil's not the best, but it should be good enough close to the creek to start a vegetable patch.'

So Ivy and Callan became freedom-fighters by default with Mortimer as communication controller while Fausto, Juan, Carmela and Adela acted as their intelligence source in town. With two rifles albeit plenty of ammo, they weren't going to make much of an impact, but they weren't going to go hungry either.

Nevertheless, their plans to just lie low were seriously jeopardised after Fausto brought the news that *Capitano* Abiati had moved into *Bella Vista* permanently.

*

'I shall keep four men here,' *Capitano* Abiati explained to Lieutenant Viola. 'We'll ensure all records and reports are in order. Right now we have no administration system at all. So what is the point of just sailing around randomly wasting precious fuel? We need to compile and file our findings, correlate, look for trends and cross-reference our intelligence.'

Viola recognised so much hokum when he heard it, but didn't say anything. He considered Abiati a useless old has-been, but it meant he'd be in charge on patrol, and boy would things change then. So the lieutenant merely nodded.

'Shouldn't we also co-ordinate operations with the other patrol-boats,' Viola suggested. 'Right now we're cruising around independently. We're lucky we don't crash into one another.'

That was a good idea and Abiati knew it, but he didn't want a bar of anything that could potentially cause him grief. The thought of dealing with more Lieutenant Violas wasn't appealing, but he'd bluff his way out of this.

'Good idea, Lieutenant,' Abiati said, 'and that is exactly why we need a larger command centre. Leave it with me. I'll contact Albanian Division and organise things.'

'I'm sure there was a sea-plane in the harbour last time we docked,' Viola said. 'It's not there now, but it could be useful.'

'Get Fausto in here and we'll ask him.'

Fausto shrugged when questioned.

'The pilot must have flown away, *Senore,*' Fausto said, which was indeed true.

'Where did he go?'

'To the mainland, *Senore,* where else could he go?'

'Italy or Albania?'

Fausto shrugged.

'The pilot did not discuss such matters with me, *Senore,*'

That was also true.

'When he returns, I'd like to talk with him. What is his name?'

'Giovanni, *Senore.*'

Again the truth, although Fausto failed to mention Johnny Witherspoon was an Allied fighter pilot.

'I will tell him when I see him again, *Senore.* I have also told Carmela and Adela to continue as normal, if that is satisfactory.'

'Yes, that will do very well, *grazie.*'

So Abiati settled into his new accommodation. He was smart enough to leave his men aboard *Santa Marcello.* Billeting them around town would have proved unpopular and the last thing he wanted was discontent. The cabins aboard were comfortable enough and probably a lot better than many of them were used to or most billets in town.

The following morning around nine o'clock, he was awakened by Ensign Russo.

'What are you up to, Russo? It's Saturday. Can't a man have a sleep in now and then?'

Abiati enjoyed the Mediterranean habit of going to bed late and rising late.

'*Capitano,* I think you must come...'

Abiati quickly dressed and followed Russo to the *cittadina piazza.* It appeared Lieutenant Viola had been up early. A crowd had been herded together by Abiati's men led by Viola. The people were all dressed in their finest clothes which now looked dishevelled indicating they been manhandled. Abiati reckoned there were at least fifty men, women, youths and children in the square.

They all looked frightened and confused, which was understandable with a bunch of rifle-toting soldiers pushing them around.

'What is this all about, Viola?' Abiati demanded above the din a yelling troops and wailing townspeople.

'Filthy Jewish scum,' Viola replied with relish. 'It's Shabbat Day, you see. I caught them all together at their synagogue.'

Viola might have felt smug, but in truth he'd only rounded up about half the Jewish community.

'Oh, that's great. Now what do you intend to do with them?'

'Eradicate them of course.'

Abiati was appalled. Sure he'd heard Germans were murdering Jews in droves wherever they found them in Europe, but then they were pretty indiscriminate and murdered everyone in droves.

'We are not barbarians, Viola.'

'Yes, but they are.'

Abiati swore. He was aware of the Jewish situation or 'final solution' as his orders had phrased it, but so far he'd been able to turn a blind eye and not bother Jews if they kept out of his way. Now damned Viola had brought matters to a head. He feared Viola would simply execute them to be buried in a mass grave somewhere out of town.

'We'll send a message to Division and ask for clarification.'

'Clarification? The orders are there in black and white.'

'You couldn't help yourself, could you Viola? What have these people ever done to you?'

The men were looking uncomfortable. If there was one thing soldiers didn't want to see, it was their officers arguing.

'Do I have to remind you I am the officer commanding this detachment and you will obey me? I shall contact Division and ask for instructions.'

'Yessir!' Viola snapped to attention and shot a *Nazi* salute skywards.

'Now send all these people home.'

'Send them home? They are prisoners.'

'You'll notice we're on an island, Viola. Just where do you think they'll escape to, or would you prefer to wind barbwire around them?'

'We can hold them in their church.'

'Oh please, who'll feed them? What about sanitation?'

'Let them starve and rot in their own shit,' Viola was red-faced by now.

'Oh very satisfactory, I must say, lieutenant. Now do as I say or would you like Sergeant Vanni to replace you?'

In fact *Capitano* Abiati was fed up with his insubordinate subordinate. Whether Italian or Albanian, Mirios' population were citizens, not enemies, who in the Abiati's opinion were perfectly law-abiding and should be left alone. Policemen didn't go looking for trouble, plenty enough came to them. There was no trouble on Mirios and Abiati had every intention of keeping it that way.

Something needed to be done about Lieutenant Viola.

*

It was noon by the time Fausto and Juan sailed around Mirios to Mortimer's hide-out with the news. Although Juan assured them Abiati was basically a decent bloke caught between a rock and a hard place, Viola wasn't likely to let the matter rest.

'So right now the Jews are the only people at immediate risk?' Mortimer asked. 'And we don't know how long it will be before Abiati is forced to do something about it.'

'*Si Senore*,' Fausto replied. 'But the harbour is guarded, so no one can get in or out without Abiati and Viola knowing.'

'You did.'

'*Si*, but two men going fishing is different to a mass migration.'

'What about the other fishermen?'

'It is the same for them. The Fascists know we have to fish and the crews are only a few men per boat.'

'What about land patrols?' Callan asked.

'None so far since the one when the Fascists first arrived.'

'There isn't much to discover, is there?'

'Now I've seen half a dozen caiques leave regularly when the herring are running,' Mortimer observed.

'*Si, Senore.*'

'I may have an idea, but first I must contact Don Rocco. Juan you have a frequency you use for...business...I believe.'

Juan smiled slyly.

'We have also developed a code since war broke out.'

'Excellent. Here's what I suggest. Let me know what you think...'

*

'It's risky, bloody risky,' Ivy said and she rarely swore.

'Everything is risky these days,' Callan observed. 'I reckon the mainland is out of the question, so it's Sicily or Albania or maybe Greece?'

'We'll let Don Rocco decide,' Mortimer said. 'C'mon Juan old boy, let's get the wireless cranked up.'

*

Mirios wasn't a rich community, but financing the operation didn't prove a problem as there was only one cost, and the townsfolk would get something for it. No one raised an eyebrow when Fausto sailed away at dawn with a two-man crew in search of sardine shoals. He took water and food for five days although he only expected to be away for two, maybe less.

Leaving the same morning Fausto sailed out of the harbour, it took Ivy and Callan two days to cross overland from Mortimer's hideout to town via several tracks which were more suitable for goats than two humans with a pack and a rifle each.

Everything hinged on Juan, who'd proved a pretty good organiser in the past. They hid in the cypress grove close to *Bella Vista*.

'It should take two nights,' Juan had said. 'Any more than that and we risk discovery.'

Ivy and Callan reached town by evening.

'You get some sleep, love,' Callan said. 'Maybe a couple of hours, each. I hope Juan is up to his usual organising genius.'

'

Chapter 16 — McAlister's Exodus

It was nearly midnight when Ivy and Callan entered town and edged toward the synagogue. A pair of soldiers patrolled the narrow streets, but they appeared to be the only troops about and weren't particularly vigilant. Why should they be, everyone was tucked up in bed. Abiati had imposed a 10 pm curfew, which was a bit early for some townspeople, nevertheless they complied.

The synagogue wasn't a large building, but the faithful barely numbered a hundred, so they didn't need much room. No light shone from inside and the door was locked. Once he judged the sentries were far enough away, Callan tapped as hard as he dared.

'It's Callan and Ivy,' he hissed, hoping they'd hear inside and not outside. He tapped again.

Shortly he heard a bolt being released and the door stood ajar. Ivy and Callan slipped inside. Moonbeams streamed through the windows just illuminating the Ark Cabinet containing the Torah Scrolls and a hard-backed copy of the text. A reading table stood in front of the Ark, but all the chairs had been stacked neatly along the walls.

About twenty people were crouched beside the chairs as if for extra protection. They consisted of three families from the Jewish community and were led by one of the family patriarchs. Juan was absent, but Callan hadn't expected him to be there.

'Right Ivy will lead the way,' Callan addressed the patriarch. 'There is just enough moonlight, but you'll have to be careful until dawn. You want to be as far away as possible by then.'

Callan heard more shuffling than he liked as the people gather their sacks of food and water and the few belongings they could carry. A baby whimpered, but was soothed by its mother.

There's always a baby crying when you don't need it, Callan thought. *But it won't matter once they're a little way out of town.*

'OK, darl. Off you go. Take care. I love you.'

'Same to you in spades,' she whispered and kissed him.

She slid through the door into the night, followed if not silently, at least quietly by the group who had now become refugees.

Ivy led them a short way, then halted and listened. The town was so quiet unlike the hustle and bustle of big cities like London, Bath, Santa Fe and Cork where she'd lived at some time or another. She saw the shadows of the two patrolmen moving away towards the wharf. A few minutes later she reckoned it was safe to continue.

Her confidence grew with each step and before long she was picking her way along a goat track leading to the interior. She saw no signs of Italian patrols on the way to town and hopefully it would stay that way. Abiati was unlikely to risk injuring his men on mountain tracks at night when there was nothing for them to look for.

After Ivy left, Callan spent a nervous hour waiting inside the synagogue. He'd never been inside a Jewish place of worship before, or a mosque for that matter. Considering he'd spent some time in the Middle East during the war it was an oversight. Apart from the Ark, there wasn't anything to mark it from any other church hall used for social gatherings and services.

If he hadn't been on edge, he'd have been bored or even fallen asleep. Finally shadowy figures started arriving in dribs and drabs until about twenty more people stood around him. This time Juan was present.

'That is it for tonight, Callan,' he said. 'The rest will come tomorrow. They'll be a bigger group, but not greatly so. We didn't want to thin the numbers down too much in case someone noticed.'

'OK Juan. Lie low until an hour before midnight tomorrow. The moon is waxing, so we'll have more light, but hopefully not too much.'

So the second exodus sneaked out of town without incident. It was slow going, but by morning they were well into the hinterland. Cypress and olive groves provided shelter although there seemed to be no danger of aerial reconnaissance because Abiati's force didn't have any planes. Unless he held a census and daily roll-call, it was unlikely he'd notice anyone was missing anyway.

Callan's group met Dennis Mortimer about half way to the hideout where Ivy's people were also waiting. Mortimer would guide the entire group the rest of the way while Ivy and Callan returned to town.

Meanwhile Fausto's boat returned with an excellent sardine catch. Word got around and people hurried to the quay and returned home with their fish baskets brimming. *Capitano* Abiati strolled to the wharf to check out the excitement.

'Nice catch,' he observed when the last of the fish had been distributed.

'*Si, Capitano,*' Fausto replied. 'There are more. The other boats will want to try their luck. I have told them where to go.'

'Don't fish move about?'

'Possibly, but maybe not. Even if they do, we'll have a good idea where they go.'

'Oh, and how do you know that?'

Fausto grinned.

'That is why you are a policeman and I am a fisherman, *Senore.*'

Abiati merely nodded and walked off. His expression suggested something was puzzling him, but he didn't ask any further questions.

Juan met Fausto after Abiati left. Although the Spaniard was pretty sure Abiati didn't remember him, he'd kept a low profile and wasn't going to push his luck.

'We're all set for the second wave tonight.'

'*Molto bene,* I have given *Capitano* Abiati a reason why the fishing boats will be leaving in numbers.'

'Do you think he believed you?'

'I don't see why not. He didn't say anything.'

'You were lucky it was such good catch.'

'Yes, but not by me. I thought I'd have to go to mainland market, but I was lucky enough to meet a trawler still at sea and used the people's cash to buy some of his haul. It saved me at least one day.'

Something bothered *Capitano* Abiati about Fausto's catch, but he couldn't put his finger on it. Maybe he'd keep an eye on the gardener. How hard could it be? Fausto spent most of his time ashore at *Bella Vista.*

And then it struck him...

*

During the afternoon the harbour emptied as half a dozen fishing caiques headed to sea. Abiati watched them leave, as did Juan and Fausto. Callan and Ivy also witnessed their departure through Mortimer's binoculars from a distant hillside.

'So far, so good' Callan muttered.

The plan ran along the same timeline as the previous night. Ivy led her group into the darkness, leaving Callan to wait for the remainder who turned up on schedule. Skulking around at night was proving successful, but Callan recalled he'd had plenty of practice during and just after the last war.

He reached the edge of town with thirty people in tow. All was going well until...

'Halt!' a voice spoke from the path in front of them. The speaker didn't shout, but his tone was authoritative and clear so it carried far enough for everyone to hear.

Capitano Abiati stood pointing a pistol directly at Callan's chest.

Shit!

Before Callan could turn and tell the other to scatter, Sergeant Vanni moved from the shadows armed with a Beretta sub-machinegun, blocking any escape.

'Nobody move,' Abiati ordered, advancing slowly.

In the dim moonlight, Abiati took a while to make out Callan and then recognise a face he hadn't seen for three years.

'I know you,' he said finally, although still uncertainly.

'I spent a night...well half a night in your gaol,' Callan replied.

'Ah yes, the American...Mc...McAlister. Is that not right?'

Callan nodded.

'Your Italian is now remarkable good, I congratulate you.'

Callan still held his rifle and Abiati hadn't ordered him to drop the weapon, but if it came to a shoot-out a sub-machinegun would win hands down. Callan was also pleased he only shown Abiati his American Residency Card which made him neutral, whereas an Australian would be Italy's enemy.

'I see you are armed, please drop the weapon.'

Callan placed his rifle against the wall beside him. That was close enough and Abiati didn't object.

'So this is where you came after blowing up my police station.'

'That wasn't me. That was Don Rocco's boys. We just got caught up in your argument with him.'

'Quite so, but what are you doing with these people?'

'Solving a problem for you.'

'How so?'

'By making it go away or more literally making them go away. I understand your Black-Shirt lieutenant is pretty keen to round up any Jews on the island and ship them off to concentration camps. Am I correct?'

'You are.'

'But you're not so keen.'

'What makes you say that?'

'Because they'd be gone by now if you were. I was told you argued with your lieutenant about it.'

'You are well informed.'

'It's a small town. But I don't see your friendly Black-Shirt around.'

'He is aboard the *Santa Marcella*. I chose not to disturb his sleep.'

Abiati didn't want to involve Viola with anything connected with Jews, because he doubted if his lieutenant would think rationally. It seemed he'd been well and truly indoctrinated by *Nazi* propaganda, even though it was unlikely Jews had ever done anything to disadvantage Viola.

'But I'm not the only well informed person around here,' Callan said. 'How did you know we'd be here?'

'There was something odd about the market this morning when Fausto returned with his catch. Fishy business if you will,' Abiati grinned. 'Everyone just came and took a share of the catch, almost as if it was pre-arranged. No one spoke other than a quick *"buona giornata"*. No money or barter goods changed hands and most of all there was no haggling. It wasn't a market sale, it was a distribution point.'

'It still doesn't explain what led you here?'

'I figured Fausto was at the centre of what was going on, so Sergeant Vanni and I followed him and he finally led us to the synagogue...and you. Where do you plan to take these people?'

'To safety.'

'There isn't any safety in Europe right now. Do you think they'll last long scattered around the island? I won't be able to keep Lieutenant Viola on a leash forever...Ah, the fishing boats. You intend to use them to evacuate everyone. What makes you think they'll be any better off on the mainland?'

'You'll have to find them first.'

'I already have.'

'So what do you propose to do?'

Callan weighed up his chances of grabbing his gun and getting a shot off before Vanni sprayed lead through the street. But at that moment Abiati stepped aside.

'Go,' he said.

Callan couldn't believe Abiati who'd chased him so vigorously from San Giovanni gaol would simply let them run away.

'I am trying to get through this war without killing anyone,' Abiati said. 'Do you know just how hard that can be? These people aren't even my enemy. They're *Italians* now. So what else am I supposed to do with them? What am I supposed to do with you, *Senore*?''

'Trust me, *Capitano*. I'll keep out of your way. The US and Italy aren't at war...yet. What will lieutenant Viola do when he finds out?'

'Leave Viola to me.'

When the party of Jews disappeared, Abiati turned to his sergeant.

'I hope I haven't involved you in something that will wind us up in trouble, Vanni.'

'We both fought in the last war, sir and we know it's between soldiers and maybe partisans. We don't kill civilians whatever their religion if we can help it. But, what about Lieutenant Viola, sir? I notice he is getting pretty uppity lately, if you don't mind me saying so.'

*

'**B**loody hell, that went better than I expected, Juan,' Callan said as they marched through the night.

'I believe *Capitano* Abiati has mellowed since we last met,' Juan replied.

'So it seems.'

They caught up with Ivy along the way and reached the hideout by noon the following day. They were met with cheers, kisses and embraces. Everyone was surprisingly happy considering they'd abandoned their homes with an uncertain future and were now camping under the stars. But they'd all heard of the atrocities in Europe and were anxious to avoid the same fate.

'What now?' Callan asked Mortimer.

'I'm still waiting for Don Rocco's people to get things organised and reply. He'd like to get them across the Med to North Africa, but things have really hotted up in the Libyan and Egyptian deserts, so it's no-go there I'm afraid.'

'Not to mention the Italian Fleet swarming all over the place. Getting across would be damned risky,' Ivy said.

'Maybe they'll try to get across Greece into Turkey or the Palestine Mandate.'

'Even there they'll get a mixed reception.'

As they day wore on, the refugees made shelters from tree branches and shared what food they'd brought along. The caiques started arriving and were able to bring some of the catch they'd made on the voyage around the island. A couple of the boats were small enough to breach the narrow inlet, while the others anchored off-shore.

They waited another full day, by which time folk grew anxious. They endured another night camping out, although the older and weaker fitted into Mortimer's tents. The following morning word came from Don Rocco.

His sphere of influence was limited to Sicily and had agreements with mainland families, so the evacuation would have to be via Sicily, Sardinia and hopefully to Spain where there'd been an expulsion edict since 1492, but in 1924 dictator *Primo de Rivera* had relaxed the draconian law. Maybe they'd find a home there or at least a jumping off point to America or Great Britain.

While Juan and Mortimer organised everyone into groups to fit the individual boats, Callan and Ivy walked the cliff-top above the beach for a fine view of the pinnacle. Only minutes later they spied a speck on the horizon steaming at full speed right towards them. It didn't take long to recognise *Santa Marcella's* silhouette. There was no way they'd get the refugees aboard the fishing boats before she arrived.

'Shit, that bastard Abiati has double-crossed us.'

'Why?' Ivy said. 'He could have just stopped you in town.'

'I bet Viola got in his ear. Now he has us all in one place.'

Chapter 17 — Real War Begins

The morning after letting Callan go, *Capitano* Abiati was busy as signals zipped back and forth between Albanian Division HQ and *Santa Marcella* moored in Mirios harbour. Finally Abiati received the answer he was waiting for and smiled with satisfaction.

'Please find Lieutenant Viola, sergeant,' he said to Vanni. 'I believe he's on the bridge with Ensign Russo planning their next patrol. I would like to speak with him here.'

Abiati had turned the forward passenger lounge into his temporary command centre until he could set up completely at *Bella Vista.* Viola strutted in with his usual arrogance.

You look like you have a broomstick stuck up your arse, Abiati thought.

'Stand at ease, Lieutenant,' Abiati said. 'Your luck is in today. Read this.'

Abiati handed Viola the latest signal. He watched Viola's expression as he scanned the decoded signal, but it was hard to judge the lieutenant's reaction. Those Fascist bastards were always so damned stone-faced.

'It says I've been transferred, sir,' Viola stated uncertainly.

'It certainly does, I've read the signal. Congratulations. It seems you're a young man much in demand.'

'Am I to assume you recommended me for this posting, sir?'

'Absolutely,' Abiati spread his arms with largesse. 'You're always saying you want action, so there you are. There's nothing for an ambitious straight-shooting warrior like you around here and now *Generalissimo* Rosi has transferred his 6th Po Corps to the Albanian border to have a crack at those pesky Greeks. He'll need all the help he can get.'

'Are you trying to get rid of me..?'

'Goodness me no, but I think you'll be of much more use to Italy in a combat unit.'

'When do I go?'

'Immediately. I'll get Russo to run you across to Durrës today. All your kit is aboard. You'll pick up your written orders and transfer papers once you reach Albania. You'll be assigned a unit when you reach Tirana.'

Viola knew Abiati was somehow pulling the wool over his eyes, and he was pretty certain those wretched Jews had something to do with it. But what could he do or say? It was what he wanted after all.

'So tell Russo to get cracking.'

Abiati saw Viola off at the gangplank when they docked at Durrës. He extended his hand.

'Good luck, I'm sure you'll prove a great asset to General Rosi.'

Viola was no sooner ashore when Abiati ordered them to cast off and head back to Mirios. He went straight to the bridge and studied Russo's charts. He jabbed his finger at a point on the north eastern corner of the island.

'What's there, Russo? You've been around the island.'

'An inlet and beach, sir, but we can't get through the bay entrance. The shoals and currents are too hazardous. Only small craft can enter at the turn of high tide. The passage is open for maybe an hour every day.'

'I thought Mediterranean tides were small — just a metre of two.'

'Yessir, but the entrance is so narrow it's still inaccessible most of the time.'

'Take me there,' he said to Ensign Russo.

*

'The caiques are still moored, sir,' Ensign Russo observed.

'So they are,' Abiati replied with some degree of satisfaction. 'Get one of the inflatables ready. I'm going ashore.'

His guesswork had paid off, but he always had a nose for tracking down people, which was why he was such a successful policeman.

Russo anchored *Santa Marcella* among the caiques and the lifeboat soon settled in the water. The fishing crews could only look on, Abiati's armed men indicated they were to stay at anchor or else. To Russo's confusion, Abiati only took Sergeant Vanni and two seamen to handle the boat. The helmsman skilfully navigated into the bay until the bow gently nudged onto the beach.

Abiati wasn't surprised to see the Fairchild floating a few metres from shore. Fausto had told him the plane was away, but then he'd been cagey about saying just where. He now had a pretty shrewd idea who the pilots were.

Leaving one sailor with the boat he climbed the rise beyond. There were signs that people had camped here. There were even two tents pitched in the ruin nearby, which was good thinking. If it wasn't about faith, Jews were resourceful and forward thinking people. They'd all gone, but very recently. In fact Abiati reckoned they were hidden in the bushes within earshot.

'Go and flush 'em out, Sergeant,' Abiati sighed.

It didn't take long before Vanni discovered a woman with two infants who'd obviously slowed her down. He led them back to Abiati who asked them sit close by.

'Senore McAlister, we need to talk,' he called. 'I know you can hear me and I don't want this to take all day.'

After a pause Abiati noticed a movement two or three hundred metres away. Ivy and Callan approached doubtfully. There was no point in trying to dodge Abiati. He knew they were on the island with their escape route blocked. Abiati made no attempt to disarm them.

'A pleasure to meet you once again, *Senora*,' Abiati saluted.

Ivy smiled and even bobbed a slight curtsy in return.

'So that was your plan? Take all these people on fishing boats across the Mediterranean to God-knows-where?'

Callan nodded sheepishly.

'I suppose it depended on whether you met an Italian or British ship first. Right now that's a fifty-fifty chance.'

'Better than none.'

'I have a better suggestion. In fact it's more of an order, a civil directive if you prefer. Take them all home, *Senore*,' Abiati said wearily. 'They no more want to leave Mirios than go to the moon.'

'Or a concentration camp.'

'I believe that can be avoided. Lieutenant Viola has been assigned to duties more suited to his talents and enthusiasm. Right now I think Mirios is the safest place for your Jewish friends. Best we all say nothing and go about our normal business. If things change, well you have an escape plan ready. I won't hinder you. I do not like fascism and have nothing against Jews.'

'Thank you,' Ivy said.

'Just take them home, *Senora*.'

He turned to go, but hesitated.

'You might as well fly the plane back to town as well. Maybe you can go back to business as usual too.'

Well some of it, Callan thought.

Abiati didn't bother to check out the tents, he had no reason to. He knew nothing about Mortimer and he certainly didn't know about the contraband radio set. Abiati wasn't lax. He had no evidence enemy agents were afoot. That was just as well. Even though Mortimer had hastily gathered his radio and dashed for cover half a kilometre away, he may have left some snippet of damning evidence.

Abiati returned to *Santa Marcella* and sailed back to port.

'What do you make of that?' Mortimer asked when Ivy signalled the coast was clear. 'But that settles it. I'll definitely have to stay out here from now on. It's a dashed shame. *Bella Vista* was just so fine.'

'Don't worry, Dennis,' Ivy said. 'We'll bring up all the comforts of home in the next few weeks.'

*

Adriatic — March — April 1941

And that was pretty much that. Ivy, Juan and Callan rented a place in town. Abiati completed setting up his command centre at *Bella Vista* while *Santa Marcella* patrolled languidly along the Eastern Adriatic. Abiati arranged a mail contract with Ivy and Callan who then flew regularly to Italy, Sicily and Albania.

Yet beneath the tranquillity a turbulent undercurrent of uncertainty rumbled as the war intensified. The Italians were bogged down on the Grecian border and didn't look like advancing at all. In frustration Hitler ordered a *Blitzkrieg* into Yugoslavia to lend a helping hand. To counter that threat a BEF force consisting of the 6th Australian, 2nd New Zealand Divisions and 1st British Armoured Brigade were sent to Greece.

Meanwhile British and Italian naval fleets continued to duke it out in the Mediterranean. Ground troops and aircraft were soon embroiled in a see-saw conflict across North Africa. No one took much notice of Mirios and the surrounding area. It was of little tactical significance and frankly neither side had resources enough to bother.

Hitler always wanted an Anglo-German Arian alliance to rule Europe. He hoped Britain would sue for peace, but Churchill steadfastly rejected anything of the kind, which caused the *Reich* a logistical headache. German U-Boats may be causing havoc to Allied shipping on the high seas, but Germany was landlocked and blockaded. It was critically short of resources, especially cereal and oil. So Hitler planned to despatch the *Wehrmacht* and *Luftwaffe* to charge across the Russian steppes where there was an abundance of both. But he delayed, worrying about his southern flank which included Greece and the Balkans.

'It's like we're in the eye of a cyclone,' Callan commented one day after a peaceful flight from Durrës. 'The war's raging all around and we're calmly sitting smack in the middle of it.'

Mortimer had made himself pretty comfortable at his hideout and it was no big challenge to keep him supplied. He intercepted a barrage of radio traffic which he relayed to Alexandria. And soon it became apparent the Allies were falling apart in Greece. Despite heavy casualties the Germans were making headway southwards through the country.

Disaster followed disaster. Greece fell and the Germans were poised to invade Crete. Meanwhile Malta hung on tenaciously despite continual battering from the *Luftwaffe*.

Ivy and Callan had accompanied Fausto when he sailed around the islands to re-stock Mortimer's pantry. Fausto regularly raided *Bella Vista's* wine cellar, sneaking off with an assortment of Mortimer's favourite vintages.

'That bastard Abiati hasn't drunk the lot, then?' Mortimer said, stashing the bottles in a small cave which always remained cool. It also accommodated his cheese and salami stocks. Ivy showed him how to make damper, so he had no shortage of staples.

'There is plenty left, *Senore*,' Fausto assured him. 'I have hidden many bottles where *Capitano* Abiati will never find them.'

'Splendid! Come and we'll share a bottle because I have some significant news...and I mean significant.'

Callan couldn't believe it.

'Jerry has overrun Greece entirely. The BEF has abandoned the country, but thousands were captured.'

'Blow me down, I wonder what happens next. Jerry doesn't seem bothered about Mirios.'

'You wouldn't think so, but maybe now they might feel obliged to interfere because of the Axis Treaty.'

'Or maybe they trust the Ities to actually manage our tiny back-water on their own.'

Despite the debacle in Greece, life cruised along as usual on Mirios. It didn't seem that many people knew what had happened. But four days later *Capitano* Abiati summoned Callan and Ivy to join him aboard *Santa Marcella.*

Sergeant Vanni ushered them to lounge chairs in the salon where Abiati awaited. A seaman poured coffee while Abiati lit a cigarette.

After a few pleasantries, Abiati got down to business.

'Our relationship has changed,' he announced.

'What relationship was that, *Capitano*?' Ivy asked, a little too pertly in Callan's opinion. He was usually the one with the mouth.

'Neighbours and possible friends..?'

Ivy raised her eyebrows.

'That's nice, I'm sure and this coffee is delicious.'

'But, we can no longer be neighbours...or friends?' Callan ventured.

'As you may remember, we had unfinished business back in **San Giovanni** where you destroyed my watch-house.'

'Hang on, we've been over that. Don Rocco's men blew up your gaol. We hadn't even met him or Sorrentino until that night,' Callan insisted conveniently omitting their ongoing business association with Don Rocco's men-of-honour.

'Yes, yes, I am satisfied on that point, but my initial investigation remained incomplete and I am if nothing else a thorough policeman.'

'That is highly commendable, *Capitano*," Ivy said tactfully

She and Callan eyed Abiati warily as he dropped a sizeable file on his desk-top.

'This took some digging and time to compile,' Abiati admitted, 'especially in the world of political turmoil we find ourselves.'

'So what's the problem?' Callan asked.

'It seems you two are not entirely who you say you are, or more correctly where you have come from.'

Ivy and Callan had become complacent and hadn't worried they'd be caught out one day. Then Callan remembered back in Spain how the Russians knew of his war record. Maybe the Italians had sourced *Nazi* archives, where he would have been mentioned as a POW during the Great War. Knowing the methodical Germans it was just like them to keep old records despite the post-war upheaval and depression. What did it matter? Abiati knew. As he kept reminding them, he was a policeman not a soldier.

'We're Americans,' Ivy protested rather too quickly in Callan's opinion.

'So you say, but I have information suggesting you, *Senora* McAlister are British and you, *Senore* McAlister are actually Australian. I cannot ignore a situation where your countrymen are fighting my countrymen in Greece and North Africa.'

'Yes, but we haven't been fighting with anyone.'

'That's as it may be,' Abiati said, 'but the fact remains Italy is at war with the British Empire and as much as I regret to say so, you are now my enemies. It's a shame, because I have come to like and admire you. But you are nonetheless Italy's enemy, so what am I to do with you two?'

Chapter 18 — Engagement at Sea

'We'll start off with house arrest aboard *Santa Marcella* until I contact my superiors. I know many Australian and New Zealand prisoners were taken in Greece and are being transported to camps in Albania and Yugoslavia. I think you may be joining them as POWs,' Abiati said.

'But we're not combatants,' Ivy protested.

'Merely a technicality.'

It was regrettable, but Abiati wanted Ivy and Callan off his patch as soon as possible. The last thing he needed was his life complicated. Ivy and Callan were appalled, because they knew now the Germans were on the scene. Fighting was hotting up in Albania and a real shooting war was under way between the Italians and Albanian partisans who grew bolder and stronger daily.

Ivy and Callan were marched to their rental home and ordered to gather as much as they could carry. Meanwhile Juan looked on mortified, and helpless. Abiati had also identified Juan, but as a Spanish neutral he wasn't a priority. He might be a spy, but that hardly seemed likely on Mirios so that investigation could wait.

'Get over to Dennis as soon as you can,' Callan whispered. 'Tell him what's happened, although I'm blowed if I know what he can do about it.'

So Ivy and Callan trudged through town to the quayside. They didn't own a suitcase after losing their travel luggage somewhere way back in Spain, so they carried a knap-sack each. Abiati led them to the passenger salon.

'Make yourselves comfortable,' he said. 'Enjoy it while you can. Sadly I don't think life in a Yugoslav Stalag will be as pleasant.'

Ivy and Callan didn't really feel like enjoying the comforts of *Santa Marcella's* salon. While details were sketchy, Balkan POW and internment camps had already gained infamy for deprivation, squalor, and starvation. So they both sulked, thinking what a crappy hand they'd been dealt once again.

'Isn't there anyone in the whole of flaming Europe who doesn't want to throw us in gaol?' Callan lamented.

Abiati's instructions arrived with distressing haste.

'We're casting off immediately,' he informed Callan and Ivy. 'I regret to say you are to be transferred to the authorities in Albania. After that it is out of my hands.'

Callan and Ivy were in no mood for a sea voyage, so they remained in the lounge feeling lower than they ever remembered. They must have dozed for a while, because they were jolted awake when Ensign Russo changed course sharply and slammed the telegraph to flank speed. *Santa Marcella* wasn't a particularly high performance vessel, but she drove through the calm waters, carving a half-decent sized bow-wave.

'What the..?'

Ivy didn't wait to hear Callan's hypothesis, she wrenched the salon door open and raced to the bow deck where Russo's crewmen now manned the forward gun.

'What's happening?' she asked.

One of the sailors simply pointed. A medium-sized diesel-powered craft lay ahead. It had abruptly veered clear of *Santa Marcella,* which roused both Russo and Abiati's curiosity. Normally it would be hopeless for a small craft to try and outrun *Santa Marcella* and why was it trying to anyway? The Italian patrols weren't in the habit of confiscating a boat crew's catch, in fact they were known to often buy fish and pay cash for them.

Ivy heard Abiati and Russo discussing the boat through an open bridge window, while Callan moved to the prow.

'Do you see anyone aboard,' Abiati asked.

'No, sir. Just a figure — maybe two — at the helm.'

But there was something wrong about the boat. Although they varied, Mediterranean caiques had a certain unmistakable character and many similar design features — one flat twenty metre deck with several hatches, a fore-mast and a stern wheel-house. The hold and cabins were below decks. This one however was more streamlined with a centre helm while its forward deck looked badly damaged. The random twisted superstructure might have appeared to be fishing tackle at a stretch if you weren't looking for something else.

'Put a shot across her bow,' Abiati ordered from the bridge.

The gunshot was deafening. Callan, who'd been looking forward nearly leapt overboard. The gun was at its lowest trajectory and the shell virtually roared past his ear. A second later a jet spray erupted skywards which stirred a hornet's nest.

'That's not a fishing boat,' Callan said to no one in particular. 'That's a...'

Figures appeared on deck. Using the gunwales as a shield they opened fire with rifles and sub-machineguns. Lethal shards ripped from *Santa Marcella's* deck and wooden structures. Other bullets ricocheted off the forward gun-shield, zinging in every direction. Callan sprinted astern, grabbing Ivy as he passed.

'C'mon, love. It's time to duck for cover!'

Callan and Ivy barged back into the salon and dived for the floor just as the window panes dissolved into glassy mist. More lead screamed overhead and slammed into the finely polished wooden panelling. All the glassware and bottles on the bar shelves exploded as they were smashed by bullets. Glass fragments covered Ivy and Callan, who had no intention of moving.

Meanwhile Sergeant Vanni manned the aft machinegun post, swivelling as far as the gun mounting permitted. As they overhauled the boat the Italian soldiers raked the decks with rifle shots — or they tried to. Fierce incoming fire hindered them and their shooting became ragged after the first concerted volley. When his machinegun came to bear, Sergeant Vanni kept the enemy heads down.

Abiati instructed Russo to drive past the unusual boat until they were beyond accurate small arms range. *Santa Marcella* was nowhere as handy as a purpose-built E-boat, but Russo made the best of what he had. The ship listed as he spun the wheel to port ninety degrees.

Callan and Ivy slid across the glass-strewn floor before staggering to their feet bleeding from some nasty glass-cuts.

'We can't stay here,' Ivy cried. 'I don't think Ensign Russo has finished shaking the boat around. We'll be cut to pieces.'

She was right. They'd just made the deck when the ship lurched and turned two-hundred-and-seventy degrees to starboard. *Santa Marcella* now charged straight towards the other vessel and Abiati wasn't messing around. He ordered Russo to reduce to dead slow speed to steady the ship.

'That's an English gunboat,' Russo said once he'd identified the forward deck wreckage for what it was. Recognising enemy vessels was an important part of his job.

'Then aim for the hull,' Abiati yelled from the bridge 'Fire when ready.'

The gun-crew had already slammed another shell into the breech. Now *Santa Marcella* bobbed gently, the gunner could hardly miss. Another shell roared from the barrel, exploding right into the gunboat's keel at the waterline. The bow vaporised into a thousand wooden splinters and the boat immediately nose-dived as water surged into the hull. The gunboat's headway contributed to its doom forcing mega-litres throughout the fissure.

Knowing their vessel was doomed, those on board tossed their weapons into an inflatable dingy before lowering it into the sea. Some scrambled into the small craft, while others simply jumped for it as the gunboat wallowed in its final death throes. Several men pulled oars from the dingy bilge and rowed away from the sinking hull. Others tossed ropes to their swimming comrades so they could be towed clear of the sinking wreck and its deadly under-tow.

With a last bubbling gasp of steam generated by the red-hot engine, the gunboat's stern rose slightly before she sank below the surface forever.

There were about twenty survivors and barely room for half of them in the dingy, which was an adequate lifeboat for a normal fishing crew, but this wasn't an average fishing crew. To everyone's relief, no blood-drenched bodies floated on the surface and Abiati's crew suffered no more than a few scratches. It turned out Callan and Ivy were the most seriously wounded casualties and they'd survive.

So who were these men?

Abiati had a pretty shrew idea. He didn't interfere while they gathered everyone to the dingy side. He'd decided the survivors could do the hard work and he'd pick them all up together. He gave Russo orders to stay at a safe distance. He took a megaphone from the bridge locker and went in to find Callan and Ivy who were doing their best to treat their cuts.

'Ooh, they look nasty,' Abiati said a little too cheerfully in Ivy's opinion. 'I'll have my medic see to those wounds, but right now I have a job for you, *Senore.*'

He handed Callan the megaphone.

'You are to tell those people in that little boat to leave their weapons on the bottom and raise their hands. Those in the water can stay where they are.'

Callan stared at him.

'*And* just who do you suppose they are?'

'I hadn't thought about it,' Callan replied rather lamely.

'They could be partisans or Greeks,' Abiati said, 'but I somehow doubt it. Not in that boat anyway. That only leaves enemy servicemen — British Commonwealth troops —although what they're doing up here is anyone's guess.'

Callan took the megaphone.

'Ahoy there,' he hailed, which grabbed the survivors' attention because they weren't expecting to hear a mid-Atlantic accent which Callan had acquired after years in the states. 'Look these blokes have got you dead to rights and can blow you to smithereens in a couple of seconds. The officer in charge wants you to lay down your guns or he's threatening to open fire.'

The men in the boat and around it looked suspiciously defiant. This wasn't the sort of surrender ultimatum they expected.

'Your fellas in the water must be freezing at this time of year. And you've probably got people needing medical attention. We'll get coffee brewing in a jiffy. No one's been killed yet. I dunno about you, but I'd like to keep it that way.'

Knowing there was no choice, the men aboard placed their weapons at their feet and allowed Russo to ease *Santa Marcella* closer until the dingy brushed along-side. A pair of Italian sailors lowered a step ladder and helped the survivors aboard. Ivy thought the Italians treated the boarding men with remarkable empathy considering the recent shoot-out.

Even though some of their uniforms were in tatters, it was obvious these men were Allied servicemen. Some still wore their caps, which were a mixture of navy, army and a couple of airman. Callan definitely recognised the soldiers as Diggers.

'Find out who they are and what they're doing here,' Abiati snapped, all stiff-backed and businesslike now.

'I said we had coffee,' Callan said, noticing that some of the men were shivering.

'They'll get coffee when I find out who they are. Take them into the lounge. They'll be warmer in there.'

'At the moment it's a death trap of broken glass,' Ivy said.

'Then take them aft out of the wind. I'll post guards to make sure they don't decide to jump back into the Adriatic. Tell them I've ordered my men to shoot to kill if they do.'

So Callan led the survivors aft while Russo delegated a team to drag the dingy aboard and retrieve the enemy weapons.

'I'll get coffee and tea brewing and rustle up some grub,' Ivy said when everyone was settled on the leeward deck.

'OK,' Callan said once she'd gone, 'firstly I'm not a traitor or one of those guys who transmits trash like Lord Haw Haw. My name is Callan McAlister and I'm originally from New South Wales.'

'You don't sound like a bloody Aussie,' one of the survivors said and he should know, because he definitely did.

'I've lived New Mexico since the end of the last war. I have an American residency, so everyone around here thought my wife Ivy and I were Yanks. We were minding our own business working on an island nearby until the ruddy Italians found out who we really were. Now it looks like Ivy and I are destined for an internment camp.'

'Tough luck, mate,' the definite Australian jeered. 'Life's a right bastard, missing out on all the shooting, ain't it?'

Callan flared.

'Oh, I've done my share of shooting, *mate!* Gallipoli, Dublin Rebellion, Western Front as an RAFC pilot and a POW, so *do* I know what it's like...and I'm a POW again... just like you.'

Normally Callan would have thought he was laying it a bit thick, but no one was calling him a shirker and getting away it. He hadn't given five years to serve king and country only to be called a coward by a total stranger. He'd been awarded a chest-full of medals to prove it.

'Right, that'll be quite enough, corporal,' a young fellow said with considerable authority considering he wasn't much more than a bearded schoolboy. He'd managed to keep his RN cap and the remains of lieutenant's epaulettes.

'Sorry, sir, and apologies to you, Mister McAlister,' the corporal said sincerely. 'I meant no harm or disrespect. I'm just a bit knackered.'

'You'll perk up when my missus brings some hot drinks. She won't be long.'

Callan's anger died just as quickly as it had flared.

'I'll vouch for Callan McAlister,' one of the survivors said.

His Canadian accent was unmistakable. Callan stared blankly at Johnny Witherspoon's grinning face.

'Sorry, I didn't recognise you in the water. Bloody hell Johnny, what are you doing here?''

'Long story, but I'd like you to meet a guy who's spending the war as my saviour.'

'I'm Lieutenant Jeremy St Chalfont-Smyth,' the young RN lieutenant said, extending his hand.

'Blimey, that's mouthful if ever I heard one,' Callan said.

'I get that a lot. Just call me Jeremy, but please not Jerry.'

'Yes, I can understand that right about now.'

'Lucky we just get to call 'im "sir",' the corporal chirped.

'I have learned to ignore cheeky Anzacs,' Jeremy said.

'OK, I know the drill,' Callan said. 'Name, rank and serial number, but *Capitano* Abiati is a decent enough bloke. He wants to know how you got here. He's pretty sure you're from the Allied force in Greece.'

'Decent bloke or not, that's all he's getting. He'll have to find out the rest for himself,' Jeremy said, accompanied by determined nods from his men. 'It'd have been a different story if our forward gun hadn't been knocked out of action and our engine damaged.'

Ivy returned with Russo's cook who'd rustled up a pot of vegetable soup and pasta, so there was a break while the survivors tucked in — and they were pretty hungry. But in the end name, rank and serial number was all *Capitano* Abiati got from his captives.

Warrior ethics aside, you could understand how the Commonwealth servicemen felt. They were indeed from the Grecian campaign and it didn't paint a pretty picture. The Germans had advanced south through Greece, making mince-meat of everything standing in their way. British, Australian and Kiwi troops retreated before the onslaught. The majority were evacuated to Crete and North Africa in true Dunkirk fashion, but many were trapped..

Lieutenant St Chalfont-Smyth was initially part of the naval evacuation, but things hadn't gone as planned. However, his and Flight-Lieutenant Johnny Witherspoon's actions were commendable and worth mentioning...

Part 2 — War at Sea and Air

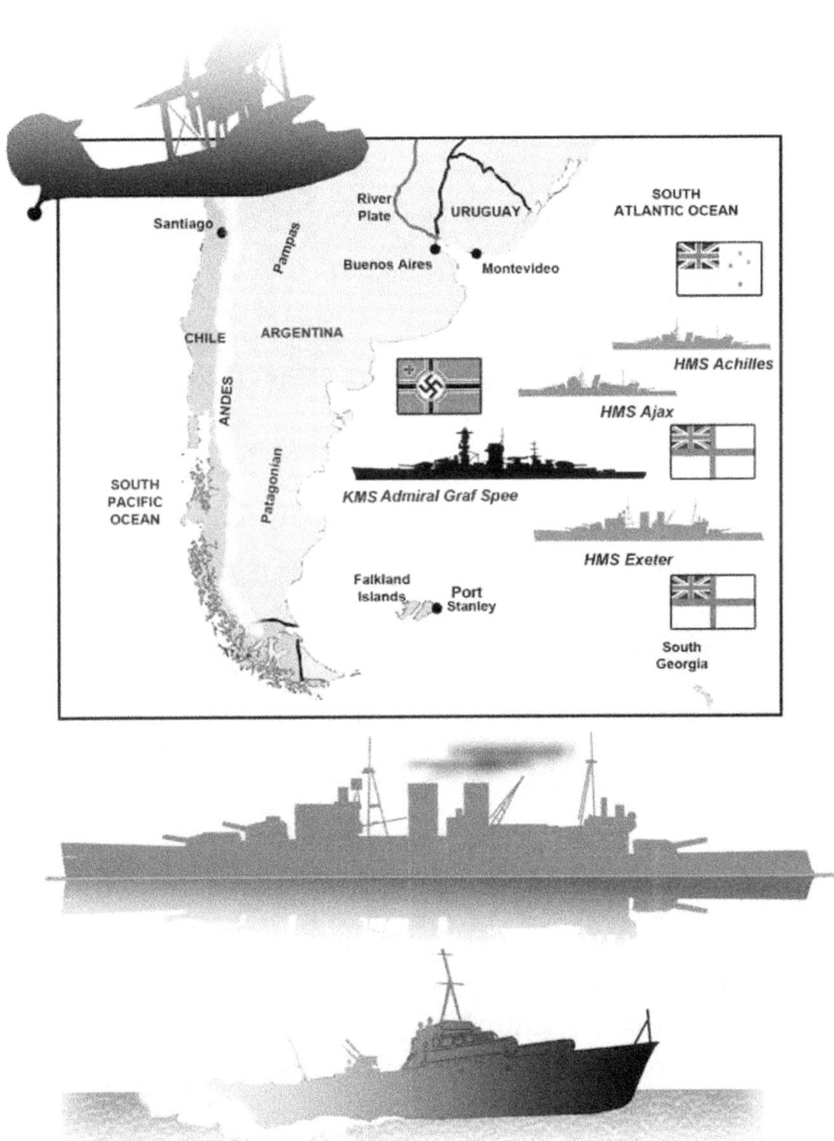

Chapter 19 — A Midshipman's Day at the Office

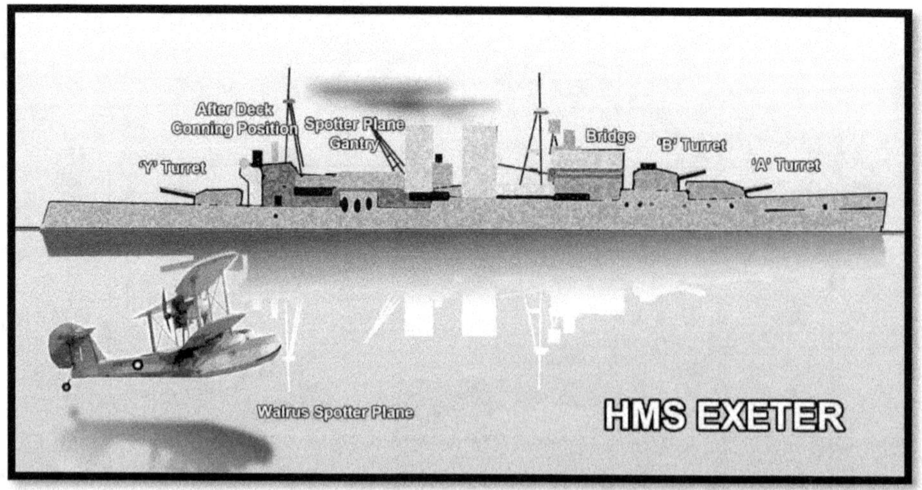

Jeremy St Chalfont-Smyth was born in Africa. He was the second son of the Earl of Fitzroy who owned a vast cattle ranch and coffee plantation in Kenya's Happy Valley. The good earl rarely visited his Kenyan holdings, but was astute enough to hire competent managers and accountants.

Like many minor noble scions, Jeremy was packed off to Eton boarding school to join his older brother and not inconvenience his parents unduly. Jeremy didn't particularly mind, the food may have been indifferent and living conditions rudimentary, but he knew no better. The other boys were all in the same boat anyway. He turned into an adequate scholar and remarkable sportsman. The latter being the more important aptitude by far.

After his brother left school for Sandhurst Military Academy, Jeremy decided the Royal Navy was a better option to avoid sibling rivalry. He successfully applied for a cadetship at Dartmouth. Again he performed well, particularly in maths and geometry, so he quickly became a competent navigator and sextant operator, which were of course great assets for a sailor. He graduated with overall fair-to-middling success.

Just as war broke out, Jeremy found himself a midshipman aboard the heavy cruiser *HMS Exeter* prowling the South Atlantic searching for the German surface raiders *Admiral Graf Spee* and *Admiral Scheer*. Two other cruisers completed Commodore Harwood's 'G' Force. Harwood had moved his broad pennant from *Exeter* to *HMS Ajax* a few days earlier and was now accompanied by *HMS Achilles* from the New Zealand Division.

At dawn *Exeter's* bugler sounded *action stations* followed by a low 'G' note indicating no enemy was in sight. As a junior deck officer, Jeremy's roles varied and at dawn on 13 December 1939, he accompanied Captain Fred Bell and several officers on the open bridge. Midshipmen spent much of their time running errands, carrying messages or simply doing what they were told while learning the ropes through experience.

Evidence of *Graf Spee's* and *Scheer's* positions was mixed, but emergency messages from two merchant ships reported being attacked by pocket-battleships. Harwood reckoned his best chance of finding a German raider was around the vital shipping lanes from Montevideo in neutral Uruguay to European ports.

'It's mostly boring work, eh St Chalfont-Smyth?' Captain Bell said, observing Jeremy diligently scanning the horizon.

'Maybe so, sir. It's chilly enough right now, but it's going to be another fine day.'

'Yes, I don't envy anyone on convoy duty out of Reykjavik at this time of year.'

'Seems funny we're going to have Christmas in the middle of summer, although it's nearly always like winter in Port Stanley.'

'The Kiwi's aboard *Achilles* will be used to it...'

Conversation with the captain was always a pleasant diversion when he was in a good mood, but not for long.

'Begging your pardon, sir, but I think I've spotted smoke...'

'Where?'

'Ten points off the port bow. Just a smudge on the horizon.'

They'd have missed it if the emerging sun wasn't behind them. One of the ratings climbed the superstructure behind the bridge, hoping the extra elevation would give a better view. All hands on the bridge crowded to the port side with raised binoculars and telescopes.

They didn't have to wait long.

'Blow me down,' Jeremy muttered. 'That's a ruddy pocket-battleship.'

'What was that, my boy?' Bell snapped.

'Could it be *Admiral Scheer*...?'

Confirmation was almost immediate. The bridge lookouts were vigilant.

'Bearing 330 degrees, sir!'

Initially *Ajax* and *Achilles* crews identified the enemy ship as a merchantman, but as the range closed it was obviously a warship, and a big one. Captain Bell immediately ordered *Exeter* to steer towards the suspected enemy at flank speed. Within minutes wireless signals flashed between the 'G' Force cruisers including one from *Exeter* declaring, '...I think it's a pocket-battleship...'

None of the captains needed to be told twice when Harwood issued the order to attack. *Exeter* turned to chase the pocket-battleship's port side, while the other two cruisers attacked on the raider's starboard flank. No one had yet identified the enemy warship.

Around 6.20 am there was no doubt about the unknown ship's hostility when it opened up on all three British cruisers with its 11-inch guns. Then shooting started in earnest and both sides were pretty accurate.

Captain Bell's curt orders gave the gun crews full discretion.

'Aim at the flaming enemy and shoot as soon as you can,' he yelled through the voice pipes. 'And get both Walruses airborne right away.'

He was no more than repeating Commodore Harwood's orders to '...attack at any time day or night...'

Exeter's senior gunnery officer, Lieutenant-Commander Richard Jennings was happy to oblige, although it was a matter of waiting until the guns came to bear and into range. Jeremy couldn't remember the exact time, but a few minutes before six-thirty *Exeter's* aft gun turret erupted with a deafening crack as the shells snarled away to their target

The shots straddled the enemy's bow. *Ajax* and *Achilles* opened up almost simultaneously. Some early shells hit the German vessel, but at maximum 8-inch gun range, it was impossible to know what damage was done. Meanwhile Captain Hans Langsdorff commanding the pocket battle ship had no intention of letting the British cruisers have it all their own way. The German raider was indeed *Admiral Graf Spee*, although *Exeter's* crew were ignorant of the fact well into the battle. *Graf Spee* was *Admiral Scheer's* sister ship, so tackling one was just as dangerous as the other.

Graf Spee's guns fired back at *Ajax* and *Achilles* then concentrated on *Exeter* alone.

Shells don't really whistle into the air, but rather roar as they carve through the atmosphere, and Jeremy heard them coming. Great gouts of sea sprayed to port and starboard.

'Jesus, that was bloody close,' one of the bridge officers muttered.

As *Exeter's* guns opened up, the crew hoisted the ship's Walrus spotter-planes onto gantries amidships. They were about to place them on the catapults when another salvo from *Graf Spee* spewed a fifty-foot water fountain, embedded with shell fragments right beside *Exeter*. Shrapnel scythed its deadly path through *Exeter's* superstructure. The Walrus sea-planes were shredded and canted uncertainly on their gantries. Aviation spirit sprayed from the ruptured fuel tanks onto the deck below creating a slimy petrol and salt-water emulsion.

'There'll be no launching the planes now, sir,' Jeremy reported to Captain Bell as the other deck officers were all paying attention elsewhere.

It only took seconds for the bridge crew to realise many of their communications tubes had been destroyed. There were no replies to Captain Bell's instructions. As a midshipman, Jeremy was generally supernumerary and assigned tasks ad hoc. Everyone was so busy he thought he'd better make himself useful.

'Would you like me to check below for damage, sir,' he offered. 'It looks like the worst is amidships.'

'Yes, lad, at the double now,' Bell replied.

Jeremy was gone in a flash. He slid down the stepladders rather than using the rungs. He instantly saw the shells had done significant damage. Shrapnel holes peppered the ship from hull to the two funnel tops. The torpedo launchers didn't appear too badly hit, but their crews were all casualties. Several sailors lay dead while others writhed, screaming as blood sprayed across the deck. The starboard torpedo launchers were certainly out of action until replacements came to man them.

Jeremy's damage report was delayed as he knelt by a rating whose leg was badly lacerated pumping crimson jets. Jeremy ripped off his jacket, flinging it aside. He pulled his shirt over his head without wasting time to unbutton it. He wrapped the shirt tightly around the sailor's wound, staunching the blood flow.

'That'll hold you,' Jeremy said, using the rating's blood to splash a capital 'T' on his forehead. 'I'll try to find the doc or stretcher bearers.'

'Thanks, sir,' the rating growled stoically. 'Not such an able seaman now, am I sir?'

'You'll be fine,' Jeremy replied, pulling his jacket back on.

'Don't forget your cap, sir,' the rating reminded Jeremy as he stood up.

That wasn't as frivolous as it might have sounded. It was important for sailors to recognise officers in the melee of battle, and wearing a cap was one of the best ways of doing so. Maybe servicemen feared death, but they were more than ready to face it if led by respected officers. And one way to gain respect was to be there in the fire-fight with them and wear your flipping hat so they can bloody well identify you.

The two Walruses swayed precariously on their gantries, threatening to crash onto the deck at any second.

Bloody hell, I'd better get a crew to jettison the birds...

Then the bridge erupted. The blast threw Jeremy hard against the deck rail, almost knocking him overboard. The grinding of tortured metal followed the explosion as massive steel plates buckled into tin-foil. Jeremy lost his senses. The concussion had momentarily blinded and deafened him. Had he not been protected by a bulkhead the injury might well have been permanent.

When he finally shook himself together, he realised any damage report was already obsolete. Clambering over shattered wreckage, he made his way to the bridge. The stepladder was twisted into a tortured spiral, making ascent treacherous. He slipped several times, but finally squeezed through the distorted bridge gate.

The sight was hell itself. Jeremy was appalled.

I could have been here!

A shell had exploded in the 'B' gun turret just forward of the bridge raking it with shrapnel. The gun turret was smashed into oblivion, killing or maiming everyone inside.

Several bridge officers lay dead, while body parts littered the area. At first Jeremy thought everyone was dead, but Captain Bell and two officers attending his wounds survived. Jeremy scanned the bridge, immediately assessing there were no working components remaining. The all-important gyro navigation system was destroyed beyond repair, while the communication tubes were just mangled scrap-metal.

Right now there were no instructions from the bridge to the rear wheel-house. The helmsmen had no idea where the ship was heading, or where it needed to go. Similarly the engine room artificers were literally in the dark although the boilers still functioned normally.

The two officers attending Captain Bell had stemmed the blood flow from his head wounds. They'd done a good job, but neither of them looked in better shape than the captain. Jeremy could only guess how their eardrums fared. Yet despite his injuries, Captain Bell was very much in control.

'We have to restore communications with the wheel-house,' Bell said.

'It'll take a while to rig a temporary telephone, sir,' Jeremy replied. 'Until then we'll have to rely on Chinese whispers.'

'What are you blithering about, lad? Has the blast knocked your brains out?'

'I have an idea to set up a manual telegraph for you, sir.'

'Very well, but make haste, Mister St Chalfont-Smyth, make haste. And keep the gun crews firing at that bloody ship.'

'Aye, aye, sir.'

'And send the surgeon,' one of the surviving officers added.

'Aye, aye, sir.'

Beyond the bridge *Exeter* was in chaos, but the gunners were keeping up steady salvos, so there was no need to pass on the captain's orders to Lieutenant-Commander Jennings. It was a different story around the torpedo tubes. Most of the crews lay dead, but Jeremy came across a gunner's mate who was in fighting shape even if a bit dazed.

'Can you find anyone to help fire the torpedoes?'

The sailor nodded, a little vaguely in Jeremy's opinion, but it'd have to do.

'Right, find enough men to get the job done. The captain's compliments to Lieutenant-Commander Smith. His orders are to fire the torpedoes as soon as there's a chance of hitting that bloody pocket-battleship.'

'Aye, aye, sir,'

Jeremy left him to it. He glanced back for a moment and was pleased to see the seaman had already found some ratings and was putting them to use. Lieutenant-Commander Smith may have commanded the torpedo stations, but his team was well trained and knew exactly what to do without waiting for orders.

On the way to the wheel-house he encountered several walking wounded who'd been patched up. He assigned them stations within easy ear-shot of one another until a line strung from the bridge to wheelhouse.

A frustrated lieutenant commanded the helmsmen.

'Do you know what's going on, Jeremy?'

'The bridge is down, sir, but Captain Bell is still OK to command. All comms are out, but I've lined men from here to the bridge. I'll get back now and tell the old man he can communicate down the line.'

And the system worked.

Captain Bell was able to issue commands by relay to the wheel-house until he felt fit enough to hobble to the after conning station and issue steering orders personally. However he still needed chains of men to contact the engine room, manual helm amidships and wireless operators' station.

Somewhere in the middle of the confusion a brace of torpedoes leapt from their tubes and sizzled towards *Graf Spee*. The German raider was now shrouded in smoke from her own guns and what looked like hits from the three British cruisers. Jeremy scanned the sea through his binoculars, but couldn't make out whether the torpedoes had hit.

'Two fish gone, sir, but there is no sign of damage,' Jeremy reported to Captain Bell.

'Very well,' Bell conceded, turning to the helmsmen. 'Hard about, we'll give Jerry a blast from the port tubes.'

But the pocket-battleship had torpedoes of her own and fired two towards *Exeter*. Luckily *Ajax's* spotter plane saw the danger and quickly radioed a warning. *Exeter's* radio station received the signal, but it was only quick running from crewmen that brought the message to Captain Bell in time. He ordered the ship hard a-starboard, turning just in time to see the enemy torpedoes shoot past only feet from *Exeter's* transom.

But if Captain Bell's woes weren't enough, the next shell from *Graf Spee* ripped into *Exeter's* forward 'A' gun turret, disabling it completely. Other shells smashed amidships. Minor explosions followed as smoke and flame billowed through hatches and ruptures in the deck. It soon became obvious there was damage below the waterline as *Exeter* started listing to starboard.

'There is only "Y" turret working aft, sir,' Jeremy reported after being instructed to inspect the damage. 'Lieutenant-Commander Jennings is still directing the remaining gun and spotting from the highest point he can find on deck. The fires are making it dashed awkward for him though, sir.'

A shadow flashed over *Exeter's* deck causing Jeremy to duck by reflex, but it was simply *Ajax's* Fairey Seafox spotter plane coming to check on the damage. *Exeter* was still in scratchy radio communications with the flagship, but it looked like Admiral Harwood wanted his aerial observers to take a look as well.

Jeremy was once again sent around the ship to report on all stations.

But he was distracted.

A shell burst through the chief petty officers' mess close to amidships followed by another direct hit further aft and yet another blasted the anchor from the bow, leaving a gaping four square yard fracture in the forward hull.

Fires broke out everywhere sending repair parties across the ship. The men were well trained and divided into fire-fighting and repair units although often the roles merged.

Jeremy ran into Archie Cameron, a fellow midshipman and chum from the middies' quarters. He and Able Seaman Bill Gwilliam were smothering flames with anything at hand. As Jeremy joined them he saw the flames leap towards a ammunition locker filled with ready-to-fire shells.

'Bloody hell, Archie, do you reckon they'll blow?'

'Good chance. You keep at the flames, Jeremy. Bill, help me toss this ammo over the side.'

Jeremy waylaid two seamen, ordering them to bring sand buckets from the nearest station. It turned out to be close by and they formed a bucket chain to douse the flames while Archie Cameron and AB Gwilliam methodically tossed shells overboard. The shells were scalding hot by then and Jeremy had to admire the two men who disregarded their discomfort until the ammunition lockers were cleared.

'Looks like you're under control, Archie,' Jeremy called. 'The skipper's ordered me to make the rounds and give him a damage report. I'll head aft now.'

'No worries, Jeremy. Bill and I can manage the last shells. Thanks for the help.'

Jeremy made his way aft...

Chapter 20 — Jack Tar of all Trades

In seconds Jeremy was back at the aircraft launch area. The catapult was just a mess of tortured steel and the planes were wrecked by shrapnel wounds. Aviation spirit still seeped from the punctured fuel tanks.

Jesus, those planes are still here. They've gotta go..?

In fact *Exeter* had only been engaged in battle for less that quarter of an hour, but other men felt the same, including the aircrews who saw the danger. It was going to break their hearts to lose their planes, but the fire risk was critical. If a spark hit the deck, *Exeter* would be a fire-ball amidships. Men resorted to muscle power pushing the wrecked planes from their launching ramps and then over the side.

An eleven-inch shell burst alongside *Exeter* before the planes were cleared. Metal fragments sliced through the hull, killing several ratings, but the huge water spray washed some fuel away, leaving a less flammable, but more slippery fuel-water sludge oozing back and forth along the main deck.

The planes weighed about six thousand pounds each, so it was tough going getting them over the side, especially as they continually snagged in tangled superstructure. Jeremy released a fire axe from its mounting point. He slashed any obstruction. Sometimes he successfully cleared the obstacle while on other occasions he enlisted the help of a dozen ratings. The planes tumbled into the ocean just as another enemy salvo exploded only yards from *Exeter's* hull.

Job done — it was time to report back to the captain.

'Lieutenant-Commander Jennings reports too much water has shorted the electrical controls for "Y" turret, sir,' was the grim news. 'He says it's tricky, and if we get hit again, it'll be pure luck if he'll be able to fire back.'

'That's it then,' Bell replied. 'No guns left, but I'm damned if I'll see the bastards get away. I might as well ram that bloody Jerry tub if I can.'

Jeremy looked horrified. He stared into the captain's icy eyes and wondered if Bell was in earnest. *Exeter* still had the means to do so. The cruiser could still make eighteen knots despite listing ten degrees to starboard. The German pocket-battleship was manoeuvring frantically to avoid torpedoes from the British warships, but was not steaming anywhere near her maximum twenty-eight knots.

'Shall I send a signal to *Ajax*, sir?'

Jeremy had no idea whether, realising his ship was no longer an effective fighting unit or his wounds, had pushed Bell over the edge. Maybe the captain simply deemed it was something he had to do if all other choices were exhausted.

Bell eyed Jeremy inscrutably.

'Go back through the ship and make yourself useful, there's a good lad,' he said. 'There's plenty to do. Report back in half an hour or if you discover any critical developments.'

How much more critical does it have to get?

Jeremy decided he'd head for the radio room. If Captain Bell planned to ram the pocket-battleship, Admiral Harwood would want to know. Also he'd make himself useful moving wounded men to the after deck along with anything that could float.

Meanwhile *Exeter* cruised with all available speed to keep up with the other three warships. The pocket-battleship was now only about five miles away but an even denser pall of smoke enshrouded her, thrown up by her own screen and fires from direct hits by *Ajax, Achilles* and *Exeter*.

But Jeremy never reached the radio station. Another salvo smashed into *Exeter* amidships and fires erupted just about along the entire length of the ship.

If we're going to ram a bloody battle ship, the best hope is astern. I dunno how the skipper plans to abandon ship, but there won't be more than a few minutes to get it done.

Jeremy gathered any seamen who weren't directly attached to a repair or fire-fighting crew, forming a general duties emergency team.

'Right men, we need to get anything that will float or we can use as a raft and pile it here at the stern,' Jeremy said. 'Anything that'll float. Then we'll need to help anyone unable to walk as far aft as possible.'

Some of the ratings looked puzzled, but obeyed without comment. However Jeremy was once more diverted when a lieutenant ordered his team elsewhere. *Exeter*'s hull was riddled with fractures ranging from small cracks to gaping fissures that needed plugging urgently. In preparation for such an event the shipwrights had constructed canvas and wood bungs which expanded when they became water-logged and plugged the hull.

What's the bloody point if the skipper is going to crash the flaming ship?

But orders were orders and *Exeter* was in real risk of capsizing if she took on much more water and listed further to starboard. It was tough, exhausting work and Jeremy lost all sense of time and anything other than the task at hand.

Just how successful Captain Bell's plan to ram *Graf Spee* might have been proved problematic. By then *Exeter* listed so badly it took the entire team of helmsmen to keep a constant course. Nevertheless she was now steaming full ahead towards *Graf Spee*. Yet Jeremy had no idea what Captain Bell proposed to do once they'd rammed the German raider. Perhaps the German eleven-inch guns would blast *Exeter* to smithereens before she could get that close.

Smash right into her and they'd all be dead. Maybe that was what the captain was prepared to sacrifice. Death before dishonour! Yes, that had been the British way for centuries, but hadn't Saratoga, Kabul, Isandlwana, Skion Kop and the flaming Western Front taught them anything?

Luckily Commodore Harwood came to the rescue in timely fashion.

From his flagship, it was evident *Exeter* was in dire straits. Communications from Exeter were sporadic due to damaged radio masts, but Captain Bell was able to send a message saying he could still make eighteen knots, just over half *Exeter's* fully serviceable flank speed. But to Harwood it was obvious *Exeter* was unable to keep up with the battle while remaining seaworthy let alone fighting effectively.

'Signal *Exeter* to disengage,' he ordered his chief radio officer. 'Proceed to the Falkland Islands for repairs at whatever speed is possible without straining your bulkheads.'

The officer returned shortly afterwards.

'Captain Bell reports he can still fire one of "Y" turret's guns, sir.'

Harwood grinned.

'You have to hand it to Freddie, sir,' *Ajax's* commander Captain Woodhouse observed wryly, 'he's a right old terrier and no doubt. It wouldn't surprise me if he'd consider ramming the bloody Jerry ship if he could.'

'The admiralty discourages its captains sinking their own ships, Charlie,' Harwood replied. 'Sinking enemy ships is just fine, but I think their lordships will prefer to get *Exeter* back and live to fight another day if they possibly can.'

'Is there a reply, sir?' the signaller asked.

'Send, "the order stands, disengage for Port Stanley. You've done more than your share. Well done, good luck and God speed.".'

Even Captain Bell had to admit that *Exeter* was no longer a fighting entity and grudgingly gave the order to turn south for the Falklands. The cruiser was by no means out of the woods. Her internal communications were shot to hell and back, she listed badly and her bow was so perforated *Exeter* was in danger of being swamped. Jeremy and his repair crew among others plugged the ruptured hull as a top priority.

Exeter's gyro steering system was also destroyed so Bell and his surviving navigation officers relied on a sextant and a rudimentary magnetic compass from one of the ship's boats. Fortunately the weather was fair, although rougher seas were expected the further south they sailed.

One of the many tasks Jeremy had virtually assigned himself was distribution of medicine and dressings to several aid-stations located throughout the ship because the sick-bay was overflowing. He discovered the rating he'd helped earlier was still alive and occupied a hammock strung to some wrecked piping.

Surgeon-Lieutenant Roger Lancashire turned up as part of his never-ending rounds.

'How're you faring, Elverson?' he asked the wounded seaman.

'Hurts like buggery, sir,' Elverson replied.

'Sorry, but we're all out of morphine. Bloody Jerry shell took the lot, I'm afraid.'

'I'll try to drum up some grog from the wardroom and messes, sir,' Jeremy suggested. 'I don't think the skipper will mind.'

'How very "bucaneerish" of you, Jeremy. Captain Bell mightn't object to a nip himself. I believe you applied the tourniquet?'

Jeremy nodded.

'Well done, it saved this young fellow's life. More than I can say for many other poor souls. The ship has taken serious hits just about everywhere.'

Not only was Lancashire a highly competent doctor, his natural cheerfulness lifted the spirits of the wounded sailors. Once his duties freed him from fire-fighting and hull repairs, Jeremy found himself assisting Lancashire on many occasions during the next three days. It all turned into a blur. Along with all the other crew members, he doubted if he slept for more than a couple of hours the entire time.

Jeremy wasn't sure when, but at some time signals from Commodore Harwood informed *Exeter's* crew they hadn't been fighting *Admiral Sheer*, but the *Graf Spee*.

'What's the difference,' Archie Cameron said. 'Pocket-battleships are like peas in a pod.'

'It means the *Admiral Sheer* is still cruising around the Atlantic and if she runs into us it'll be curtains for sure,' Jeremy replied.

'It's a big ocean, Jeremy. I'm a glass-half-full bloke. We'll be fine.'

Archie grinned and slapped Jeremy on the back before dashing off. He too was keeping busy.

Most heartbreaking of all, over the next three days the survivors buried over sixty of their shipmates at sea, while many of the wounded looked unlikely to make it to Port Stanley Hospital. The dead were laid on the open desk covered with tarpaulins and weighted with chains. Many of the sailors had been messmates for three years and more than a few tears were shed as bodies splashed into the waves.

'The ship is such a wreck,' Lancashire lamented. 'The regular sick quarters are now totally unsuitable. Men will die if we can't make them comfortable.'

'I have an idea, sir,' Jeremy suggested.

Lancashire eyed him curiously.

'Well sir, when I thought the skipper might ram *Graf Spee*. I got a team together and moved a lot of material to the after deck. There are rafts mattresses and all sorts of useful stuff to make shelters and temporary pallets. It'll be out of the wind as well.'

So Jeremy formed another work party. They turned out to be a useful bunch with carpentry, welding skills as well as just plain common sense. Two ship's boats were overturned and secured to act as shelters. The sailors laid wooden pallets beneath the boats and covered them with mattresses, blankets and cushions from the wardroom and sailors' mess-decks. Soon about thirty wounded men lay in comparative comfort, especially after Jeremy organised tarps to be rigged across the deck for shelter. They'd freed up the remaining space Lancashire was able to use as sick-bays.

Able Seaman Elverson was among the men transferred to the make-shift accommodation.

'Thanks, sir,' he said accepting a cigarette.

'You're looking much better after such a short time,' Jeremy said, lighting the smoke.

'Lieutenant Lancashire says I'll live sir, and reckons I'll keep my leg thanks to you. A couple of rum tots worked wonders too.'

'I'm pleased to have been on hand to help out,' Jeremy replied. 'Keep the fag-packet. You'll need 'em and I know where to scrounge more.'

Elverson grinned.

'You're all right sir,' he grinned, 'for an officer.'

High praise indeed.

'Cheeky bugger. Now take it easy I'll be around regularly checking on everyone for Lieutenant Lancashire.'

Jeremy wasn't a smoker, but he knew where cigarette packs were stored. With the supply of morphine gone, it was the best anyone could do to relieve the wounded men's pain.

Towards the end of the third day, the weather, which had been so benign, turned against *Exeter*. The wind backed from a light north-easterly to an icy south-westerly and the swell picked up to several metres. Bell, who continued to command from the after conning station, still had only a boats rudimentary compass to navigate by, so relied on sun and star shots. All deck officers were engaged in sextant work to ensure any errors were eliminated.

Now cloud covered the skies most of the time, celestial navigation was sporadic and brief on those occasions the weather cleared sufficiently for a decent reading. As the swell picked up, making the wounded comfortable was vital, especially if they were in danger of tipping out of their hammocks onto the rolling and pitching decks.

But they reached Port Stanley and docked safely, which said much for the captain and crew's seamanship. The wounded were immediately disembarked and transferred to Port Stanley hospital.

Captain Bell allowed most of the crew to go ashore and let off steam in town. Many sailors had made friends of islanders who happily accommodated them, eager to hear every detail of the battle. The pub and cafes overflowed with the ship's company thirsty for beer and the companionship of the island girls.

Bell wasn't being particularly generous. Exeter was so damage there simply wasn't enough room to accommodate the entire crew even with their reduced numbers. Nevertheless all able-bodied hands reported for duty the following day and got to work to make *Exeter* seaworthy for the long voyage back to

England. There was talk that the proud vessel was a right-off, but not from Captain Bell.

'We'll take her home even if we have to paddle all the way,' he said before appointing his specialist officers to their duties.

With no particular assignments ashore, Jeremy and Archie Cameron took it upon themselves to report to each repair crew and ask if they needed any help. Most of the petty-officers figured a couple of midshipmen would probably get in the way, but all complained they needed more materials especially metal plates to weld over the cracks and holes caused during the shelling.

'The army blokes are doing what they can,' one CPO informed them. 'Patching up tanks is one thing, but repairing a ruddy great cruiser is quite another.'

'We'll hunt around and see what we can rustle up, Chief,' Jeremy said. 'C'mon, Archie, let's see what's lying around town.'

As it turned out, they were quite successful, finding several tons of steel plates at an abandoned rail depot. Port Stanley residents considered themselves very British and were more than ready to lend a hand. Soon truckloads of metal plates, timber beams and rivets along with iron-workers' and carpenters' kit arrived at the quay-side.

Jeremy was in the middle of yet another scavenger hunt when a seaman tracked him down.

'Beggin' your pardon, Mr St Chalfont-Smyth,' he said as he saluted. 'The captain sends his compliments and would like you to report to 'is cabin right away.'

Jeremy followed the rating, wondering what he'd done to gain the skipper's attention.

Chapter 21 — MGB-10

'It'll take a couple of weeks — maybe more, but we'll jury rig *Exeter* somehow and sail her back to Plymouth for a complete refit,' Captain Bell explained. 'One task will be to disperse the crew to other units. I'll be interviewing every man before we reach home port. It's a big job, but there'll be time enough.'

Bell told Jeremy to stand easy.

'It's wartime, so there isn't much choice in the matter. Sailors will go where they're bloody well told.'

'Aye, sir.'

'But in your case I see in your record you've indicated patrol-boats as your preference. Looking for a quick command, I presume?'

'Yes, sir, but it's still an honour to serve under you.'

Bell grinned.

'You don't have to butter me up, young man, but from the reports I've received you acquitted yourself well during and after the battle.'

'It was pretty chaotic, wasn't it, sir?'

Bell scanned several papers on his desk.

'Quite so, yet you proved useful in many areas. Helping wounded, organising repair gangs and doing your share of fire-fighting and dirty jobs. It looks like you knew when to lead and when to follow, which is commendable.'

'Thank you, sir.'

'I'm mentioning your conduct in despatches, which I'm sure their lordships will give a few moments of their time. However, I can't have midshipmen running amok on my ships, can I?'

'Er...no sir,' Jeremy had no idea how to take the captain's comment. He wasn't sure if it was just the old man's way of keeping junior officers on their toes, so it was best just to agree with him.

'I'm also recommending you be posted to the Channel MTB division. What do you think about that?'

'Thank you, sir. I wouldn't want to waste the war ashore waiting for *Exeter* to return to operational status.'

'We'll get her seaworthy enough to stagger home, but I agree it'll take some months to get her back to fighting shape.'

Bell studied another sheet, furrowing his brow.

'Surgeon Lancashire says here you organised a temporary sick-bay on the after deck. That was good thinking. What gave you the idea?'

'Well sir, it wasn't my initial intention.'

Bell eyed Jeremy sceptically.

'It was when you said you'd ram *Graf Spee*, sir. I knew if we did hit her or got blown out of the water before then, any survivors would be in the drink and we'd need as much floating material as we could lay our hands on. I thought the after deck was the best place to stow it. As it turned out all the pallets, tarps, mattresses and everything else came in handy to accommodate wounded men, sir.'

'Fair enough. Well done.'

'Sir, may I ask a question?'

'Go ahead.'

'Were you truly going to ram *Graf Spee?*'

'To paraphrase Admiral Lord Nelson, in war every man is expected to do his duty. Now off you go. Commander Graham will assign all crew members their specific tasks in the next few days. There'll be a lot of reshuffling to fill the gaps. So just keep making yourself useful until then.'

Jeremy saluted, leaving the captain's cabin none the wiser.

*

Several days later news came that Captain Langsdorff had scuttled *Admiral Graf Spee* just outside Montevideo harbour. He believed his ship had been damaged to such an extent it would not be able to take on *Ajax* and *Achilles* now reinforced by another cruiser, *HMS Cumberland*. Langsdorff feared he'd lose his entire command, with no strategic result. Knowing the *Reich* preferred to sacrifice their military personnel in meaningless fights-to-the-death, Langsdorff reckoned the *Nazi* hierarchy would take the news badly so he planned to go down with *Graf Spee*.

His officers persuaded their captain to abandon ship with them. Nevertheless, five days before Christmas Langsdorff shot himself in his room at the Naval Hotel, Buenos Aires.

By late January *Exeter* was ready to sail north. She was initially accompanied by the cruisers *Dorsetshire and Shropshire* before joining a convoy with a frisky destroyer escort, which despatched a couple of prowling U-boats along the way.

And what a reception awaited *Exeter* when she docked at Plymouth. A huge flag-waving crowd lined the quay-side and even the First Lord of the Admiralty, Mister Winston Churchill, turned up to greet the crew. Cigar firmly clamped between his teeth, he doffed his hat every few seconds and shook hands with the sailors as they disembarked.

A parade through Plymouth was planned, but Jeremy wasn't to take part. He was transferred to the Coastal Forces MTB and MGB flotilla, assigned to MGB number 10 as its first officer. As he boarded the bus for Dover which was to be his new base, a motorcycle courier handed him an envelope containing his transfer documents and confirming his promotion to sub-lieutenant.

On arrival he was met by Leading Seaman 'Billy' Bones who snapped to attention and presented a business-like salute.

'I'm to escort you to your billet and then to meet the skipper, sir.'

'Very good, lead on...Billy...Bones..?' Jeremy said uncertainly as the rating took his duffle.

'Well no, sir. I'm Charlie Bones, but...you...know...the name kinda stuck.'

'I see. Which do you prefer?'

'Well I've got used to "Billy", sir, but I ain't usually on a first name basis with officers.'

'It's a one-way street when it comes to "first-name-basis", Billy. I understand we're a ten-man crew, so I think we can indulge in a little informality.'

'Aye aye, sir, but the skipper 'as 'is ways,' Bones said enigmatically.

Jeremy let it slide, as friendly as he was he certainly wasn't going to discuss his captain's personality with a rating.

'And what's your role aboard?' Jeremy asked as they strode through Dover's streets.

'Forward gunner, sir,' Bones said with pride. 'Three pound cannon for'd, sir. Twin twenty-mil Oerikons anti-aircraft mounted aft, double .303 Vickers amidships port and starboard.'

'She's not called a gunboat for nothing then?'

'Not forgettin' the depth-charges. 'Ere we are, sir. Your 'ome for the duration.'

Jeremy dumped his duffle in a room with a single bed, wash-stand, dresser and cupboard and nothing else other than fair enough view of Dover harbour. A friendly middle-aged woman oversaw the place, which she told him housed several other officers from various service branches, but no one was around right then.

Jeremy and Billy Bones soon reached the wharf which had been secured by barbed-wire with a sentry post at the gate. An armed guard examined Jeremy's papers and seemed to know Bones well.

It was early days and the phoney-war still vacillated from day to day as if no one was quite sure how to go about it. Considering the *Nazi Blitzkrieg* in Eastern Europe, the German high command was in no hurry to start trouble in the west. Indeed many in England including Prime Minister Neville Chamberlain believed Hitler would sue for peace any day now. Winston Churchill on the other hand left no one in any doubt about his opinion of Hitler and the *Nazis*.

Still, several anti-aircraft gun placements were installed in strategic locations around Dover along with a large number of barrage balloons.

Jeremy counted four MTBs and two MGBs moored at the time. MGB Number Ten was among them. The craft were either made by the British Power Boat Company or Vosper and Number

Ten was the latter. She was a sleek sixty-eight foot craft capable of thirty-five knots without breaking a sweat and forty under the whip.

Her skipper was Lieutenant Arthur Cuthbert, a truculent Geordie with two gold zigzag stripes on each sleeve indicating he was a naval reservist as were many serving mariners.

'Well, the hero of the River Plate, I presume?' Cuthbert growled.

He extended his hand, but in such a way that made Jeremy feel it was under sufferance.

'Dunno about "hero",' Jeremy said honestly enough, 'but I was a participant.'

'We aren't as glamorous as a cruiser, no doubt, but a lot less moving parts. You'll be learning on the job. As number-one you'll need to know all the ropes including managing the guns and the engine room.'

'Aye, aye, skipper.'

'The flotilla's heading into the Channel to escort a troop convoy across to Calais. Just an afternoon's work and we'll be back for opening time, but Jerry can be pretty cheeky, so we'll be on the alert for E-Boats and U-Boats.'

The MGBs had no crew accommodation. Their range was less than five hundred miles at around twenty knots, but as they spent most of their time at higher speed their range was limited to inshore operations. Before departure Jeremy met the crew.

MGB-10 Complement

Lieutenant Arthur Cuthbert RNR — Master

Sub-Lieutenant Jeremy St Chalfont-Smyth — Executive/Navigation Officer

Chief Petty Officer Andrew Scott — Marine Engineering Artificer

Leading Seaman Barry Hagman — Engineer's Mate/Gunner

Petty Officer Garry 'Snowy' White — Chief Gunner

Leading Seaman Charles 'Billy' Bones — Gunners Mate

Able Seaman Phil Becker — Wireless Operator/ Gunner

Able Seaman James Ruddock — General Hand/Gunner

Ordinary Seaman Kevin Jones — General Hand/Gunner

Ordinary Seaman Oliver Wilcox — General Hand/Gunner

Andy Scott gave Jeremy a quick tour of the engine room which consisted of three massive diesel marine engines and very little room to service them.

'Don't put on any weight, chief,' Jeremy said, 'or you'll never squeeze in between all that hardware.'

'Not likely on Navy rations, sir,' the chief was a garrulous fellow, exuding goodwill. 'But not to worry, that's what I've got Hagman for.'

'Everyone seems to be a gunner,' Jeremy remarked after he'd met the entire crew.

'It's a gunboat ain't it, sir?' Billy pointed out.

Two gunboats, a single MTB and two destroyers formed the escort for three troopships and several freighters. It seemed inconceivable they'd run into danger with the French coast almost visible, but the convoy was slow moving and U-Boats were the *Reich*'s most successful warships so far.

Cuthbert handed Jeremy the helm. It was simple enough, engine throttles and the wheel, which was unexpectedly heavy.

'I thought she'd be more responsive,' Jeremy said.

'Don't be such a girl, number-one,' Cuthbert snapped. 'It's all we've got so you'd better used to it.'

'Aye, aye, skipper.'

Over the following weeks Jeremy's MGB sea-trials proceeded and at first things went smoothly enough. Channel crossing became routine. Jeremy was a conscientious trainee and soon mastered MGB-10 from stem to stern. He ensured he was just as proficient at the helm as he was with the guns, engine room, depth charges, and even the galley. Eventually Cuthbert gave his grudging approval.

Which was just as well, because the phoney war was about to end.

*

The Allies should have seen it coming, because Germany had been building its forces along the border for some time, but such was their faith in the impregnable Maginot Line, they weren't paying sufficient attention. Anyway someone forgot to tell the Germans the Maginot Line was impassable. While the Allies clustered around the Low Countries, Panzer divisions blasted their way through the Ardennes.

Even when the *Panzer* assault stalled waiting for petrol to catch up along their stretched supply lines, the Allies still squandered the opportunity to stop the advance dead in its tracks.

In what was to become a classic *Blitzkrieg* manoeuvre, the Germans walloped the French and swung north to trap the BEF against the English Channel.

By mid-May the situation was desperate. More Germans poured into Holland and Belgium, which quickly capitulated and were in for some harsh treatment from their conquerors.

MGB-10 was busy as German E-Boats, merchant raiders and destroyers grew bolder although destroyers weren't Germany's strong suit. In February Operation *Wikinger* turned into a fiasco when a destroyer flotilla sailed into the North Sea to round up a bunch of fishing boats acting suspiciously around Dogger Bank. Due to poor Navy and *Luftwaffe* communications, two destroyers were lost to friendly fire. The *Reich* had also lost ten destroyers to the RN at the Battle of Narvik in April. But the Germans persevered and despite their shortcomings in range, firepower and manoeuvrability in heavy seas, destroyers were causing mischief in the Channel, although U-Boats were the biggest threat.

A couple of MGBs and an MTB could usually see off an enemy destroyer.

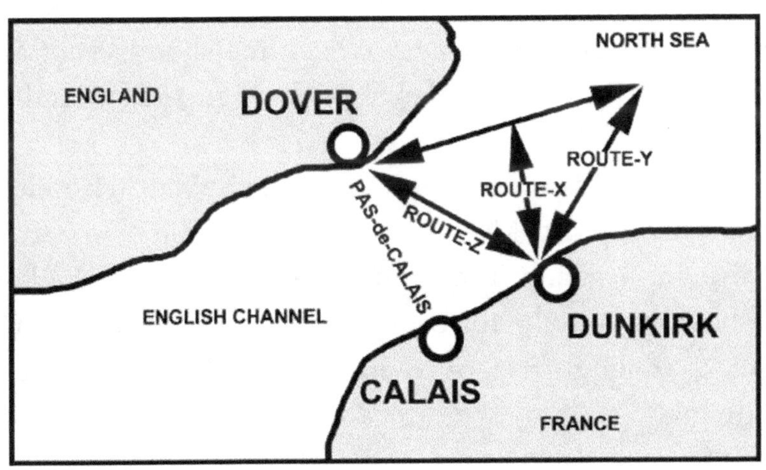

'**B**loody hell,' Cuthbert grumbled. 'Playing nursemaid to a bunch of pleasure boats. The Admiralty has got to be kidding.'

Sure enough all manner of small ships were setting sail for France from harbours along the South Coast.

'We're going to need 'em,' Jeremy commented. 'There is only one pier that extends far enough for large ships. These little fellows'll have their work cut out ferrying troops from shore.'

'Yep, that's the plan. Load as many of those poor bastards trapped at Dunkirk onto as many boats as possible and sail back through the U-Boats and minefields. Operation Dynamo — bloody brilliant.'

'I can't think of a better idea,' Jeremy said but actually thought — *I bet you can't think of a better idea either, Mr Smart Arse.*

MGB-10 was allocated the port flank and had range enough to stay on station most of the day. Because of the expected congestion there were three evacuation routes between Dunkirk and Dover — X, Y and Z. MGB-10, its convoy and escort were assigned Route-Z which may have been the shortest, but also the most heavily mined with a dangerously high U-Boat and E-Boat population.

The first U-Boat periscope was sighted about ten miles from the French Coast and MGB-10 with the two other escort motor boats swung into action. The U-Boat skipper spotted the advancing enemy, but was steering towards a group of small craft. Unable to turn quickly enough to face MGB-10 the U-Boat fired a torpedo before diving.

The missile sliced through the small ships, but they all managed to dodge aside or were just plain lucky and no damage was done.

'One hundred yards, ten degrees to port,' Able Seaman Phil Becker called from the ASDIC screen. Jeremy relayed the position to the other boats that encircled the U-Boat, slowing to 5 knots to reduce engine and wake noise. MGB-10's job was to act as spotter while the other vessels stealthily glided in for the kill.

'They'll be right over it in one minute,' Becker said.

Cuthbert nodded in acknowledgement which was the signal for Jeremy to give the drop order.

'Clear to drop two hundred yards ahead on your present course,' he said into the wireless mic, trying to sound as calm. It wasn't easy as they were about to drop several hundred pounds of high explosive on top of an enemy sub. Hopefully two hundred yards would be enough lead for the sub to move into the kill-zone.

The two motor boats dropped their depth charges simultaneous and then gunned their engines heading out of range at flank speed. The charges were set to explode at different depths for the maximum chance of damaging or destroying the sub.

An eerie calmness followed what seemed like an over-long time. But then the Channel erupted with the first explosion, followed by five more in quick succession. The combined impact sent a ragged shock wave outwards that rocked MGB-10 which was now closest to the attack location.

Once the waves settled Jeremy and Cuthbert scanned the surface for signs of a hit, which weren't long in coming. At first the sea frothed with air bubbles followed by a black oil slick.

'What do you reckon, skipper?' Jeremy asked.

Cuthbert shrugged.

'Oil doesn't necessarily mean we got the bastard. He may have released it to fool us. What's on the scope, Becker?' he called to the wireless operator.

'Nothing yet, sir. The water is still churning and messin' up the returns.'

'Keep your eyes peeled to that screen and report the second something turns up.'

'Aye, aye, skipper.'

But Becker wasn't needed. At that moment the U-Boat's stubby bow reared out of the sea and splashed down as the entire hull settled, listing to starboard.

'Right we've got the bastard,' Cuthbert said. 'Forward gunner, there's your target. Give it all you've got!'

The sub was only two hundred yards away, which was pretty well point blank range for a 3-pound armour-piercing cannon shell. As chief gunner, Petty Officer Snowy White manned the forward facing gun and in seconds he'd ripped several jagged holes in the sub's hull. Water began pouring through, flooding the U-Boat. The accompanying gunboat joined the turkey-shoot. In minutes it was clear the U-Boat was doomed.

'OK, that'll do,' Cuthbert ordered. 'Cease fire. Don't waste ammo.'

Both MGBs veered away from the stricken sub which was now sinking quickly with only its conning tower visible.

'What about survivors, skipper?' Jeremy asked.

'No time for luxuries, Number-One. We're needed back at our escort station. If anyone gets out they'll have to float around the Channel for a bit or swim ashore.'

Chapter 22 — Blood on the Beach

Jeremy's concerns about drowning U-Boat crewmen soon faded, as they were approaching shore where threats were not just below the waves. The evacuation had been in progress for two days and the Germans were trying to stop it with artillery, Junkers Ju-87 *Stuka* dive-bombers and ground attack Me-109s.

Jeremy's information was correct. There was only one long jetty from shore reaching far enough for destroyers to dock. Other merchant ships were also involved, but so far the RN destroyers, frigates and corvettes had done the lion's share of evacuations, carrying up to a thousand troops at a time. The evacuees crammed the open decks braving bomb shrapnel rather than risking being trapped below decks if the ship was damaged or sunk.

Lines of soldiers stretched from the beach until they were chest deep in water. From there the first small boats hoisted shivering men aboard. In the scramble boat crews had to be pretty forceful to ensure the evacuees didn't capsize their vessels. The heart-breaking moment always came when skippers had to tell the next man there was no more room and he'd have to wait for another boat.

MGB-10 patrolled close to their flotilla which soon had their decks crammed with soldiers. Some men were wounded, but there was barely enough room for them to lie down, so most were carried into whatever cabins the small craft had.

'Skipper, they're 'ere!' Billie Bones called from the aft gun platform.

'Where away, man.'

'Dead ahead, looks like they're turning into their dive right now.'

Sure enough, a dozen specks blinked into view as a squadron of Ju-87 *Stukas* plunged to earth. Even from ten thousand feet the screaming sirens heralded impending destruction. The *Stuka* was a clever piece of kit. Its wind-mounted air-breaks and automatic pull-out system allowed the planes to drop their bombs almost on top of their targets.

The first planes shrieked down into a blaze of tracers from the MGBs and destroyers. MGB-10's rear and side guns all swivelled to aim at the planes. A bomb tumbled from the leading aircraft as it pulled six or seven 'Gs', probably blacking out the pilot and gunner who relied on the pull-out system until the g-force reduced.

One explosion followed another, spraying water and shrapnel throughout the fleet. Fortunately there were no direct hits, but one small boat was swamped and others damaged.

MGB-10's gunners followed the planes as they pulled up, one trailing smoke and flame from the engine cowls. The *Stuka* sank below the horizon. It looked in trouble, but was soon out of sight and no one saw if it crashed or not.

Moments later a flight of RAF Hurricane fighters flew overhead and raced after the *Stuka*s.

'Now they bloody turn up,' Cuthbert growled.

'They should make mincemeat of the *Stuka*s, skipper,' Jeremy observed. '*Stuka*s are slow.'

'Maybe, but there'll be one-o-nine escorts around somewhere...'

To prove him correct two Me-109s flew only feet above the beach, strafing the soldiers who had no cover other than to dive onto the sand.

'It doesn't make any sodding difference,' Cuthbert fumed. 'They're just as big a target standing, sitting or lying flat.'

The Me-109s were gone in seconds, but they'd be back.

'Looks like our boats are all full,' Jeremy observed.

'Right, let's get cracking and lead this lot back home,' Cuthbert said. 'Keep a sharp eye out for mines. We were lucky on the way out.'

'Couldn't we take some survivors aboard?' Jeremy asked.

'We could, but that's not our role. Like I said before, we don't have the luxury of time. We need to get these boats home ASAP. And we need the decks cleared for action in case we meet the enemy from either air or sea. We won't be too effective with our decks cluttered with men.'

The small boats didn't really sail in formation, but rather turned in a ragged line and followed one another as best they could. Cuthbert cajoled them, blaring orders from his loud-hailer, but to be fair the craft were so different, keeping a consistent speed was impossible.

'Bloody hell, they're all over the place like ruddy Brown's cows. How the hell are we supposed to protect them? Even if we don't run into another U-Boat, don't they know the Channel is riddled with mines?'

'Anything on the ASDIC, Phil?' Jeremy asked Becker, whose eyes were still focused on the screen.

'It's turned to shit, Number-One. There's wake interference all over the shop. I'll be lucky to pick up a sub, but no chance of getting a ping off a mine.'

'At least it'll be dark soon and we won't have to worry about bloody dive-bombers.'

MGBs and MTBs had been developed from wooden hulled racing boats and pleasure craft. So they were vulnerable if they struck a mine, but with a weak magnetic field, could pass right by one without setting it off. Many of the small craft were also made of wood.

'We're heading back the same way we came,' Cuthbert said without sounding particularly enthusiastic about it. 'We didn't hit anything on the way out so maybe...'

Crump!

A trawler a hundred yards to port was lifted out of the water by the explosion. The entire bow was blasted to splinters which sprayed in every direction as deadly spears. Water flooded into the vessel which sank within a couple of minutes. The long summer twilight crept in, but there was still enough light to see the surface was littered with debris and possibly men swimming for their lives.

'We'd better go and check them out, skipper,' Jeremy suggested.

'No, we keep going.'

'But there might be survivors, and they're on our side this time.'

Cuthbert glared at Jeremy.

'I'm unused to having my orders questioned, Number-One. I will not tolerate insubordination. Is that understood?'

Jeremy had no choice. He was pretty close mutiny right then.

'Aye...aye...sir.'

They cruised north-westwards into the setting sun. By the time they reached Dover it was fully dark.

A reception crowd had assembled along the quay-side. Every available inch of dock was used to disembark the troops. Many wounded weren't critical, because they'd been fit enough to wade into the ocean and survive wet-to-the-chest for hours in some cases. Stretcher cases took priority.

Red Cross volunteers were ready with cocoa and bully-beef sandwiches, while ambulances and medical teams stood by to receive wounded men from larger ships. Soon the wharf was packed with refugees and MPs were hard pressed to organise their dispersal. These men had seen serious combat and been harassed by air attack and artillery barrages, so they weren't in any mood to be pushed around by officious officials.

But move they must, because vessels both large and small kept arriving. Fortunately Admiral Bertram Ramsay was in charge, directing operations from a series of tunnels and bunkers constructed below Dover Castle. Bertram had an eye for detail and knew how and to whom to delegate responsibility.

Before reporting to Bertram's HQ with other commanders, Cuthbert drew Jeremy beyond earshot.

'Now you may reckon you're a big hero of the River Plate, Number-One,' Cuthbert said through clenched teeth, 'but remember I'm MGB-10's skipper. Don't ever question my orders aboard again. Do you understand?'

'Aye, aye, sir.'

What else could Jeremy say?

'Very well, now get the boat refuelled and moored while I go and see what they want us to do next.'

It didn't make Jeremy feel any better when the MTB escort pulled alongside. The vessel was only slightly larger than the gunboat and their decks were almost level.

'I say Jeremy,' the cheerful MTB skipper, Peter O'Sullivan hailed, 'there's no space to park this tub right now. Do you mind awfully if we lay a couple of gang-planks across to you, so these poor blighters can get ashore?'

Sure enough about forty men crammed the MTB top-deck and a few others were below.

'Fished them out of the drink about half way across,' the MTB skipper continued as the shivering men scrambled from the torpedo boat to MGB-10.

The crews were attentive, making sure no one slipped into the harbour.

'Poor sods hit a mine. Anyway we got 'em all, which was pretty damn good luck, I'd say. I'm sure they'll perk up with a good feed and hot cuppa inside them.'

The survivors were indeed in surprisingly good spirits, nodding their thanks to the seamen with more than a few grins. Numerous Red-Cross volunteers stood by with cartloads of sandwich-boxes and tea urns while Civil Nursing Reservists were ready to tend any injuries.

'We'll be heading back to get your mates just as soon as we've refuelled,' Billy Bones said as the survivors passed by, which was thoughtful because many of the soldier's comrades were still stranded on the Dunkirk beaches.

But Jeremy harboured dark thoughts towards Lieutenant Bloody Arthur Cuthbert.

The torpedo boat crew rescued everyone from that fishing trawler and we passed right by. They could have done it in half the time if we'd leant a hand.

But he kept his thoughts to himself when Cuthbert returned with orders to escort another convoy of small ships to reach Dunkirk at first light.

'Better get some food and a kip. It'll be time to cast off around midnight,' Cuthbert told the crew.

Jeremy was only too happy to oblige. MGB-10 was refuelled and rearmed, while shore mechanics checked the engine and ancillary systems. The crew had swabbed the deck and prepared the under-deck spaces. Jeremy recalled dozens of barrage balloons protected the harbour from air-attack, so sleep was the most sensible thing to do right then.

Jeremy couldn't help himself.

'Pete Sully picked up those blokes from that trawler. Got 'em all too,' he said as he passed Cuthbert who just glared at him.

In the morning they were joined by two tugs each towing about ten small craft.

'They'll slow us down,' Cuthbert grumbled.

'Saving petrol I guess,' Jeremy observed, but the skipper didn't respond.

The armada was vast that day. The Dover boats were joined by many from Folkestone, Margate, Ramsgate and other Channel ports along with other warships.

And so began four days of blurred mind-numbing, terrifying and heart-breaking maritime action. The escort boats could easily cross the Channel three times during the long summer days, but it depended on the evacuation boats and...the enemy.

At times there were lulls allowing the troops to board the small ships and larger vessels along the jetty which became known as 'The Mole'. But at other times planes filled the sky unloading bombs and strafing the beaches. Additionally inshore German artillery barrages landed in town and as far as the shoreline.

Every day wreckage and dead bodies sloshed around the shallows ebbing and flowing at the tide's whim. U-Boats tended to prowl at dawn and twilight when they were hardest to spot, but that didn't mean they didn't pop up randomly. Sometimes the escort vessels drove them off or destroyed them with depth charges, but on other occasions a torpedo would blast a boat to splinters and cherry-coloured human mush while the U-Boat glided away undetected.

Yet the evacuation continued. Everyone expected the *Wehrmacht* to come boiling through town and overwhelm the beaches at any moment. But the French and British rearguards were putting up stiff resistance, so the Germans weren't getting it all their own way.

Initially only British troops were evacuated causing resentment among the French, but by June French soldiers joined the evacuees. On the second of June the last BEF members sailed for Dover, but tens of thousands of French still remained in the Dunkirk enclave.

'Well, that's that,' Cuthbert said as the final British troops boarded destroyers from the Mole.

'What do you mean?' Jeremy asked.

'The Admiralty won't risk British lives or His Majesty's ships on a bunch of Frogs.'

Before Jeremy had time to debate the matter — which was probably a good thing — Phil Becker called from the bow where he was on lookout duty.

'Signal from the Mole, sir. They want us to come alongside *Gallant*.'

'What the hell do they want?' Cuthbert grumbled. 'We're scheduled to head back.'

As they pulled alongside the destroyer *HMS Gallant*, several ratings secured MGB-10's bow to the destroyer's aft deck which wasn't much higher than the gun boat's. An officer with four gold bars on his coat epaulettes clambered aboard, saluting in naval tradition. This brought the gunboat crew to attention.

'At ease,' the officer said. 'I need your boat for a while, Lieutenant.'

'Aye, aye, sir,' Cuthbert replied.

No one had met the senior officer before, but the crew knew he was Captain William Tennant, the Dunkirk beach master, whose skill and common sense had done much to steer the evacuation to its remarkable success.

'Take her in as close to shore as you can, Mister Cuthbert,' Tennant ordered. It was typical of Tennant that he bothered to find out who the MGB's master was. 'I'll need a loud hailer, if you please, Number-One,' he added addressing Jeremy.

'Take her right along the shore,' Tennant said.

A large number of men still dotted the beach and were easily identified as French troops by their unique helmets.

'Are there any British men ashore?' Tennant called through the loud hailer. 'All British troops to the Mole!'

MGB-10 patrolled the beach for several hours until Tennant was satisfied no British soldiers remained ashore— at least any with earshot. Whether the French troops understood him or not was problematic, but most of them were too exhausted to show any resentment. They just looked stunned and resigned to either die or be captured where they were.

Just as Tennant appeared satisfied he'd done all he could, a flight of four Me-109's flew in low to strafe the beach.

'Open fire all guns as you bear!' Cuthbert yelled. 'Cover the beaches.'

Who'd have thought he cared? Jeremy thought absently, as the aft and port guns opened up on the Messerschmitts. Tracer bullets slammed into the leading plane which immediately erupted in flames. One wing tumbled from the fuselage which rolled hideously over the beach, slamming into the sea only yards from the French soldiers.

But the following planes managed to rake the beach with cannon and machinegun fire. Great gouts of blood-drenched sand spewed up along the beach, leaving untidy lines of dead and wounded men in the planes' wake. MGB-10's gunners kept firing until they risked hitting the troops below the German planes.

'Poor bastards. There's nowhere for them to take cover,' Tennant muttered. 'Take me back to *Gallant* if you please, Mister Cuthbert. We've done all we can here.'

Chapter 23 — Master Mariner

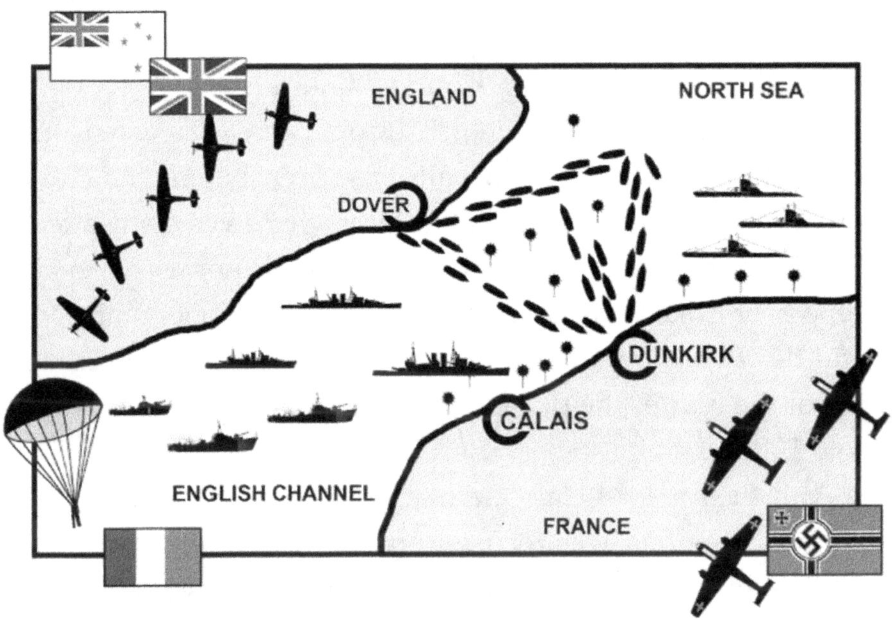

MGB-10's crew were in for a shock when they arrived at Dover. The evacuation wasn't over for them by a long chalk. Vice Admiral Ramsay wasn't satisfied with just evacuating the BEF. He wanted to get as many French troops away as possible. No one was going to say he didn't do a thorough job. There were still over a hundred thousand Frenchmen stranded at Dunkirk. The weather was overcast, so air attacks were minimal. Above the cloud and out of sight RAF Hurricanes and Spitfires dealt with German bombers.

'Back we go, Number-One,' Cuthbert sighed without enthusiasm.

MGB-10's crew had lived on only a couple of hours sleep in every twenty-four, but now most things were in their favour. As well as fewer air attacks, miner-sweepers had cleared the Channel considerably, although there was no guarantee they hadn't missed a few. However the Germans still hadn't advanced onto the beaches. Without aerial reconnaissance, they seemed unaware of the dwindling allied numbers around Dunkirk.

So, seventy thousand French troops were evacuated on 3-4 June. But by the night of 4 June, all those Frenchmen who chose to leave were aboard the last naval and merchant vessels headed for Dover. Forty thousand men remained on their home soil to either surrender or duke it out to the last bullet and bayonet point. MGB-10 and her two companion vessels of the past week were ordered to patrol the rear of the departing armada for any lurking U-Boats or bold E-Boats.

And then a 1934 class German destroyer showed up. While everyone's attention was focused on the evacuation, it cruised in from Frisian waters. The German commander sensed the RN warships were reluctant to start a fight laden down with evacuees. The first thing he did was launch a batch of torpedoes towards the disappearing fleet. One merchant steamer was blown to pieces while a destroyer received serious damage, but managed to steam on at reduced speed.

'Shit,' Cuthbert hissed, 'those bastards aren't getting away with that.'

What happened next confounded Jeremy and perhaps the entire MGB crew, but revealed Cuthbert in quite a different light.

'Man all guns,' he ordered, 'and standby the depth charges. Set for three fathoms!'

Jeremy stared at Cuthbert for a second. MGB-10 was equipped with twin stern-mounted delivery racks each loaded with three depth-charges ready for use. Just shy of twenty feet was incredibly shallow for the depth-charges which were simply released over the transom, there was a chance MGB-10 could be damaged by its own detonations.

Steering directly towards the destroyer, Cuthbert gunned the MGB to top speed. 1934 class destroyers were normally fitted with a single 5.8 forward gun, not much larger than the MGB. Cuthbert was relying on superior speed and agility. Although the MGB was heavy at the helm, Cuthbert was a seasoned master and whipped around the sea with skilful dexterity.

'OK Number-One, I'm going right under that Jerry bastard's hull. Go aft and release the depth-charges just as we come abeam her. And for Christ's sake, don't let 'em go too early...or too late. Got that?'

'Aye, aye, skipper.'

Bloody hell, first Captain Bell wants to ram the Graf Spee and now Cuthbert wants to play charge of the Light Brigade with a Jerry destroyer!

'Hop to it, man,' Cuthbert chided, 'we don't have all night.'

The German ship was only a mile away, but it took a few moments for its crew to work out what the MGB intended. By then two shells from Billy Bones' forward gun had already exploded into the destroyer's bow and forward deck.

'Keep it up, Bones,' Cuthbert yelled with almost manic frenzy. 'Stand by machineguns. Open fire as soon as you come to bear. We're in range now!'

Seconds later the rattle of gunfire erupted from MGB-10's side guns. But the *Kriegsmarine* warship reacted with a shot that exploded just feet along the starboard side. MGB-10 bucked madly nearly tossing Jeremy overboard, but he hung on and stayed upright.

With his hand on the release trigger, he saw the destroyer rushing towards them. Another shell splashed and erupted astern.

With Cuthbert slamming the throttles through the safety gate, MGB-10 was now doing close to forty knots and the German gunners misjudged the closing speed.

Not so Billy Bones who scored two more hits. But the Germans now opened up with small arms and heavy machineguns. Bullets zinged past Jeremy while others pinged off the boat super-structure, ricocheting in all directions. The engine roar was deafening while the water around MGB-10 boiled with bullet strikes.

Jeremy had no time to think. Suddenly the destroyer hull loomed ahead and then it seemed to rear up like a massive steel wall. Cuthbert steered so close it looked as if the two ships would collide.

Wait....wait.....wait....now...

He pressed the release trigger just as MGB-10 scraped the destroyer's hull. The motor boat lurched to port, but all the depth-charges tumbled into the sea before the MGB rushed past in a hail of bullets and several hand grenades tossed from the destroyer.

With a three fathom fuse the depth-charges exploded almost instantly. A tidal wave surged up the destroyer's hull, spewing death and destruction across its decks. Bodies and wreckage hurtled overboard. More explosions rocked the destroyer. She was in trouble straight away, but Jeremy had other problems on his mind.

He turned from the scene of carnage astern to see to his horror MGB-10 was heading on a straight course at flank speed. She was in urgent danger of hitting a mine or running aground. The beach was not far away.

Why hasn't that lunatic reduced speed? He'll blow up the wretched engine.

Jeremy raced to the helm to find Cuthbert slumped over the consol. His coat was caught on the wheel, holding him partially upright. Jeremy grabbed the skipper who felt like lead. His right shoulder was a mess shattered bones, mangled cartilage and muscle. He'd lost a lot of blood. Jeremy had no idea when the skipper had been hit, but he'd still steered MGB-10 with minute precision.

There was no time to spare, Jeremy pulled the throttles to idle and took the wheel.

'The skipper's in bad shape,' Jeremy called to the crew. 'I'm taking command. Snowy, grab one of the lads and get him below. Staunch any blood flows.'

Snowy White and Ollie Wilcox were there in seconds. Manhandling Cuthbert was heavy going. The skipper was unconscious so literally a dead weight.

Jeremy steered MGB-10 around and headed after the main fleet. The German destroyer looked in a parlous state. Fire belched from her hatches. Men were manning boats or jumping overboard. Everyone seemed to be abandoning ship. Jeremy knew they didn't have room for an entire destroyer crew, or the manpower to guard them. They were close to shore anyway and it looked as if sufficient boats were away to ferry the sailors ashore.

And then a mighty blast shook the sky and sent a ten foot wave outwards. One of the ammunition magazines exploded and ripped the ship apart. The shock wave washed past the motorboat crew, while Jeremy struggled to control the helm when the mini-tsunami struck. After the sea settled little remained of the destroyer.

'Jesus, Number-One,' Billy Bones said. 'If we'd been a little closer, I reckon we'd have gone up with that lot.'

'Absolutely, Billy. Get some help and take Lieutenant Cuthbert below. Chief, what is the engine status?'

'She's had a right going over, sir,' Andy Scott replied, 'but she'll get us home if we're gentle.'

'Gentle it is, Scotty,' Jeremy grinned.

Snowy White appeared and reported Cuthbert was alive, but needed urgent medical attention.

'OK, we'll go as fast as we can. Meanwhile check for hull damage and if anyone else is hurt.'

'Aye, aye, sir.'

Shortly Snowy White returned.

'Deck has more holes than a colander, sir and we're taking water from hits below the waterline. Ollie's looking after Mister Cuthbert and Jonesy has the pumps going. He's keeping up with the flow. Jimmy Ruddock has a nasty shrapnel gash, but Phil has bound it up for now. All other hands are shipshape, sir.'

'Thanks. Well done all hands. I'm damned proud of this crew. Now let's get back to Dover. I want two lookouts forward. We don't want to run into a mine or a Jerry torpedo after today's excitement.'

'Aye, aye to that, sir.' Snowy said.

'And do you think we can rustle up a hot cuppa by any chance?'

'I'm sure we can accommodate you, sir.'

'Excellent.'

They caught up with the fleet before reaching Dover and signalled to the destroyer flying Captain Tennant's broad pennant Cuthbert and Ruddock had been wounded in action. Ambulances were waiting at the wharf. Along with MGB-10's casualties there were many other wounded to be treated.

*

Military Medical Centre, Dover Late June 1940

Arthur Cuthbert lay in the officers' ward. He was pale and had lost some weight, but he seemed in good spirits when Jeremy visited. He'd come most days, but only after extensive surgery and a fortnight in bed was there any noticeable improvement in Cuthbert's condition.

'How're you feeling, Arthur?' Jeremy asked.

Naval protocol allowed off-duty junior officers to address one another by their Christian names, so Jeremy wasn't being over-familiar.

'Like shit actually, although it's relative. Last week was murder, but they saved my arm and I've got my appetite back, although the food here isn't that posh.'

'I'm pleased to see you're on the mend. When do the medicos say you'll be up and running.'

'Dunno about running, but they're talking about getting out of bed in the next day or two. I won't be sorry to see the end of a ruddy bed-pan.'

'Great. Jim Ruddock's been discharged and rejoined the crew,'

'Good for him. I'm pleased to hear it, but I've been told I'm desk-bound for the duration.'

'I'm sorry.'

'Why? You'll be given command of number ten I guess.'

'Yep, we're just waiting for her final repairs and we'll be operational by next week.'

'Congratulations. At least this way you won't be questioning some other poor bugger's orders.'

'Yes, sorry about that...'

'Don't be. Now you'll be able to sail your own ship. You're you and I'm me. We all fight the war differently.'

'You've trained a great crew for me.'

'Yes, they're all good lads. I've seen you working well with them and they like you, but more importantly they respect you.'

'I heard they've put you up for a gong,' Jeremy changed the subject.

'Did they just, now where did you hear that?'

'A WREN from Admiral Ramsay's staff who fancies me.'

'Lucky you. But at least I'll see the missus and kids a bit more often. Their lordships in their infinite mercy and wisdom are posting me to Tyneside to do some pen-pushing.'

Jeremy left the sick-bay feeling satisfied Cuthbert and he'd parted on cordial terms. The Newcastle man may never regain full use of his left arm, but he was returning home to his family a hero, which was not the case for thousands of dead and captured servicemen...and the war had hardly started.

*

So it was time to regroup, recoup and retrain the BEF and their French, Dutch and Belgian Allies along with men from Poland and Czechoslovakia. The Channel was still busy. It was the fastest supply route from the world to London and eastern ports. E-Boats and U-Boats had a field day sinking an alarming number of merchant ships and generally being unpleasant. MGB-10 was busy discouraging *Nazi* miscreants and escorting convoys once they came within motor boat range.

French resistance grumbled under the *blitzkrieg*. Paris fell by mid-June and the rest of the country quickly followed.

By this stage no one knew what went on in Hitler's mind, but he seemed to lose interest in Britain after Dunkirk. Maybe he was concentrating on France and swinging his evil eye eastwards. Some said he reckoned the BEF was done for and Britain would negotiate a treaty. And that might have been the case if Chamberlain was still prime minister, but Winston Churchill had taken over and he was a right old firebrand when it came to dealing with *Nazis*.

Jeremy and his crew saw action in many spiteful clashes with E-Boats and claimed another U-Boat, but during July he noticed more and more German planes crossing the Channel to bomb seemingly random British targets. By August hundreds of Heinkels, Dorniers and Junkers bombers streamed overhead along with their ubiquitous Me-109 escorts.

Hawker Hurricane and Spitfire squadrons swarmed up to meet the attacks as the Battle of Britain hit full stride. MGB-10 also found it had an unexpected side-line. German bombers seemed to lose interested in Channel shipping, preferring to leave that to surface craft. So it was business as usual for Jeremy and his crew. They still performed escort duty and U-Boat harassment as the skies about became laced with vapour trails tracing dog-fights on high. Often flaming wreckage tumbled into the sea and, if they were lucky, aircrew drifted down afterwards. Over the weeks MGB-10 among other vessels picked up a number of airmen.

Unlike the Germans who had specialised sea-planes dedicated to air-sea rescue, the RAF and RN hadn't given the matter much thought. True the Channel was dense with shipping, but vessels might not always be in a position to pick up ditched pilots, especially if they had an E-Boat hot on their heels.

'Look there, sir,' Billy Bones said pointing to a particularly dense vapour-trail pattern. 'I wonder how they stop bumping into one another.'

'I think they do...often,' Jeremy replied.

Just to prove him right a plane exploded although it seemed less than a fire-cracker at high altitude. Whether it was a collision or just a plane being shot to pieces was anyone's guess. An almost undiscernible speck hurtled from the blaze. It plummeted earthwards for a few seconds, before a tiny mushroom emerged.

'Keep an eye where he lands,' Jeremy said. 'We'll go and fish him out of the drink.'

It didn't matter what side the pilots fought on, they were valuable assets. If they were British they lived to fight again, if they were German they became POWS and out of the game. War planes could be built quickly, but pilots took months to train and were less easily replaced. RAF pilots weren't equipped with life-rafts. Mae West life vests may have kept them afloat, but didn't protect them from cold...and the Channel was cold even in late summer.

The parachute had opened at around ten-thousand feet, so it took a while to descend and also drifted with the changing airflows as it passed through different levels.

'You'd think the bloody thing would stay in one place,' Jeremy complained.

'I hope he doesn't drift over to France, skipper,' Jim Ruddock said.

'No, it looks like he's coming our way now,' Kev Jones said from the bow.

But the downed pilot wasn't the only thing coming their way. A Me-109 pilot, perhaps the one who'd shot down the parachutist, pulled his fighter into a tight turn to draw a bead on the parachute. Shooting parachuting airmen was considered bad form by aviators generally, but after weeks of air-to-air combat, some pilots weren't inclined to such sportsmanship.

The first burst shook the parachutist up, but the shells sped past as did the Me-109. But it only took seconds to climb and return for a second go.

'Blow me down, that's a bloody poor show,' Ollie Wilcox said. 'Reckon we can do something about it, skipper?'

'Fill your boots,' Jeremy said, following the incident through his binoculars. 'All gunners take out that Jerry bastard, but for heaven's sake don't hit that poor blighter on the 'chute.'

It was times like those Jeremy was glad he had a good gunnery team. The *Luftwaffe* pilot had made a cardinal mistake in his excitement to get rid of another RAF flyer. In a dog-fight altitude was paramount. Foot soldiers have a saying — never surrender the high ground — and the same applies in the air. Not only was the Me-109 now at risk of enemy fighters from above, but he was well in range of ack-ack fire. MGB-10's brace of twin machineguns blazed skywards. Rounds raked the under-fuselage and ripped the wings, rupturing the fuel tanks.

The Messerschmitt blew apart. The pilot had no hope. He was either incinerated or blasted to pulp. Jeremy's crew whooped and cheered at their kill. And fair enough too, it was damn fine shooting...but there was collateral damage.

'Oh, shit,' Billy Bones muttered.

Fragments of the German plane had scythed through the parachute, tearing the canopy. Wind whistled through the gashed nylon and the pilot's descent rate doubled.

'Bloody hell, he's a goner,' Phil Baker said.

It looked like the wind was shredding the parachute further. Nylon ribbons now trailed above the pulsating canopy. In seconds it would disintegrate. It was a race against time and the parachute was losing. The crew all differed about the height the chute finally collapsed and was reduced to its shrouds leaving the pilot hurtling into the sea. He dropped for several seconds and disappeared below the Channel surface.

Jeremy thrust the throttle to full ahead. MGB-10 surged forward and planed immediately, reaching the wrecked parachute in a moment. At first there was no sign of the pilot other than his trailing parachute shrouds, but he bobbed to the surface. He lay face down, seemingly dead. If the fall hadn't killed him, he'd drown in seconds.

Jeremy slammed the throttles to idle.

'Take the helm, Barry,' Jeremy said to Hagman who stood beside him. 'All hands, keep your eyes peeled for more planes or E-Boats.'

He stripped off his jacket and threw his hat onto the deck before diving into the sea and reaching the pilot in a few strokes. Grabbing the pilot's collar, Jeremy turned him over and inflated his Mae West.

'Grab hold, sir,' Billy Bones called, accurately tossing a life-line within feet of Jeremy.

Bones hauled Jeremy to the gunwale where it took three pairs of hands to drag the pilot aboard. Seconds later Jeremy was manhandled onto the deck. He started shivering and someone handed him a blanket and towel which settled the shakes.

Billy Bones was attending the pilot. He pulled off the thick leather bomber-jacket to check for broken bones. The pilot wore the single shoulder bar of a flying officer and a Royal Canadian Air Force badge on his uniform upper arm. Billy bent close to check for a pulse.

'He's alive, skipper, but breathing real shallow.'

'Lie him on his side and see if any water flows out,' Jeremy suggested.

It seemed to work, because the pilot started coughing up sea-water by the mouthful.

'Bloody hell,' he muttered, 'I feel like shit.'

'Take it easy, sir,' Billy said. 'You've had a hard day, but I reckon you'll make it.'

After warming up and a cuppa, the pilot recovered remarkably.

'Thanks, chaps,' he said. 'You sure saved my arse. Howdy, I'm Johnny Witherspoon. I think I left my Hurricane somewhere up there around fifteen thousand feet.'

Howdy? Jeremy thought, *he didn't really say howdy, did he..?*

Chapter 24 — Mission to Mayhem

Johnny Witherspoon was duly returned to No 1 Squadron RCAF, given a medical once-over and resumed flying duties the following day. Over the next three months he proceeded to shoot down ten enemy planes, was promoted to a flight commander and was awarded a Distinguished Flying Cross. Not bad for a Saskatchewan farm boy.

Although the *blitz* continued, by the end of September 1940 the German attack lost its intensity due to attrition. By the end of November the *Luftwaffe* simply ran out of puff and newly elevated *Reichsmarschall* Herman Göring was distracted by the Führer's next bold step down the road to perdition.

The squadron had been in continuous action for over four months including a detachment to North Weald in Essex where they were in the thick of the action, taking heavy losses before returning to Northolt. All sections of the squadron were exhausted. Mechanics had worked wonders to keep the Hurricanes airborne while all support units had toiled tirelessly to see the aircrew were nourished and fit enough fly their planes. So now they enjoyed a respite after August and September's frenetic dog-fights.

King George VI and WWI Canadian ace Air Marshal Billy Bishop, who'd been awarded just about every medal invented including the Victoria Cross visited Northolt. Both men shook Johnny's hand and chatted for a moment or two. Johnny thought was nice of them to take the time. His Majesty was especially appreciative of the *Few* as Battle of Britain pilots had become known.

Rumours suggested the squadron was to be transferred to Prestwick for R & R. Johnny was ambivalent about that particular development as they moved through autumn. Scottish winters could be bleak. But he was from a Canadian prairie province, so what could be worse than that? As it turned out Johnny Witherspoon wasn't to spend his winter rugged up against snow and sleet.

It was sometime in autumn, although Johnny didn't remember the exact date. He lounged around the crew room, with no sign of enemy raids in the offing. One of the mess-orderlies sought him out.

'CO wants to see you sir,' the orderly said.

'Oh, what does he want?'

The airman gave Johnny a *yeah-he's-going-to-tell-me* look.

'One way to find out, sir.'

Squadron-leader Ernie McNab looked a quintessential fighter pilot, less than middle height, pencil-thin moustache and hat cocked at a jaunty angle. As a senior flight commander, Johnny and the boss were on a first name basis in private and the officers' mess.

'We're re-locating to Scotland in a couple of days, Johnny.'

'I heard the rumour, Ernie. When do you want my flight ready to fly out?'

'That's the point. You're not coming with us. We'll be sorry to lose you, but we go where we're told.'

'Where am I going, then?'

'No idea,' McNab replied looking at his watch, 'but a car is picking you up and taking you to Whitehall after lunch, so you'd better get spruced up in service dress uniform and make sure you comb your hair and polish your shoes. Who knows what our lords and masters want? As far as I know there's no one below group-captain in London.'

What did Whitehall want with a lowly flight-lieutenant? He belonged to 11 Fighter Group commanded by Air Vice Marshal Keith Park whose headquarters were at Uxbridge only a few miles away. Anyway senior officers usually only summoned junior officers to give them a right bollocking, but Johnny couldn't think of anything he'd done to merit that level of attention.

A khaki Hillman Minx pulled up to the officers' Mess and a pretty young woman from the ATS got out of the driver's seat. She smiled as she saluted smartly and went to open the rear door.

'Flight-lieutenant Witherspoon?' she queried.

'That's right, do you mind if I sit in the front?' Johnny said. 'It'd be nice to chat along the way.'

'Absolutely sir. Some officers prefer silence to do paperwork while we drive.'

'I'm not a paperwork kind of guy.'

'Good for you sir. We all need to shoot Germans, not use up fountain pen ink.'

'Does that include you?'

'I manned an anti-aircraft gun close to Tilbury until last week. I've been rotated to the motor-pool for a spell. Then I'll go back to ack-ack again.'

'What is your name?' Johnny asked as they sped away. 'I can't call you sub-leader all the way to London.'

'My name is Amy Potter, sir.'

Amy, now that's a pretty name.

ATS members wore the same insignia as regular army ranks, but were named differently. Amy's rank was equivalent to a corporal.

'Well, Amy did you shoot down any Jerries?'

'It was sometimes hard to tell, but our battery has three confirmed kills and a number of probables or shares.'

'You deserve a medal.'

'It seems you've beaten me to it, sir,' she said eyeing the purple-blue and white striped ribbon below Johnny's pilot insignia.

It was only a short drive and should have been a pleasant one. Spending time with a pretty girl was something Johnny had enjoyed on Mirios Island, but had little chance to pursue since joining the air force. But as they arrived at London's inner suburbs, the damage from German bombs became more and more apparent. Initially they'd pass a single bombed out home or shop, then totally flattened buildings and, finally in the city entire streets had been razed to rubble.

Salvage crews worked everywhere clearing brickwork, concrete and steel reinforcing. Bulldozers, fire trucks, excavators and ambulances were parked everywhere or busily at work.

'Nasty raid last night, sir,' Amy said.

'So I see. We got some of the Dorniers and Heinkels, but obviously not enough.'

'Think how much worse it would be if aircrews weren't doing their bit.'

Johnny sensed that even though Londoners suffered dreadfully during the *Blitz*, they all seemed cheerful and just needed a fag and hot cuppa to give them the will to defy the worst the *Reich* could throw at them.

Amy had a pass to drive into the Ministry of Defence. They were often stopped by armed guards who examined both Johnny's and her credentials. Considering the guards and warders had endured months of chaos they were efficient and not officious, snapping a smart salute as they sent the car on its way.

'Will you be driving me back to Northolt?' Johnny asked.

'Would you like me to?' she replied coquettishly.

'That would be nice. Perhaps we could have a pint afterwards. Our local does good pub-grub if you like bangers-and-mash.'

'Sounds mouth watering, but we'd better see what their lordships want first. You never know, you might be whisked off on a secret mission and I'll never see you again. But to answer your question, yes I've orders to wait and drive you back to your base.'

'Is that also a yes to bangers-and-mash?'

'How could a girl resist?'

Johnny thought she had the most beautiful smile of any girl he'd met.

Once inside the War Office grounds, Amy was directed to a parking bay. She accompanied Johnny into a rather grand foyer a-buzz with people who all appeared to be very busy. A few secretaries glanced Johnny's way. It wasn't often they saw a dashing young fighter pilot among the top brass. Johnny showed his authorisation papers to a WAAF sergeant receptionist and was surprised she looked genuinely relieved to see him.

'Flight-lieutenant Witherspoon is here, sir,' she said into one of half-a-dozen phones on her desk.

Within minutes a wing-commander staff officer appeared.

'Good, you're here, Witherspoon,' the wingco said rather unnecessarily in Johnny's opinion. Of course he was bloody well here. 'Come with me, please.'

Amy didn't quite know where she fitted in, but the wingco solved the problem.

'If you'd like to wait in the canteen, my dear,' he said in a kind uncle sort of way. 'You can grab a cuppa and wait for your flight-lieutenant there. Janet will show you the way, won't you Janet?'

'Certainly sir,' the receptionist replied.

Everybody seemed so polite and not at all toffee-nosed as Johnny had expected.

Johnny was led through a maze of corridors until he reached an office guarded by two armed MPs. They were expected and one of the sentries opened the door without knocking. That surprised Johnny, because seated at a large desk was none other than Air Chief Marshal Sir Hugh Dowding, the most senior officer in fighter command.

And that wasn't all. Sprawled in a leather lounge-chair was a man unmistakable by anyone in the Allied armed forces.

Chomping a mega-sized cigar sat the British prime minister, Winston Churchill! A glass of whisky had been placed on a coffee table beside him, but looked untouched.

Johnny snapped to attention and shot up his smartest salute.

'At ease, Witherspoon,' Dowding said wearily. He certainly looked care-worn, but it'd been a trying few months. Johnny only had his flight and himself to worry about, but Dowding was responsible for thousands of pilots and support personnel. Mind you Churchill, whose task was even more encompassing, seemed very much at ease to Johnny. The room reeked of cigar fumes, but Churchill wasn't the kind of man to ask permission.

'Thank you for coming,' Dowding said, sounding as if he actually meant it. 'Do sit down.'

Dowding dismissed the wingco who hovered uneasily behind Johnny. Surprisingly Churchill hauled himself to his feet and shook Johnny's hand vigorously.

'Wonderful to meet you, young man,' Churchill gushed. 'You have no idea what a service you have done for the British Empire.'

It was no secret how highly the prime minister regarded *the Few*. He'd coined the term after all.

'Thank you, sir,' Johnny said because he couldn't think of anything better.

Churchill returned to his seat and made himself comfortable. He still didn't touch his whisky.

'What you're about to hear is top secret, Witherspoon,' Dowding began. 'You can't tell anyone including friends and squadron chums.'

Johnny nodded. He'd already signed a document acknowledging he'd not divulge official secrets during or after his period of service.

'We have intelligence the Italians are setting their sights on Greece, although they're still having trouble with the Albanians.'

'Do you mean they intend to invade?'

'That is precisely what I mean.'

'Seems like they're asking for trouble.'

'Not from the Axis point of view,' Churchill said. 'They see Greece as our access to the *Reich* through the Balkans. We believe Hitler has told Mussolini to plug the gap.'

'The Italians are also keen to expand their territory into an empire,' Dowding said.

'Mussolini thinks he's Julius Caesar,' Churchill scoffed. 'Anyway, we believe there's going to be trouble in Greece and the BEF may have to intervene. The Greeks are playing cagey because they don't want to provoke the Germans into invading by inviting an Allied force onto Greek soil.'

'From my limited experience the Germans will do whatever they bloody well please whenever they bloody well please,' Johnny replied. 'But I fail to see how a lowly flight-lieutenant can influence Mussolini's grand plan, sir?'

'It has come to my attention you know the area well, and that is a qualification in short supply in British airmen right now,' Dowding said. 'Our source informs us you ran a small air service throughout the Adriatic before the war.'

'Yessir.'

'Right, that settles it. You have an excellent record, Witherspoon, as that DFC attests. In a nutshell you are to report to Air Chief Marshall Tedder's headquarters in Egypt and from there deploy to Eleusis Field close to Athens. Your task will be photo reconnaissance and intelligence gathering.'

'We need to know what the Italians are up to,' Churchill said, 'and more importantly whether the *Nazis* start sniffing around. We must be informed, Witherspoon. I don't want another debacle like France.'

The Balkans hasn't been too good to you in the past either, Johnny thought.

'Your orders will await you in Alexandria,' Dowding said. 'The details will be explained when you get there. The less you know right now the better. Any questions?'

'Only one, sir. How did you know I was familiar with Greece?'

'A business colleague of yours apparently,' Dowding said evasively.

'Dennis Mortimer, the sly old dog. And all this time he was a spy and never let on. I suppose he's an MI-6 secret agent.'

'We also know about a couple of Australian chums of yours posing as Americans, which is a dangerous game. But what he or they are is irrelevant. You will keep this information to yourself — all of it. No pillow talk, no careless chatter to your messmates, no one is to know where you're going. Do you understand?'

'Yessir.'

'Good. The *SS Stratheden* sails from Plymouth shortly. Your travel documents are available from Sergeant Wilson at reception.'

That seemed to be that. Johnny wasn't quite sure what to do next, so he waited to be dismissed. Dowding had plenty to keep him occupied on his desk. Luckily Churchill lumbered out of his chair — his drink still untouched — and shook his hand.

'Come on, dear boy,' he said jovially, 'I'll see you out. I understand you've been on continuous stand-to for nigh on six months, so enjoy a few days leave while you can.'

Churchill escorted Johnny to Janet Wilson's desk where she and Amy were chatting over a cuppa. Amy sprang to her feet and saluted.

'At ease, my dear,' Churchill said. 'You nearly spilt your tea. Now sit down and enjoy it while it's still hot.'

About then a bunch of civil-service and security minders guided the prime minister away to other paramount duties.

'Gosh,' Amy said, 'I've seen Mr Churchill when he's inspected bomb damage or our Flak stations, but he actually spoke to me. He seems nice.'

'He can be charming,' Janet said with a wry smile, 'but get him on a bad day and that's a quite another story. Here are your orders, Flight-lieutenant Witherspoon,' she added, handing Johnny a plump manila folder.

They'd hardly walked down the Ministry of Defence steps when air-raid sirens began to wail.

'Bloody hell,' Johnny said. 'They're early today.'

'They can be random, as you know,' Amy replied. 'Come on, we'd better get down the tube. Westminster Station is right over there.'

'I should have been back at Northolt so I could have had a go at the sods,' Johnny grumbled.

'Well you aren't,' Amy said, grabbing his arm, 'and you'll be no good to the war effort getting blown to pieces. And you're taking me out for a meal, remember.'

The German raids seemed random, but it didn't really matter with so many worthy targets at their mercy. Some bombs plunged harmlessly into the Thames, but many more struck indiscriminately. Even if the official *Nazi* spin was only docks and military targets, rows of terrace houses packed the dockside area.

Civilian terror bombing had grown throughout the first months of the *Blitz*. The Germans claimed their first London raid was an accident from an off-course plane. But now it was tit-for-tat because of Bomber Command's retaliatory Wellington raids on German cities. The ethics of what was to become known as carpet-bombing would be argued for decades afterwards.

The drone of aero-engines soon drowned the sirens. Amy and Johnny had barely made the Underground station with an orderly procession of Londoners whose calmness Johnny admired, when bombs started dropping.

Docks and shipping erupted in flames, while warehouses and loading bays were gutted. The air-raid also claimed hapless victims unable to reach shelter in time. Johnny and Amy squeezed onto the Circle Line platform. At night people would sleep anywhere they could find a spot, even on the lines, but right now trains still ran and you had to watch your step close to the platform edge.

But Londoners were well drilled and stoically hunkered down to wait for the *Luftwaffe* to be on its way. Suddenly the scream of falling bombs and thudding growls from explosions rocked Westminster Tube Station, sending shock-waves shuddering through the rail tunnels and along the platforms.

Johnny and Amy had taken cover just in time.

Chapter 25 – London at Night

Bombs fell for what seemed like hours. Often the impact was just a distant crump, but other explosions close by, rattled the tiled Underground walls. Amy grabbed Johnny's arm, holding him close.

'Ain't you in the wrong place, mate,' a cloth-capped old-timer beside Johnny said, eyeing his uniform and pilot wings.

'You sure got that right,' Johnny replied.

'Shouldn't you be up there shooting them bastards down?'

'I'd rather be doing that than stuck down here. How do you stand it night after night?'

'You get used to it, I guess.'

At first Johnny thought the old boy was accusing him of shirking his duty, but it seemed he was just garrulous.

'I don't mean to gas on, but it 'elps take me mind off things like.'

Others had the same idea and soon usually reserved Londoners introduced themselves and an impromptu party developed. A black-clad bearded fellow began to play a squeeze-box accordion and everyone sang along. It turned out he was a Jewish refugee from the Sudetenland who'd got his family across the border to Yugoslavia then Greece and on to relatives in London. He'd quickly learnt all the pub songs even if his English was still rudimentary and heavily accented.

Darkness fell quickly in autumn. It looked like the first bomber wave had simply mistimed their raid and got to their target early. But others followed into the night and it was late when the all-clear sounded.

People streamed from the Underground, hoping they'd find their homes had survived the bombs. Amy and Johnny made their way back to her car while all around buildings crumpled in flames. Ambulances and fire engines with bells clanging sped to new hot-spots.

The car and Ministry of Defence remained unscathed, but getting back to Northolt through streets cluttered with debris and rescue teams wasn't going to be easy. They hadn't gone far when they were stopped by a warden.

'You won't get no further, miss,' he said with practised resignation. 'Bombs 'ave flattened the whole row of 'ouses. The fire crews are 'avin' a dickens of a time controlling the blaze. There's folk trapped too.'

'Do you need a hand,' Johnny asked.

'We always need a 'and, sir,' the warden replied.

'Park the car and wait for me here, Amy,' Johnny said. 'I might as well make myself useful because we're not getting through. It'll take hours to make a detour...and then there are no guarantees we'll make it.'

'I'm coming with you,' she said resolutely.

Johnny was going to argue, but thought better of it. It might be dangerous work, but nowhere was safe in London during the *Blitz*. At first Johnny wasn't sure what to do with the folder containing his secret orders, but found room in his gas-mask case. He crushed them in, but he knew he'd be in deep trouble if he left them in an unattended car for anyone to find.

The warden led them to a blazing street where firemen hosed the flames which stubbornly refused to subside. The intense heat and choking smoke hampered the rescue effort, but Johnny and Amy joined a team clearing rubble. They stood before a house with its roof blown away. The terraces on either side were gutted while the front and rear walls were just a pile of bricks and timber. The side walls stood like battered sentinels at risk of giving way at any time.

'We think there're survivors under that lot, sir,' a home guard sergeant said.

'OK, we'll help move the brickwork,' Johnny offered.

'That'll be helpful, sir, unless you want to take charge,' the sergeant said, deferring to Johnny's commissioned rank.

'No sergeant, you're the expert. This is your show.'

They started moving the rubble brick by brick, aware that if the remaining walls gave way anyone trapped below was doomed. Other members of the sergeant's crew used collapsed beams to shore up the walls. After a while about ten men and women formed a line and tossed bricks from one to another where they finally formed a growing pile. A gas main erupted close by, but luckily didn't explode. The flames, although dangerous, added some illumination to help the rescuers.

''Ang about,' the sergeant cried. 'Quiet everyone.'

They all stood still, but the sound of roaring fires, random explosions and sirens still filled the air. The sergeant bent forward.

'Anyone there?' he called.

'Yes,' replied a woman's muffled voice, remarkably calmly in Johnny's opinion. 'There're five of us. Me and my kids. We took shelter in the cellar.'

'Right you are missus, we'll 'ave you out in a jiffy.'

It took longer than a 'jiffy' but after two hours of painfully slow work, a dust-covered woman and her four children scrambled to safety. She sported a livid bruise on one leg.

'Is that everyone?' the sergeant asked.

The woman nodded after accounting for her family.

'Right, everyone stand clear,' he added with a sixth sense for danger after months of rescue work among crumbling ruins.

He was right. Just as the last of the fire trucks backed away, the two side walls groaned and smashed down in a spray of choking dust, smoke, ash and sparks.

'Now let's be gettin' you to safety and a hot cuppa,' the sergeant addressed the children's mother.

'Where's the nearest shelter?' Amy asked.

'Notting Hill Gate, miss. About 'alf a mile away.'

'I'll take this family in my car. They look completely worn out.'

'Thanks miss. Do you know the way?'

'Yes, I'm a London girl.'

'Amy when you get there, don't move. You'll be as safe as anywhere. I'll come and find you when I can,' Johnny said as they ushered the survivors into the Hillman.

'But sir...'

'No "but sirs", Amy. I'm pulling rank this time.'

As it turned out Johnny needn't have worried. When Amy reached Notting Hill Gate, willing hands took care of the woman and her family. She gratefully accepted a cup of cocoa and a camp chair. She was exhausted and only adrenaline had kept her going. She finished the drink and immediately fell asleep. The tin cup dropped from her fingers and clattered on the concrete floor.

'Oh bless,' one of the tireless volunteers said as she gathered the cup. 'The little angel is all in.'

Someone found a blanket to cover Amy and that was where Johnny found her before dawn. His team had rescued others, but also recovered bodies of men, woman and children who were just in the wrong place at the wrong time. The home guard sergeant saw his team was reaching the end of their endurance and no longer functioned effectively. They were becoming a danger to themselves and those they tried to rescue. Someone — Johnny never discovered who — recognised they'd done all they could and stood them down while a replacement crew took over.

It took Johnny some time to find the Underground station. Street signs had been removed either for security reasons or from bomb damage. But eventually after several wrong turns and many inquiries, he made it. Most of the Londoners taking shelter were heading home, but Amy slept on.

'I'm looking for my driver,' Johnny said to the kindly volunteer.

'There's an ATS lass just over there. Poor lamb,' the volunteer said. 'You don't look so flash yourself, if you don't mind me saying so, sir.'

Johnny's uniform was covered in dust and grime, not to mention blood from victims he dragged to safety. His rank and flying insignia were barely visible, but the volunteer recognised him as an officer.

'You should see it from my side,' Johnny grinned.

'You look like you could do with a cuppa and a corned beef butty,' the woman said.

'Thanks. I have to get back to camp, but it can wait a bit and we'll let Amy sleep for a while longer. How do you endure this every night?' he added.

'Listen, sir.' she said. 'I see you're a pilot. How many months have you trained to go up after them bastards? How many 'ave yer shot down?'

'Over a dozen,' Johnny replied without trying to brag — he was simply stating a fact.

'So 'ow many bombs 'ave yer stopped?'

'I hadn't thought about it.'

'We 'ave and it's bloody 'undreds. So we all does our bit in our own way.'

For some reason Johnny didn't know what to say. He leant forward and kissed the woman lightly on her cheek.

'Thank you,' he whispered, 'you've made everything I do worthwhile.'

He woke Amy after he finished his sandwich.

'Oh goodness me,' she said. 'I'm sorry sir, I must have nodded off.'

'Good thing you did,' Johnny replied. 'I don't want you falling asleep while you're driving me around.'

Johnny climbed into the car while Amy checked with the nearest air-raid warden to avoid any road closures. When she returned to the car he was snoring softly and was still asleep when they reached Northolt. As they drove through the camp gate thundering Merlin engines jerked Johnny awake as one Hurricane flight after another roared skywards.

'Bloody hell! The squadron is up early,' was all he could think to say.

Support crews were packing equipment and engines into canvas covered and flat-bed lorries. All the pilots were airborne including the CO. Just one administration clerk remained. He handed Johnny his pay-book.

'We took the liberty of packing your kit, sir,' the orderly said, indicating Johnny duffle leaning against the wall. 'I've arranged accommodation for you at the Plough on Mandeville Road just off the A-40, sir. I haven't been instructed to supply any travel vouchers. All I know is you won't be following the squadron to Prestwick.'

'I've already been issued with all my orders and docs, thanks. What about you?'

'I'm holding the fort so to speak, sir. To tie up loose ends then I'll rejoin the squadron up north ASAP. Your driver is authorised to drive you to the pub, sir. It's not far away.'

'Yes, I've had a pint or two there. Well, good bye and the best of luck to you and the squadron.'

Johnny extended his hand.

'And to you, sir,' the orderly said, shaking Johnny's hand.

'Still fancy bangers and mass?' Johnny asked Amy when they reached *The Plough*. 'This is where I planned to take you.'

'I'm usually off-duty by five, sir. And I certainly need to "freshen up" as the Yanks so quaintly say. Would you like me to meet you in the snug around five?'

'That sounds "swell" as the Yanks say. They're mostly nice folk, but we Canadians don't like to be confused with them Also it's probably time you stopped calling me sir.'

'We'll see, sir,' she replied with a cheeky smile. 'The bus runs right by here, so I'll see you this evening.'

She saluted and drove away.

Johnny's short nap had revived him. He checked with the pub landlord who showed him a small but comfortable room.

'Thought you might like a double bed so you can stretch out, sir,' the landlord said.

'That's very considerate, Mister Barry, but right now I need a bath.'

'Right you are, sir. I'll get the missus to boil a kettle.'

'Boil a kettle..?'

'Yessir, I'm afraid you're only allowed five inches of water a week for a bath.'

'Are you that short of water?'

'Ain't water, sir. Heating it up is the problem.'

Johnny then stopped to consider some aspects of wartime shortages and rationing. At Northolt officers had a communal shower and there always seemed enough hot water any time of day.

'I tell you what, Mr Barry, I'll nip back over to camp — it's only a short walk — and shower there. You can keep my ration for someone else.'

'Thank you, sir — much appreciated. It's a right 'eadache tryin' to run a pub with no facilities for guests.'

'I have a date with a young lady tonight...?'

'No problem, sir. We've got bangers 'n' mash with vegies from the garden tonight. There's plenty of best bitter on tap and I'm sure we can rustle up a G-'n'-T if your lass prefers.'

So Johnny returned to base marvelling at how cheerfully Mr Barry accepted his five inch bath, ration book including bully-beef, powdered eggs and potatoes. The Canadians received supplementary supplies from home — even maple syrup at times. It was a brisk autumn day. Gazing upwards he spied vapour-trails streaming south to intercept another wave of German bombers. John felt a little guilty, but was relieved he didn't have to go and face them today.

He felt much better when he returned to *The Plough*. Mrs Barry took his uniform to brush down and press and laundered his shirts, socks and underwear.

'Oh my, sir, whatever 'ave you been up to. Your uniform is a right disgrace.'

'I'm sorry, Mrs Barry, but I hadn't planned spending all last night digging around London rubble for survivors.'

'Oh my sir, forgive me. I'm never meant to scold. I know you done your bit. You're one of the *Few*, ain't yer?'

Johnny nodded although he wasn't feeling particularly brave right then.

'What you need sir is a good afternoon nap. Don't you worry we'll wake you in time for a pint and I'll 'ave your uniform looking tickety-boo for your young lady.'

Johnny smiled.

My young lady...word gets around...but it's a nice idea.

271

*

Amy arrived looking fresh in a smart, clean uniform with her usual gas-mask container slung over her shoulder. Everyone seemed to be in uniform at the time and she wore her over-coat as the evenings were chilly now. She kissed Johnny on the cheek when he rose to meet her. It seemed the most natural thing in the world.

She refused a gin-and-tonic and chose a half-pint lager-and-lime.

The first thing she did while her drink was poured was visit the ladies room and change her opaque cotton stockings for her prized pair of black-seamed nylon hose a self-opinionated spiv had bought her before the war. He'd reckoned sheer stockings were enough to get a girl into bed — well not Amy Potter. She'd rejected his advances, but kept the stockings. Nylons were a serious luxury. The war began the following month and she'd yet had an opportunity to show them off.

The evening went well and the couple got along famously from the start. As closing time approached Amy seemed unconcerned about the last bus back to her billet.

When Johnny mentioned it was getting late, Amy simply lit another cigarette.

'I don't have to go back tonight,' she said.

'Won't you be AWOL?' Johnny said, initially missing the point altogether.

'I applied for forty-eight hour's leave,' she replied coquettishly. 'And...actually got it!'

Johnny wised up about then.

'Are you sure you want to..?'

272

'Listen, Johnny,' she whispered placing her hand over his. 'This is when I stop calling you "sir". I'm twenty-one and free to do as I choose. Last month three ATS girls were killed during a raid. That could be me next week or next month. This war isn't going to end quickly. I don't want to die never having known...well, what all the fuss is about.'

Johnny was silent for a second.

'You *do* like me don't you, Johnny Witherspoon?'

'As a matter of fact I really liked you from the moment I first saw you. Do you believe in love at first sight?'

'I'm sure it happens, but I don't think those involved know it at the time...and let's not get ahead of ourselves.'

'What about our landlord...or more especially our landlady?'

'I'm way ahead of you. While you were in the loo, Mr Barry and I came to a discreet arrangement.'

'And what about Mrs Barry..?'

'Mr Barry reminded her how they'd met under similar circumstances during the last war, how they were young then and not so old now. He rather implied romance might be infectious tonight. I'm wearing beautiful nylons so I don't want my legs to go unappreciated.'

*

So Johnny and Amy spent an idyllic two days just enjoying themselves. Amy had come prepared with a change of underwear, toothbrush, basic toiletries and most importantly a decent supply of prophylactics to last a young enthusiastic couple through the nights...and days. The Germans even cooperated by deciding to set their targets on other industrial centres for a while. The skies over London remained clear of *Luftwaffe* planes.

They spent their time walking through nearby parkland, lunching at leisure, chatting and getting to know each other, and of course lovemaking. Amy was charming, vivacious and interesting along with her girl-next-door beauty, who could ask for more? But their joy was over in a flash and it was time for Amy to resume her ATS duty and Johnny to catch the train to Plymouth.

'Now Johnny you don't have to make any promises,' Amy said before their farewell kiss. 'I've had a wonderful time and can certainly see what all the fuss is about.'

She smiled wantonly.

'But Amy, I do want to see you again...I...I think I love you.'

He didn't care whether he sounded like a callow schoolboy.

'Like I said, let's not get ahead of ourselves.'

She pulled sheet of note-paper from her uniform breast pocket.

'I wrote down my mum and dad's address and phone number. I didn't know whether I'd give it to you or not. I guess it depended how the last couple of days turned out.'

He took the paper.

'I know you're a genuine bloke now, I'm awfully fond of you and you certainly know how to keep a girl smiling. '

You have the most gorgeous smile.

'But you see I don't know where you're going or for how long...or if you'll even make it back. So after this beastly mess is over and you come back to England...and...if you still feel the same way about me, come and find me through my parents.'

'I'll try to write,' Johnny said lamely. 'You could write back care of the Air Ministry. It doesn't seem like it sometimes, but mostly they know where their pilots are.'

'That would be lovely, sir,' she replied genuinely. 'Adieu, Johnny Witherspoon, until we meet again.'

She kissed him as her double-decker pulled up. One last embrace and she was gone. Johnny waved at the departing bus then turned towards Northolt Park Railway Station. He felt absolutely wretched, because former ladies' man Johnny Witherspoon had fallen in love.

Chapter 26 – Sea Trials

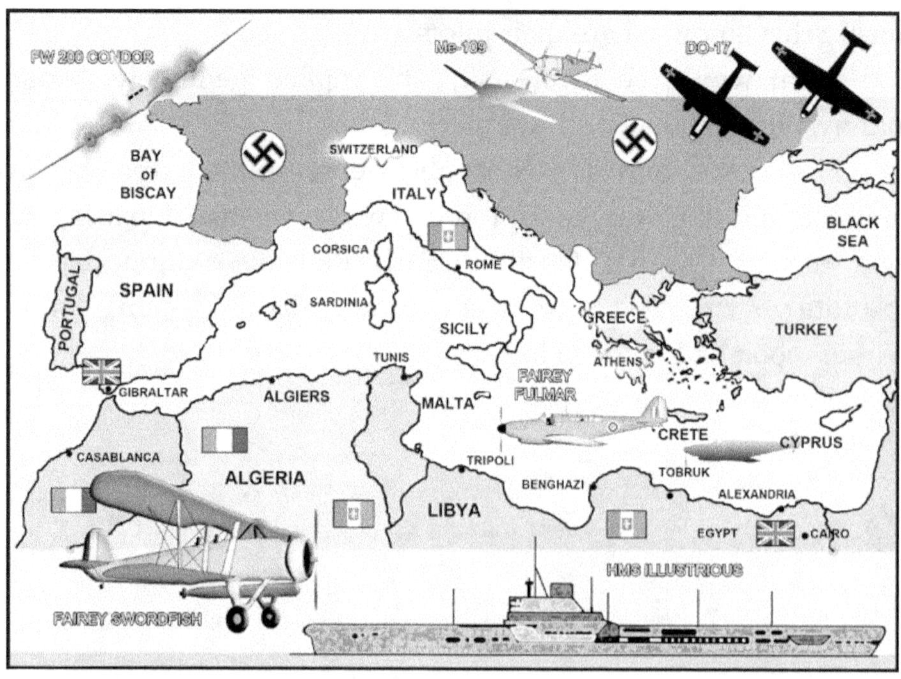

New Year 1941 – Bay of Biscay

*B*loody *hell the Atlantic is colder than Canada,* Johnny thought as he leant against the *SS Stratheden* side rail. It had taken longer than expected assembling the fifty ship convoy and escort, which delayed their departure from Plymouth. Johnny nearly went crazy killing time around town thinking about Amy.

I could have stayed in London, it's no safer here. Bloody Jerry's got his sights on every port and city in Britain as far as I can see.

But now Convoy AP-02 ploughed their way through thirty foot waves with decks awash with spray. Johnny found a spot behind a bulkhead relatively sheltered from wind and spray. He preferred to be on deck, because he shared his cabin with three Army officers bound for the North African Campaign. Below decks was claustrophobic and although Johnny wasn't prone to sea-sickness, The Bay of Biscay was notorious rough. The stench of over-flowing latrines was enough to make anyone throw up.

SS Stratheden carried over a thousand wretched servicemen who'd have rather faced the entire Italian army than another moment at sea.

But Convoy AP-02 was a magnificent sight as breakers crashed right over ship bows. There were twenty escort vessels, destroyers, corvettes and three motor boats. Johnny even saw MGB-10 stencilled on the bow of one boat. It must have been misery in the small open-bridge ships, although MGB-10 had rigged a canvas shelter over the helm.

He waved to the MGB-10's crew when it had come within a few hundred yards of the *Stratheden*. An officer waved back from the helm and Johnny recognised the young sub-lieutenant with the posh name who'd rescued him from the Channel.

The merchantmen carried munitions, food, vehicles and servicemen in two troops-carriers. A tanker accompanied the convoy bound for refuelling operations in the Mediterranean, but also topped up the smaller escort vessels.

SS Statheden's first mate stopped for a chat during his rounds.

'Decided to risk being washed overboard than face life below decks,' he said far too cheerfully in Johnny's opinion.

'It'd be nice if the sea settled a bit.'

'No way, old man. The rougher the better, it'd be a bloody lucky U-Boat to hit anything in this swell. Recce planes can't spot us through this overcast either.'

The first mate had a point. Since late 1940 Admiral Dönitz had developed a new tactic where U-Boats formed packs of ten or more, causing headaches for escort vessel crews. The *Luftwaffe* also utilised converted Fokker Wolf 200 Condor airliners for long range maritime reconnaissance missions. Once the Condors spotted a convoy, they used HF radio to guide the U-Boat packs in for the kill.

For the past few months U-Boats had sunk shipping by tens of thousands of tons in what the *Kriegsmarine* called its 'happy time'.

The weather cleared close to Gibraltar, which was just as well, because a Condor recce-plane turned up and buzzed around just beyond accurate anti-aircraft range. Fortunately Convoy AP-02 reached Gibraltar before a U-Boat pack formed.

Although Britain had reduced the Vichy French threat by destroying its Fleet in North Africa the previous summer, *Regia Marina* was proving troublesome and naval battles erupted regularly throughout the Mediterranean. Thus Convoy AP-02 was joined by two battleships and the aircraft carrier *Illustrious* armed with Swordfish torpedo bombers and Fairey Fulmar multi-role monoplanes.

The mighty carrier *Ark Royal*, pride of the Royal Navy, was also in port refuelling and rearming for Mediterranean operations against *Regia Marina*.

Johnny really wasn't under any particular chain of command at the time, so he thought he'd take a look around Gibraltar while *Stratheden* was being replenished. He didn't get far. He'd just set foot on dry land when a dapper Fleet Air Arm lieutenant-commander greeted him.

'You're Witherspoon I believe,' the naval officer said cheerfully offering his hand. 'Rodney Hardy — pleased to meet you.'

'A pleasure, sir. I thought I'd take a spin around town to see the sights.'

'Sorry, there won't be time for that, old boy. You've been transferred aboard the *Illustrious*. You'd better grab your kit.'

As they boarded the ramp to one of *Illustrious'* lower entrance hatches, the carrier's immensity became evident.

'Impressive,' Johnny said as he saluted at the gangway. He'd remembered it was a Navy thing to salute when boarding a vessel.

'It certainly is,' Hardy replied with obvious pride. 'Seven hundred and fifty feet stem to stern and nearly a hundred abeam and she'll do thirty knots without raising a sweat. It's jolly handy if you're taking off at max weight.'

'I can imagine so.'

An extra thirty knots headwind was a great asset for taking off and landing. Even so with just under seven hundred feet landing distance, Johnny didn't envy the Fleet Air Arm pilots.

'You're welcome to it, sir,' he said to Hardy who gave him a smug and suspicious grin.

'What?'

'I'll explain after we stow your kit,' Hardy seemed to enjoy being enigmatic.

After clambering through passageways and bulkhead hatches, Johnny dumped his duffle on a bunk in a four-berth cabin much like the one aboard *SS Stratheden*. Hardy showed him to the wardroom where several FAA officers lounged around sipping cocoa. Hardy claimed to be a descendant of the legendary Sir Thomas Hardy of 'Kiss *me Hardy*' Trafalgar fame and was christened Rodney after Admiral George Rodney, another eighteenth century RN power-house.

'So you're off to Greece,' he said after introducing Johnny around.

'Begging your pardon, sir, but I'm not at liberty to discuss my orders.'

'That's OK, old chap. We've got your plane parked on the flight deck.'

'I thought I'd be assigned a kite when I reached Alexandria.'

'Change of plan and an opportunity Admiral Cunningham isn't prepared to pass up.'

'Opportunity..?'

'Yes, right now we're doing a steady job with our *Swordfish* that work fine as torpedo bombers against shipping. The *Fulmars* are versatile as dive-bombers, reconnaissance and ground attack platforms. They'll hold their own against anything the Ities can throw up at them, but they're vulnerable against Me-109s.'

'Do you think one-o-nines will come into the picture, sir?'

Hardy shrugged.

'Best to be prepared.'

'I still don't see what this has to do with me. I'm RCAF.'

'We're developing Hurricanes for carrier-borne ops...and we'd like your help.'

Johnny didn't like the way this was going at all.

'You want me to fly my Hurricane off *Illustrious*..?'

'Good man,' Hardy said, 'I knew you'd be up for it. Two G-and-Ts, please,' he added to a nearby mess steward.

'But I'm not a test pilot. You have to be some sort of ace for that,' Johnny protested.

'I disagree,' Hardy declared. 'That DFC on your chest and a dozen kills over the Channel tells me differently. Air-Vice Marshal Park rates you very highly. The cream of *The Few*, no less. Just the chap we need. Don't look so glum. We operate Fulmars off the deck all the time. They may not be red-hot little performers like your Hurricane, but their wing-loadings are almost identical, so take off and landing speeds are much the same. And don't forget we catapult you airborne and we've just introduced a hook-wire to pull you up on landing. How good is that?'

Johnny wasn't convinced. He got the feeling this was a volunteer's job and he'd just been volunteered by Hardy. And who was he to disappoint Admiral Sir Andrew Cunningham, Commander-in-Chief of the Mediterranean Fleet?

Johnny accepted his fate stoically enough. How hard could it be, especially after he inspected his new Hurricane? The aircraft remained on deck because unlike the Fulmars and Swordfish its wings didn't retract to accommodate the critical hangar space below. The plane looked pristine, indicating the navy mechanics took pride in their work. Now it was just a matter of waiting for *Illustrious* to be ready for sea.

*

Late January 1941

When *Illustrious* finally set sail, Johnny Witherspoon's sea trials began. Initially Lieutenant-Commander Hardy flew a few Fulmar training sorties with Johnny in the observer's station. After the initial horror of landing on a postage stamp, Johnny discovered the catapult and arresting-cable worked well. Hardy drew Johnny's attention to the landing signals officer holding two paddles at the deck threshold.

He explained the signals for guiding the plane's glide-path, speed, undercarriage and flap operation and most importantly, the go-around signal in case of a completely botched approach.

After that Johnny was introduced to the Fulmar trainer with a high set rear cockpit for the instructor. With some trepidation Johnny clambered into the forward seat. Ground crew helped with his seat belt and parachute straps.

It didn't take Johnny long to get the feel of the Fulmar, which although it didn't have the Hurricane's punch, was a likeable enough plane to fly. After half an hour of general handling Hardy told Johnny to make an approach to within a few feet of the deck then apply power and overshoot. Once he was satisfied Johnny could fly a consistently stable approach, it was time for his first carrier landing. There wasn't anywhere else to land in the middle of the Med.

Johnny was pleased his landing wasn't any different to Hardy's. After three or four more successful approaches, Johnny was well and truly used to the catapult's discomfort and thumping the aircraft onto the flight-deck. There was no room for fancy greaser-landings on a seven-hundred foot runway. *Illustrious* was a pretty stable platform, but it was still subject to sea swell and the Mediterranean wasn't always calm.

'You catch on quickly,' Hardy said. 'I think we're ready to set you loose on that Hurricane of yours. It's all up to you from now, old boy.'

And it was, because Johnny was soon to face action.

A Fulmar recce pilot radioed he'd spotted a lightly protected Italian convoy making a dash from Naples to Palermo. Admiral

Cunningham couldn't resist letting his Swordfish and Fulmars have a crack at it. He only had one Hurricane, but an ace to fly it so Johnny became operational overnight.

The navy was already conducting trials at Scapa Flow with machines that would become known as Sea-Hurricanes, but here was an opportunity to test one in the Med. The Fulmars were to fly escort for the torpedo-laden Swordfish and take on any Fiat G-50 *Freccia* or Macchi C-200 *Saeta* fighters that might show up. The Fulmars and Italian fighters were more or less evenly matched, with the Italians having a slight edge. Johnny was the Admiral's trump card flying above the Fulmars ready to dart down and give the Italians a nasty shock with at least another fifty miles an hour speed advantage.

Illustrious' flight deck was frantic. Firstly the Swordfish came up from the hangar and lined up along the flight deck. One by one their engines coughed into life until the air pulsed with the vibrations from shuddering prop. Several minutes passed before the engine oil and cylinder-head temperatures rose to operating limits. On-board hydraulic jacks unfurled the first plane's wings. It taxied to the catapult and was immediately airborne. Other planes followed at precise intervals. Once the Swordfish were airborne to fly into formation, the Fulmars took their turn, following the same procedure.

Being fastest Johnny was the last away, but soon caught up with the leading aircraft. It was nice to feel a fully armed and fuelled Hurricane strapped to his back once more.

The recce plane had reported the Italian convoy accurately. Twenty merchant ships steamed southwards with four escort destroyers. Once they entered ack-ack range the Swordfish dropped to the wave tops. Their speed wasn't spectacular, but their pilots were well trained and truly battle-harden by then.

Through scattered cloud, Johnny saw the torpedoes drop and carve their way towards their targets. The destroyers opened up, but were unable to depress their big guns low enough to hit the Swordfish. Nevertheless lighter guns laid down a barrage of lead into the oncoming bi-planes.

While one Fulmar flight maintained altitude, alert for fighters, a dozen other planes attacked, dive-bombing and strafing the decks in turn. Johnny estimated most of the ships including two of the escort destroyers had been hit and some erupted in flames. The FAA looked like it was having things all its way until a *Freccia* squadron flew in and a dog-fight was on.

Time to go to work, Johnny boy.

He picked a target. A *Freccia* had latched onto a Fulmar, worrying it with short machinegun bursts. No one was expecting an attack from above, so Johnny easily tucked in behind the Italian fighter. The enemy pilot was so intent on finishing off the Fulmar, Johnny flew within yards and squeezed the control stick trigger button. A two second burst was enough. Shells scythed from the *Freccia* cockpit to its engine cowls. Flaming debris exploded from the front section slicing into the wing fuel tanks.

Johnny pulled up and banked to starboard, avoiding any shrapnel from the enemy plane which broke in two sections that tumbled into the sea. There was no parachute. Johnny used his excess speed to climb above the dog-fight. Whether the other Italian pilots were aware of his Hurricane was unclear. They still seemed intent on duking it out with the Fulmars. To be fair the Italians weren't expecting to come up against a Hurricane, and in the mind-spinning melee of a dog-fight, a Fulmar and Hurricane looked similar. The *Freccia* pilots had only a split second to decide which aircraft to engage. Whether it proved to be an evenly-matched Fulmar or the lone Hurricane was just a matter of luck.

Johnny took out two more *Freccias* in much the same way as the first, by which time the Swordfish had all completed their torpedo runs and were heading back to *Illustrious*. The Fulmars didn't hang around. Their job was done and they broke off the fight to follow the Swordfish, weaving randomly to shake off any tenacious Italians.

Johnny formed the rear guard. He damaged another *Freccia*, but the Italian was able to turn clear and limp back to base. Johnny never discovered whether he made it or not.

Now comes the flipping dangerous bit, Johnny thought as *Illustrious* appeared on the horizon. He radioed his fuel status and was placed in a landing queue by the carrier's air traffic controller.

'That went well,' Commander Hardy said rather too smugly in Johnny's opinion.

The FAA aircrews had assembled in the briefing room looking pretty pleased with themselves. Reconnaissance photographs confirmed they'd destroyed half a dozen enemy ships including a destroyer. Some had sunk while others were reduced to blazing hulks. Several other vessels were damaged and either at a stand-still undergoing repairs or steaming back to Naples. They'd lost interest in Palermo and North Africa for the time being.

The FAA aircraft had suffered some damage, but all pilots had flown back to the carrier successfully. One Swordfish's controls were too shot up for the pilot to attempt a deck landing, so he ditched beside the carrier. The aircrew were recovered in just minutes.

'The convoy didn't get through,' Hardy continued, 'which means the Ities will be denied vital supplies for some time to come. And I must say a special thanks to our Canadian chum,' Hardy continued. 'The sooner we get Sea-Hurricanes operational, the better.'

'I'll prepare a report, sir,' Johnny said. 'Things like beefing up the undercarriage and salt eradication. Stuff I've noticed. They've probably come up with the same thoughts at Scapa Flow, but I'll add my two bob's worth.'

'Excellent,' Hardy beamed.

He was already planning another raid on the Italian convoy to mop up any stragglers or finish off immobilised ships. However the FAA was going to have to do without Johnny Witherspoon.

'Your orders just came through,' Hardy informed him. 'Take off tomorrow at first light for Eleusis Field.'

'I was expecting to ferry a plane from Alexandria.'

'It seems their Lordships have other ideas, old boy. Things are hotting up in Greece. We'll have sailed within range by tomorrow morning. Our tech-boys are fitting a new fangled Sherman Fairchild camera and a shutter switch wired up to your joy-stick. It's a bit of a jury-rig, but our intelligence boffins would like you take some snaps if you see anything interesting, or even if you just think it's interesting.'

'Sure, but I'm not an aerial recce trained pilot.'

'Just play it as you see it, there's a good chap.'

Johnny went on deck to check out his plane. The camera casing was bolted to one of the belly covering panels, using the existing screw holes, so when it was removed the aircraft would be returned to its original configuration.

Once satisfied the camera was secure, Johnny turned to face half-a-dozen FAA aircrew, three pilots and three observer-navigator sub-lieutenants. They were barely more than teenagers, but so were most of the pilots Johnny had flown with — and against — during the Battle of Britain.

'We'd like to thank you,' one of the pilots said offering his hand.

Johnny hadn't had time to meet many of the navy aircrew, which included these young men.

'You're very welcome, I'm sure,' Johnny replied. 'For whatever it is I've done for you.'

'Just saved our lives,' one of the observers blurted.

'We were all in Fulmars trying to shake off Ities when you sorted them out.'

'In that case I'm only too pleased to have been of service.'

'Yep, the Fulmar is OK for ops way out to sea where there's no fighter cover, but we're not much of a match for purpose built fighters.'

'We hear the Ities are putting bigger engines in their *Freccias* and *Macchis*,' the observer said.

'So the sooner you get Sea-Hurricanes the better, eh?'

'That's about it. Come on, we'd like to buy you a drink — each.'

*

Johnny wisely stuck to beer and turned in early. The following morning dawned fine and the forecast was for clear weather all day. Johnny checked with *Illustrious'* duty navigation officer who supplied the carrier's exact position and route maps to Eleusis Field. He didn't expect any navigational problems as he was familiar with the area and had visited Athens on a number of occasions.

What he didn't want to run into was an Italian fighter squadron. Despite its extra speed, a lone Hurricane wouldn't stand a chance — it wasn't *that* much faster than **Regia Aeronautica** machines. So Johnny climbed to thirty-thousand feet, which Italian fighters were capable of reaching, but the air was so thin, no one would be dog-fighting at that altitude. Indeed, care had to be taken controlling the airspeed. Above twenty-thousand feet the performance dropped off as Johnny flew closer to the stall speed. The Hurricane could actually climb higher, but Johnny reckoned he was safe enough.

Soon he started picking out landmarks as he reached familiar territory. Athens spread out before him and he started descending, spiralling down over Eleusis Field. He wasn't over-impressed after he landed and taxied to his parking area. A dozen other Hurricanes were dispersed randomly and covered with camouflage netting studded with tree branches and foliage.

The workshops, mess accommodation and admin facilities were all under canvas or in a couple of nearby stone huts. Diesel generators chugged in the background supplying electricity via some suspect-looking power lines strung along poles which sloped this way and that.

But the ground crew were sharp enough. After marshalling Johnny's Hurricane to its parking spot, a fitter climbed onto the wing to help with the restraint and parachute straps.

'Welcome to the sunny Med, sir. I'm Corporal Abrams, engine fitter.'

'Thanks, Abrams you're just the bloke I need. Will you give the under-cart a thorough going over? The last half-a-dozen landings have been on a carrier flight deck.'

Abrams winced visibly.

'Say no more, sir. I'll get our riggers right onto it and I'll check out the Merlin with a fine tooth comb. I expect we'll find salt in the nooks and crannies.'

'Good man. I'm Flight-lieutenant Witherspoon. I'm attached to 80-Squadron. I hope I've come to the right place.'

'Well, you've come to 80-Squadron, sir. But I dunno if I'd call it the right place.'

'Is anywhere while this bloody war lasts? The navy techs attached a camera to the under fuselage. Could your blokes remove the film, please? The *intelo* will want to have a look. Also I'll have to get my duffle from the starboard ammo magazine.'

Abrams looked aghast.

'You came across the Med with unloaded guns, sir?'

'Less weight. I cruised above pretty well anything they could send after me.'

'Not to worry, sir. I'll get one of the lads to drop your kit at the O's.'

'Thanks, I'd better report to the CO.'

'HQ is just over there sir,' Abrams said, pointing to a ramshackle hut sited in an olive grove which was handy for extra concealment.

Squadron-leader 'Tap' Jones turned out to be an all-business sort of man. A South African flight-lieutenant lounged in a director's chair beside Jones' folding table he used as a desk. The officer introduced himself as Pat Pattle.

'The OC's sending Pat over to 33-Squadron to straighten them out, so I'll give you his flight, Witherspoon,' Jones said. ' You'll get your fair share of dog-fights and glory, but we multi-task around here. We escort our Blenheims on bombing raids, ground attack, intercepting Dago bombers, recon and anything else our lords and masters desire. Normally we'd take you for a few *famil* flights, but we're stretched pretty thin and I believe you know your way around.'

'No sweat, sir. I was sent here because I know the area. I've flown in and out of Athens dozens of times from the Albanian Coast. The FAA techs installed a camera to my plane to gather photos and *Intel* about what Jerry is up to.'

'You think they'll join this show? We've just been up against Ities until now.' Pattle asked.

'That's what Whitehall fears, so it's up to us to find out, isn't it?'

Just then a young flying officer entered the CO's office. He saluted and turned to Johnny.

'Dave Coke, blow me down,' Johnny said, pumping the young man's hand.

'Obviously you know each other,' Jones observed.

'I met Johnny when I was with 257-Squadron at Northolt, sir,' Coke said.

Johnny was pleased to find a friend in Dave Coke, because chums were hard to come by in 80-Squadron. It had been the same during the Battle of Britain and in most operational units. Aircrews often avoided close friendships, because so many of them failed to return from missions, it was just too depressing.

So once again Johnny was put to work doing what he did best. The following day he flew to Tikala only about sixty miles from the Albanian border. 33-Squadron was the other Hurricane equipped unit and both squadrons operated from Tikala from time to time. The 80-Squadron technicians modified the camera pod to a permanent fixture with a more reliable control-column shutter switch.

Johnny flew several sorties a day over the Albanian, Yugoslavia and Bulgarian borders. Without any particular training he soon got the hang of aerial reconnaissance. He photographed Italian positions on the western front and the Eastern flank along what was called the Metaxas Line on the Macedonian and Thracian border. It was named after Ioannis Metaxas, Greece's Prime Minister and general tough guy who'd died of a throat disease in January leaving a bit of a power vacuum in the Grecian hierarchy.

The Metaxas Line served the same purpose as the French Maginot Line except the Greeks had made a better job of it. The Italians had given up on the Eastern front to concentrate on the Albanian border. But they were also bogged down there, slugging it out with the Greek Army in a desultory stalemate. To be fair the winter had been unusually harsh and the border mountain passes were often snowbound and impassable, but Hitler was growing impatient. It was a pretty badly kept secret he wanted to invade Russia before summer, but feared being outflanked from the south. So he needed Greece as an impenetrable bastion between Axis territory and Allied forces in North Africa.

And if the Italians weren't up to the job, he'd have to send his own boys. In March the *Reich* launched another *blitzkrieg* from

Yugoslavia. The *Nazis* had already brow-beaten Yugoslavian Prince Regent Paul into allowing German forces to pass through his country, using the railway network while they were at it.

The winter may have been severe, but once again no one had bothered to tell the Germans. *Wehrmacht* and *Waffen SS* storm-troopers were a tough crowd who weren't going to let a little frost-bite stand in their way.

Then one day, which was proving no more remarkable than any other, Johnny spotted a speck a few miles ahead and several thousand feet below him. As the image grew closer and larger, Johnny recognised the plane as a Focke-Wulf 189 *Uhu* which translated as Eagle Owl. It was a twin engine, twin tail boom aircraft with an almost entirely Perspex central fuselage. Black cross insignia definitely identified it as a *Luftwaffe* machine.

The *Uhu* wasn't fast, but the clear fuselage and multi-crew made it difficult to sneak up on. Well Johnny was going to have a go at it anyway. Any German recce plane needed to be disposed of.

Johnny banked his Hurricane and dived towards the enemy plane. He was soon spotted and the rear gunner sent a couple of blasts to meet him, but the shots fell short. Johnny knew his machinegun shells had gravity on their side, so he squeezed off a short burst just as he reached the German gunner's range. After a second burst the *Uhu* pilot banked into a sharp starboard turn.

The German plane was impressively agile and as much as Johnny tried to follow he flashed past and was forced to climb again for another pass. Once again Johnny dived towards the enemy. This time he waited to open fire. German tracers streamed past, but Johnny held his nerve. A sixth sense told him the German pilot was going to take avoiding action at any second. Johnny squeezed his gun trigger.

Bingo!

Shells ripped into the Perspex fuselage. Johnny was now so close he saw blood smeared over the greenhouse panels. He figured he'd hit the pilot as the *Uhu* pitched forward and nose-dived almost vertically. The pilot was most likely slumped over the controls as it continued heading earthwards accelerating far beyond is maximum structural limit. Finally the fuselage could bear no more and the wings ripped from the main spar and the sections plummeted to their fiery doom.

But Johnny had fallen into bad habits. Although his wing magazines had been fully loaded, his job was to take photographs, not go glory hunting. Suddenly tracers flashed past his cockpit.

Bloody hell!

Johnny peered into his rear view mirror then spun his head as far as possible. Two twin engine planes were on his tail. From their profile he knew exactly what they were — Messerschmitt-110s. Maybe not quite as fast as his Hurricane, but fast enough, well armed and there were two of them right on his tail. Turning wasn't an option.

Johnny rolled the Hurricane on its back and pulled through the bottom half loop, carving thousands of feet in altitude. He hauled the column back with all his strength until he greyed out. All colour drained from his vision due to blood-loss. He tensed his stomach muscles to help circulation to his upper torso.

The airspeed indicator flickered in the red zone well above maximum IAS. Johnny used that excess speed to gain precious altitude. As he pulled from the dive the G-force lessened and colour returned. He quickly picked up the Me-110s which had turned one-hundred-and-eighty degrees and now flew directly towards him.

Johnny knew each Me-110 was armed with two cannons and four forward facing machineguns. He'd faced them over the Channel. He knew he could out-fly a single machine, but two—and maybe more he hadn't seen —was a big ask.

Time to cut and run. Yeah, but just one more go...

Johnny now played a game of cat and mouse with the *Luftwaffe*. He didn't fly directly towards the oncoming fighter-bombers, but banked erratically. One of the Me-110s opened up, but a little too soon and the tracers ducked away. Once again Johnny used his instinct for the optimum time to open fire.

His first burst smashed into one of the Me-110s. Johnny didn't hang around to see if the plane was destroyed. He dived, gathering speed then banked away, climbed rapidly before the remaining German could latch onto his tail and made a full throttle dash for home.

After Johnny landed a quick inspection of his Hurricane revealed no bullet holes, but everyone was very eager to hear what he had to say. Indeed his observation of German encroachment was confirmed by many of the eccentric Englishmen, including Dennis Mortimer, who roamed the Balkans as un-official secret agents spying on anything anti-British. Now signals were received, either through Bletchley Park or directly from Alexandria that the *Wehrmacht* was on its way.

All through February Johnny picked up more and more evidence that German units were advancing towards Thrace and Macedonia. He also encountered more German reconnaissance planes sniffing around, but now they usually had a Me-110 escort, so he ensured he led his flight when he tackled them. The RAF fighters had chalked up an impressive record with Pat Pattle claiming a prolific number of kills, while Johnny added two Fiat G-

50 fighters and three Italian bombers. But more *Luftwaffe* planes showed up every day.

Then Me-109s joined the fight, meaning the German lines had advanced within the fighters' limited range. If the 109 and 110s weren't bad enough, they were joined by Ju-88 twin engine multi-role aircraft. Their speed almost matched the Hurricane and they were heavily armed with forward machineguns supplemented by upper and lower rear guns. And the *Luftwaffe* had squadrons of them.

Chapter 28 — The Last Hurricane

In March the BEF had launched *Operation Lustre*, transporting what was known as 'W' Force consisting of the 2nd New Zealand and 6th Australian Division elements along with the British 1st Armoured Brigade across the Mediterranean to help the Greeks stop the German advance. However there was no talk of bolstering the RAF's strength in Greece.

Soon boisterous and independent Australians and Kiwis were streaming northwards. They were confident and keen to give the *Wehrmacht* a bloody nose, but just two divisions seemed pretty thin on the ground, from what Johnny had spotted on his recon missions over Albania, Yugoslavia and Bulgaria.

'Ruddy hell, I hope it's not going to be France in '40 all over again,' Johnny commented one evening.

'I dunno,' Pattle replied. 'I mean how many bloody Jerries are there? They've occupied just about the whole of Europe all the way to Norway. There can't be too many of them left to spread around.'

'I'd be a lot happier if we had more crates.'

Johnny was right. Air superiority was to prove decisive. Although the RAF still gave a good account of itself they were hopelessly outnumbered. German raids over military targets, ports and Athens itself were now daily events. Sure the *Luftwaffe* lost planes, but the Hurricanes were being whittled down as well.

Johnny couldn't remember the exact date, but sometime in early April reinforcements arrived in the form of a lone Hurricane. The pilot parked the plane close to the maintenance tents and slid the cockpit canopy open.

'I say, would you mind awfully giving me a hand,' he called to the ground crew. 'My ruddy legs have gone to sleep.'

Johnny joined Abrams and an aircraft rigger who finally extricated the pilot from his seat. No wonder he was cramped, he was a long limbed, gangly maybe six-and-a-half-foot tall pilot-officer.

'I wasn't designed to sit for nearly five hours in this ruddy crate,' he complained as he stomped around to regain blood circulation. 'Thanks awfully,' he added addressing Johnny. 'Pilot-Officer Roald Dahl, reporting, sir.'

'Pleased to meet you and call me Johnny. Save "sir" for the old man. He's over in that hut beside those tents. Don't expect him to be overjoyed to see you. What he wants are a few new fighter wings.'

'You should 'ave joined Bomber Command, sir,' Corporal Abrams addressed Dahl cheerfully. 'Plenty of leg-room in a ruddy great 'Allifax, there is, sir.'

Dahl had flown from Palestine which had just about doubled his Hurricane hours, so it was fortunate he was a quick learner because the air battle for Athens was imminent. 80-Squadron had barely a dozen serviceable Hurricanes to protect the city.

Throughout April Italian and ever increasing *Luftwaffe* bombing raids pounded Athens, the surrounding ports and military units which not only included the Anzac divisions, but RAF airfields. Several times a day 80-Squadron Hurricanes were scrambled to deal with them. For a while planes took-off arbitrarily to be ready for the enemy, but sometimes the Italians arrived late and the Hurricanes had to land and refuel before they'd finished off the invaders.

'We're between a rock and a hard place,' Johnny complained. 'If we get airborne in timely fashion we risk running low on petrol. What hope is there with no radar, and only a few local enthusiasts with binoculars on a hill north of the city? By the time they spot the enemy inbound and phone the message through it's too late. We're caught with our pants down.'

'Why don't *we* just send up a look-out?' Pilot-Officer Dahl suggested. 'He'll have time to climb to altitude and spot anything coming for miles. He'll be in line-of-sight VHF range, so even with our rubbish wireless comms he should get the message through. If the rest of the squadron stay close to our kites, we'll have a good chance of meeting the bombers head on. We rotate the spotter planes when they're low on fuel.'

So they tried Dahl's plan which worked pretty well especially after the squadron started getting more and more timely warnings from the Enigma code breakers at Bletchley Park and Mediterranean MI(R) operatives like Dennis Mortimer. They were occasionally let down by the poor quality of their radios, but it was the best they could do.

Nevertheless air-raids intensified now German fighter protection was within range, so dog-fights were back on the agenda. Newly promoted Squadron-leader Pat Pattle soon licked 30-Squadron into shape and they joined the fight with 80-Squadron. Pattle did a sterling job reviving 30-Squadron's discipline and moral and the unit now performed admirably.

*

20 April 1941

Johnny awoke to all sorts of clamour around the base. He sprang from his camp bed, donned his cap and rushed outside still in his pyjamas. Airman busied themselves dismantling storage tents and packing spare equipment into awaiting lorries.

'What's all the fuss about?' Johnny called to Corporal Abrams as he rushed past.

'They're abandoning Athens, sir. The CO wants us to start packing non-essential kit. He reckons we'll be pulling out anytime now. We can't stay here without the army to defend our position.'

'Bloody hell, it *is* France all over again. Shit!'

Roald Dahl walked by.

'CO wants everyone in his tent right now,' he said, eyeing Johnny appearance. 'PJs and all,' he added with a grin.

Johnny was appalled to see Air-Commodore Jack Grigson standing next to Tap Jones. Grigson had been around from time to time and Johnny had met him once.

Grigson however had more important things on his mind. He'd travelled to most of the Allied positions and knew just what a parlous situation confronted them. He was also painfully aware how pitifully small his air force was. The Anzacs were withdrawing in good order, but a detachment of Kiwis was already surrounded at the legendary Thermopylae Pass in grave danger of suffering the same fate as the heroic 300 Spartans.

'We're scrambling right away,' Tap Jones said. 'Admiral Cunningham is sending anything that can float to Piraeus Harbour to evacuate whatever and whomever they can take south. Spies are crawling all over the city, so Jerry'll find out in no time.'

The pilots exchanged looks.

'The sky'll be black with Jerries before we know it. Let's get up there and shoot down as many of the buggers as we can. C'mon what are you standing around for? Get upstairs!'

Johnny had just time to jam on his flying boots. The pilots flew in shorts and shirts anyway. Mediterranean springtime weather was clement and dog-fighting was sweat-raising work. In moments fifteen Hurricane engines roared into life. In minutes the planes rattled down the strip spearheaded by Pat Pattle. Tap Jones was very much an operational control CO by then, leaving the gung-ho cavalry charges to Pattle.

Yet before half the Hurricanes were airborne a speck popped above the horizon. A lone Me-110 looking for trouble streaked towards the airfield as ground crews raced to their machinegun posts.

Johnny's plane led the last flight of four Hurricanes to line up for take-off. There were no radio communications between aircraft or the ground, so there was no warning of the German attack. Visibility was always a problem from nose high tail-wheel aircraft and Hurricanes were no exception. The ground personnel saw the threat before the taxiing pilots.

Just at that critical moment Johnny was distracted as Air Commodore Grigson marched to the edge of the take-off strip with a .303 rifle in hand. He was accompanied by Corporal Abrams and another airman, who both had rifles slung over each shoulder.

What the blue blazes?

But there was no time to speculate. Johnny's flight turned into wind and began their take-off roll. As they built up speed Johnny spotted the incoming *Messerschmitt*.

Oh shit!

As the Hurricanes sped past, Grigson levelled his rifle and emptied the five-shot magazine towards the oncoming *Luftwaffe* plane. Without hesitation he handed the empty rifle to Abrams who held out a loaded weapon. Grigson emptied a second magazine just as Johnny's Hurricane flashed by.

Luckily the Hurricanes reached take-off speed before the *Messerschmitt* opened up. The flight now had speed and manoeuvrability making them difficult targets. Nevertheless tracers streaked by uncomfortably close. Although now out of view, the German shells gouged into the airstrip, hacking out turf and rock. Grigson seemingly oblivious of the machinegun fire erupting all around him kept firing while Abrams and his admirable companion reloaded the rifle magazines with remarkable composure.

The action was over in seconds. The Me-110 roared overhead only feet above Grigson then soared skywards heading back northwards. Remarkably the Air-Commodore and his two stalwart loaders remained unscathed.

Meanwhile Johnny's flight caught up with the squadron although even with all 30 and 80-Squadrons' aircraft combined, fifteen planes hardy merited the title. One advantage was it didn't take long to sort themselves into formation and head for Piraeus, Athens' main port. There was no sign on the maverick Me-110 which had brassed up the airstrip moments before.

The city sprawled below the Hurricanes with smoke billowing from unquenched fires of previous bombing raids. Ahead lay Piraeus crammed with vessels including tankers, freighters, destroyers, brand new Fairmile dog-boats and lowly caiques. Although the vessels were armed to different levels, they were all sitting ducks.

Soon the *Luftwaffe* showed up in spades.

Bloody hell! There must be more than a hundred of the buggers.

Johnny Witherspoon's estimate was pretty close. No one knows for certain, but estimates of between one hundred and two hundred German planes led by Ju-88s were reported from several sources. The sight of so many German planes was as magnificent as it was terrifying. Accompanying the 88s were flights of *Stuka* dive-bombers and dependable Dorniers. The entire sky was speckled with sinister black shapes in a spiteful mood.

How does the Luftwaffe have so many planes and we have so few?

As the Germans approached it became clear Piraeus was their target, not the city. The Hurricane pilots realised there was no time for fancy formations, it was dive in and shoot down as many planes as possible. There was no time to look out for your pals. It was every man for himself.

The choice of enemy targets was almost confusing. Johnny knew he must select a target and stick to it. Changing his mind in mid-air was just a wasted opportunity.

Like sharks chasing a sardine bait-ball, Johnny grinned as he saw his shots rip into a *Stuka* fuselage. The dive-bomber spiralled away, but there was no sign that the crew escaped. There was no time to dwell as Johnny climbed to mark his next victim. He glimpsed other hurricanes in the chase, but couldn't follow their progress. The Ju-87 *Stuka*s were beastly, deadly-accurate weapons platforms, but they were slow, easy targets so Johnny concentrated on them.

After taking another one out he was feeling pretty cocky until the Me-109 and 110s arrived. Now the hunters were in danger of becoming the hunted and it all became a haze of punishing flying, aiming his guns and avoiding fighters trying to get on his tail and into their gun-sights. Mid-air collisions were an extra hazard.

The dog-fight lasted around half-an-hour, but Johnny felt he'd flown all day. He was exhausted and drenched with sweat. His plane was also exhausted. Flying at full throttle guzzles gas and it was time to return to Eleusis field.

Johnny touched down with near-empty tanks, bumping over the rough spots of hastily filled bomb craters and turf ripped to shreds by cannon fire. Roald Dahl landed close behind him. The tall fellow was almost in a daze and Johnny knew exactly how he felt.

They inspected their aircraft for damage with Corporal Abrams who tut-tutted as he stuck his fist through various cannon-shot holes.

'Just as well they're bloody 'Urricanes,' he commented. 'Your ruddy Spits might be glamorous equipment, but they wouldn't take the damage your planes 'ave. Blow me down you're both lucky to get 'ome. But we'll get 'em airborne again in a jiffy.'

'How did you go?' Dahl asked Johnny.

'Bagged two for certain and maybe another, but in the melee I can't be sure. What about you?'

'Not a clue, old boy — No bloody idea at all.'

Dahl was inclined to be refreshingly honest.

'Never mind, you're back in one piece and you probably scared the shit out of a few Jerries.'

Johnny Witherspoon and Roald Dahl may have returned safely, but that was not the case for others. One third of the squadron failed to land at Eleusis Field. Pat Pattle was among them. There was always hope that missing aviators had managed to bail out, but when that could be established was anyone's guess.

There was little time to feel miserable. While Abrams and his ground crew patched up the damaged Hurricanes, everyone pitched in to squeeze whatever would fit into the lorries, ready to move south. Evacuation points were established at any feasible port, but the drivers had yet to receive orders to a particular destination. Unfortunately the *Luftwaffe* now completely controlled the skies and all ports were fair game.

The next day the remaining Hurricanes were dispersed across the field, under tree cover wherever possible. The Germans strafed a couple of times causing considerable damage, verifying the writing was on the wall. So Tap Jones gathered his remaining — some said pathetically few — pilots for a final briefing.

'There's no point in prettying this up,' he began. 'We're hopelessly outnumbered and vulnerable here, so we're pulling out to Argos.'

He jabbed the map on his folding table, pointing to a spot across the Isthmus of Corinth. I can't say it'll be much better, but those are the AOC's orders.'

It was only a short flight to Argos, but the trucks took all day to relocate.

'Bloody hell,' Abrams complained. 'The roads are sod-awful at the best of the times, but they're clogged solid with retreating Anzacs, refugees and there's abandoned kit all over. We had to clear the way a dozen times. Jerry blasted the road everywhere, but missed us.'

Corporal Abrams assessment was spot on. The Germans surged into Greece ploughing any resistance aside. On 24 April Grigson gave the order to cut and run. By then only half-a-dozen Hurricanes remained.

'Fly 'em to Crete,' he ordered Tap Jones. 'Choose your best and most experienced pilots for the job. All other pilots will be flown to North Africa where we hope we'll reform the squadron and have another crack at Jerry in decent numbers.'

Tap compiled a list of six ferry pilots including Johnny Witherspoon and the other five most experienced pilots. Later in the day a de Havilland Rapide light transport plane landed in a nearby field to hopefully avoid being noticed by roaming *Messerschmitts*. The pilot was a nervous fellow who couldn't wait to take off. To his credit he took everyone who could squeeze on board including the six-and-a-half foot tall Roald Dahl who'd probably be as cramped on the evacuation flight as he was squashed into his Hurricane cockpit for nearly five hours.

'What about you, sir?' Johnny asked Tap Jones as he hadn't included himself in the ferry pilots.

'Don't worry, the AOC and I have a rendezvous on the coast. A Sunderland will meet us and we'll fly to Alex from there.'

Privileges of rank, Johnny thought, but realised it was unworthy. Whatever their personalities, the RAF needed all its senior officers right then.

The critically overweight Rapide barely scraped the tree-line on take-off. But they got away and reached North Africa safely.

Before clambering into the cockpit, Johnny farewelled the ground crew who'd take what they could to an evacuation point and destroy everything else.

'Good luck to you, corporal,' he said pumping Abrams' hand. 'I hope to see you in North Africa.'

'Me too, sir. Don't worry me and the lads'll be fine. Look after yourself.'

The six planes roared into life and once again the *Luftwaffe* decided to make an appearance...

Chapter 29 — Sea Cruise

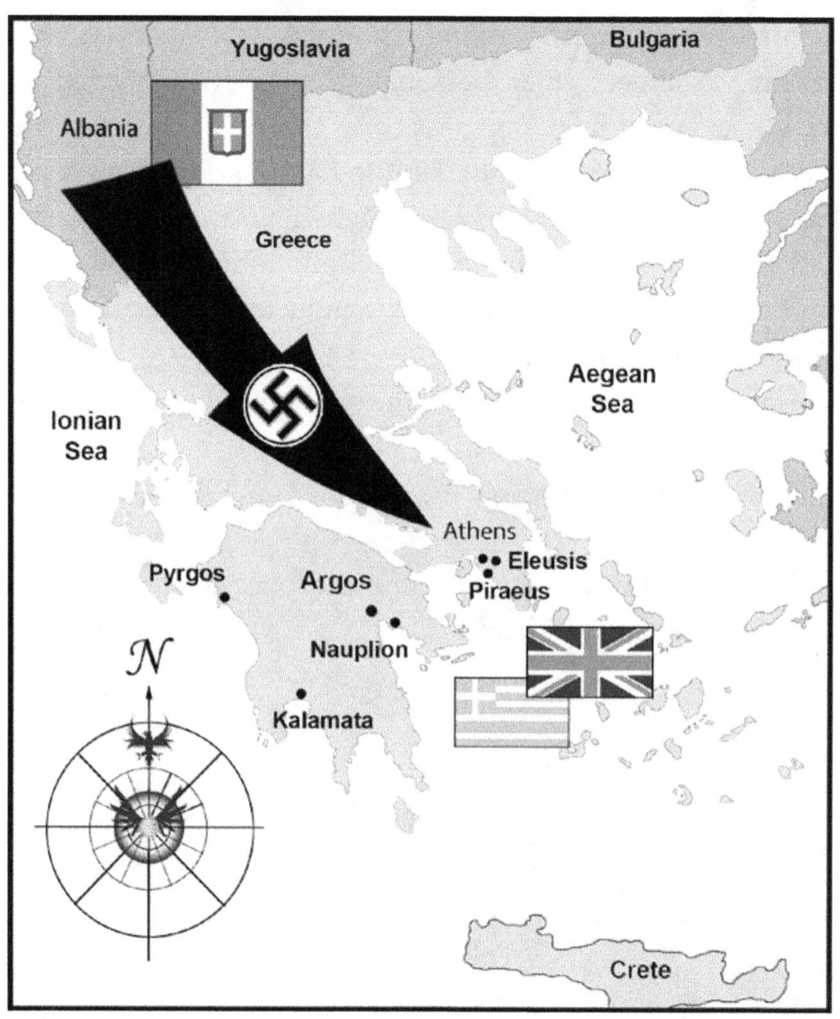

Five Hurricanes began their take-off roll as two flights of Me-109 and 110s roared in for the kill. The wing leading edges erupted in smoke and flame as cannon shells and machinegun bullets streaked towards Argus Field. Johnny piloted the sixth plane to taxi forward. Abrams had barely pulled the chocks from the

Hurricane wheels when the air was filled with shrieking bullets tearing through the plane's wings and ruptured its fuel tanks.

The wing exploded in flames and tumbled for yards after it was ripped from the fuselage. Abrams was blasted face down into the dirt as the ball of flame swathed over him before dissolving into oblivion. Abrams' hair was singed, but otherwise he was none the worse for wear. Recovering his wits he leapt to his feet and dashed to the Hurricane which now lay slewed to one side.

Johnny wasted no time. He tried to leave his seat before remembering to unbuckle his lap strap and shoulder harness. The cockpit was still open so he clambered onto the remaining wing and jumped, landing right on top of Abrams.

'Time to get out of Dodge, corporal,' he yelled. 'The other wing and reserve tanks will go any second now.'

Johnny was wise to exit the aircraft in haste. A twenty-eight gallon reserve petrol tank was fitted just behind the engine. If it ignited the entire cockpit would be engulfed in flames.

Along with the other aircraftmen they dashed for a nearby olive grove and dived for cover just as the *Messerschmitts* rolled in for a second strafing run. Gunfire rattled once more as the enemy flew in unopposed. The remaining five Hurricanes were away safely, but didn't hang around to tackle the German pilots who'd worked out the survivors were hiding under tree-cover.

Bullets raked the olive groves shredding branches, leaves and fruit into lethal confetti. Two men were hit by cannon fire, their bodies exploding into crimson spray, leaving only a smudge of pulp where a living being once lay. Mercifully fighters have limited endurance and their raid was short-lived. As they peeled away in triumph, Johnny was left to count the cost.

He tried to retrieve the dead men's dog-tags, but they were nowhere to be found. Nevertheless Abrams identified them from what was left. He'd served with them for over two years now and they'd been his pals.

'Kraut bastards,' he snarled. 'I wish I could kill every stinkin' last one of 'em.'

'Come on, Henry,' Johnny said using Abrams Christian name for the first time. 'We'll get even, just wait and see. But right now we've got to get cracking if we're going to live to fight another day.'

Abrams' truck was unscathed and as the other surviving vehicles pulled away there was only Johnny left to hitch a ride. Abrams' two chums were to accompany him, but there wasn't even time to bury their remains.

'Where to, Henry,' Johnny asked. 'I'm in your hands. I was supposed to fly out remember.'

'Nauplion, sir. It's the closest port. We'll get there easily.'

Henry Abrams couldn't have been more wrong. Nauplion was indeed only a few miles from Argos, but they'd barely left the airfield when the road became jam-packed with refugees, yet Johnny saw very few soldiers and they looked bewildered, lost and nervous.

Motor and pedestrian traffic clogged every foot of the road which was sometimes sealed, but often gravel-base or just a dirt track. Countless bicycles, horse and hand carts and even baby carriages edged forward surrounding trucks, buses and cars. An abandoned Mk1 Matilda tank stood smouldering beside the road and ignored by the seething mass of passing humanity. Drivers moved at a crawl, fearful of crushing the refugees on all sides.

Shortly a harassed RN lieutenant clambered onto the running-board. He didn't have to flag Abrams down as his truck was hardly moving at the time.

'How long will it take to the port, sir?' Abrams asked.

'I'm afraid that won't happen, corporal. Nauplion is clogged with refugees and we've orders to divert all military personnel to Kalamata further west. We're trying to prioritise and get combatants away first. All evac ships have been sent there.'

'My officer 'ere's a combatant. The last fighter pilot.' in Greece.'

'Quite so I'm sure, but you'd better head for Kalamata as quickly as you can. It's about sixty miles and you might get there by night-fall. No one will be boarding until after dark anyway. The evac ships are standing off-shore where they at least stand a chance against the bloody bombers.'

'You're sure there will be ships at Kalamata?' Johnny asked warily.

'As I said according to my intelligence, all available vessels have been despatched to Kalamata or Pyrgos, but for how long is anyone's guess.'

'What do you reckon,' Johnny asked Abrams who merely shrugged with a *you're-the-officer* expression.

'Can you take those chaps with you?' the naval officer asked.

It was only then Johnny noticed a squad of Diggers crouched on the grass verge, smoking while eyeing the RAF lorry with suspicious intent. They'd walked a long way in a short time and their boots were worn to tatters, but they were all well armed with Tommy guns, ammunition bandoliers and hand grenades clipped to their shoulder straps.

It seemed the Diggers may have been retreating, but they were ready for a scrap if it came to one and this group of Anzacs looked in a bellicose mood. Perhaps justifiably they felt they'd been let down by high command and lack of air support.

'Henry, what exactly do we have in the back of this truck?' Johnny asked.

'Everything got tossed in so quick I ain't done an inventory to the last detail, but mostly just tools, spare plugs, gaskets, bolts, you know — small stuff.'

'So nothing that'll really help Jerry if he gets his hands on it.'

'Dunno, anything might 'elp the bloody Krauts, sir.'

'Not if we blow it up.'

'With what?'

'I'm going to talk to those Aussies.'

The Australians didn't stand or show any sign of acknowledging an approaching officer. There were eight of them, which was light on for a squad, so Johnny was under no illusions these men had seen bitter fighting and suffered losses.

'Do you fellows want a lift to Kalamata?' Johnny offered.

'What bloody well for,' one of the soldiers replied sullenly. 'We might be shagged out, but we'll outrun that bloody heap of shit you've got there.'

'Valid point, in fact I sometimes wonder if we'll get much further.'

The Australian spokesman merely shrugged.

'This bottle-neck will be a turkey-shoot if the *Luftwaffe* shows up and you're right in the middle of it.'

'What's bloody well new? We've been strafed every bloody mile since leaving the front.'

'That naval officer I just spoke to reckons there'll be no more evacuations from Nauplion. We have no choice but to head over to Kalamata. You can come with us if you like.'

'Is that an order?'

'I somehow think you blokes haven't been taking orders for a while, but if you join us, that'll have to change.'

Johnny was sure he'd made any impression, so he thought he'd explain the ground rules.

'Now I know you don't think much of the RAF, but that's not because we haven't been in the sky all day, every day doing our share of fighting...and dying. There just weren't enough of us. My Hurricane was destroyed when I tried to take-off this morning. I was lucky not to be roasted alive.'

The Australians mellowed a little once they heard they were not the only ones doing it tough. So they set about unloading Abrams' lorry and dumping everything in a sizeable pile.

'I 'ope Jerry don't get 'is ruddy 'ands on that lot,' Abrams lamented. 'It mightn't be much, but I don't want to give them bastards nothing.'

'She'll be right, mate,' one of the Aussies said, unclipping a grenade from his shoulder strap. 'Tell them buggers to stand clear,' he added to his mates who shooed away passing refugees.

He pulled the pin and casually tossed the bomb under the jetsam while everyone dived face down in the dirt. He hadn't really thought it through. The grenade explosion wasn't huge in artillery terms, but the spray of shrapnel including nuts and bolts turned into deadly missiles. Luckily the refugees had moved far enough to avoid danger and the only damage was a number of perforations in the truck's canvas canopy.

'All aboard,' Johnny yelled after the final tinkle of tumbling metal subsided. 'Next stop Kalamata!'

*

By the time they reached Kalamata, the truck radiator was boiling and every dash-board caution light blinked constantly.

'Well Jerry didn't get us, but I think she's 'ad it, sir,' Abrams conceded. 'Engine, gearbox and diff are all shot, tires are worn bare and there's 'ardly no fuel left. I don't think we'll even 'ave to scuttle 'er.'

'Let's find a ride out of here before we talk about scuttling anything, Henry,' Johnny said. 'I'm sure there's life left in the old girl yet. But get the chaps to bring all the weapons and ammo.'

The Aussies piled out of the lorry and formed up in good order. They followed Johnny and Henry to the wharf where a number of Fairmile dog boats and caiques lined the harbour wall. The small vessels ferried soldiers and refugees to two destroyers prowling just beyond the port.

An animated row flared between a platoon of Greek troops about to embark on an older Vosper model RN gunboat. It appeared some wished to leave while others insisted they stay and fight. A young bearded RN lieutenant strode down the gangway, service revolver in hand. He raised the weapon and fired a shot into the air.

'Will you all shut up,' he yelled. 'I don't care what you do. Just make up your bloody minds.'

Whether the Greeks understood what he said, they were in no doubt about his meaning. Yet they remained uncertain.

Blow me down, I know that bloke and that boat, Johnny thought and he was going to take advantage of the situation.

'If they don't want to go, we're ready and willing,' Johnny said, moving quickly to greet the naval officer. 'Nice to see you again, Jeremy. Can I impose on you to bail me out again?'

'Goodness me, Johnny Witherspoon, isn't it?' Jeremy St Chalfont-Smyth grinned, pumping Johnny's hand.

But there was no time for pleasantries.

'I don't have time to wait for these fellows to stop arguing. How many people do you have with you?'

'Ten including me. Aussies, but they're well armed and in a punchy mood.'

'Good, just the ticket. Get 'em aboard quick as you can while I sort these Greek chaps out. I hope at least one speaks English because I'm damn sure I'll need an interpreter.'

Johnny should have been paying attention. He was so grateful to find a familiar face and get onto a ship, especially a well armed and agile one, he didn't consider why Jeremy would need an interpreter. As it turned out the Greeks weren't arguing about who would go or stay, but where they would go if they boarded Jeremy's gunboat.

Meanwhile Henry and the Aussies were settling in. They were all getting along fine especially when Seamen Kevin Jones brewed tea and served up bully-beef sandwiches, that good old military staple.

MGB-10 still retained its original crew and although they'd seen action aplenty, so far they'd suffered no casualties. Jeremy was promoted to lieutenant somewhere along the line, but he'd quite forgotten when.

The Greek translator turned out to be a nervous, scholarly private called Loukas who didn't look at all happy to be going along. He cheered up after a cuppa and something to eat.

Jeremy didn't waste time in clearing Kalamata breakwater. Turning right, MGB-10 flashed past the destroyers and powered into the Gulf of Messina. It was pitch black until the moon rose at about ten o'clock, so Jeremy had no real idea of their course.

'Clear to starboard, skipper,' Billie Bones hailed from the bow after an hour.

'Thanks, Billie,' Jeremy acknowledged. 'Make course 220, Andy,' he added to CPO Andy Scott who manned the helm.

As the moon rose the shoreline became visible five miles away to the right. The Aussies dozed wherever they felt comfortable. They didn't ask questions, but simply slept when they had the opportunity. Strangely for all their insubordination, they were content if led by a competent officer, which they deemed Johnny Witherspoon to be.

Johnny joined Jeremy on the bridge just in time to hear the young skipper alter course once more.

'Bring her round to 330, Andy. That'll keep us well off-shore.'

330 degrees, that's bloody north-west!

'Uh, Jeremy, I don't want to tell you your business, but isn't Crete *back* the other way.'

'Absolutely, old boy,' Jeremy replied, altogether too cheerfully in Johnny's opinion.

He shot Jeremy a *well?* expression.

'A bit of a jolly detour I'm afraid, Johnny. We received a message from Alex to pick up some chaps in Pyrgos.'

Johnny eyed Jeremy suspiciously.

'When exactly did you receive this message?'

Jeremy looked decidedly sheepish.

'Let me help you. Was it *before* or *after* we got aboard?'

'Maybe a teensy-weensy bit before. Oh all right, Johnny, we were supposed to take a squad from that Greek detachment, but you saw how they were. I think they've had the shit bombed out of them.'

'I'm interested to see how the Aussies will react when you tell them you've shanghaied them into riding shotgun on your wild goose chase.'

'Steady on, old boy, I don't think you should call my orders a ruddy wild goose chase.'

'Sorry, Jeremy,' Johnny slapped the skipper on the back and grinned. 'Do you want to tell them or should I?'

'I'd better. You haven't exactly heard the worst of it yet...'

The Australians took the fact they were heading north surprisingly well in Johnny's opinion. Being part of a unit with meaningful work seemed to please them. Also they'd had their best meal in a fortnight, which perked them up and they weren't too concerned about sailing to Pyrgos. It was still a designated evacuation port and maybe they'd transfer to a bigger ship there. Another big plus was the Germans hadn't reached Pyrgos yet as far as anyone knew.

Indeed that proved correct, in fact they spotted no Italian warships en route and weren't bothered by the *Luftwaffe*. When they arrived half-a-dozen caiques were taking soldiers aboard. They appeared to be the remnants of random units who'd been separated during the retreat.

MGB-10 pulled alongside the jetty. Although the gunboat carried spare fuel drums, CPO Andy Scott quickly arranged refuelling to ensure the tanks were full. The fuel depot was still manned by a squad of sappers who'd blow up anything left before the Germans arrived.

Meanwhile a fellow hailed Jeremy. He looked to be in his mid-thirties beneath an unkempt and dubiously hygienic beard. He was followed by four equally shabby individuals Johnny took to be partisans. The leader however spoke with a plummy Eton-imbued accent. It also appeared Jeremy and the ill-kept aristocrat were acquainted. In fact they were close family friends.

'Hello there, Jeremy,' he greeted. 'Thanks for coming so promptly, we're in a bit of rush, don't you know?'

Aren't we all? Johnny thought — *in a hurry to get out of here.*

'Think nothing of it, Peter. The word from Alex is they're pretty keen we pull our finger out. Is this all of you?'

Jeremy looked doubtfully at the small group.

'More than enough. We don't want a crowd giving the game away.'

The five men boarded as Jeremy and the stranger shook hands.

'Welcome aboard. How's brother Ian?' Jeremy asked.

'Oh he's doing some hush-hush thing or another. If he told me I think he'd have to kill me.'

'Same as you, I suppose?'

'Exactly. Did you manage to get an interpreter along the way?'

'Yes, but he didn't seem too keen about it all.'

'It's up to him. Between the lads and me, our Greek's probably adequate, but nothing eloquent. Are we expecting air cover?' the stranger added observing Johnny's pilot insignia.

'No, this is my Canadian chum Johnny Witherspoon who's hitching a lift. Johnny, meet Peter Fleming. My father went along on his Amazon and Asia expeditions...'

'No time for stories, Jeremy. I hate to be a bind, but it looks like your chaps have finished refuelling so we'd better get cracking before some collaborator spots us. Jerry is right on our tail.'

Peter Fleming squeezed between Johnny and Jeremy.

'There,' he said pointing to a spot on the coast over fifty miles north of Pyrgos. 'That should do nicely. According to my chaps there's a cove that'll give us excellent cover.'

'But that's way behind enemy lines,' Johnny couldn't help blurting.

'Why, that's entirely the point, dear boy,' Fleming said cheerfully as he packed his pipe and lit up.

'Actually I've been fishing there,' Johnny added rather smugly.

Jeremy and Fleming stared at him.

'I ran an air service out of Mirios further north. The local lads went there occasionally. It's why I was posted to Greece in the first place, although it didn't change things much. The Jerries were already on the way and I didn't get far beyond Athens in the end.'

He pointed to the inlet on Jeremy's chart.

'Yes, it is sheltered and you shouldn't have a problem getting your boat in there. So what's the plan, or do you have to kill me afterwards?'

'Nothing complicated, Johnny,' Jeremy said. 'We just drop Peter and his chums ashore and then skedaddle for Crete. What could possibly be simpler?'

'What indeed?'

Both the Fleming boys were mixed up in military cloak-and-dagger ops. While Ian worked for Naval Intelligence, Peter was part of Brigadier Colin Gubbin's Auxiliary Units which specialised in commando raids and guerrilla warfare. Although Johnny didn't know it at the time that was precisely what Peter Fleming and his comrades were up to.

A born adventurer, he liked nothing better than roaming around behind enemy lines blowing up anything the Germans might find useful. Other Englishmen who'd lived around the Med between world wars also encouraged sabotage and resistance in German occupied territory.

That was the easy bit. Jeremy found the cove before dawn. Seamen Jim Ruddock and Ollie Wilcox ferried Fleming's team ashore in an inflatable dingy before waving them off and God speed. Once the guerrillas, including Loukas melted into the darkness Jeremy turned seawards where two Italian destroyers waited for them...

*

Blam! Blam! The destroyers simultaneously open up with their 4.7 inch forward guns. They blocked any chance of escape to the south, so Jeremy was forced to turn hard to starboard and race northwards at flank speed. MGB-10 had a good chance of out-running the destroyers, but not their forward guns.

Two water-spouts bracketed the gunboat as their first shells landed far too close for comfort. The shells exploded and shrapnel sizzled across the gunboat deck. Jeremy started zigzagging for all he was worth as another salvo roared past. Despite his wild manoeuvres, the Italian gunners knew their stuff and every shot drew closer as if they'd anticipated Jeremy's every move.

The destroyers cranked into full speed ahead. Although they stopped MGB-10 powering out of range, the acceleration made the gunners' job harder. The gunboat inched ahead, but agonisingly slowly. At first it looked like they'd get away and circle round the destroyers later. But then the Italians got lucky, after so many near missed they fluked one true shot.

A shell smashed into MGB-10's gun turret. To everyone's amazement it failed to detonate, but the impact ripped the gun from its mounting, sending it tumbling overboard in a mess of tortured metal. Able Seaman Jim Ruddock manning the gun at that time was swept away with the shattered steel and disappeared with the wreckage.

All aboard were stunned by the blast, but Jeremy kept the gunboat at full throttle. Although the vessel's streamlined silhouette was mangled beyond recognition, the engines still functioned but now vibrated badly. Nevertheless Jeremy didn't reduce speed until he was certain they'd left the destroyers behind. The foredeck was a mess of jagged debris, but more distressing for Jeremy's crew, there was no way to turn around and see what had happened to their shipmate, Jim Ruddock.

Worse still CPO Andy Scott reported the engines did have shrapnel damage. It wasn't terminal, but they would have to continue at reduced speed to keep the juddering to an acceptable level.

'We'll never get back around those bloody destroyers now,' Jeremy said. 'We're going to have to find a spot to make repairs.'

'Why not Mirios,' Johnny said. 'I know the Dagoes have a small detachment stationed there. That was according to the last letter I got from a couple of pals who live there. Mind you it was over a year ago.'

'Let's hope the Jerries haven't taken over.'

'There's a cove on the north east corner of the island. It'll be a squeeze, but I reckon you'll get in there at high tide, so I doubt if the Ities will be guarding it. There's a workshop on the quayside where I used to fix my plane. I reckon we can scrounge extra tools if you need 'em and we're careful.'

Johnny reckoned with any luck he'd be able to secretly contact Callan, Ivy and Dennis Mortimer to get a lay of the land.

'It's a long way into enemy waters,' Jeremy said doubtfully.

'What else do you reckon?'

Jeremy was loath to abandon MGB-10 and wanted to preserve it as a naval asset. So he took Johnny's advice and motored slowly north towards Mirios where Captain Abiati aboard the *Santa Marcella* awaited...

Part 3 — the Peacemaker

Chapter 30 — POWs

*I*f them bloody destroyers 'adn't done our gun in, we'd never be in this mess,' Billie Bones lamented as the truck rattled along a particularly rough piece of road. 'We'd 'ave blown that Fancy-Nancy boat right out of the water.'

'I'm pleased you didn't. We were on board *Santa Marcella*,' Ivy reminded him.

Abiati had ordered Ensign Russo to sail back to Durrës because that was where his immediate superior was based and they needed to make repairs. *Santa Marcella's* crew received quite a welcome. The colonel commanding the Durrës detachment met them at the wharf. He chanted to be part of the action when Abiati radioed they'd captured twenty enemy servicemen after a naval shoot-out. Technically Ivy and Callan hadn't been captured during the fight, but Abiati didn't see the need to quibble over details.

Two trucks awaited the prisoners who were bundled aboard en route to a POW camp somewhere inland. Abiati muttered his apologies to Ivy and Callan, but their fate was out of his control.

The colonel was so pleased with Abiati, he shared a bottle of half-way decent wine in his quayside office and the conversation went something like this.

'That was well done, Abiati,' he gushed, pouring the first glasses.

'Thank you, sir,' Abiati replied, assessing the wine, which may have been the colonel's best, but wartime standards had dropped considerably.

'I understand you have the situation well under control on Mirios.'

'Yes sir, we have suppressed any suspected unrest.'

Abiati didn't see any reason to mention there was no suspected unrest to suppress.

'Anything I should know about?'

'No sir. Of course if a situation develops I'll send a signal immediately,' Abiati said without meaning a word of it. He was happy with his independent command and the last thing he needed was a senior officer butting in and throwing his weight around.

But the colonel had other issues on his mind.

'So your men aren't taking any unpatriotic nonsense from the locals.'

'Absolutely not, sir. I run a tight ship.'

'Good. I take it you can manage if I reduce your strength on the island as it's so well under control.'

'Reduce my strength, sir?'

'Precisely, Abiati. I won't pretend the border campaign against the Greeks went well. We had losses which need to be replaced.'

'What about the Germans, colonel?'

'It's no secret they will invade Crete next and we're to be involved either directly or to counter any insurgency on the mainland. So I've been ordered to transfer all your men of combat age to General Rosi's 6th Po Corps.'

'How many men, may I ask, sir?'

'I'm leaving you with Sergeant Vanni and your two oldest men. That should be ample.'

Abiati stared at the colonel.

'You said yourself everything was under control. Mirios is nothing more than a police beat and you, dear Abiati, are a highly respected police officer according to our records.'

What could Abiati say? The colonel was correct and it would make his life so much simpler.

'What about the *Santa Marcella*, sir?'

'Once the vessel is repaired Russo will continue patrolling the area, but report to the senior naval officer here at Durrës.'

'It'll take a few days to get *Santa Marcella* ready for sea again, so I'd better commandeer a caique and return to Mirios immediately,' Abiati said.

'Excellent idea. Tell your men to gather their kit and weapons. They'll be transferred to the front immediately. They'll be re-equipped with anything extra they need.'

The colonel was being optimistic. Italian troops on the Greek front were poorly equipped and many had died during the winter of exposure not Grecian bullets. But truth be told, losing his men wouldn't make much difference to Abiati. He only kept half-a squad to guard Mirios when *Santa Marcella* was away on patrol anyway. The rest were doing their job keeping an eye out all along the coast.

Meanwhile the trucks carrying Callan, Ivy and the other POWs lumbered through Tirana towards the Yugoslavian border. A reconnaissance vehicle led the small convoy. A machinegun was mounted on the rear of the leading machine. Two Italian guards sat in the rear of each truck while two more were in the cabin beside the drivers.

Their progress was unimpressive. The vehicles were underpowered and the petrol of dubious quality. They stopped whenever the guards felt like relieving themselves and Ivy just had to just get used to peeing with an armed guard beside her. It was no time to be coy. When they reached mountainous country the track grew rougher as the trucks struggled upwards.

Callan and Ivy just about jumped out of their skins when they heard the explosion only meters away. The recce vehicle had detonated a mine. It bucked into the air, crashing onto its side. The driver and front seat guard were tossed into the scrub beside the road, but the machine-gunner wasn't so fortunate. He was instantly crushed to death under the wreck.

But the driver and guard's luck didn't last. A blaze of Tommy-gun bullets sprayed from cover, cutting them down in seconds. Each man must have been hit at least a dozen times, shredding their torsos to crimson tatters.

The truck guards leaped over the tail-gates. Two died instantly in a blizzard of lead. The remaining pair dived for cover under the trucks, but by then men and women leapt from hiding and made short work of the survivors. There was no question of surrender. One of the attackers was a woman barely five feet tall. Pistol in hand, she stood over each Italian solder and fired a coup-de-grace with a single shot into each forehead.

Some bullets whistled through the truck canopy and everyone inside ducked from their seats, landing in a messy scrimmage. It was all over before the POWs could react. They quickly realised hiding on the truck-bed was pointless. In any event heads appeared at the truck tailgate.

'Everyone out!' the petite woman shouted in heavily accented English. 'Quickly!'

Callan jumped to the ground to be greeted by about fifty suspicious looking individuals brandishing Tommy-guns with itchy trigger-fingers.

'Welcome back to Albania, *Senore* McAlister.'

Major Abaz Kupi strode through the partisans and extended his hand. After shaking Callan's hand vigorously, he embraced Ivy, kissing her on both cheeks. Meanwhile the partisans were picking over the Italian dead. They salvaged ammunition and guns while stripping the bodies of any clothing not too badly mutilated to be of use. Boots were especially popular.

Callan thought they were lucky not to have been collateral damage in the ambush, but apparently Kupi knew the trucks carried POWs.

'You're very well informed,' Ivy said with relief.

'Not at all,' Kupi replied. 'We have friends in Durrës and it was simply a matter of them picking up the telephone. The lines are up unless we choose otherwise. But now we have to dispose of the bodies and destroy any evidence. If you disappear we may get away with it, but if they discover dead Italian soldiers there will be reprisals.'

The dead Italians were dumped into a nearby deep ravine, where it was unlikely they'd ever be discovered. With all the partisans and Aussies pitching in, the lead vehicle followed. It was a write-off anyway. The partisans commandeered the trucks. Turning off the main road and crawling over backwoods tracks for several kilometres. It was almost dark when they reached the partisan camp. It was a temporary affair, with just canvas lean-tos for shelters.

'We have to be ready to move in a hurry,' Kupi explained.

'Quite understandable,' Callan agreed.

The Albanian scouts reported there were no Italian patrols anywhere close by, so everyone settled down for the night. They'd bagged a wild boar and an antelope, making supper something of a feast. Needless to say there was no shortage of wine.

'So how have things been going?' Callan asked Kupi as they sat around a campfire.

'It's complicated. I was sent to Yugoslavia after the invasion. I've been trying to organise resistance forces ever since.'

'And how's that working out for you?'

'Something of a nightmare. We have Communists, Catholics, Royalists and dozens of other factions all wanting to be in charge. I've only just come back to Albania this year and I don't know whether I'll be able to stay.'

'So no one is co-operating against a common enemy.'

'No, and it's the same in Greece. I think the partisan groups hate one another almost as much as they hate the Italians and Germans. Not to mention the Russians who've been sniffing around in the east.'

'Rather you than me,' Callan said.

'So what do you plan to do?' Kupi asked. 'We can always use extra hands.'

'I can ask the others, but they're not guerrilla fighters. Johnny Witherspoon, Jeremy and his crew are specialists. I think they'd better serve the war-effort if we can get them back to doing what they're trained for. It's impossible to tell what the Australians will decide.'

So what do you intend to do?'

'Can you lend me a guide?'

*

Durrës Waterfront — May 1941

The Australians, probably wisely, decided a partisan's life was not for them and stayed with Callan, Ivy, Johnny and Jeremy's seamen. They were significantly less armed than before, but the partisans had few weapons to spare and ammunition was always precious. However they were confident they'd be able to scrounge more fire-power along the way.

Major Kupi issued them with three days rations, which was enough to get back to Durrës. At times it was slow going because they stuck to mountain tracks and avoided the main road where they'd almost certainly meet Italian troops. Their guide left as they approached town. He was keen to get back to the relative safety of his mountain hide-out. He wished them good luck before making himself scarce.

'Now what we need is a boat,' Johnny said. 'We've got plenty of chaps to sail it.'

Although the Italians didn't patrol in great numbers or with any particular regularity, the ex-POWs were a light platoon, which would have difficulty moving around Durrës' narrow streets unnoticed. Johnny, Callan and Ivy had dealt with Albanian fishermen over the years and it was time to deal again. And there were more than a few Albanians happy to pull the wool over their oppressor's eyes.

The first problem was to get everyone into mufti, which came with risks. Servicemen caught behind enemy lines out of uniform could be shot as spies. The Aussies, seamen and Johnny all wore dog-tags, but it was a risk nevertheless.

Leaving the servicemen hidden in a vineyard outside town, Ivy and Callan headed for harbour. This was hazardous, because allegiances could have changed since the Italians arrived. They were generally likeable fellows similar to Albanians. The Germans on the other hand were quite a different kettle of fish. Luckily being too preoccupied in Greece and possibly Crete, they left Albania to the Italians.

Callan held a wild card — those he sought out were Don Rocco's people who knew how to keep a secret.

Callan and Ivy arrived at a waterfront cafe by mid-morning. Few people were around except some elderly male patrons. Albanian men didn't really seem to do anything else with their leisure time unless they were partying late.

Ivy and Callan were relieved to discover these folk were delighted to see them back. They were of course all aware of the couple's arrest, but careful not to ask how they got away in case unwanted eavesdroppers were around.

So they hatched a plan...

It was pretty simple really involving a caique, its crew, a few sacks of rough clothing, some sneaking around and a decoy just in case.

By evening the escapees were all kitted out with assorted garb and hessian sacks to carry their uniforms. The caique crew were among Don Rocco's trusted men-of-honour who'd make sure word didn't spread about fugitives being in town. By nightfall they were ready to move.

About half-a-dozen village girls entered one of the occupation soldiers' favourite drinking spots. The girls didn't need much encouragement to behave coquettishly with a stern proviso not to take things too far. The Italian troops were easily distracted and soon it was wine, ouzo, balalaika-strumming and dancing all round.

The Allied servicemen crept to the wharf in small groups towards a caique. By ten o'clock they were all aboard, the boat cast off and set sail for Mirios. The revelry ashore continued until concerned parents came to fetch their daughters before they took their wantonness too literally.

Don Rocco's henchman had eyes and ears all over Durrës and he provided Callan with a vital piece of information... *Capitano* Abiati now had only Sergeant Vanni and two soldiers garrisoning Mirios. The island was no longer a military post, but reduced to a mere police station. Now that was intelligence that might be worth exploiting.

*

The caique dropped anchor at sea just beyond the inlet passage to Dennis Mortimer's hideout. With only one small inflatable dingy at their disposal it took several trips to ferry everyone ashore. Johnny, Callan and Ivy were among the first boat load and quickly headed for Mortimer's tent concealed by the ruins and cypress trees.

'Goodness me, how lovely to see you again,' Mortimer greeted drowsily when they shook him awake. He'd received Juan's message that, Callan and Ivy had been taken as POWs and didn't expect to see them again until war's end, if they survived at all.

'Yeah, it's been an interesting few days, Dennis and we need you to get your wireless warmed up.'

'We need to get a message to Alex, you old rogue,' Witherspoon said.

'Well, I'll be damned, Johnny where the blazes did you come from? Aren't you supposed to defending England's green and pleasant shores?'

'Long story, Dennis but right now we need your help to get me back to do just that. We've also brought some chums along who need a lift out of town.'

'I'd better make a cuppa then,' Dennis offered.

'You get onto the wireless, Dennis,' Ivy said. 'Callan and I'll sort out the catering.'

Sending messages was a tedious business as messages had to be coded, and Dennis' books were out of date. Up until the German advance new books had arrived by submarines, which Dennis had kept secret for everyone's protection.

'What you don't know can't be tortured out of you,' he explained blandly.

Complex identification protocols followed, accompanied by seemingly random frequency changes. Nevertheless with Johnny and Jeremy's help, ably assisted by Phil Becker, MGB-10's radio operator they got the message through and even identified themselves.

Once communications were established Becket took over the headphones, Morse-key, pencil and pad. Although Dennis was proficient, Becker was an expert telegrapher. After frantic tapping Becker handed a message to Mortimer.

'They've got it all mixed up, sir,' he said. 'They think we're still aboard number-ten and have a job for us.'

'What do they want us to do?'

'You know them fellas we dropped off before we were shot up?'

'Peter Fleming's crew?'

'Aye sir, well they've got themselves into a right fix. Apparently Jerry is closing in on 'em and they need immediate extraction.'

'You'd better put them straight, Phil,' Jeremy said. 'And mention *we* need immediate extraction too.'

'Can't they send a sub?' Johnny asked.

More tapping and Phil's fast handwriting...

'They're all committed picking up stragglers everywhere, sir. Reckon it'll be days before they can get up here. They're going to get back when they've got something available.'

'Hang on,' Johnny said. 'Dennis, is the Fairchild still in the harbour?'

'As far as I know.'

'It was when they took us off the island,' Ivy said, 'and that was only a few days ago.'

'Well, how about this for an idea..?'

Chapter 31 — McAlister's Truce

'The caique can get us to Mirios Harbour by tomorrow,' Johnny said. 'I can make the rendezvous tomorrow night.'

'Landing a floatplane on water at night...?'

'It's a three-quarter waxing moon, so that'll be light enough, I guess. Anyway it'll have to do.'

'You're nuts,' Callan said, but Johnny instructed Becker to make the arrangements for dusk the following night. The Fairchild radio comms weren't compatible with the set Fleming's men carried, so they arranged torchlight signals.

'Now what about the Italians stationed at Mirios?' Mortimer said. 'They aren't going to just let Johnny take his plane, are they?'

'We won't give them a choice in the matter,' Callan said. 'There are only four men left and we have our tough Aussie squaddies to make sure of it. They'd better get back into uniform.'

*

It was siesta time when the caique chugged into Mirios Harbour and few folk were about. As soon as they moored the vessel, Callan led Ivy, Johnny and the eight Australians ashore, while Jeremy and his crew searched the Quayside buildings. The caique skipper didn't hang around. He'd done all Don Rocco's henchman asked him, now it was time to skedaddle. He steamed his boat past the harbour breakwater reaching open sea in minutes.

All the port offices were locked except one where the sailors baled up a surprised soldier enjoying coffee and chatting to Juan Vargas. There was no apparent need for security and everyone seemed getting along fine. Mind you Juan was a born negotiator and could probably ingratiate himself anywhere.

The Aussie squad hurried through town towards *Belle Vista,* passing a lad who was maybe ten years old herding goats to pasture. The boy eyed them curiously, but showed no signs of alarm. It was doubtful whether he knew the difference between the two warring army uniforms.

The villa was silent as Callan tried the front door. It was unlocked, so the squad eased through the portal with well practised stealth. The men fanned out, their stolen weapons at the ready. They carried an assortment of rifles and pistols, but no automatic firearms, which Major Kupi insisted were too valuable to give away.

The soldiers silently investigated every room. Callan was pretty sure where to start. He darted up the grand staircase leading to first storey corridor. He gingerly turned the master bedroom door handle. Dennis Mortimer had favoured this room because of its grandeur and magnificent balcony view. Abiati undoubtedly felt the same way.

Bingo, Callan smiled.

Abiati dozed on the grand double bed dressed only in his underwear and socks. Callan inched to the bed-side and placed his pistol barrel an inch from *Capitano* Abiati's temple.

'Rise and shine, my dear *Capitano*,' Callan whispered.

Abiati stirred from siesta then sat bolt upright. He cast his eyes to the holstered pistol on the bedside table only a foot or two away

'Easy there, *Capitano*. Don't even think of doing anything foolish.'

Abiati gathered his wits with remarkable speed.

'McAlister, what in God's name are you doing here?'

'Fighting the war it seems.'

'So you have come to kill me.'

'That's rather up to you.'

'*Senore,* you are joking surely? My men will not hesitate to shoot you on sight,' Abiati insisted. 'Surrender now before you regret your rashness.'

At that moment Ivy entered the master bedroom.

'We've rounded up Sergeant Vanni and his two men. They're in custody downstairs,' she said rather formally in Callan's opinion.

'In custody', where did she get that from?

He turned back to Abiati and grinned.

'Nice try, *Capitano*, but it looks like we've called your bluff.'

'Perhaps if I dressed before we discuss the matter.'

'By all means.'

Carmela and Adela were initially distressed to have their home invaded, but Ivy calmed them down. Fausto, who'd been working in the vegetable patch rushed to joined them and see what all the fuss was about. Ivy helped Carmela prepared coffee supplied by Don Rocco's black-marketing enterprises although Abiati was unaware of the fact. She remembered her way around the kitchen. Adela was delighted to see Johnny Witherspoon as she was one of the local lasses who'd cast an amorous eye his way.

Ivy joined Callan, Jeremy and Johnny who sat around the dining room table with *Capitano* Abiati.

'The way I see it is you have three choices, *Capitano*. You can try to fight it out, but I think that ship has sailed. The other is to accept life as a POW somewhere in Australia or South Africa...'

'Forgive me, *Senore*, but how do you propose to transport us to Australia or South Africa?'

'I'm coming to that, bear with me. Option three is we declare a truce.'

'I'm listening.'

'Well, I was thinking how nice it would be if life on Mirios continued undisturbed by this stupid war.'

'Go on.'

'I think you're just the man for the job, *Capitano* Abiati,' Callan declared with largesse. 'Mirios needs someone to protect its citizens...including the Jews.'

'What about your...army, *Senore*?'

'I fancy they're wanted elsewhere.'

'And how do you plan to arrange that?'

'Leave that to me, *Capitano*. What I need you to do is let the war run its course. The Germans are too busy in Greece and now maybe Crete to take any interest in Mirios. You need to keep it that way.'

'So what you're really asking is for me to commit treason.'

'Perish the thought! Let's just call it international co-operation and goodwill in a time of crisis.'

'Very well, but I promise you I will not commit one act against Italy.'

'I'm not asking you to. All I'm asking is none of us gets involved. We live in peace in the middle of a war.'

'For as long as we can,' Abiati observed. 'What about you and your dear wife?'

'We came here as refugees, *Capitano*,' Ivy said. 'The people here welcomed us when they could have turned the other way. It's our job to help protect them.'

Callan stared at her. He might agree, but it was the first he'd heard about staying and protecting people.

Leaving the MGB-10 crew to secure the port, Jeremy and Juan turned up about then. Juan looked as surprised as anyone to find *Bella Vista* occupied by Aussie troops. Callan drew him aside and explained what needed to be done to get the Fairchild ready for flight with full fuel tanks. Then he turned to Ivy and beckoned her to follow him out of earshot.

'Did you mean what I think you meant, love?' he asked.

'I know you said you didn't go to war anymore, but someone has to keep an eye on Abiati and make sure there's no back-sliding,' she smiled.

'But we're hundreds of miles into enemy territory.'

'I won't tell if you don't.'

'If we're discovered we'll be shot as spies.'

'Not if we tell them we just got cut off up here.'

'We've already played that card. We're escaped POWs remember?'

'These people may need our help and I know Juan, Fausto and Dennis will appreciate us being here. Look, *Capitano* Abiati thinks we're harmless and I'm sure he'll vouch for us.'

'You and Johnny Witherspoon are off your flaming rockers.'

Callan heaved a sigh. This was the craziest idea she'd come up with so far. He returned to the kitchen table where Abiati eyed him with a mixture of suspicion, curiosity and amusement.

It seemed Abiati had nothing against Callan's proposal that he and Ivy would stay on Mirios. He couldn't see why they wanted to, but then he didn't know about Dennis Mortimer and his radio set. Maybe they didn't want to run the gauntlet of Italian ships trying to escape south, but the McAlister couple didn't strike him as being afraid of anything. Or at least if they were afraid, they'd tackle the problem head on. It was something he could investigate at his leisure.

'So I really have no option,' Abiati conceded. 'Four — now unarmed — men can hardly take on twenty.'

'I'm pleased you see it that way,' Callan said.

Shortly afterwards Callan and Jeremy held a confidential council-of war.

'The important thing is Abiati doesn't know about Dennis and his wireless,' Callan said. 'He won't sit still until he finds it if he knows about it.'

'Don't worry, we'll make ourselves scarce, but are you sure you want to stay here?' Jeremy asked.

Callan shrugged.

'I'm not, but Ivy is.'

Before dusk, two craft prepared to leave Mirios Harbour. The first was the Fairchild followed by Fausto's caique commandeered by His Majesty's Navy.

'You know this is a suicide mission, Johnny?' Callan said. 'Your plane is slow with no guns.'

'I'll fly so low no one will spot me. Don't worry it can't be any more dangerous than taking on a dozen Me-109s at the same time.'

Ivy hugged him and maybe cried just a little. He only took Henry Abrams with him and soon they were gone.

As the Fairchild disappeared southwards Jeremy said goodbye. Fausto made a great fuss about losing his beloved caique. Words like robbery, compensation, and a few expletives were bandied around as the Aussies and MGB-10's crew squeezed aboard. They took all the Italian weapons they found. Soon the caique too was gone, leaving Abiati, Sergeant Vanni, Juan, Ivy and Callan standing together on the quayside.

'So now what?' Abiati asked. 'We are totally undefended. We have no weapons, so we're entirely at the mercy of the world.'

'We'll be fine, *Capitano*. Ivy and I still have hand guns. You'll have to make do like English Bobbies.'

Callan neglected to mention his hunting rifle was still stashed away.

'Bobbies?'

'English policemen. They manage to maintain law and order admirably with no guns at all.'

'I confess there has been no call to draw a gun against anyone here...except you of course. But you're telling me that their plan is to sail that caique south until a British warship picks them up.'

'Yep.'

'And they were going to take my men and me prisoners as well? I don't know where we'd fit. There's hardly room enough aboard as it is.'

'Fausto's boat was the biggest in the harbour,' Callan replied.

'Why come here in the first place? You'd obviously already stolen a boat.'

'Johnny Witherspoon wanted his plane back and, yes it was an oversight not putting a guard on the caique skipper to stop him buggering off. I'll just have to make my peace with Fausto.'

Callan had to be careful he didn't give away where Johnny planned to fly the Fairchild or Jeremy and his men were planning alternate transport south. So far he'd covered their tracks pretty well. Abiati seemed to believe they'd all simply escaped and returned to Mirios for Johnny's plane as Callan said.

'He took his mechanic, but didn't take any of the other men with him..?'

'They preferred to take their chances on the boat. At least they're armed after pinching most of your weapons.'

'Nice touch to leave us a rifle each, which are useless without ammunition.'

'Like I said,' Callan smiled, 'London Bobbies.'

*

Meanwhile Johnny Witherspoon navigated southwards along the Albania coast until he reached Peter Fleming's drop-off point. There was just enough twilight to put the Fairchild down and water-taxi close to the water's edge. He took care not to ground the floats on the beach while Abrams lowered a metal step ladder.

'Seems quiet, sir,' Henry said, 'but where are the buggers?'

'Too quiet for me, Henry. I hope they haven't been wiped out.'

Then a torch light blinked from the trees close to shore, followed by the rattle of small arms fire and the distinctive crack of a hand grenade.

'You were sayin', sir,' Abrams said, grabbing one of the rifles they'd brought along just in case. 'I'll cover them.'

He checked the magazine was full before slamming it into place. Just then four figures dashed from cover. The beach was narrow so they didn't have far to go, but two men were supporting one of their companions while the fourth blazed away into the scrub behind them. Abrams saw several muzzle flashed. The bullets zinged past before he heard the pop-pop of gunfire. He aimed several rounds into the bushes, which kept the enemy heads down for a few vital seconds.

A hail of lead ripped into the Fairchild, but the bullets passed clean through and didn't damage any flight cables or fuel lines. Abrams helped haul the wounded man aboard. The others scrambled after him. Loukas the interpreter bled from a shoulder wound, but it didn't look fatal. Henry reached for the first aid kit for a dressing while Fleming's men emptied their machineguns towards shore.

'Is that all?' Johnny yelled from the cockpit.

"Fraid so, old boy. We had to leave our dead behind,' Peter Fleming said bitterly.

Johnny didn't wait for Abrams to close the fuselage door. The Fairchild was accelerating through forty knots when Abrams finally got the job done. Hugging the coast made navigation to

Kalamata easy enough. To the east distant flashes sparked periodically indicating artillery fire or bombing raids.

'The place is swarming with jerry's' Peter Fleming explained. 'We dodged them for a bit, but then ran into a patrol. We were lucky to get a wireless massage off.'

'And even luckier I was able to get hold of this plane,' Johnny said and told Fleming their story.

'I hope Kalamata is still bloody open,' Abrams muttered gloomily.

It was — just.

The Germans had reached the edge of town where they met harsh resistance from Greek troops. The quayside was chaotic as men jostled for a place on the gangways to the remaining ships. Sappers sweated to dump any useful equipment into the harbour, or simply torched anything that would burn. The noise was appalling. Officers yelled orders which were sometimes obeyed, but often ignored. The situation was just short of panic and it wouldn't take much to tip it over the edge.

With Peter Fleming's tough guerrillas to force the issue, Abrams found one of the few remaining drums of aviation spirit and a hand pump. He'd never refuelled a plane so quickly.

Artillery shells exploded into town buildings and the sea beyond. The last freighters steamed seawards while three remaining destroyers loaded the last refugees aboard. As the first warship cast off its rear guns roared, firing shell after shell towards the German lines.

'She's full, sir,' Abrams yelled, dropping the fuel line. 'Time to get out of Dodge as you'd say.'

'Damn right. All aboard!'

And not a moment too soon. Incendiary shells thumped into the docks in the Fairchild's wake. The remaining fuel drums exploded blasting full tanks fifty feet into the air where they erupted in a grotesque fireworks display. Before the Fairchild was a hundred yards from the wharf, the remaining destroyers cast off. Figures silhouetted against the flames darted frenetically as the Germans and Greeks slugged it out to the bitter end. No one took prisoners.

When the Germans finally overran the wharf, surviving Greek troops and partisans jumped into the sea only to be mown down as they swam away. Soon the tumultuous splashing and screams died as the Germans reloaded their Mauser machineguns ready to kill again.

But they didn't have it all their own way, the departing destroyers fired until they were well out to sea and many German soldiers were blown into oblivion or swept from the docks.

Johnny Witherspoon banked the Fairchild to avoid the navy salvos before setting course for Heraklion airstrip on Crete's northern coast.

Chapter 32 — Island in Isolation

Mirios — May 1941

There were a few details Callan had to iron out. Abiati had moved his command centre, including the radio to *Bella Vista*. Fausto told Callan Abiati had little need to communicate with the Albanian headquarters other than a routine 'ops-normal' call every morning. As Callan and Ivy now spoke and read Italian fluently and after many years of aviation were experts in Morse code, they monitored every radio transmissions with ease.

Abiati made no move to change the situation although he was torn between his civic duty to protect Mirios' citizen, including the Jews and his patriotic duty to Italy. As he despised fascism he let matters slide for the time being. Right now no harm was being done also he liked Ivy and Callan and would regret it if they were recaptured or worse — shot.

As a citizen of neutral Spain, Juan did pretty much as he pleased, especially as Abiati had decided he wasn't a secret agent. With the Fairchild gone and Ivy and Callan fugitives, they were no longer free to fly at will anyway, so business prospects were limited. Nevertheless, Juan still wheeled and dealed with the town merchants and fishermen.

The problem of Fausto's caique still bothered Callan. Obviously they couldn't retrieve it from Dennis Mortimer's bay and sail back into Mirios Harbour. Abiati wasn't going to ignore that event, but Fausto needed the boat to fish. However commerce found a way. A few days after Jeremy's crew and the Australians left, Callan and Fausto borrowed a caique and sailed around the island.

Fausto's boat was anchored just outside the bay. The sailors had gone, but left the boat spotlessly shipshape. The nets, ropes, sails and onboard kit were all neatly stowed and ready for use. GPO Andy Scott had given the engine a thorough service and it now ticked over as never before. Mortimer told them a submarine hadn't surfaced until the night of the full moon, so the sailors and Aussies used their time to repay Fausto's hospitality.

They also left all the weapons and ammunition they'd confiscated from *Capitano* Abiati's armoury.

'Jeremy thought you might need them,' Mortimer explained, 'and they had no use for guns in a submarine.'

'Well God bless the Navy and those Diggers,' Callan said, 'we'll take the guns back to town and stash them somewhere handy just in case. But it's going to be a bind for you, Fausto, not being able to use your lovingly restored boat.'

Fausto wasn't fazed in the slightest.

'I will simply base my boat at Durrës. It's where I sell most of my catches anyway. I can always rendezvous with other boats to bring what I need back to Mirios. *Capitano* Abiati doesn't have to know a thing.'

'We'd have trouble explaining your boat had been abandoned,' Callan said. 'He'd put two-and-two together and come looking, whatever I threatened to do. I'm sure he knows I'm not going to shoot him or his men.'

Fausto's expression suggested he had no such reservations.

'I've discovered Abiati's wireless Channel, so I can intercept his messages,' Mortimer said. 'So far so good. And by the way, Johnny completed his mission and got to Crete safely, although how safe Crete will be is anyone's guess. The sub took your Navy chum, his crew and the Aussies back to Alex. I'm sure they'll find something useful for them to do.'

'Yep, I guess they'll get back to fighting the war where they're most needed. I'd better get back to see ours doesn't start. We'll take the hardware back and stash it. I hope we never have to use it.'

After that Mirios settled into a peaceful routine. Security wasn't necessary, because the entire island population realised their safety depended on discretion. Abiati appeared relaxed and happy to let things tick over as usual. He often met Ivy and Callan at a waterfront cafe for coffee or a glass of wine. Normally they discussed the island's daily situation like town elders. The war quickly faded into the background.

There was little need for people to sail to the mainland other than sell their surplus catch, which was small enough these days. Flour for bread and pasta was in short supply, but corn grew easily on the island and the resulting carbohydrate products were acceptable. Goats supplied milk, cheese and meat as ever. Every household grew their own vegetables and fruit as well as raising chickens. Vines grew everywhere and some of the local home-made wines weren't too bad at all. Callan continued to cull feral goats for the local market. He regularly led a team of local lads on hunting trips lasting a day or two. In short Mirios might not have been the lap of luxury, but it was self-sufficient.

So the war raged around the Mediterranean. Dennis Mortimer kept Callan updated with the bitter slaughter on Crete after the Germans carried out an airborne assault on the island's northern coast. Casualties were horrendous until the Commonwealth and Greek troops were once again driven into the sea and evacuated to North Africa leaving thousands of dead or captured. The subsequent German reprisals were merciless and long lasting.

'We don't seem very good at this at all,' Mortimer lamented to Callan and Ivy on one of their visits. 'We keep getting chucked out of countries and things aren't going that well in the desert campaign either. General Erwin Rommel's heading up a new Jerry unit called the *Afrika Korps*. He was successful in France and seems to be Hitler's blue-eyed boy.'

'Yes, the Germans do love their blue-eyed boys,' Ivy commented acidly.

So days ran into weeks, with nobody bothering to pay Mirios any attention. As far as Albanian high command was concerned *Capitano* Abiati was keeping a lid on things with just four men who were all WWI veterans. This meant he wasn't wasting young and energetic men needed to quash rebellious partisans on the mainland.

Abiati finally reconciled his ambivalence and decided not to rock the boat. He was actually doing his duty, which was to keep order on Mirios and subdue any anti-Italian behaviour. Callan was worried Abiati's men would grow bored and restless, but nothing could have been further from the truth. They helped townsfolk whenever needed and joined in the many festivals to countless saints, while Sergeant Vanni courted a recently widowed woman renowned for her spaghetti sauce widely considered the tastiest on the island

Both warships and freighters passed Mirios by. There was nothing to interest them on the island. The Germans were too busy being beastly on Crete while the struggle for North Africa waged from east to west with more blood soaking into the sand daily. But *Capitano* Abiati wasn't feeling sanguine.

'You're not going to get away with this, you know,' he said to Callan and Ivy over coffee one afternoon.

'So far, so good,' Callan said rather too glibly in Ivy's opinion.

'We can't stay cut off for ever,' Abiati insisted. 'The army is bound to send someone to inspect this post.'

'Why?'

'It's what the army does. They'll want reports and paperwork. We aren't producing enough.'

'But, isn't that what you've been doing? It's just there isn't anything much to report.'

'I don't think the army cares about that. It'll bet some junior administration officer is itching to justify his existence so he doesn't get issued a gun and sent to the front — especially now Operation Barbarossa is in full swing.'

'Yes, but surely Russia's a German show, not Italian?'

'The *Nazis* have all sorts of units serving in Russia now — Italians, Poles, Croats, Czechs and even French units.'

'You're very well informed,' Ivy said suspiciously.

'Oh, I don't have any special intelligence sources, my dear,' Abiati replied with a shrug. 'Right now I'm getting most of my intelligence from our fishermen coming back from Durrës.'

'So you reckon some military heavyweight will come sniffing around sooner or later.'

'It's possible.'

'What do you suggest?' Callan asked.

'Firstly we'd like our weapons back so we can at least look like a military unit. A couple of empty rifles aren't going to fool anyone especially uppity officers who like nothing better than inspecting rifles. I just know those ex-POWs kept some back for you.'

'Maybe...'

'Vanni tells me he can easily run the orderly room and generate just enough paperwork to look convincing — pay records, sick parades, leave entitlements and even ration requisitions.'

'How do I know you won't double-cross Ivy and me?'

'You don't, but if I had that in mind, I'd have done it already. I know where a dozen rifles are stashed and could have used them against you any time...'

Ivy and Callan stared at him.

'You keep forgetting I'm a policeman. I pay attention and learn things when I have a mind to.'

'Fair enough,' Callan conceded.

'Look I don't want you to be interned and so far as the authorities are concerned, you've joined the partisans on the mainland. We can keep it that way, but I have to convince anyone who cares that we're a viable military unit. And even if you are found out, I'll just plead ignorance.'

Abiati had a valid point, so Callan returned the stolen guns. It was a huge gamble, which Ivy reminded him repeatedly. But Abiati kept his word, so Ivy and Callan were hidden in plain sight. The Italian soldiers weren't inclined to make a fuss. They'd found probably the most comfortable wartime billet of all at *Bella Vista* and they were happy to keep it that way.

So Abiati organised a caique to send and receive any written correspondence although it turned out there was precious little, but it kept the *Capitano* up to date. Occasionally a gunboat moored at Mirios harbour, but the crews only stayed briefly while Callan and Ivy slipped into the background unnoticed.

*

13 December 1941 — Dennis Mortimer's Hideout

'Blow me down,' he said, 'the bloody Japs have declared war on America. They attacked Pearl Harbour with carrier planes last week. Now that's stirred a hornet's nest.'

Callan, Ivy and Dennis sat around a campfire dining in style as the hide-out vegetable patch was in full production. It turned out Mortimer had a green thumb as well as being a successful chicken breeder. There were always fresh eggs when visitors popped in for a chat

'It's stirred a hornets' nest all right,' Callan said. 'Abiati's on tenterhooks because Germany and Italy have both declared war on the States as well. He's worried it might change things on Mirios.'

'I don't see why,' Mortimer said. 'The Yanks will be kept busy in the Pacific and we'll have to sort out Africa before we can have a crack at Europe.'

'Don't forget the Russians,' Ivy reminded them. 'The Germans might have *blitzkrieged* their way to Moscow, but winter has stopped them dead in their tracks. They should have gone sooner, not wasted all that time in Greece and Crete.'

'*Capitano* Abiati says that awful Lieutenant Viola has joined one of the Italian battalions in General Paulus' German 6th Army in the Ukraine or the Caucuses or somewhere like that,' Ivy added.

'He was after combat glory, maybe now he'll get it,' Callan said. 'Looks like Abiati is keeping tabs on Viola in case he comes back to haunt him.'

Capitano Abiati was pretty sure America's entry into the war spelt the eventual death-knell of the Axis forces. The next twelve months were to prove him right.

*

Christmas 1942 — Dennis Mortimer's Hideout

'Things seem to finally be looking up,' Dennis said. 'Monty and the Yanks are finally stitching up the desert campaign and the *Wehrmacht* looks like it's in big trouble at Stalingrad. US marines have got a foothold into the South Pacific at Guadalcanal and the Aussies are holding the Japs in New Guinea. Considering all the practice we've had over the centuries for a while it didn't seem like we Brits were very good at this war lark at all.'

'Don't sell yourself short, Dennis,' Callan said.

'Dunkirk, France, Greece, Crete and then Singapore surrendered in February. I mean the Japs had only been in the war for three ruddy months.'

'I just wish it will be over,' Ivy sighed. 'I hope Johnny Witherspoon is staying safe and that nice Jeremy whatever his long name is.'

'They seem quite capable of looking after themselves,' Dennis reassured her. 'Now cheer up and show me what you've brought in that hamper.'

*

9 September 1943 – Mirios Waterfront

Ivy and Callan were enjoying a drink on a balmy late summer evening. They were aware a blood bath had gone on around them. Earlier in the year Prime Minister Winston Churchill had ordered a joint force operation to recapture selected Greek Islands in the Aegean Sea. It had ended badly with a huge butcher's bill and Germany retaining control of the Aegean. Once again Churchill's Adriatic bogey-man had reared up to bite him.

The Americans had steered clear of that operation, concentrating on Sicily and Italy. Commonwealth troops joined in and were now going head-to-head with the *Wehrmacht* in central Italy. The North Africa was pretty much wound up with tens of thousands of Axis troops bound for South African and other faraway Commonwealth POW camps.

'Gosh that was nice, darling,' Ivy said putting down her empty glass. 'I do believe I'll have another.'

'Me too,' Callan said. 'According to Abiati we're not expecting any generals to visit today.'

'We never have any generals, silly. The only top brass to visit Mirios in nearly two years was that poncy major who strutted around for five minutes while the *Capitano* saluted a lot, shouted orders to his men and Sergeant Vanni raised a flag.'

'By the way where is our good captain? It's not like him to miss happy-hour.'

Almost at the mention of his name, Abiati marched along the road from *Bella Vista* with Vanni and his two men bringing up the rear. To their credit his men were always immaculately turned out when in uniform. Despite the fact they were all middle-aged they marched well and kept physically fit. In this case they were dressed in their finest uniforms, their boots were spotless and Abiati even wore a sword clipped to his belt buckled over a red-white-and-green sash around his waist

Where he found the sword was anybody's guess, but it looked in good condition and the hilt flashed as it caught the evening sunlight. The four soldiers stomped to a halt in front of Ivy and Callan's table. Abiati snapped a sharp salute in the conventional manner and not a straight arm *Nazi* version.

'Goodness me, *Capitano,*' Ivy said. 'You and your men look very smart. Is there a special occasion and if so please come and join us.'

'I think you will have cause to celebrate, *Senora,*' Abiati replied formally, 'and I have a duty to perform.'

The *Capitano* unclipped his sword, stepped forward formally and laid the weapon on the table. Callan stared at the sword and then to Abiati.

'I have come to offer you my surrender,' Abiati declared. 'The Grand Council has removed Mussolini and King Victor Emmanuel resumes the post of commander-in-chief. However the Italian High Command deems the war no longer viable and yesterday negotiated an armistice with the Allies. So it appears we are now your prisoners. We will lay down our arms.'

'I knew things weren't going well for you, but I never saw this coming.'

Abiati shrugged, neither had he.

'Look, you hang onto your guns for now,' Callan said after a moment's consideration. 'You may need them because I don't think the Germans are going to take an Italian surrender well.'

Abiati stood his men down and joined Callan and Ivy for a drink. He was greatly relieved in a way because they could now become true friends.

Callan was right. Germany still controlled Greece, Crete, Yugoslavia and the other Balkan states. And they ruled with an iron fist, executing partisans, Jews and innocent civilians indiscriminately. A day later Abiati received a message from Albanian HQ that Italian troops could continue to serve with the *Reich* or become POWs.

'So they'll come for you as soon as they decide to ask you whose side you're on,' Callan said.

'So it seems,' Abiati replied. 'Maybe it's so chaotic on the mainland it'll be a while before anyone bothers with a tiny outpost like Mirios.'

'What are you going to do?' Ivy asked with genuine concern. Over time she and Callan had grown sincerely fond of the Italian military contingent.

'As you know I was never a fascist and neither are my men, so we'll be damned if we'll serve with the *Nazis*!'

'Then we need to plan for the worst.'

Chapter 33 — Plan for the Worst

'The first thing we need to do is bring Dennis in from the wilderness,' Callan said. 'And Fausto can sail his caique home.'

Abiati looked at him suspiciously.

'We would have got around to telling you all in good time, but we kinda had help from the other side of the island.'

'Someone with a radio?' Abiati suggested.

'Well, yes and it's going to come in damned handy because it seems the boffins in England know the Jerry codes, which might just mean we'll find out what they're up to.'

The upshot was Fausto sailed his caique with Dennis aboard back to his beloved *Bella Vista* to reclaim his master bedroom. Abiati moved into the room next door, which was only slightly less opulent with French windows opening onto the same balcony. Dennis set up his radio next to Abiati's so they could monitor both British and Axis messages.

Meanwhile Callan and Ivy organised several weapons caches so townsfolk could arm themselves at short notice.

'What about trenches and booby-traps?' Abiati asked.

For some reason people seemed to defer to Callan for leadership when the chips were down.

'It depends how they come,' he said. 'If there's anything much more than a squad we'll have to head for the hills and ask the Navy for help. I think that'd be a good move anyway, because we'd never take on a company of storm troopers.'

It turned out nearly everyone on Mirios was armed to some extent and were happy to drink any number of wine bottles dry and convert them into Molotov cocktails. Alex informed Dennis that although there'd been radio chatter about securing the Ionian Sea islands, it appeared the Germans had virtually no warships or freighters in the area and the Italian Fleet was not an option since the armistice.

'It looks like the Allies are by-passing Greece and Yugoslavia,' Dennis reported one day, 'so Jerry will be desperate to hold onto any territory they can. This island has suddenly become important especially as an observation post.'

'So they'll come by air,' Ivy said.

'It's the most probable case, but even then the Germans have lost much of their air superiority. How many planes can they spare?'

'I think we need to call Alex for some extra kit,' Dennis said.

*

However the Germans *did* have enough planes. It took some months for them to figure out that no one occupied a number of the Ionian Sea islands including Mirios. It took even longer for them to do something about it. And although he wasn't German, they had just the man for the job.

Lieutenant, now *Hauptman* Enzo Viola had made what would have been an unimaginable transfer to the 1st Division of the *Luftwaffe Fallschirmjäger*. The elite parachute Corps was very much the domain of blond, blue-eyed Arian boys, but by spring 1944 the *Nazis* were less fussy. In fact they welcomed anyone who'd fire a gun for the *Reich* and was prepared to jump out of a plane. Viola had built up his credentials as a dyed-in-the-wool *Nazi* warrior.

He'd marched through the Ukraine to Stalingrad where he made a name for himself by killing whoever stood in his path. Amid the rubble of Stalingrad's utterly devastated western Volga bank a sniper's bullet ripped past Viola's right cheekbone, melting his eye socket and ripping off his ear above the lobe.

A medic staunched the wound and left him to fend for himself as snow fell and the temperature plunged way below zero. Along with pitifully few other wounded men, Viola staggered to the rear ignoring the pleas of men so badly hurt they were simply going to freeze to death where they lay.

Viola had no idea what happened to the other casualties, but he was alone when he finally reached an Italian staging station. A skeletal, exhausted surgeon bandaged his wound before assigning him to a truck crammed with groaning, shattered men. After fifty gruelling kilometres along the Don Riverbank they reached *Tridentina* Divisional headquarters. The Italian force, comprising several units including elements of the *Alpino* Corps, was held in reserve at the time.

With no anaesthetics or morphine left, Viola only remembered a nightmare of hideous pain and confusion. The surgeons did what they could, but his eye was beyond repair other than stitching the wound in rudimentary fashion. How Viola endured the bitter New Year proved he was nothing if not a tough guy and he was going to have to get a lot tougher.

By January 1943 General Zhukov's Russian army had nearly surrounded the Germans and their allies. Air support was all but non-existent and incapable of even resupplying a fraction of the German needs. Russian planes commanded the sky and shot down *Luftwaffe* transports before they could make their parachute drops.

Stalingrad was a busted flush, but Hitler ordered every soldier to fight to the death. Most of them noted cynically that it wasn't *his* death. But the Italian senior officers were having none of it. Along with the remnants of Romanian and Hungarian units, German stragglers and a few Panzers, the Italians fought their way through a town called Nikolajewka which no one could pronounce.

Losses were huge, but the Italians pushed on despite harassment from Red Air Force fighter planes while losing their few Panzers to bombs, mines and breakdowns. One-eyed Lieutenant Viola spearheaded a rag-tag company comprising the dregs of many decimated battalions. In desperation his men charged in a human wall, killing the enemy with their bare hands if they ran out of ammunition. Then they fought on with captured guns, bayonets, and grenades.

Miraculously some of them broke through the Russian cordon. The Reds let them go, turning back to Stalingrad to finish off General Paulus' trapped 6th Army. The Italian division was the only unit to escape the Russian encirclement. Viola reached the Axis lines snarling like a wild animal, his face awash with blood and his one eye blazing insanely. He was volatile enough to begin with, but Stalingrad had pushed him to total sadistic madness.

Hitler may have been displeased that a few thousand men had failed to die gloriously for the *Reich*, but the front-line officers were more sanguine. Viola was hailed a hero. There was even talk of an Iron Cross, but that might have been a bit optimistic for an Italian. So Viola spent his convalescence redeeming himself by leading *Nazi* death squads. They rooted out partisans, Jews and anyone else he disliked before either packing them into cattle trucks bound for labour-camps, or simply shooting people at will.

The German commanders had a pretty good idea their Russian invasion was doomed and the best way to solve their problem was kill as many Russians as possible. So that's how Viola gained his reputation as an A-Grade *Nazi* and was inducted into the *Waffen-SS*. When he applied for an airborne regiment, the *Luftwaffe* accepted him without hesitation.

Parachute training had reached a pretty abbreviated form by then and after a few jumps, Viola was promoted to replace a captain killed during the Crete invasion. So in May 1944, as soon as word went out that the Germans planned to secure any unoccupied Aegean and Ionian islands by airborne assault, Viola volunteered to lead the raid on Mirios. He knew the place well enough and he also knew a bunch of Jews were most likely still hiding out on the island.

*

Meanwhile Dennis' appeals were answered. He'd convinced the Allied decision-makers Mirios' citizens were bona fide partisans in desperate need of fire-power. He was pleased to receive the reply that the British were happy to oblige, although the Americans weren't interested in becoming involved in the Eastern Mediterranean theatre.

Nonetheless, a few days later a Dakota transport plane accompanied by a flight of Hurricane fighters flew to Mirios. Soon parachutes cascaded from the plane, settling all around town. Ivy, Abiati, Juan and Callan organised the townsfolk to unpack crates of machineguns, rifles, ammunition and grenades. They also discovered medical supplies and army rations, which everyone accepted graciously enough. They may not have thought much of the food quality, but times were hard and even on Mirios folk sometimes went hungry.

Once the containers were unpacked the newly qualified partisans gathered the parachutes and began folding them to store around town.

'I'm sure they'll come in handy even if we never use then,' Juan said, thinking himself very droll.

Just then the leading Hurricane peeled away from the formation. The pilot dived earthwards to tree-top level. The fighter plane skimmed over roof-tops while the townspeople waved and cheered. The pilot drew back the cockpit canopy and waved back.

Callan noticed a cylinder tumble from the plane and bounce along one of the cobbled streets. The cockpit slammed shut as the pilot gunned the engine and the plane swept away. It climbed steeply and, after a couple of neatly performed rolls shot skywards to join the Dak and its escort.

Juan retrieved the cardboard cylinder, which although a little dented, was intact.

'It's addressed to you,' he said, handing Callan the cylinder.

Callan pulled open the tube and withdrew a rolled note which read:

Hi Guys,
My Hurricanes are escorting this Dak to make sure these presents reach you folks safely.
I hope you don't need to use this stuff. I can't tell you where I'm based, but get Dennis to try and call if you get into trouble.
I'll come if I possibly can.
All the best
Johnny

The Dak droned away and banked to set course back to Italy.

'Oh that Johnny Witherspoon is such a show-off,' Ivy declared. 'He'll kill himself if he doesn't stop being so silly.'

'I wonder if he's still in touch with the girl he fancied in London,' Callan said. 'That should make him more careful.'

'I don't remember fancying a girl making you any more careful,' Ivy said, taking his arm as they walked through town to organise the supply distribution.

While the townsfolk busied themselves gathering the supplies with Juan and Ivy supervising to see nothing was overlooked, Callan returned to see how things were going at *Bella Vista.*

'Alex is reporting a lot of chatter from Jerry in Greece and Crete,' Dennis said. 'From what I can gather, they're hard pressed to stay in the Med with the Russians driving them back from the east and the Yanks and us belting away in Italy.'

'They're clinging onto Greece and the Balkans to protect their south-eastern flank,' Abiati surmised. 'But from what I can gather they'd like to withdraw back through Yugoslavia.'

'Dennis, *Capitano* Abiati,' Callan said, 'we must monitor the radios twenty-four hours a day. *If* they send a force to Mirios we need to know when and most importantly what their strength will be.'

'Righto, old boy,' Dennis said rather too nonchalantly in Callan's opinion. 'I'll nag Alex every hour or so.'

'I'll get back to town and see how Ivy and Juan are getting on.'

Then, on the 4 and 6 June, two game-changing events occurred. The Allies captured Rome, and two days later General Dwight D Eisenhower's joint force successfully stormed the Normandy Beaches during Operation Overlord, which became known as D-Day, although it was a term used for the date of any major military operation.

Now fighting on south, east and western fronts the *Reich* was on the skids, but once again someone forgot to tell the Germans, and Hitler wouldn't listen anyway.

'We should be pretty safe now,' Abiati observed as he and Dennis monitored their respective wireless sets at *Bella Vista.*

'Maybe,' Dennis replied, 'but Jerry still holds on to Greece and we're picking up Intel about paratrooper units training on the Ionian Coast.'

And they did come …

Chapter 34 – Airborne

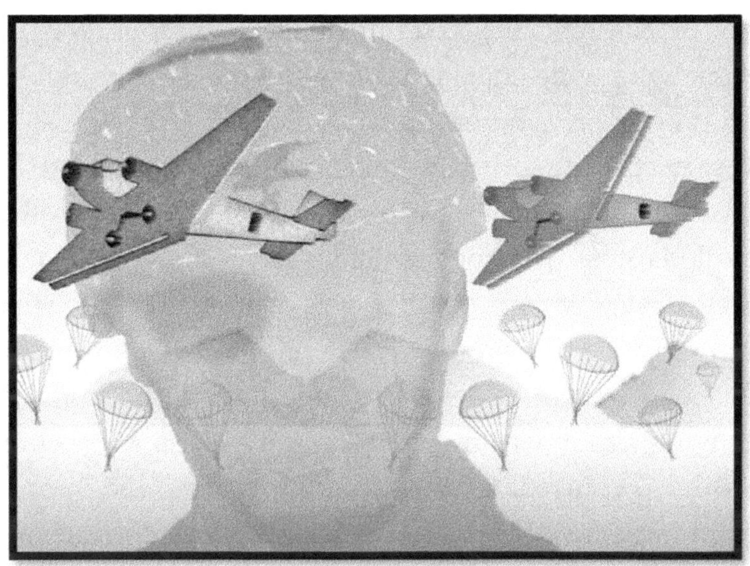

'This is you target, *Hauptman* Viola,' the SS Intel officer said, jabbing a finger at Mirios on the map. 'The coastal strip north of Mirios Harbour is ideal. Two Ju-52 transports with a twelve-man stick each. You will drop at first light. You occupy and hold the island. Your task will be to crush any resistance and set up an observation station to monitor enemy shipping and aircraft.'

'I have been assigned just two squads,' Viola explained. 'A light platoon. Will that be sufficient?'

'It is all we have to spare. You volunteered for this duty, so deal with it.'

The Intel-O was probably right. Although there had been no reports from *Capitano* Abiati since the Italian surrender, there was no evidence that the Allies had showed the slightest interest in Mirios either. Nevertheless, Viola was under no illusions about his men.

To be honest his troops weren't the cream of the SS crop. In fact they were mostly in disgrace for having shown a shred of humanity or common sense, both qualities discouraged by *Nazi* ethos. Some who were considered malingerers and trouble-makers had been on one punishment detail after another for most of their military service. One private, Jonas Wolf, even claimed to be a pacifist, thus qualifying him for front-line combat duty in the hope he'd be killed on his first engagement.

After Crete, where paratrooper casualties were appalling, joining an airborne division was only one step away from suicide. Not only had German losses been huge during the initial assault and following ground action, but Cretan partisans executed any Germans they captured. Crete's brutality became the template for how warfare was now conducted around the Mediterranean.

'What about re-supply, sir?' Viola asked.

'You'll have to live off the land to start with. Radio your situation once you've secured the area. Understand one thing, the Fuehrer demands every man's absolute commitment. There will be no retreat, no extraction. You will hold the island to the last man if necessary.'

Viola eyed the Intel-O glumly.

'But don't worry Viola, we have no intelligence indicating British or American forces are anywhere near Mirios. They're just a bunch of passive peasants. Feel free to shoot as many as you please if they cause trouble. I'll try to organise a supply drop within a week.'

'Unless we're all killed.'

'Yes, there is that but try to stay positive, won't you.'

Viola shrugged.

He despised his men. In his opinion they were nothing but sloppy back-sliders and not fit to wear a uniform. He viewed them strictly as cannon-fodder. As for his own life, he'd survived Stalingrad and there weren't too many people who could claim that. It'd take a lot more than the rabble on Mirios to concern *Herr Hauptmann* Viola.

So at 4 am this unhappy band of misfits boarded two ponderous Ju-52 tri-motor transport aircraft. Each plane carried twelve paratroopers. Viola led the first stick while the second was commanded by a resentful sergeant who considered an Italian platoon commander as unnecessary as it was distasteful.

The paratroopers lit cigarettes and pipes as the Ju-52 engines spluttered to life. The men showed nothing but resigned indifference after the planes lumbered skywards, droning towards Mirios Island.

*

Callan kicked himself afterwards. Despite their preparations Mirios townsfolk grew more complacent as each day passed. The town was short of meat, so he, Fausto and a group of Mirios sharpshooters went hunting. Abiati and Dennis had nothing to report, so Callan reckoned it was safe enough to leave town for a couple of days. It was dawn when the hunting team returned from their night camp with a decent haul of wild goat carcasses. It was enough to last at least a week. The loaded cart made slow going, but they weren't in any particular rush.

That was until they heard growling aero-engines and then they raced on. A dozen men knowing they'd be caught unawares and dreading what they were about to see as they topped the ridge above *Bella Vista* overlooking the town.

The Ju-52 transports droned over the harbour just as Callan topped the ridge. They were cumbersome, slow moving beasts. Callan reckoned they were easy targets even for his rifle if only they were in range. Beyond town black specks drifted downwards. Not a huge force by Callan's reckoning, but his group would never reach town in time to organise its defence.

Meanwhile Viola wasted no time. He led his men to town. There was no way two dozen men could round up everyone, but they did a pretty good job. Dividing into three-man groups, they smashed down doors and herded drowsy townspeople down to the harbour, which Viola decided was the best place to keep everyone together. A couple of hundred hostages should keep others from trying something foolish.

Occasionally a shot cracked through the dawn air, but it seemed they were just to get everyone's attention and keep them moving along. The Germans hadn't killed anyone…yet.

When Callan and his companions reached *Bella Vista*, the roundup was well underway. The paratroopers hadn't reached the villa by then and didn't appear in any great hurry. Things were going their way. Dennis Mortimer sat ready with his Morse key.

'Do you know what's happened?' Abiati asked.

'We saw two sticks drop. Maybe twenty or twenty-five men. No more. Dennis, try to get hold of your bosses in Alex or Rome or wherever the hell they are now and put 'em in the picture.'

The key-pad clicked into action.

'I'd better go down there and see what's what,' Callan said.

'No!' Abiati said. 'I'll go. At least I'm supposed to be here even if my status is problematic.'

'What do you think we should do?' Ivy asked.

She was still in her pyjamas.

'Look, they don't know we're here,' Callan said, 'and it's best we keep it that way, but I've got an idea. I'll get our lads organised, and anyone who hasn't been caught in the net. We'd better get cracking before anyone starts shooting.'

Callan issued instructions to the men who'd come down the hills with him. Abiati gave them some time before he headed for town. He too was in no hurry.

*

Mirios wasn't a particularly large town, but it still took two hours to clear every house and march the occupants to the quayside. Although he didn't care, Viola was amazed no one had yet been shot. His men may have been loafers and bar-room brawlers, but they didn't have the ice-cold ruthlessness of indoctrinated storm-troopers. Undoubtedly people had fled out of town, but phase two of Viola's operation would track them down.

The crowd gathered, eyeing the machine-gun toting soldiers nervously. The first arrivals had now been at the wharf long enough to be suffering from the summer heat. Children cried and parents asked for water, while things could get very unsanitary at any time. Appeals from the townsfolk fell on deaf ears. The whole sorry bunch of them could wet themselves as far as Viola was concerned, especially as he'd identified a number of Jews.

Eventually Viola's men had gathered everyone who was going to be caught in the first cordon. Hundreds either got away or remained undetected, but still the harbour was jammed with people. Some sat while others stood and shifted about despite the German's efforts to keep them still.

And then things got ugly.

Viola began separating anyone he considered to be Jewish and assembling them beside the harbour building that had once been *Capitano* Abiati's quay-side office. The fact the Jews were herded into one place wasn't lost on anyone and when two storm-troopers mounting a Mauser MG-42 a machinegun on its Lafette tripod at the edge of the sea-wall their suspicions were confirmed.

The townsfolk had two choices. They'd either try to take on the Germans or see their Jewish neighbours massacred. They'd heard the stories from the mainland, and knew the Germans showed no mercy to Jews and others they considered inferior. A few hundred citizens would probably overrun two dozen soldiers, but the cost would be horrendous, especially as half were women and children. An MG-42 could spray lead at twelve hundred rounds per minute.

Viola's men then got rough, forcing the two groups apart. They slammed their rifle butts into anyone moving too slowly. Several people, young and old fell, and were in danger of being trampled. Women and children screamed as the wharf dissolved into a panic-stricken mass of seething humanity. Viola took no notice. He ordered his machine-gunners to load the ammo-belt and take aim.

Right then *Capitano* Abiati marched into the harbour square. He wore full dress uniform, sash and sword-belt, riding breeches, brilliantly polished boots, kepi and campaign ribbons pinned above his tunic breast pocket. He was accompanied by Sergeant Vanni and his two erstwhile soldiers. Abiati strode straight up to Viola, grabbed his arm and spun him around. Abiati recognised his old lieutenant, eye-patch and all, even before he saw his face. Viola's strutting manner hadn't changed.

Viola glared, brushing his sleeve as if Abiati had left something distasteful on his arm.

'Couldn't keep away, I see,' Abiati said conversationally. 'What's all this about?' he added indicating the milling crowd of fearful townsfolk.

'I no longer answer to you,' Viola snarled smugly. 'In fact you are under arrest and will hang for treason.'

'Treason?' Abiati raised an eyebrow.

'You know perfectly well all Italians must either serve the *Reich* or be considered traitors.'

'And how have I not served the *Reich*?' Abiati asked, knowing he was goading Viola, but also playing for time

'This Jewish filth still lives. That is evidence enough. In fact I think you should join them.'

Viola ordered two paratroopers to manhandle Abiati and his men to where the Jews stood. They were shoved into the group. Abiati stumbled, but recovered and stood rigidly to attention glaring defiantly at Viola.

Screams came from both groups as the Germans took aim. Viola raised his arm, but only those close by heard a dull *thunk* as he froze and dropped to his knees before collapsing onto his face. No one saw the neat red hole in his forehead, but everyone saw the mess of bone and brain tissue sprayed from the back of his skull.

A barrage of lead riddled the two machine-gunners who flopped grotesquely over their weapon. Several flaming Molotov cocktails dropped onto the square, exploding in front of the Germans, giving the hostages time to run for it. Viola's men sensed rather than saw the danger was from the rooftops. As they bolted for cover, they sprayed gunfire into the terracotta tiles, shattering vermillion shards everywhere. The troops guarding the crowd were unhurt. It looked like whoever was shooting wanted to avoid collateral damage.

The townsfolk scattered. Some dived into the harbour and swam to nearby boats while others raced down alleys, through doorways and open windows. Wherever they went, the harbour emptied within minutes.

Viola's sergeant needed to gather his men and consolidate their position. He was left with only one wireless phone. The other lay abandoned on the quayside. The Germans had no idea how many partisans they faced so the sergeant decided he'd retreat to the drop zone and consolidate with good visibility and cover behind the stone wall running beside the road they'd come to town on.

His only communication was to yell for his men. Some responded, while others were scattered even beyond his bellowing voice. About half the force joined him as they made their way through town, hugging the walls and darting between shadows. Shots rang out continuously, sometimes distant but on occasion shells ripped past, smashing into masonry and cobblestones.

And the Germans' nightmare worsened.

Reaching the outskirts of town they were met by a hail of rifle fire. One man died instantly while another was wounded in his thigh. Private Wolf, acting as medic, staunched the bleeding and administered pain-killers, but the Germans now had two more men out of action.

Then the Sergeant sensed movement to the German's rear. To his dismay partisans had barricaded the streets with barrows, a truck and anything else they could lay their hands on. With such a narrow fire-zone, the Germans would be annihilated if they turned back. From the amount of shooting so far the enemy had plenty of guns and ammunition. It was a face-off.

'We won't be able to break out until dark,' Wolf observed.

The sergeant told him to shut up.

'We need to get inside,' he said, but the Germans didn't get the chance…

*

Beforehand it hadn't taken Callan long to work out where the townspeople were being taken. He just followed the yelling. Harsh German voices barked commands amid the wailing and protests of Mirios' citizens. Occasionally a rifle shot cracked to move things along.

'What do you think they're planning?' Ivy had asked.

'They'll check everyone's papers and God know half the people here don't have any,' Callan replied. 'They'll be lucky even to have their births registered with one of the churches.'

'They'll ship the Jews off to labour camps,' Juan said.

'I'll get my rifle and scope,' Callan said. 'Juan, get hold of anyone who escaped the Jerry roundup. Arm them from the nearest cache and get to the harbour. We need as many people on the roofs or upper windows as possible. We'll need men in the streets too.'

'And women?' Ivy said with intent.

'Yes, and women. Anyone who can fire a gun. Fausto can you organise the street fighters? Ivy, get people to man a roadblock on the edge of town. If things go well, we need to stop any Jerries escaping. Make sure you have plenty of cover.'

Fausto nodded and was gone.

'Where are you going?' Ivy asked.

'To church.'

He kissed her.

'Now get going!'

The Catholic steeple wasn't huge or ostentatious, but it was the highest structure in town and only a street away from the waterfront. Someone had suggested the Catholics chose the site to beat the Orthodox, Muslims and Jews to any sailors seeking solace for their sinful souls.

He dodged a couple of Germans who he noted were spread thinly, sometimes in pairs and sometimes alone. They were all heading to the wharf and would be there in moments.

That's worth remembering, he thought.

Luckily Mirios Catholics didn't feel the inclination to lock their church. The good father maintained God was happy to receive callers at any time. The priest wasn't there as the Germans had already scooped him up with many others. Callan didn't have time to worry. He squeezed through the stone arch leading to the clock tower steps.

The church was designed centuries ago when people must have been smaller, but Callan worked his way up the spiral stone staircase to the belfry where a single bell hung. A narrow ledge ran around the tower with just enough room for Callan to shuffle along until he faced the harbour.

The belfry opened on all four sides, giving Callan not only a good view of the wharf, but the town in all directions. As he watched he quickly understood the horror that was about to unfold. He'd promised Ivy he was done with killing, but it looked like another war had landed in his lap.

Should have gone on the bloody sub, while we had the chance.

But he knew that wasn't true, he was here because Mirios needed him. He sighed, checked the magazine and clipped into the rifle breech. He identified the one-eyed German officer in charge quickly enough. There was something familiar about him…what was it?

Then Abiati arrived and Callan made the connection.

It's bloody Lieutenant Viola in an SS uniform!

There was no time to waste. After a brief discussion, Callan saw Viola's men dragging Abiati towards the Jews and the machine-gunners preparing to fire. He aimed. It was no big deal at such close range. He squeezed the trigger just seconds before gunfire exploded from the rooftops and second-storey windows…

Chapter 35 — The Last Rifle Shot

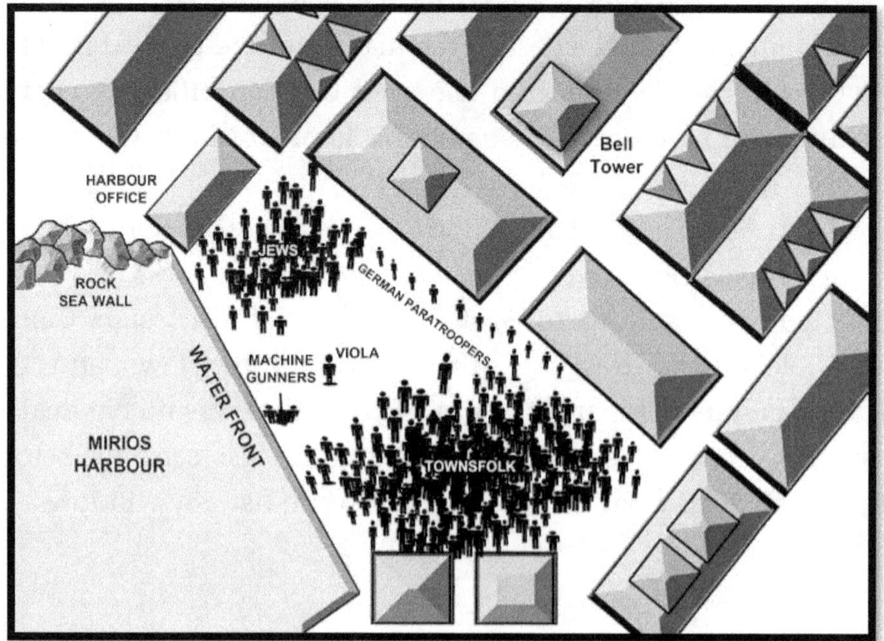

Mirios' citizens were seriously pissed off. Their blood was up and they were well armed. The Germans were perhaps slightly better equipped, but woefully out-numbered. By the time Callan reached the street, Ivy had established fifty people behind make-shift barricades between the last row of homes and the paratroopers' drop-zone, blocking any escape.

Meanwhile Fausto's men clambered from the roof-tops and upper storey windows covering the street leading back to the harbour. The Germans were trapped in an impotent stalemate furthermore they'd lost their hostages and any bargaining leverage.

Callan gathered a dozen men and began extracting individual stragglers who'd taken cover in doorways or broken into buildings.

Callan remembered a little German he'd learnt from a farmer's wife after he escaped from Holzminden POW camp during the Great War. They found half-a-dozen frightened men who'd lost their Teutonic bravado once they were alone and cornered. It was no secret partisans summarily executed any Germans they captured in Crete, and no one expected things to be different on Mirios.

But Callan didn't want to kill anyone else. He felt badly enough about Viola who was right proper bastard, but what was the choice? Most of the confrontations went something like this:

Callan:

You're surrounded. There's no escape. Throw down your weapons and come out with your hands up.

German Soldier:

Bugger off you'll kill me if I do.

Callan:

We'll kill you if you don't. We're not Cretans. I'm American. No one else has to die.

After some haggling, the Germans all surrendered and were marched to the harbour to be guarded by sword-toting *Capitano* Abiati, Juan and a handful of stern, pistol-packing Mirios goodwives. That just left the largest group bottled up between Ivy and Fausto's people.

Unfortunately the tough-guy sergeant had been in the first wave during the Crete invasion where he was wounded and had only recently returned to active duty.

The paratroopers took cover in a street building. That was easy enough, but what to do then? They tried escaping through the back door into a line of walled courtyards, but were driven back by a hail of gunfire and exploding Molotov cocktails from snipers on the roof-tops.

So, braving random rifle fire they formed a redoubt around the front doorway of the building they held. They piled furniture from inside onto the street for cover and manned the front windows.

This was by no means ideal because Ivy and Fausto's groups were on either flank while the Germans faced the narrow street. But as their barricade extended with everything they added to it, they were able to shoot at the townspeople, who'd erected their own barricades and were pretty well protected by then.

Callan checked Fausto's position which was well set up and it would be pure suicide for the Germans to try to storm in along such a narrow street. The only chance was to inch their redoubt forward, which would take hours if not days.

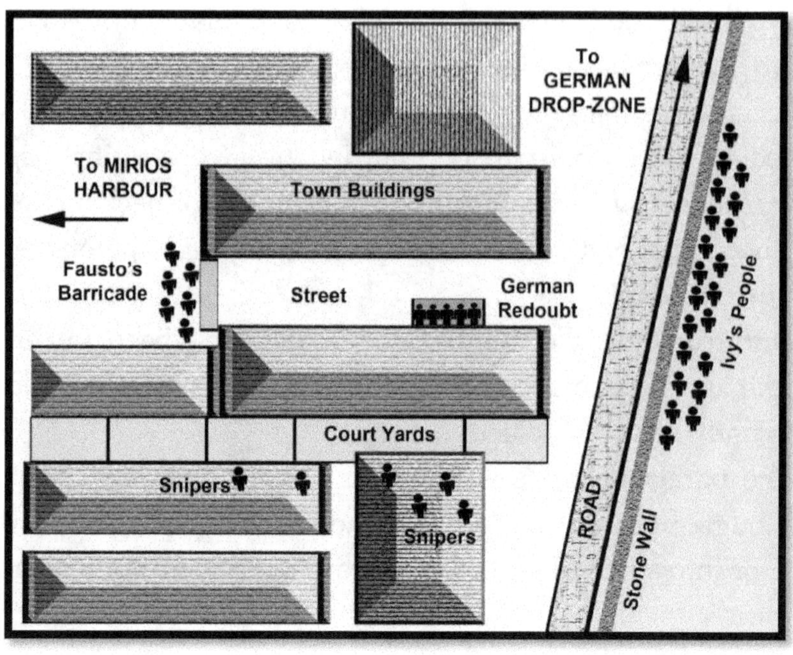

He detoured around town and reached Ivy's people who were well dug in behind a stone wall augmented with upturned carts for extra protection. This was the Germans' only chance if they spread out and moved quickly a few might get past, but where would they go then? Did they have wireless communications to call for reinforcements? Callan didn't know.

'It's time to parley,' he told Ivy. 'Has someone got something we can use for a white flag?'

'Don't be silly,' Ivy chided. 'They'll shoot you. We've got them bottled up. We can get extra people on the roof-tops to lob more Molotov cocktails onto them.'

'It might come to that, but maybe a bit of horse-trading will avoid further killing. I don't really want to see those men burn to death, do you?'

Ivy agreed so he walked towards the German redoubt alone. A white apron hung from his rifle barrel which he'd loaded with a full magazine. You can never be too careful.

Yeah, right. Here I am walking towards a bunch of desperate trigger-happy Jerries who aren't known for reasonable behaviour.

'Don't shoot,' he called in poor German. 'We need to talk.'

'Don't come any closer or we'll shoot!'

Callan was surprised the reply was in English.

'You speak English?

'Better than you speak German. I recognised your accent is English, maybe American.'

'We need to sort this out before anyone else is killed.'

'This is war! People are supposed to be killed.'

'Not innocent people.'

Callan sensed he was only talking to an interpreter because there were pauses during the exchange when he heard mumbling from behind the German barricade. After a longer pause, two men edged past their cover and faced Callan.

'I am Private Jonas Wolf,' one of the soldiers declared, 'and this is Sergeant Dekker who is now in command.'

'My name is Callan McAlister and I have to tell you we've captured your other men. There is no way out for you. If you surrender, we can arrange for your safe transfer from the island as POWs.'

Private Wolf and Sergeant Dekker conferred, although the German NCO didn't appear to be in a particularly negotiable mood.

'My sergeant says you'll murder us if we surrender just like Crete. He says he'd rather die fighting.'

'This isn't Crete and you haven't committed any atrocities to anger these people...yet. You have my word you won't be harmed.'

More discussion.

'I believe you, but my sergeant does not,' Wolf said.

'What do the others think?'

Callan saw Dekker was enraged by the idea of any form of democracy.

'He says the *Waffen SS* do not vote. They obey orders...'

Then Dekker made his move, but Callan saw it coming. Dekker stepped clear of the redoubt for a better aim. He raised his Erma-Werke MP-38 machinegun as Callan dived and aimed his rifle.

'*Nein!*' Private Wolf yelled barging Dekker aside just as Callan fired.

The bullet ripped through Wolf's body and he lay still, while Dekker staggered to regain his balance, spraying lead ahead of him. The bullets flew over Callan, but Dekker saw his error and lowered his aim. Suddenly he jerked like a rag-doll as his body was ripped to scarlet shreds by gun-fire from both Ivy's and Fausto's people. Dekker was hit by dozens of rounds. His torso dissolved into mush oozing over the cobblestones.

With guns blazing Fausto's men charged up the street and stormed the redoubt. The Germans were driven back through the bullet-riddled door, slamming it behind them. A German stick grenade tumbled from the shattered front window pane and clunked onto the street, but Fausto grabbed it and tossed it back inside.

The explosion blasted shrapnel and shattered glass from inside. Screams and choking curses pierced the smoke-filled building. Fausto's people blasted the door to chips. They kicked the tortured wood aside and fired randomly through the smoke before charging in. The fight was over in seconds. All the Germans were wounded or stunned by the blast.

The Mirios men could have finished the Germans off in an orgy of bloodletting, but they relented. When they saw the enemy was finished, they disarmed them just in case before helping them outside.

'Get the doctor,' Fausto said. 'I don't think these men are in any condition to complain about being treated by a Jew.'

Meanwhile Callan scrambled to where Private Wolf lay. The bullet had gone straight through the young man's shoulder and exited cleanly.

'You'll live,' Callan assured him.

'It hurts like hell.'

'Hang in there. We'll get something for the pain.'

'Thanks,' Private Wolf even managed a quick smile.

'Your English is very good,' Callan said, because wasn't sure what else to say.

'Thank you, my mother insisted I learn.'

'It came in handy.'

Ivy raced forward and flung her arms around Callan.

'Darling, are you hurt?' she cried. 'I saw you fall over in all that shooting.'

'No, I'm fine thanks to this young chap here. Let's get him somewhere comfortable.'

*

Bella Vista Villa Lunchtime

'We've contacted the navy and they're sending a ship in couple of days to pick up the Germans,' Dennis Mortimer reported. 'The wounded men are doing OK. Your saviour young Private Wolf is recovering well I'm happy to say.'

'None of our people was seriously hurt and other than four Germans and Lieutenant Viola killed, we didn't come out of this too badly. The doctor expects everyone to get better completely,' Ivy said.

'What if they send more paratroopers?' Callan asked.

'It's unlikely now,' Dennis said. 'The Allies have just landed in Southern France. They called it Operation Dragoon and it was nearly as big as Normandy. It all seems to be going well according to what I hear on the wireless. Jerry's pulling men back through Yugoslavia, so they'll have no time for our little backwater.'

'Private Wolf has volunteered to stay and man the radio set to reassure the German commanders the paratroopers are doing fine here.'

'Doesn't he feel that's just a teeny-weeny bit treasonable?' Callan said.

'He says it's all over for the *Reich*, but Hitler and his cronies just don't want to face the fact,' Abiati said. 'There's no way even the Germans can hold back the Russians and Allies on all fronts. The *Luftwaffe* is stretched to the limit. They've simply lost too many planes and aircrews to dominate the sky anymore.'

'Funny about Private Wolf, though,' Ivy said coyly. 'He told me his mother was a farmer's wife in Schleswig Holstein. Her husband was killed on the Western Front. Didn't you stay with a Frau Wolf when you were on the run after you escaped that POW camp?'

'It's a common name and Schleswig Holstein covers a lot of territory,' Callan said.

He'd failed to tell Ivy that Frau Wolf had often shared his bed until he returned to the Allied lines.

No, it can't be. No way.

'He said he has two sisters, who were teenagers when he was born,' Ivy prattled on. 'Apparently they married pure Arian men to produce pure Arian citizens for the *Reich*. Jonas wasn't taken in by the *Nazi* hokum and was always getting into trouble for not joining the party.'

Yeah, Frau Wolf did have two girls and she did take a fancy to me. It can't be. What are the odds? He doesn't even look like me...does he?

Luckily Dennis changed the subject.

'What do you think we should do about our Jewish community if Jerry returns?'

'It depends how big a ship the navy sends for our POWs. They won't even fit a quarter of them aboard a dog-boat or a sub.'

But the war had turned significantly by then and the navy was happy to spare a frigate and two corvette escorts which steamed right up to Mirios Harbour, anchoring just beyond the breakwater. None of the ships flew a broad pennant, but such a modest flotilla hardly warranted a commodore, let alone an admiral.

A boat pulled away from the frigate carrying the ship's skipper. Ivy and Callan were delighted to welcome Lieutenant-Commander Jeremy St Chalfont-Smyth back to the island.

'There'll certainly be room for everyone on board,' Callan said, 'but I dunno if they all want to evacuate.'

'Won't be up to them, old boy,' Jeremy said. 'I have orders to ship out all Jewish civilians for their own protection.'

'That's seems harsh,' Ivy said.

'Not really. At least they'll be safe. Admiral Cunningham doesn't want to have to drop everything and come to their rescue again.'

'The Germans are unlikely to come back,' Ivy insisted.

'The Admiral isn't going to take that chance. He's not an "unlikely" sort of chap. He prefers certainties.'

'Where are you taking them?'

'Palestine. Apparently there's a Jewish community kicking off there, hoping to make a permanent go of it.'

'You mean start a new country.'

'Nothing's set in stone yet, but yes something like that.'

'I wonder what the Palestinians think about that,' Ivy said.

'If our top brass and politicians are true to form, I doubt if anyone has bothered to ask them,' Jeremy added.

Callan was surprised to find all the Jews, including the elderly who'd called Mirios home all their lives, wanted to leave.

'I guess they can always come back when the war is over, and we can certainly see the light at the end of the tunnel now,' Callan observed.

'They won't want to come back,' Ivy said.

'How can you be so sure?'

'Their Rabbi says it's a prophecy fulfilled. He called it Zionism, a movement to form an independent state of Israel. Apparently Old Testament profits, Leviticus, Jeremiah and Ezekiel all foretold the Israelis return to the Holy Land after they'd been kicked out on and off throughout history. Well a bunch of Zionist zealots have jumbled the prophecies together and come up with a return date to Israel any time now.'

'What, they want to take over a chunk of Palestine and call it Israel?'

'Apparently so — just as soon as the war is over. There are Jewish refugees who've escaped concentration camps all over the world, just itching to start their own homeland.'

'Like I said, the Palestinians ain't going take that lying down,' Callan said.

'You can bet your life on that,' Jeremy said, 'but I'd better get my chaps to start loading. Those Jerry POWs don't seem too concerned.'

'I think they're happy you aren't Russians and they recognise the *Reich* is finished. They probably just want the whole thing to be done and dusted. I dunno what'll be left in Germany for them to go back to though.'

'I'll drop by to say cheerio before we go. Are you sure you don't want to come with us?

'No thanks, Jeremy. We'll stay and give Dennis a hand. *Capitano* Abiati is going back to Sicily to be a policeman again. I think he still really wants to catch Don Rocco, but I don't fancy his chances. His men have decided to stay now they're officially civilians.'

Excerpt from Ivy Brown's Journal, August 1945

Dear Diary,
It's finally over, but the Americans had to drop two hideous bombs to
force the Japanese into surrender.

Greece, Italy and Albania are all making claims for Mirios, so who
knows where it will finally wind up. I fancy the Allies will hand the
island over to Greece despite Albania's opposition. Everyone is ignoring
Albania as if it's just too small to matter.

Darling Callan and I are packing up and heading Stateside He is so
disappointed after all we did through those awful war years. No sooner
were the Germans beaten when the Greeks started a bitter civil war.
Royalists against Communists.

There's talk of forming a United Nations to replace the League of
Nations, which was hopeless. The victors are already carving up territory
hell west and crooked. France and Britain want their colonies back
although they've done precious little to deserve them.

Johnny Witherspoon sold the Fairchild in Egypt and plans to start a
charter business with the money. He has asked us to join him in British
Colombia. He was quite the fighter ace and won heaps of medals, but now
he just wants to fly float-planes out of Victoria Harbour on Vancouver
Island to servicer the western seaboard. He promises us British Colombia
has much nicer weather than Saskatchewan.

He found that nice girl, Amy Potter, who'd waited for him. He's taking her to Canada and we're invited to their wedding.

Callan is thrilled about teaming up with Johnny again. He doesn't believe we'll run into any wars in Canada. I agree absolutely and what girl doesn't love a wedding. I hope I don't cry, and if Johnny's Amy is half as lovely as he claims, she'll be a stunning bride.

Dennis Mortimer was awarded the George Cross for his work on Mirios. It turned out that many of his wireless messages contributed to successful operations in the Med. And he never said a word about it to anyone!

Jeremy plans to stay in the navy. I wouldn't be surprised if he's an admiral one day.

Juan isn't returning to Spain. He said life under General Franco would be heart-breaking as all his family are gone now. There's talk he'll become Mayor of Mirios.

And so, dear Diary, I will pack you away in my valise until we are reunited aboard our trans-Atlantic steamer. Canada awaits.

If you'd like to discover how Callan and Ivy met and the possible mystery of Private Jonas Wolf, I recommend *McAlister and the Great War* so you can judge for yourselves.

Jeremy St Chalfont-Smyth appears in *McAlister's Siege* and *McAlister's Allegiance,* although he doesn't seem to link Danny McAlister and his Great-Uncle Callan, but seven years had passed and McAlister is a common enough surname.

Gene McAlister also appears in *McAlister and the Great War* while his father Sam McAlister features in *McAlister's Trail.*

We must wait to see if Zach and Angela come up with any more stories from:

The McAlister Line

For more details and artwork, visit:
www.richardmarman.com
www.richardmarman.net

By his fifteenth birthday, Danny McAlister escapes from a draconian Rockhampton boarding school after seriously injuring the principal. His flight takes him through Northern Queensland to the New Guinea Highlands in search of his father, lost while fighting the Japanese on the Kokoda Track.

Thrown into an adult world he becomes embroiled in union wars between cane cutters, joins the crew of a prawn trawler in the Gulf of Carpentaria, gets mixed up with smugglers and the hazardous burgeoning New Guinea aviation. He teams up with 'Mad' Monty, an eccentric Afro-American pilot and Angela, the stunning teenage daughter of an English missionary. Together they endure a series of harrowing adventures as they journey through New Guinea's Central Highlands and the Bismarck Sea archipelagos where they face their final challenge against vicious Filipino pirates and discover the secret of Danny's missing father.

Only months after escaping from Frenchy Duval's band of cut-throat pirates, Danny McAlister and Angela Holyman are once again thrust into a thrilling, helter-skelter adventure in their tropical, South-Sea paradise.

Following only the flimsiest clues they embark on a perilous treasure hunt to save the lives of some new friends in a desperate struggle against old enemies.

Danny McAlister and Mad Monty are on the run once more. They wind up working for General Claire Chennault's *China Air Transport* only to be dragged into the last throes of the Chinese Civil War and then on to Korea where Danny learns first-hand the horrors of battle. Far worse is yet to come. After the Korean cease-fire General Chennault assigns Danny to Vietnam where he rejoins his old flame Angela Holyman. Unwittingly Danny and Angel are thrown into the desperate blood climax of the siege at Dien Bien Phu.

After recovering from his injuries suffered at Dien Bien Phu, Danny is straight back into action. Joined by Monty and Angela, they plunge headlong into another non-stop, roller-coaster odyssey across five continents, landing in one desperate scrape after another. Finally all three must face heart-breaking decisions that ultimately define their true allegiances.

In an instant the developed world is destroyed and plunged into anarchy. Can Zach McAlister, Karen Davenport and Mike Farrow survive as they're thrust into a feral, deadly new order? Not only must they come to terms with their Stone Age environment and the use of only medieval technology, but also face the terror of marauding tribal gangs, whose only method of survival is violence and conquest. Will they forge a future for themselves and their descendents? The question can only answered through their courage, determination and friendship. But, is that enough?

Zach McAlister and Angela Holyman have uncovered another thrilling story of Lieutenant Jonathan McAlister during the Napoleonic Wars Peninsular Campaign at the beginning of the 19th Century. Severely wounded and trapped behind enemy lines, two common soldiers' wives are his only chance of salvation, but the entire French Army and marauding bandits stand between them and freedom.

Set against the panoramic backdrop of New Mexico, Sonora, Arizona and California in 1867, Jubal Quinn is desperate. He's a black trooper in the newly formed 10th Cavalry accused of murdering a white man. Behind bars and doomed to hang, his only chance is to escape from the stockade with the help Billy Songbird, a wayward, half-breed Kiowa teenager. Hot on their heels is Lieutenant Sam McAlister, a man whose devotion to duty has turned to obsession. Blasting a trail of blood headlong through the southwest, not even the love of a beautiful Mexican girl can deter Sam. The chase can only end when either he or Jubal Quinn is dead.

1914. On his seventeenth birthday, New South Wales farm boy, Callan McAlister, joins the AIF and is swept off to war. He endures the trials and deprivations of the Sinai Desert, Gallipoli, the Dublin Easter Uprising and finally the ultimate carnage along the Western Front. Callan falls in love with beautiful English girl, Ivy Brown, but their path to future happiness is perilous when they are torn apart by aristocratic prejudice and the brutality of war. Can Ivy and Callan struggle through the years of turmoil, or will they become just two more casualties among millions?

<u>**McAlister's Hoard**</u>

'Thanks Richard, just to let you know I finished *McAlister's Hoard* – started at 9.00 am and put it down all done at 5.00 pm great read, a real *Boys Own* book... the novels have certainly caught my interest as I seem to relate to Danny and Ange. Maybe they were part of my Day Dreams growing up in Tully and NQ and they get me away from some the Deep, Dark and Sombre books that are written these days. I also purchased "The Story of Two Turtles" for my Grand Children - Girls aged 10 and 7 - I will get you to sign it with a little note if you would.

Once again thanks for a NEW experience

Peter Mullins

'

This is a fast paced, thoroughly enjoyable adventure that will take you through strange places where smugglers do their dirty deeds and pirates are not far behind. Where beautiful ladies are hungry for life and young men find adventures unlimited. There are plenty of hazards along the way to leave you wondering 'what will happen next'. The characters are lovable, humorous and there are desperado's amidst then too. I highly recommend you get your copy ASAP

Ian King

Refreshing to read a story that reminds of yarns spun from storytellers when the tale was the highlight in itself. Enjoyed this read and the language used. Enjoyable read.

AJ Mouse

<u>*McAlister's Siege*</u>

The McAlister Line series continues. And it's great to see my old favourite characters - Danny, Angela, Mad Monty, Long Li ... and even Frenchy Duvall - return.

This book is set in the Indo-China wars, a period I'd never heard much about before the time when the Americans (and Australians) entered the war. Richard Marman pulled the story together well. Danny and Monty escape some heavies in PNG to do a job in Indo-China — a job that would set them up with significant cash. The action escalates when they find the war comes to them. Then our other favourites come along, including ANGELA! I'm beginning to see this series as an action-adventure-romance between Danny and Angela, and I'm cheering and booing them from the sidelines. It's a great read, plenty of action and intrigue, with a dash of romance. I'm looking forward to reading the next instalment

Chris Johnson, author

An excellent fast-moving tale, plenty of details to keep the military nerd happy.

Kevin Colbran

<u>*McAlister's Trail*</u>

'A decent read and a fun romp across the Southwest.'
Sandy Whiting for Western Writers of America *Roundup Magazine*

'This is a great and interesting novel written in an easy-to-read way. I loved the characters and settings as well as the action-packed events. Really enjoyed reading it.'
Amazon.com review
<u>*McAlister's Spark*</u>
McAlister's Spark is a fast-paced, action-riddled amazing read you will struggle to put down.'
Wade Reynolds, Brisbane

'A great action read for teenagers and great graphics — a great literary effort.'
Amazon Review

<u>*McAlister and the Great War*</u>

'A very good and well researched read. I enjoyed it very much.'
Squadron-leader Mark 'Cowboy' Willcocks, RAAF ret. Chief Pilot and CEO Fubilan Air Transport PNG

Hi Richard, I was the guy who drank whiskey with you till 4am after which you gave me a copy of McAlister *and the Great War*. I needed a break from work, went to Sydney with Colleen this weekend and devoured your wonderful book in almost a day. Thank you for the wonderful book. Kind regards
Paul Coppens

Other Tittles by Richard Marman

The dreaded dragon, Brimstone is terrorising the sleepy village of Oak Tree, so it's up to Prince Roger and his sister Princess Crystal to hunt down the fiery beast.

They are aided and hindered — as the case may be — by an evil knight, a mysterious good-guy, the local sheriff, loyal men-at-arms, forest brigands, a pair of trusty — and not so trusty — chargers, ogres, trolls and Oak Tree's citizens with a bunch of attitude. There are thrills, spills, romance and a heap of rollicking good fun to be had by all.

I just finished reading Richard Marman's *Dragon Stalkers* and gave it a resounding five stars on Amazon and Goodreads. It's an awesome book, hilarious with the writer's wicked sense of humour *Dragon Stalkers* is eminently readable and oh, so funny. It presents a refreshingly original tale out of a kaleidoscopic jumble of common fairy tale clichés. It is cleverly done storytelling that entertains on every page. The humour is light but sharp with loads of double entendres that would not be out of place in a *Carry On* movie.

I don't remember a book I finished as quickly and enjoyed so much. I would love to read more in this style. I seriously believe Richard Marman has hit on something special.

Salman Shami, author

Approaching his sixteenth birthday, Henry is thrust into a perilous quest when his village chief's wife is abducted. Joined by three companions and his pet wolf, he vows to track down the sinister kidnappers. With no magic or special skills, they can only rely on their courage determination, wits and friendship to survive in a cruel realm which makes no concessions for youth or innocence. Danger mounts with each challenge until ultimately they face a seemingly unconquerable foe at the gates of a hostile, alien city.

I didn't party this NYE, unless you count staying up to finish reading a novel, which is what I did.

The novel I read is "The Wealth" by fellow Australian author Richard Marman. Yes, he happens to be a friend of mine, but he's a fantastic storyteller, and I'm in awe of how he strings a yarn together. (I particularly loved the battle scenes near the end. They're not gory, which is good, but one of them was so entertaining! It reminded me of the old Cisco Kid serials I used to watch as a kid on the telly.)

Check it out at https://www.amazon.com/Wealth-Richard-Marman/dp/1925833046 it's also available through Kobo, Apple, and other good bookstores. **Chris Johnson**

Wave and Web Series

Available at online bookstores

Children's Books Illustrated for other authors

Illustrated for Rita Hayward   **Illustrated for Elle Burton**

Story by Judith Bandidt
The
Littlest
Bandit
Illustrations by Richard Marman

Max
Visits the
Zoo
Story by Judith Bandidt
Illustrations by Richard Marman

An
Excellent
Awesome
Adventure
Story by Judith Bandidt
Illustrations by Richard Marman

Max and the Princesses
Story by Judith Bandidt
Illustrations by Richard Marman